Kate Furnivall was born in Wales and studied English at London University. She worked in publishing and then moved to TV advertising, where she met her husband.

In 2000, Kate decided to write her mother's extraordinary story of growing up in Russia, China and India, and this became *The Russian Concubine*, which was a *New York Times* bestseller. All her books since then have had an exotic setting and Kate has travelled widely for her research. She now has two sons and lives with her husband by the sea in Devon.

Visit Kate's website at www.katefurnivall.com

The —

LIBERATION

Kate Furnivall

**SIMON &
SCHUSTER**

London · New York · Sydney · Toronto · New Delhi

A CBS COMPANY

First published in Great Britain by Simon & Schuster UK Ltd, 2016
A CBS COMPANY

3 5 7 9 10 8 6 4 2

Simon & Schuster UK Ltd
1st Floor
222 Gray's Inn Road
London WC1X 8HB

www.simonandschuster.co.uk

Simon & Schuster Australia, Sydney
Simon & Schuster India, New Delhi

A CIP catalogue record for this book
is available from the British Library

Paperback ISBN: 978-1-4711-5555-0
Trade Paperback ISBN: 978-1-4711-5556-7
eBook ISBN: 978-1-4711-5557-4

Typeset in Bembo by M Rules
Printed and bound by CPI Group (UK) Ltd, Croydon, CR0 4YY

For Norman
with love

CHAPTER ONE

SORRENTO, 1934

Caterina Lombardi didn't want Nonno to die. Not here. Alone. Not lying lost and broken somewhere on the moist black earth with beetles for company and wet leaves as a shroud. Her head twisted from side to side, searching for any sign of him. She expected him to leap up out of the mist, a tall erect figure who would laugh away her fears with a shake of his head and demand a glass of Marsala to warm his chilled bones.

But there was no figure. No laughter.

The sides of the ravine were steep. Caterina skidded and scrambled, and clung on to stalks and branches that lashed out at her as she descended in a wild rush through the dense under-growth. Crashing into rocks. Skinning her elbow. Uttering no sound. Her heart pounding. She had to keep up with the search party or Papà would send her home.

'She's too young. She shouldn't be here,' Augusta Cavaleri had declared with disapproval.

1

Standing at the top of the ravine, Papà had rested his callused hand on Caterina's damp head and bent down so that his eyes were on a level with hers. But they were not his usual bright affectionate eyes that knew how to make her laugh with just a well-timed wink. No, these were a stranger's eyes. They made her nervous. So full of shadows she could barely find him behind them.

'You really want to help with the search, little one?' he asked softly.

'I am ten today, Papà. I am old enough.' She glanced warily at the tall grey-haired woman in the long black coat who wanted to send her home. Augusta Cavaleri possessed a livid white scar on her forehead that always frightened Caterina because it looked like a silver snake slithering across it. 'He is my grandfather. I want to search for him.'

'It is dangerous terrain here,' Augusta Cavaleri pointed out with annoyance at having her will thwarted by a child.

The Lombardi and Cavaleri families were firm friends. Papà and Roberto Cavaleri, who was Augusta's son, worked in their own wood-inlay businesses in Sorrento, but Caterina had learned to tiptoe with care around this matriarch of the Cavaleri clan if she wanted to keep her knuckles intact.

'Look down there.' Augusta Cavaleri directed a cold finger at the rocks below. 'She'll break her neck.'

'I won't, Papà. I promise.'

They gazed down into the ravine, a steeply wooded gash in the volcanic rock with a tall-chimneyed mill nestling at the bottom, abandoned and in ruins now. Everywhere was overgrown with bushes and briars, and trees spread their stunted canopies over whatever secrets lay below. It was a sombre world. Shapes were blurred by the ropes of mist that trailed across the floor of the ravine and by the relentless drizzle that had made the descent wet and slippery.

Somewhere in that dark and tangled underworld lay Caterina's grandfather.

She'll break her neck.

The words swelled in Caterina's head. Fear caught in her throat and she pressed a hand over her mouth to keep it in. Her fear was for Nonno.

Was his neck broken? Somewhere down here? Was that why they huddled in groups, the searchers? Whispering. Falling silent when they noticed her nearby. They didn't want her to know. The searchers had spread out in a line, calling to each other, shouting Giuseppe Lombardi's name, and beating the undergrowth with sticks as they marched forward at a steady pace. Light rain pattered down on to their shoulders and caps and speckled the foliage, dripping on to shoes and spiders.

Caterina ducked under ferns so tall they closed over her head, locking her into a world of greens and greys and silvery webs, a world where the edges had become liquid and unstable. Sounds became slippery. She moved forward quickly, jinking to the right, taking a route of her own, away from the shouts and the boots. Crouching low, she scrambled through the thick undergrowth and the shouts dwindled as she was swallowed by the silence at the far end of the ravine.

'Nonno!' she cried. 'Where are you?'

She listened. No answer. Just the chatter of the rain. But a shape flickered just out of sight. Wreathed in mist. Caterina's pulse jumped. Her feet stumbled. Was it a person? Or only the wind stirring the leaves?

A noise. Behind her.

She spun around but could see nothing through the veil of rain. Was that a whisper? Her grandfathers' voice?

'Nonno,' she shouted. 'Nonno!'

Nothing.

A small animal trail opened up under a forest of ferns and she ran along it, bent double, her long hair twining dark wet tendrils around her neck. That was when she saw the splash of white through the green stems. It was at the base of an outcrop of grey rock towering over her and she plunged through the ferns, trampling them down into the mud to get to it.

Her grandfather always wore a white shirt.

Her feet wanted to slow. To stop. To turn back. Before her eyes saw what she knew they would see. She forced them on towards the splash of white, but when she reached it her knees buckled and she knelt on the ground, trembling, next to the body that lay stretched out on the sodden floor of the ravine.

It was Nonno.

On his back. Crumpled into impossible angles. It was Nonno's face, but its strength had vanished. It was weak and slack, his nose off-centre and blood streaming in the rain from his nostrils, down his cheek and pooling at his neck, soaking into his white collar. Turning it pink. His black suit was soaked and torn, one eye-socket was shattered and pieces of bone poked through the wet skin.

Caterina stopped breathing. She picked up his hand in hers. Held it tight. It was heavy and cold. She touched his cheek.

'Nonno,' she whispered. 'Nonno, it's me.'

No answer. No flicker of an eyelid. There were streaks of blood on his white hair.

She tore off her raincoat and spread it over his chest. She kissed his cheek. Water was running down her face and she didn't know how much was rain and how much was tears, but as she bent over him, unaware of her own sobbing, a long strand of her wet hair trailed across his ashen lips and she saw it lift for a fraction of a second. Lift, and then lift again. No mistake.

'Nonno!' she screamed. 'Nonno, wait for me. I'll get Papà. Wait, Nonno, wait, wait . . .'

She was still screaming 'Wait' when she crashed through the ferns, tearing down the veil of mist between her father and herself.

Voices drifted up from downstairs. Caterina sat on the floor in the darkness of her small brother's bedroom, huddled against his cot, knees tucked up to her chest. He was five months old and could sleep the sleep of the innocent, so the voices didn't wake him. They didn't scare him. Didn't drive his heart up into his throat the way they did to Caterina.

They were her parents' voices. Her mother's was loud and high-pitched, her father's a low rumble that was impossible to decipher. The house relaxed around her, creaking its joints, but she was tense, twisting the hem of her new birthday nightdress into a tight roll. Her parents often argued. She knew that. It was nothing to be frightened of.

5

But her stomach was in knots.

There was something different this time. In her mother's voice. Some shift of tone that she had never heard before and it gripped something in Caterina's mind, gripped it and wouldn't let go. Earlier she had sat on the wet earth in the rain with her grandfather, refusing to release his cold hand, even after he was transferred to a stretcher. Only at the hospital did she relinquish her hold on him, and allowed her father to take her home.

Nonno was alive, he said. Drifting in and out of consciousness. Broken bones, a damaged skull from the fall. Maybe internal injuries, it was too early to tell yet.

'What happened to him, Papà?'

'He says he was walking around the edge of the ravine, you know how Nonno likes to walk, but he lost his footing on some loose rock.' Papà had wrapped his arm around her and she could smell brandy on his breath. 'He fell. That's all.'

'Poor Nonno.'

Her father had rested his cheek against hers, so she could not see his eyes when he murmured, 'Yes, poor Nonno.' But in a voice she scarcely recognised. 'Thank God you found him.' He'd kissed her hair and she'd wound an arm around his neck. 'Nonno will get better,' he'd added, 'you'll see. He's strong. Lombardis are made that way.'

But now she heard her mother's voice, clear and distinct as it drifted up the stairs.

'You are weak, Antonio. You and your father. Weak and spineless.'

*

Caterina perched on the stairs in the darkness, arms tight around her shins, chin on her knee to stop her teeth chattering. From here she could see into the living room, only a slice of it, a brightly lit triangle, but it was enough. She could see her mother stalking back and forth across the room, in and out of the triangle, drink in hand. She was wearing her red dress. She only wore her red dress when she was angry. Or when she was going away.

Caterina gripped one of the banister rails hard with both hands, as if by doing so she could stop her world falling apart. There was a brown leather suitcase standing by the front door, her mother's scarlet umbrella propped against it.

'Don't go, Lucia.' Her father's voice sounded tight. Hoarse. As though he had a string tied around his throat. 'Stay.' He paused and though Caterina couldn't see him she imagined him trying to swallow past the string. 'Please, stay.'

Her mother's laugh was harsh, panicky. 'And fall off a cliff like your father. No, thank you. There's a certain person I have no wish to see again.'

'You should have stayed away from him, like I warned you. This would never have happened if you had managed to keep yourself from wagging your fancy tail in his face.'

'Don't be coarse, Antonio. Though God knows why I expect any better from a southern peasant with wood for brains.'

'I am not a peasant, Lucia.' Still patient. 'I am an artisan, a master craftsman.'

Her mother's red dress flashed into view, her figure slender, her full breasts on show in a way Caterina didn't like, though she couldn't say why. Even angry, her mother was beautiful, with huge blue eyes that could pin you to the floor, and a mane of silky blonde hair that fanned over her pale shoulders. In her hand she still carried the glass of red wine and for two seconds she stood still long enough to drain it before starting her prowling once more. She disappeared from sight.

'Don't go.'

'For Christ's sake, Antonio.'

'What about the children?'

'What about them?'

'They need you.'

Her laugh was raw. Not finished properly. 'All Caterina needs is you and all Luca needs is Caterina. They won't even notice I'm gone.'

'Of course they will. Don't be so selfish, Lucia.' His anger was seeping into his words now. 'Don't you love them?'

Caterina held her breath and pressed her face between the banister rails.

'You love them enough for both of us, Antonio. They don't need me.' Another flash of red and then it was gone again. 'Caterina doesn't even like me.'

'Dear God, you are her mother. Of course she likes you. That child adores you.'

Caterina was nodding. Willing her mother to believe her father.

'No, you're the one she adores,' her mother insisted. 'You and your stupid woodwork and your stinking yellow fish glue. She can't get enough of it.'

'Don't make us your excuse, Lucia.' Caterina heard him light a cigarette. 'Stay with us.' His voice was clipped, painful. 'I'll keep you safe, I promise you.'

'Yes? Like you kept your father safe.'

'I'm begging you, Lucia. Stay for the children's sake.'

Her mother strode into the triangle of light without the glass this time and remained there, staring back at her husband. She broke out a wide beguiling smile. 'What's the matter, Antonio? Can't you bring yourself to ask for your own sake?'

A long pause, so long it seemed to Caterina that he must have fallen asleep.

'I love you, Lucia,' he said softly. 'You are my heart and soul. Stay for my sake.'

'I am tired of you, Antonio. Sick and tired of your dull wood and your dull conversation and this dull small-town life of yours. I am leaving right now.'

'No.' Sharp. Urgent.

'Yes.'

She turned toward the door and Caterina scooted back up three stairs. Her father suddenly strode into the triangle and placed his hand on his wife's shoulder. She shrugged it off. Caterina couldn't see his face.

'At least say goodbye to the children.'

'I think not. What's the point?'

He grunted. As though she'd punched him.

'Where will you go?' he asked.

'To Rome.'

'For how long?'

'Forever.'

'Lucia, I love . . .'

'Roberto is coming with me.'

The stairwell abruptly became darker, the shadows deeper, though Caterina could not be sure whether they were in her head or not. A pain like a burn was growing behind her ribs.

Her father's back was rigid. 'Roberto? My good friend, Roberto Cavaleri?'

The smile was mocking. 'The same. Not such a good friend now, it seems.'

'Lucia, he is married. Have some decency.'

It was at that moment that Caterina saw her mother give up. It was like a string snapping. One moment she was still part of the Lombardi family, the next she wasn't. A visitor in their house. Caterina wanted to fly down the stairs and cling to her. But she didn't, any more than she would cling to a stranger. She backed up to the very top of the stairs.

But she watched the red dress shimmer in the hallway, saw her mother shrug on an elegant black coat, noticed the way her hand smoothed down a wayward lock of hair before seizing the leather handle and lifting the case.

Lucia Lombardi didn't say goodbye. She opened the door and walked out into the night without a word. When the door clicked shut, Caterina's father reacted as though he'd been shot. His body flinched, his broad shoulders shuddered and he released a howl of pain.

Quietly Caterina walked down the stairs and went to him.

CHAPTER TWO

Eleven years later

NAPLES, JUNE 1945

Caterina Lombardi had never fired a gun.

But she didn't hesitate. She plunged her hand deep into the heavy sack at her feet, snatched her grandfather's Bodeo revolver from inside it and cocked the hammer, yanking at it hard with both thumbs the way she'd practised. The heat of the sun had warmed it within the sack so that it felt alive against her skin. She pointed the long muzzle straight at the boy's chest. Except that *boy* was the wrong word. He had the shell of a boy, it was true. He was dressed in an oversized army shirt with the sleeves ripped out, but his limbs still possessed the girlishness of youth. He was probably no more than twelve, but he had eyes stolen from a man. Pale, hard eyes that had lost track of the child he had once been.

'Come no closer,' she warned.

The boy's eyes grew huge with purplish specks of fear and she could hear the sound of his rapid breathing. The gun was old and heavy, a relic from the Great War, its metal ridges unfamiliar in her hand. She had never pointed it at anyone before but she had good reason to now. A blade flicked back and forth between the boy's hands.

'That's not friendly,' he said and licked his lips.

'It's not meant to be.'

Between them stretched three metres of no-man's-land. It was part of a grey and grubby wasteland of rubble, of shattered lives and jagged stones that had once made up a row of dwellings. That was before the American bombs had rained down on them from the B24 Liberators day and night. Twisted chunks of masonry lay in the strong sunlight ready to slice into unwary feet, and Caterina noticed a snake of blood coiling around the boy's bony ankle.

He took a step forward.

She said loud and clear, 'If you take one more step, I'll pull the trigger.'

'No, you won't, *puttana*.'

The youth's voice was high and nervous.

'Don't,' she ordered bluntly. 'Don't force me.'

The gun didn't waver. But as each second ticked by she saw the fear draining from the boy's pale eyes and pooling in the dirt at his feet, until he uttered an arrogant snort of contempt. Was it genuine? Or just bravado? She couldn't tell. But she couldn't take a chance.

She could smell his hunger, like she could smell the smoke

that drifted from the fires among the city's ruins, where its desperate inhabitants huddled in ragged groups to cook small mammals they had snared in the sewers. The boy's hunger was not for her, not for her skinny body, she knew that. No, this boy's hunger was for the cumbersome sack that sat tight against her leg and she knew that he would not let it escape.

Her lips were dry. He wasn't alone. The five friends, who had been slinking through the bomb-site with him, shuffled forward now to stand stiff-legged beside him, shoulder to shoulder. Behind them the morning sun threw their shadows at Caterina and the boy's mouth took on a smile of macho scorn.

'Leave the sack,' he ordered.

'No, I will not. I have my family to feed.'

The knife in his hand edged closer.

'I want that sack.'

'It is mine,' she told him firmly. 'Not yours.'

She wanted to warn the boy, to shout at him to flee. *Don't push me.*

He took another step forward.

'Don't.' She said the word quietly.

'You got no guts.'

With a swagger of his narrow hips he came at her, the knife in his hand leading the way. The sun glinted on its razor-sharp edge.

Merda!

Caterina pulled the trigger.

*

13

Earlier that morning Caterina had fastened the neck of the sack with string. She'd hoisted it on her shoulder and squeezed on to the Circumvesuviana train that ran from Sorrento to Naples, gripping the sack tightly in her arms.

The smell of old clothes and empty stomachs filled the crowded carriage. The heat turned the air solid and sweat slithered between the shoulder-blades of the passengers crammed inside, grimly seeking a change of fortune in the big city. That hope lured them from their villages for a chance to make a few lire. Just as it lured her. They were desperate to sell a tired pair of shoes or to barter a few cabbages for a chicken head which they could sell for three lire, or a sliver of soap if they struck lucky.

Caterina was well aware that some would even beg, because they had nothing to sell except their gaunt face. She had seen them. They would stand hour after hour outside one of the palatial hotels where the military were billeted, where foreign soldiers smoked real American cigarettes and stuffed their mouths with real meat. The villagers would stand out there in the burning sun with expressions as empty as graven images. And beg.

It wasn't what Italians had expected, this shame. Not now the war was over. Shame made eyes furtive. It silenced tongues. The journey was oddly quiet.

Outside, the silvery green of olive groves rippled past the windows, drawing lustful eyes to their ripening fruit and Caterina heard her stomach growl. It was a rattle-bucket train that skirted the fertile volcanic plain at the base of Mount Vesuvius and clanked its way into Garibaldi Station in the centre of Naples. The tranquil pearly beauty of the morning was flipped into a buzzing hive of activity the moment Caterina stepped out into Piazza Garibaldi. Instantly she became more alert and looked around sharply. A young woman alone in this city was fair game, but a young woman clutching a bulging sack was a honey-pot. Shoulders jostled her. Hands grasped. One man with heavy dark pouches beneath his eyes and a patched khaki shirt leaned so close he breathed garlic in her face.

'*Benvenuto a Napoli*, signorina,' he said in honeyed tones and uttered a rasp of laughter. 'Let me be your guide to our beautiful city.' He gestured towards the roofless ruins of the houses nearby and tweaked a corner of her sack.

'*Va via!*' Caterina hissed.

She elbowed him aside and strode away through the city's shattered streets, past grey landslides of rubble from bombed buildings. She headed purposefully westward, aiming for the port. That's where she'd find them – the loud, strange-smelling foreign soldiers and sailors with money in their pockets and a ready eye for a young woman's smile.

She turned down Corso Umberto in the centre of Naples, but the traffic was jammed. Horse-drawn carts battled for space with the hefty Bedford trucks of the British army that belched out smoke, and everywhere the more nimble American jeeps swerved and blared their horns. Hawkers dodged back and forth through the dust between them, thrusting chunks of pagnotta bread through drivers' windows in exchange for a few lire. Or, with a sly smile, dangling strings of nude photographs to tempt a sale.

Much of Naples was made up of elegant boulevards and wide avenues that before the war used to rival Rome, but at the city's heart lay the old quarter, an ancient maze of lanes so narrow you could spit from one side to the other.

Caterina hurried down one of the side roads into Via Vicaria Vecchia, and from there she ducked into the tangled lanes that were miraculously untouched by bombs. The mediaeval stone buildings towered four or five storeys above her and seemed to lean towards each other, sharing ancient secrets. Wooden shutters rattled in the breeze, paint peeling, and a forest of washing flapped noisily above her head between balconies, blocking out the sun, while a big-busted woman was leaning out of an upstairs window singing a Neapolitan song in a full rich voice.

So much of modern Italy felt disjointed to Caterina. Dislocated. An alien landscape that they all had to relearn. But here in the deep shade of old Italy, she could hear the ancient pulse of Naples, feel it vibrating in the smooth black lava slabs beneath her feet. Bombs. Gunfire. Death and starvation. Blood in the streets. Defeat and destruction. Italy had had a gutful of them all. Caterina found it hard at times to control her anger and her despair, but the end of the war in Europe had finally been declared last month, the country liberated with great fanfare and wild tossing of flowers in the air – May 1945, a date branded into history. As she hurried with her sack along Spaccanapoli she felt a kick of excitement, an odd clenching of her heart.

She glanced up at the crumbling baroque façades of the old buildings, up past the blood-red geraniums and the gaudy purple zinnias that splashed and curled over iron balconies. She looked up to the pencil-thin strip of blue sky above. Today would be her own new beginning.

So. It was true. The rumours.

Caterina stood in what was left of the port of Naples and stared at the devastation. It was as bad as they said. How many had died here? And how in God's name would they ever shift the mountains of smashed masonry or the ships beached like dead whales in the glittering blue waters of the bay. She'd heard rumours, but rumours could always be lies. Italians were good at lying. But not this time.

The American B24 Liberator and the British Bristol-Blenheim bombers had done their worst, day after day, night after night, and their worst had been more than good enough. By bombing Naples they cut off the German supply route across the Mediterranean from Naples to troops in North Africa and shortened the war. That's what they said. More than two hundred bombing raids on the city. No one, not even Ivanhoe Bonomi, head of the new caretaker Italian government, saw fit to argue, but it was hard to take, an invader's boots crushing the life out of you. The docks were hectic with activity now as fresh vessels anchored in the bay, troop ships and supply ships that had the quayside swarming with uniforms of every hue – green, khaki, buff, navy and white. Stick a pin in them, her grandfather said, and they all bleed the same colour of arrogance.

Caterina turned her back on the wide sweep of the bay with

its startlingly blue waters and the islands of Ischia and Capri floating in the distance, just as a truck piled with rubble roared towards her, its wheels jarring in the pot-holed road. It sent a whirlwind of stone-dust skimming over her and to escape it she stepped behind a jagged shoulder of wall. It was all that remained standing of what had once been a run-down block of apartments.

Immediately she felt uneasy. Yet there was no reason to fear. Nothing here but broken stones and weeds, a playground for rats. Maybe it was the long shadows that stretched like dead dogs between the shattered doorways, or maybe the smell – the stench of damaged drains was bad. Or the crows circling overhead, watching her, flecks of soot against the bare blue sky. Or maybe it was just hunger.

She was always hungry. The kind of hunger that sucked the marrow from her bones, but she was used to that. When she spotted a snail, fat and luscious, hiding away between broken slabs, she reached out to snatch its shell. Nothing, absolutely nothing that could be devoured by the human stomach was ever wasted in Naples. It was only in recent years that Caterina had learned that you don't know what food means until you have none. Until you hear your young brother crying in his sleep, until you see your grandfather reduced to fragile skin and bone. Until you are ready to stick a knife into a man for a loaf of bread. You change. You become a different person, and she didn't always like the person she had become. But she felt a flutter of black wings at her cheek and a crow stole the snail, rising through the bright shimmering air with a caw of triumph.

'What's in your sack?'

Caterina swung round to see who had crept up behind her on silent feet. To her surprise it was a small boy with filthy black hair sticking out like a hedgehog's spikes. He wore a torn scrap of material that must once have been a shirt, a pair of ragged shorts and he had bare feet. He was so thin, his arms and legs looked like pins stuck in him, but on his face beamed a wide grin.

She could not resist returning the smile. 'What's your name?' she asked.

'Tino.'

'Hello, Tino. Looking for food?'

'*Si*. You?'

She shrugged. 'All of Naples is looking for food.'

'You have food in your sack?'

'No.' With her foot she nudged the bulges that deformed the hessian. 'Just some things I want to sell.'

He spread his spindly arms out wide. 'No one to buy things here.'

Caterina glanced around. It was true. Only weeds lived here now.

'So, young Tino, what are you up to?'

His bright eyes shifted to her sack. 'I find things. I sell them.'

'Not here, you don't.'

Her smile remained in place, but the little urchin must have heard something in her voice because his attention shot back to her face. His grin crept back.

'You got a *sigaretta* in your sack, signorina?'

'No, no cigarettes. You're too young to smoke.'

He puffed out his chest. She could see his ribs. 'I'm nine.'

She laughed. 'More like six.'

He looked at her sideways, as if squeezing past the lie. 'How old are you, signorina?'

'Twenty-one.'

'You smoke?' He mimed puffing on a cigarette with grubby fingers.

'I'd rather eat.'

'And me.' He skipped closer to her, as a truck roared past carrying troops, its canvas flapping like the sound of rifle shots. 'I can help you sell,' Tino said. 'I know good bars. Lots of Yankee soldiers there.'

'No, thank you.'

This close she could see his bones almost jutting through his skin. With a sigh she reached into the pocket of her dress and pulled out a handkerchief. It was a square of pristine white cotton, carefully ironed, with fine cobwebs of lace at each corner.

'Here,' she said and held it out to him. 'Have this.' She would regret it later, she knew, but right now it seemed the least she could do for the child. 'You can sell it.'

He snatched the dainty square from her hand.

'*Grazie*, signorina.' He hopped from foot to foot with pleasure.

'It was my mother's.'

His small face adopted a solemn expression. 'Is she dead?'

'Yes.'

It was easier to say yes.

Dead to her daughter. Dead to her son. Though no doubt sipping champagne in Rome with a hundred other lace hand-kerchiefs tucked inside her perfumed drawer.

He pushed the handkerchief into his filthy pocket quickly for fear she might change her mind.

'I know someone you will like to meet. His name is Vanni. He will help you sell,' he said. Again the grin. It was his only weapon against the world. 'Wait here. I fetch him.'

He pointed a finger at her to make her stay and then scamp-ered off, clambering over the sun-baked rubble with the agility of a weasel. But the moment he was out of sight Caterina knew that she had lingered too long. Tino was clearly one of the *scugnizzi*. These were the feral packs of children that ran wild on the streets of Naples. They roamed the back alleys, orphaned or abandoned, and lived off their wits, stealing, scavenging, beguiling with their smiles. Where there was one, there would be others. She hoisted the sack on to her shoulder and hurried towards the battered road that skirted the harbour, but she was too late. She heard them behind her. The scratch of stone against stone as they scrambled closer.

Children, she told herself. That's all they were, no need to fear them. She swung around to face them.

CHAPTER THREE

The sound of the gunshot from Caterina's Bodeo tore through the bombsite, sending the seagulls tumbling through the clear blue sky like flashes of sunlight. The bullet had gouged a hole the size of a fist in the ground in front of the boy, Vanni. Two centimetres to the left and it would have shattered his foot. Both stared at it in shock. A jeep swerved off the road and ran up on to the edge of the bombsite with a squeal of tyres. Two soldiers leapt out. Instantly the *scugnizzi* turned and fled, melting into the heaps of rubble like mice by the time the soldiers reached Caterina.

'Put down the gun.'

The one who gave the order was wearing an American officer's uniform. He was dark-haired, his eyes watchful, his voice stern. He was around thirty and his skin was deeply tanned, as if he'd been one of those who'd done their fighting against Rommel and the Afrika Korps in the punishing deserts of North Africa. He spoke in fluent Italian.

'I didn't hurt anyone,' Caterina explained.

She gestured at the hole. 'It was just a warning shot to . . .'

The American officer calmly drew his pistol and pointed it at her. 'Put the gun down, lady. On the ground.'

She put down the gun. On the ground.

'Back away from it.'

She backed away.

He picked up her grandfather's pistol, stuffed it in his belt and inspected her with narrowed eyes.

'They were trying to steal my sack.' Caterina pointed to it.

'So you were going to shoot him?'

'No, of course not. He pulled a knife on me. I was . . .'

'Look, signorina,' the other soldier stepped forward with an easy soothing smile, 'we can't have people running round waving guns in people's faces, can we?'

He was British. Softer at the edges. His hair was fair and short under the peak of his officer's cap, and his sandy-coloured khaki drill uniform with two pips on the epaulette was crisp and clean. He was of a similar age to his companion and also spoke fluent Italian, but with a stiff English accent.

'I wouldn't shoot anybody. I have to return the gun to my grandfather.' Caterina held out her hand for it.

The tall American shifted his attention to the sack at her side. He indicated it with a nod of his head. 'Open it.'

The English captain laughed softly. 'You'll have to excuse my companion, Major Parr. He left his manners in Milwaukee, it seems.'

'What's in it?' the major asked.

'Some things to sell, that's all.'

23

'What kind of things? Stolen ones?'

'No.'

He stepped closer and prodded it with his US army boot. 'Open it.'

'Please,' the English officer added with a firm but polite smile.

With a shrug Caterina bent down and opened the sack.

'Exquisite.'

The British captain let the small wooden musical box sit on the palm of his hand. On its lid the Amalfi coast was depicted in wood inlay, the towering cliffs picked out in mahogany and olive veneers, the billowing sail of a yacht glistening in white holly wood.

'Utterly exquisite,' he said with satisfaction.

Caterina said nothing. She was frightened the soldier would take it from her. She never liked people handling the boxes. Looking, yes. Handling, no. Leaving their heavy fingerprints on the pristine sheen of the polished surfaces. She was tempted to snatch it from him, wrap it back in its straw overcoat, stuff it into the sack with the others and run.

But there was the cigarette box too. She couldn't leave it behind. It had taken a lot of work. She glanced at the American. He was holding it at arm's length, balanced on his fingers, studying it with the same kind of quiet intensity with which she selected her veneers. He still had her gun.

'What wood is it constructed from?' His thoughtful gaze was on the box.

'Burred walnut.'

'And the figures on it?'

'They are veneers. Maple. Ash. Pear. Yew. Cherry.' She could go on.

On the lid of the cigarette box was a wood-inlay picture of three soldiers sneaking a moment of relaxation. They each wore a different army uniform – American, British and Italian. The Italian soldier was leaning on his rifle and smoking a cigarette. Her little joke.

'*Bellissima*,' the American major murmured. Not to her. To the box. Caterina liked that.

'Where did you get these?'

'My father made them.'

There. The lie was told.

They both laughed, the arrogant American and the Englishman.

'It's true,' Caterina insisted.

'Are they stolen?' the major demanded.

Caterina licked her dry lips. If he believed the boxes were stolen, he would confiscate them. All of them. He'd sling the sack in the back of his jeep and vanish.

'My father is a master craftsman,' she said. 'And he is teaching my brother.'

'So your brother worked on these boxes?'

Her hesitation was so slight. They wouldn't notice.

'Yes. He applies layers of varnish and polishes them. It takes a long time. He is good.'

The American gave a small smile and Caterina thought he was going to say something nice about the boxes.

'So,' he said quietly, 'how much of that damned garbage is true?'

'Jake, watch your mouth!' the Englishman exclaimed. He turned to Caterina. 'Please excuse my ill-mannered friend.'

'Don't be a fool, Harry.' The major scowled at Caterina. 'Signorina, we are lied to a hundred times a day. You Italians lie as readily as you drink your wine. Good or bad lies, good or bad wine, it makes no difference.'

'Everything I told you is true,' she lied. 'I didn't steal these boxes. I know everything there is to know about working with wood.'

'Is that so?'

'Yes, it is. I can draw you a dovetail or a mitre joint, I know the difference between a scroll saw, a coping saw and a razor saw. I can tell a good quality veneer from a bad one that will buckle, and I have heated up more fish glue than you've had cold beers.'

There was a stunned silence. Only the rumble of machinery from the docks stirred the stone dust at their feet. Then the Englishman slapped his comrade's shoulder, his blue eyes bright with laughter.

'Who looks a bloody fool now?' he chuckled, reverting to English. 'Major Parr, she has you by the short and curlies.'

The American nodded but offered no smile. 'So, signorina, it seems you have a talented father. Yet he sends his daughter out on the streets of Naples to sell his boxes? That could be dangerous.'

'That's why I carry a gun.'

She reached out and took back the musical box from the

Englishman, encased it in straw once more to protect it and replaced it in the sack. But when she moved to reclaim the cigarette box from the American, he lifted it out of her reach.

'I will buy this one,' he said. His fingertips caressed the wood. 'How much?'

Caterina considered his request. She needed to sell more than just one box.

'Take me to where your troops are,' she urged. 'Take me to whatever bar they like to drink in. In exchange you can keep the cigarette box.'

He frowned.

'Major,' she continued quickly, 'everyone knows that soldiers are the only ones with money in Naples. No tourists come here since the war started, just ships crammed with your Allied troops with your Am-lire burning holes in your pockets.'

Everyone was aware that the Am-lire was the official currency issued by the Allied Military Government for Occupied Territories, one hundred of them to the US dollar. Printed in America, hundreds of tons of the notes had been crated up and flown out on cargo planes to Italy. Caterina knew they were intended to assist Italy's recovery, but instead they were having the damaging effect of unbalancing the economy and causing inflation. It was a sore point.

The American gave her a hard stare, searching for a lie hidden inside the maze of her words. But he could find nothing. He shrugged his broad shoulders.

'You've got yourself a deal.'

*

Caterina rode in the jeep.

Whore.

Her grandfather's voice sounded in her head.

You bring shame on your father's name.

Her grandfather was strict about a woman's honour. He laid down rules and, as sure as bells toll for the city's dead, Caterina knew that riding in a car with two strange men – two *foreign* strange men – brought disgrace. Throats had been cut for less.

But the old times are brittle, Nonno, they are cracking wide open. This country is changing. Mussolini has gone and women are fighting to be heard. Italy herself is lying on her back with her skirts up round her hips and holding out her hand for Allied gold. So don't talk to me of whoring. Italy needs to eat. And you, dearest Nonno, you need to eat before your old bones poke through your skin.

She sat upright in the back of the open jeep, hugging her sack as they hurtled through the streets, the wind snagging her hair as Naples came at her in a rush. The sights and smells of a busy but fractured city darted in and out of her senses. They overtook a woman on a bicycle, wearing a man's scarlet dinner jacket and a pair of bloomers, probably the only clothes she had salvaged from a bombing raid. A one-armed man singing opera for centesimi was standing on the corner of a cobbled alleyway, and the rich garlic aroma from cooking stoves on the street mingled with the eye-watering stench of broken sewers.

They drove past the massive brooding towers of Castel Nuovo, the thirteenth-century fortress that loomed up out

of Naples' violent past, and along Via Partenope, with the sea
shimmering like plate glass on the left, in contrast to the skeleton buildings that rose like rotten teeth on the right. Caterina
kept her hands tight on her sack as the jeep's front bumper
dodged past a cart pulled by two scrawny goats and missed it
by less than a whisker.

'Are you all right?' the Englishman asked from the front seat,
swivelling round to face her.

'Yes,' she smiled at him. 'I'm enjoying the ride.'

The bar was for British and American servicemen. It was called
Leo's, a small name for such a huge place. It sprawled over the
ground floor inside a gently crumbling seventeenth-century
palazzo. But the moment Caterina stepped inside its ornate
interior she felt her heart quicken. Today she would not be
going home hungry, she was certain of that.

She walked into the bar. She didn't notice the beautiful
high-ceilinged room or its lavishly Baroque decoration with
frescoes, ornate scrollwork and gilded cherubs, all faded and
peeling now. The tall mirrors on the walls were speckled like
birds' eggs, but she saw none of it. She had eyes for only the
crowd of men in uniform in the room, heard only their loud
voices and strong easy laughter. Above their heads cigarette
smoke hung like lace netting, though a pair of sluggish ceiling
fans tried to tear it to shreds.

'Would you like me to introduce you to a few of our chaps?'
the English captain asked kindly. His name was Harry Fielding,
she had discovered.

She smiled at him. 'No, thank you. I can manage myself. Don't let me keep you from . . .'

The American gave her a brisk nod. 'Come on, Harry, she'll do better without us. Let's get a beer.' He glanced at her. 'Join us when you've finished fleecing the poor saps.'

He headed for the bar, drawing Captain Fielding with him. She knew it was better that way. Without the officers breathing down her neck, the soldiers would welcome her more readily and empty their pockets more willingly. She was wearing a cornflower blue dress, one that used to belong to her mother. Caterina had sold the rest. And the hats. Tipped the perfume down the drain in a rage. But she had hung on to this one summer dress because it belonged to a time of laughter, before things went bad. It hung too loose on her thin frame but these days no one noticed that. Everyone's clothes hung too loose on them.

She pushed back the long strands of her dark hair and bent over her sack to untie the string, but when she straightened up, she found four British tommies had abandoned the long bar and surrounded her with broad expectant smiles.

'*Buongiorno*, signorina.'

'Hello, boys,' she said in English. 'I have something to show you.'

They laughed. And Caterina laughed with them.

It took her an hour. That was all. An hour of smiling and speaking her uncertain English, an hour of brushing against their muscular arms and tossing her hair at their jokes that she didn't understand. She liked their straightforwardness. Their energy. Their comradeship. It filled the room, rising from their khaki and buff shirts along with the smell of beer and cigarettes. Some had haunted eyes, eyes that had seen too much blood, and when one young smooth-faced gunner bought a musical box for his mother, he cried when he heard it play '*Come back to Sorrento*'.

She didn't mind the women. Not the ones with dyed hair and dresses tight as second skins and hard professional smiles. At least the prostitutes smelled nice and spoke to her. It was the others that made her uneasy. The ones in the shabby workaday skirts, the ones with the hollowed-out smiles and the white marks on their finger where a wedding band usually sat. They were the Neapolitan women who had families to feed and nothing to sell but themselves. They didn't speak to her and kept their eyes averted. Shame did bad things to people.

'Here. I saved these for you.'

Caterina placed her last two boxes on the low table where Major Parr and Captain Fielding were seated nursing beers. It was the musical box for the captain and the cigarette box with the soldiers inlaid on the lid for the major.

'*Grazie!*' Harry Fielding immediately took possession of his, smiling at her. 'How much do I owe you?'

'Nothing. Take it as a thank you. I couldn't have asked such prices if I were selling them on the streets.'

'No, I insist.' He drew a fold of Am-lire notes from his pocket.

'For God's sake, Harry,' Major Parr interrupted, 'let the girl keep a shred of pride, can't you? Italian women don't seem to possess much of that right now.' He glanced at the women in their drab clothes, then turned to Caterina. 'Sit down, signorina. Join us. I'll get you a drink.' He moved off to the bar.

Caterina sat down reluctantly. She snatched up her grandfather's Bodeo that lay on the American's vacated seat, and tossed it into her empty sack. She was tempted to throw the cigarette box in after it.

'Don't take offence,' Captain Fielding said.

'Why not?'

He shrugged and gave her the kind of graceful apologetic smile that only an Englishman can master. 'He hasn't always been so . . .' he hesitated, 'so ungentlemanly.'

'What happened? What makes him so rude?'

He leaned forward, keeping his voice low amid the noise and chatter around them, his fine-boned face suddenly growing older, his clear blue eyes sad. 'Nine months ago here in Naples Jake helped a woman in the street. Just like he helped you. She was being knocked about by her husband and no one was lifting a finger to help her. He put a stop to it. And do you know how she thanked him?'

'How?'

'She took one look at Jake's uniform, pulled an army pistol from her shopping bag and shot him point blank in the chest. It seems an American bomb had destroyed her parents' house, killing them both.' He exhaled hard. 'And her two brothers.'

'I'm sorry,' she said.

'Our foolish Yank survived, as you see. Broken ribs and a collapsed lung. I thought we'd lost him for a while, I must admit.' He laughed to lighten the solemn mood that had descended. 'They build them tough in Milwaukee, it seems. His grandmother over there is Italian, so maybe that helps.'

She heard something in his voice, an affection that he was too British to express, and she thought the rude Yankee didn't deserve such loyalty. They were very different, these two Allied soldiers.

'What is it you do together?' she asked. 'I didn't think that the American and British forces were . . .'

'*Amici*? Friends?'

She nodded.

'We are Intelligence Officers,' he explained. 'We work together.'

A champagne glass materialised on the table in front of Caterina. Major Parr sat down opposite her, stretching out his long legs, and raised his beer.

'To your good health and wealth, signorina.' His eyes still regarded her with suspicion, but he didn't mention the gun.

'Thank you,' she said in English.

The champagne looked inviting. It would taste wonderful, but if he'd bothered to ask her, she'd have requested coffee. Now that she'd sold all her boxes, she'd have to go back to work this afternoon, so she needed a clear head. At least he'd thought to bring over a dish of olives. She made herself take no more than one. It was as she bit into the deliciously oily olive that Caterina noticed the woman who had sidled up to stand next to the American's chair. She was running her hand up and down the back of his neck.

'Hello, Jake,' the woman murmured.

'Hello, Maria.' He tipped his head back and smiled up at her.

She was fortyish and had a good face, strong-boned with a generous scarlet slash of a mouth. Her hair was coloured an over-dramatic black, but it was a mistake. It made her face look naked and weary, despite the lipstick. Heavy brass earrings jangled as she moved and she wore a lilac blouse that was cut too low. Caterina was acutely aware of the ample layers of flesh on the woman's limbs and the full curve of her breasts. No shortage of food there.

'So, Maria, *como esta*? How are things?'

'I'm good, Jake. *Sto bene*. How about you handsome soldiers?'

She was laughing in an easy manner that was infectious, but her eyes were fixed on Caterina as she circled the two men.

'So who do we have here?' she asked.

'This is . . .' the Englishman started.

'Caterina,' the woman finished for him.

With no warning she leaned over, gripped Caterina's chin in her hand and tilted it up to the light to take a better look. 'Just like your mother.'

Caterina's heart froze.

'Don't look like that, girl. When I last saw you, you were only a gawky kid but look at you now. *Bellissima*. I'd know you anywhere – you are the spit of your beautiful mamma, Lucia Lombardi.'

Caterina raised her hand to the woman's wrist and removed the grip on her chin. Where the fleshy fingers had touched, her skin burned.

'You knew Mamma?'

'*Si*, long ago in Naples' nightclubs. But I hear she left Sorrento and caught herself a big fat fish in Rome – a German general, that's what they say.'

There was an awkward silence. Caterina stood up, snatched the sack and started to head in the direction of the door, but abruptly she whipped round.

'Do not speak to me of Lucia Lombardi,' she said fiercely. 'Ever again.'

'Caterina, I . . .'

But Caterina was striding away, her heart racing in her chest, while her throat burned. She pushed open the heavy door and tumbled out on to the pavement, but not before she'd seen the look of interest on the American army major's face.

CHAPTER FOUR

It was hard for Caterina to explain. Even harder to understand. But it happened every time she returned home to her small hometown of Sorrento. The moment her foot hit the warm pavement outside the railway station and she made her way through the crowds along the elegant Corso Italia, past the row of shops to Piazza Tasso, the beautiful beating heart of the town, she felt the outer layer of her skin slough off.

She left it there, lying in the dirt. Without it she could move freely, not just her limbs, but her mind. She could think more clearly. Here in the pure clear air of Sorrento she could at last breathe.

Sorrento was a town like no other in Italy. It sat perched up high alongside the seabirds on top of a sheer limestone cliff. Far below, the dazzling Tyrrhenean Sea heaved itself against the rocks and tugged at the colourful fishing boats moored in the small marina. The town's ancient Roman and mediaeval history was stamped on each narrow street and on every one of the mediaeval walls, as well as on the great arched doorways that hid courtyards and iron staircases from view.

Even the great slabs of stonework from which the houses were constructed, hewn in the *bugnato rustic* style of grey volcanic blocks, bore pock-marked indentations as though a hundred thousand fingers had trailed over them. It was a town that had gazed out over the spectacular sweep of the Bay of Naples and the brooding hazy presence of Mount Vesuvius for more than a thousand years, a town so exquisitely beautiful that people came here to die.

Caterina believed that was what her mother had done. Come here to die. Not literally, of course not. But in every other way. In her twenties Lucia Neroni had abandoned the wild parties of her youth in Florence and the sophisticated salons of the north, and buried herself in the peasant world of the south. She swapped her dancing shoes and pearls for goats and lemon groves, for blood feuds and the shadow of the Camorra mafia. And she found herself a man who smelled of fish glue and linseed oil instead of cigars and caviar.

Why, Mamma? Why did you do it? You hated every minute of being incarcerated with what you called mindless donkeys. You always told us we were peasants, Papà and me, with dirty fingernails and souls made of wood.

You left, eleven years ago. On my tenth birthday. You walked out on us. Not just us, on Luca, your new son. *Your new son.* You sprayed scent on your long white throat and left. I worked hard to scrape you out of my head. Out of my heart. To core you out of it, the way I core an apple with a sharp knife.

So don't think you can walk back into it now just because I crossed paths with one of your Naples nightclub friends.

But a German?

A German general in Rome.

Mamma, what were you thinking?

Caterina turned into the street where she lived. It was narrow and lay in deep shadow. The houses, which opened straight on to the black flagstones, were so tall that they blocked out the light, except for a few joyful minutes at midday when the sun squeezed itself into the slender gap to daub the street with gold. Yet the heat was fierce, trapped there, with nowhere to go, and the inhabitants retreated behind their closed shutters, awaiting the sweet coolness of evening.

'Hello, Caterina, where have you been all day?'

She swung round. 'Carlo! Don't creep up on me like that.'

But she laughed at him because it was impossible not to. He was holding a white rose between his teeth.

'For you, *cara mia*.'

'*Grazie.*'

She accepted the rose and slid an arm through his as he fell into step beside her. Carlo Cavaleri was handsome – even she had to admit that – with swarthy skin and fine black eyes that he rolled with amusement at every opportunity. He possessed glossy black curls worn too long and a careless charm that turned girls' heads. He was the same age as Caterina and she had known him all her life, but these days he only came to seek her out in deepest shadow or after dark.

'You weren't at your workshop today,' he said.

'No, I went to Naples.'

'Selling?'

'Yes.'

'Any luck?' He glanced at the sack.

'Yes. But Carlo, it's bad there. Really bad. The city is nothing more than the skeleton of what it used to be and its people are wretched. There are no jobs for them because the factories and offices are in ruins, and the churches and hospitals have been destroyed and . . .'

'Don't, Caterina,' Carlo said gently. 'I hear that the Allied troops daren't turn their back on their equipment for even a second or it is snatched from under their noses.' He laughed and shook his shaggy curls at her.

Caterina pushed her hand into her pocket, feeling her day's spoils tucked safely in there, and pulled out a packet of cigarettes. English cigarettes, a golden yellow pack with the words 'Gold Flake' on the front. They lingered in a shadowed doorway, smoking and talking quietly, while heat radiated from the stone walls of the house. A black tom cat used to stalk the lane before the war, but no more. It had probably been eaten long ago. When the cigarettes were finished they walked to her door.

'How's Luca?' Carlo asked.

'My brother is out on the fishing boats today.' She looked at him closely. 'Why?'

He shrugged. 'Nothing.'

'Why, Carlo?' She punched his arm just hard enough to make him rethink his answer.

'I saw him hanging around at the Hotel Vittorio Excelsior earlier.'

'With the soldiers?'

He nodded. 'Don't be hard on him.'

'I'll skin his lazy backside, the little layabout.' But she smiled. 'Why don't you come in for a glass of wine?' She dangled her sack at him. 'I've bought a bottle for Nonno.'

'Are you mad?' He ran a finger across his own throat. 'I would rather cut my throat than set foot in your house.'

He kissed her cheek, then loped off back to the piazza and the sunlight with a wave of his hand.

'Do you think I am deaf, as well as blind, Caterina?'

The old man was standing in the hallway, leaning heavily on a mahogany cane, and a dusty shaft of light had turned his thick white hair into polished silver. His voice boomed off the terracotta tiles as Caterina closed the door behind her.

'Do you think, Caterina, that your grandfather is too old and foolish to know who you were with?'

'No, Nonno. Of course not.'

Giuseppe Lombardi was nearly eighty but he was still an impressive figure, forceful and straight-backed, in a spotless white shirt and crisply pressed trousers. He raised his cane and pointed it straight at Caterina.

'You disobey me.'

She shook her head. 'You shouldn't be eavesdropping.'

'Don't be impudent, young lady. Giuseppe Lombardi does not eavesdrop. I heard voices in the street but not the words.

I would recognise the filthy tones of a Cavaleri voice even in the fires of hell itself.'

'Is that where you intend to meet them all eventually, Nonno? All those Cavaleris you hate so fiercely?' She grinned at him. 'In hell?'

He lowered his cane, sending dust motes spinning across the hallway. 'Impudence!' he snorted.

But one side of his mouth tilted up into the slightest of curves that he couldn't quite suppress and Caterina could sense relief in it, relief that she was safely home out of harm's way in Naples. She wondered how long he'd been standing alone here behind the door, cane in hand, waiting for her.

'I mean it, Caterina. I won't have you consorting with that Cavaleri brat,' he commanded.

She sidestepped the cane and laid a hand on his arm. The muscles under his sleeve were still as hard as the wood he'd worked all his life, hard enough to knock down a man with his cane last week in Via Correale. She took no offence at his tone. Instead she felt an overwhelming warmth of affection for this proud man who was reduced to waiting in his dark world for his granddaughter. He had once owned a flourishing business. Giuseppe Lombardi had been head of the family business that was respected throughout Sorrento, a person of stature in the town, a man to whom the mayor, the lazy *sindaco*, hastened to doff his hat. But now it grieved her heart to look at her grand-father. His once-black eyes were as opaque as a turtle's egg and the wood-inlay business bequeathed to him by his father and by his father's father lay in ruins at his feet.

Of course he was angry. He had every right to be, in Caterina's opinion; angry at the men in uniform – the black ones of Fascism or the khaki ones of the Allied troops – who had brought her beloved country to its knees. So she held tight to his arm and kissed his cheek.

'I have bought you wine,' she said cheerfully. 'And olives.'

'How so?'

'I sold all my boxes, every single one of them, and for good prices. To soldiers.'

He scowled at her, his forehead a canyon of creases. 'Caterina Lombardi, I ordered you to stay away from the soldiers.'

'They are the only ones with money right now. Don't worry, no one was rude or disrespectful to me.'

Not quite true. An English sergeant with lonely eyes and a whisky-soaked mouth had placed his hand on her backside and squeezed hard, but he was the only one. She was surprised at how civil most of them were. Not like Italian soldiers who could make you feel dirty just by the way they looked at you.

'*Molto bene*, little one. But you shouldn't spend your money on wine for me.'

'*Our* money, Nonno. Without you, I'd know nothing.'

At that he smiled and allowed her to steer him into the living room. She seated him in his ancient armchair whose arms and feet he had carved himself when he was young. Its fine burgundy velvet was worn thin now and possessed a whitish bloom like his eyes. She poured them both a glass of wine and made for each of them a plate of fresh bread with a wafer-thin slice of salami, two olives and half a tomato. The wine tasted sour and the salami was all pig fat, but for Caterina and her grandfather it was a feast.

She knew she should be in her workshop but she was reluctant to leave him alone again, so she sat sharing the moment and told him about her day. Except for the ride in the jeep. She didn't mention that. She wasn't stupid.

Later in the quiet living room, which possessed only basic furniture because anything of value had been sold, Caterina knew she had to say more to her grandfather.

'Nonno.'

The old man raised his head. He was sanding a piece of boxwood that he had carved into the shape of a running deer. Caterina loved to watch his hands. The way they spoke to the wood he was holding, the way they flowed over its surface. His fingers were his eyes.

'What is the matter, *cara mia*? Tell me.'

His ears were sharp. In her one word, he had heard the turmoil she tried to hide.

'Nonno, when I was in Naples I met a woman.'

'What woman?'

'Her name is Maria. She said that years ago she knew Lucia Lombardi.'

Lucia Lombardi. Not *my mother.* The words *mia mamma* scourged her tongue.

'No! No, Caterina, no!' Her grandfather lifted the heavy cane that rested at his side and slammed it down hard on a small wicker table in front of him. One of its legs buckled. 'Do not

43

speak that woman's name in this house,' he bellowed. 'Never! Do you hear me?'

'Yes, Nonno. I hear.'

In silence she returned to stitching a new sole on to her brother's shoe while the sound of her grandfather's laboured breathing stalked through the room.

'Nonno.' She didn't look up.

'What now?'

'I am frightened. I am forgetting what she looked like. It's been eleven years.'

He released a short sharp hiss. 'That is no bad thing.'

'Papà burned all the photographs.'

'It was for the best. To rid our home of her.' He added angrily, 'Why keep any trace of a woman who brought shame and disgrace on the Lombardi name?'

He jabbed at the floor tiles with the ebony tip of his cane, as if he could prod out the offending woman's heart. But Caterina hadn't finished. Not yet.

'The woman in Naples,' she muttered.

'What about her?'

'She told me I look just like . . .'

She heard her grandfather's quick hiss of breath.

'Is it true?' she asked. 'Do I look like her?'

'Yes.'

She waited for more, and was aware of a painful ticking at the base of her throat.

'Yes,' he said again, 'you have her high forehead and her fine cheekbones. Your mouth is all your own but you have the same oval shape to your face and, worst of all, the same sapphire-blue eyes with that look of . . .' He halted.

'That look of what?'

'That look of sadness.'

Caterina forced herself to swallow. The ticking stopped.

'But you cannot see me, Nonno. How can you say my eyes are sad?'

'I am blind, not deaf. I can hear it, little one. In your voice I hear it.'

She bowed her head and rubbed the heels of her hands into her eyes, as if she could scrub the sadness out of them.

'You are wrong,' she told him. 'I am not sad at all. I am glad she is gone. She did me a favour when she left.'

'How?'

'If she had stayed, I would never have been allowed to work with you and Papà all these years.'

A low rusty chuckle escaped the old man's chest.

'Then she did me a favour, too.' He pushed his cane out in front of him as far as it would go, until it nudged the cap of Caterina's knee, a quick little stab. 'Because, my granddaughter, without you and your boxes the boy and I would starve.'

It was early evening when Caterina heard the front door open and soft footfalls creep across the hall floor, heading for the stairs.

'Luca!' Giuseppe Lombardi roared.

The skinny figure of a boy slunk into the doorway of the living room and remained there, approaching no closer. He was barefoot. Luca was a bright and energetic boy of eleven with the sunny nature of his father and the nose for an opportunity of his mother. He looked at his repaired shoes that sat by the door. He said nothing but one hand hung behind his back and he was chewing gum.

'Boy,' his grandfather demanded, 'where have you been all day? I told you to go down to the fishing boats, to make yourself useful, mending nets to earn a few lire. Maybe get a fish-head or two. I smell no fish on you, boy, no scent of the sea on your shirt.' The old man sniffed the air. 'I smell cigarettes,' he announced. 'And beer.' He reached for his cane. 'So where have you been, boy?'

Luca didn't move but his jaw stopped chewing and his thin shoulders sank. His usual smile that had been lurking on his lips crumpled and his expression grew cautious. He flicked a quick glance at his sister.

'Luca, answer Nonno.'

'I've been running errands for the soldiers.'

'Come over here at once,' Giuseppe Lombardi ordered.

Luca edged forward. His feet were filthy.

'When I was your age,' the old man said angrily, 'I was working twelve hours a day in my father's workshop and breathing the grain of the wood into my soul. Stay away from those damn soldiers, I've told you that before.'

'Why?' Luca retorted. 'They are kind to me. They give me ...'

The cane lashed out, aimed low. It caught the boy across his calf, raising a scarlet welt, but he uttered no sound.

'No, Nonno,' Caterina cried out, 'don't . . .'

But Luca drew his hand from behind his back and tossed what was in it onto his grandfather's lap.

'I kept this for you.'

He ran from the room. Caterina stared at the small rectangular object wrapped in brown paper and aluminium foil that now lay between her grandfather's fingers. On it were printed the words *U.S. Army Field Ration D.* He tore off the paper. It was an American chocolate bar.

'Don't be hard on him, Luca.' Caterina was perched on a low stool in her brother's bedroom.

The boy was sitting hunched on his bed, knees tucked under his chin, his dirty feet on the white sheet. When had his spindly legs sprouted so long?

'Why not?' he demanded. 'He's hard on me.'

'It's because he loves you. He sits here and worries. You know he does.'

'I know.' Her brother stuck out his chin stubbornly and picked at a scab on his ankle, making it bleed. He possessed their father's face, the same broad forehead and large nose, with deep-set dark eyes that regarded the world as something to be moulded to fit his needs. Right now it seemed that Luca's needs included the Fifth Army. He was still chewing gum. Caterina wanted to snatch it from his young mouth.

'So you went down to the Hotel Vittoria?'

He nodded, then shot her a sudden bright-eyed glance. 'I saw General Clark. He marched past me in the hotel gardens.'

'How exciting for you.'

He nodded vigorously. General Clark was the head of the American Fifth Army, as close to God as you could get.

'You got your hair cut too, I see.'

He ran a hand over his tightly cropped black hair. No childish curls left for her to stroke.

'A G.I. haircut,' he boasted.

'Yes.'

'And I rode in a jeep.'

Her heart slowed. 'A jeep?'

'Yes.' He was grinning now.

Who was she to say a ride in a jeep was wrong?

'That must have been fun.'

He giggled at the images in his head. 'Look. They gave me this.' He dragged a comic from under his shirt. '*Captain America*,' he announced proudly.

He touched it the way a priest would touch a Bible. Caterina stared at its garish colours. On the well-thumbed cover posed a hero-figure with a star on his chest, an A on his head and a shield of red, white and blue. He looked ready to take over the world.

'Lucky you.'

'I didn't steal it,' he insisted.

'Of course you didn't.'

'I helped them,' he laughed.

'What kind of help?' she asked.

'Like I told Nonno, I ran errands.'

But a flicker of guilt was blinked away.

Caterina smiled and kept her tongue clamped between her

teeth. I am not his mother, she told herself, I am his sister. Their mother had abandoned him when he was only five months old, and ten-year-old Caterina had been the one to raise him while her father and grandfather laboured in the workshop. She'd made mistakes, she knew that. Lots of them.

She stood and moved over to stand beside his bed. 'What kind of errands?'

'Just boring errands,' he muttered and threw himself on his back on the bed, holding the comic above his face, blocking out her questions. 'Have you ever been in the Hotel Vittoria?'

He was changing the subject.

She shook her head.

'It's like a huge palace. I wasn't allowed in but I peered through the windows. It was all gold and big rooms and ...' He rolled his eyes in ecstasy. 'If I were Captain America I'd live in a house like that.' He lowered the comic and looked at her over its edge, suddenly worried. 'Do you think Nonno will let me have some of the chocolate?'

She smiled. 'Yes, if you're good.'

'I'm always good.'

'Hah!'

They both laughed. She sat herself down on the edge of the bed.

'What kind of errands, Luca?'

The comic shot back over his face but she firmly lowered it again. 'I'm waiting, Luca.'

His thin cheeks flushed scarlet, but whether it was annoyance or guilt, she couldn't tell.

'Just taking things to people, that kind of thing.' He said it casually. 'Nothing else.' But he wasn't yet good at lying.

'What kind of things?' She rested a hand on his bare knee, pinning the question on him.

'Oh, you know, army stuff.'

'Like what?'

'Blankets. Boots. Spanners. Electric lamps. Nothing much.'

'Luca, selling things on the black market is illegal.'

Luca abandoned his comic. 'They gave me money. And it's not illegal if the troops do it. They make the rules now.'

Caterina rose quickly and opened the window wide to rid her brother's room of the stink of corruption.

'What is it, Caterina? What's wrong?'

'No more black market,' she said sharply. 'Tomorrow you work on the fishing nets, you hear me? We need bread as well as chocolate. School on Monday.'

She walked out of his room, her footsteps on the bare boards sounding loud in the silence, and she closed the door behind her. To keep him safe.

CHAPTER FIVE

Morning came to Sorrento, and dispersed the clouds that had built up overnight, clouds that would have eased the heat of the day. Caterina left her bed early, restless and on edge after yesterday. The first thing she did was check the pouch under her mattress. Yes, it was there. A bundle of Am-lire notes nestled in her fingers. She counted them. This week they would eat. There were bills to pay, overdue bills that marched through her head at night when she couldn't sleep.

She made herself a drink of hot water spiked with a slice of lemon and headed out into the fresh dawn air just at the moment when the sky was balanced on the tipping point between night and day. She pulled a scarf around her shoulders and set off for work, but took a detour through Piazza Vittoria and halted at the parapet on the edge of the cliff, breathing deeply. The wide panorama of the horseshoe Bay of Naples far below spread out before her. To her left the Sorrentine peninsula hunched black against black, still belonging to the night, but to her right the dawn light spilled like fine silk over the surface of the sea. The twin-peaked cone of Vesuvius was draped in a lilac haze and she could almost smell the volcano's sulphurous breath drifting across the water.

She stood there thinking about the two soldiers of yesterday, the polite Englishman with the charm and the smile, and the curt American major with the hole in his chest. She loathed their well-polished boots, the way they marched over the rich earth of Campania with such arrogance. She hated their full petrol tanks while most Neapolitans were forced to go about on foot, and she could not rid her mind of the image of the extravagant glass of champagne or of their smooth steak-fed cheeks.

Yet Luca was right to hang around with the soldiers instead of the old fishermen. The military broke down barriers, they made things happen, they opened doors for change. The soldiers smelled intoxicatingly of the future. And Italy needed a future.

Caterina turned her back on the fuchsia-tipped waves and faced the ancient walls of Sorrento, steeped in tradition and old family ways. A sea breeze fingered her neck and lifted the drowsy leaves of the palm trees. It was time to wake up.

The Lombardi workshop was a smallish space in an old stone outbuilding, though its high vaulted ceiling had at first made it feel too big for her, but she had grown into it now after more than two years on her own. She liked its high windows. She kept it neat. Everything in order. The long sheets of veneer were stacked in racks, each wood accessible at a glance, and around the walls was a hook or slot or shelf for every tool – the numerous handsaws, spiral and cog-wheel drills, rifflers, files, chisels, calipers, cutters, clamps – and many more, each an old familiar friend. Every morning Caterina's sharp eyes skimmed over them, automatically checking their position and condition, and when she was satisfied, she set to work.

Today she was to decorate a jewellery box. She had constructed it out of a length of exquisite burr walnut, part of the stockpile her father had had the foresight to squirrel away in his workshop before the war.

'We will have nothing, Caterina,' he had warned her. 'When the guns start, they will blow our business to hell.'

It was her idea to hide the wood. When Mussolini took Italy into the war in June 1940, hand in glove with Hitler and Nazi Germany, Caterina and her father had bundled their stock of veneers, along with a crate of music box mechanisms and many of their tools, under tarpaulins in their house instead of keeping them in the workshop. In case the Germans came scavenging. Oh, they came all right, in their jackboots and their Kubelwagens, but they missed the stash in the house.

Caterina muttered a curse under her breath at the memory of how the German troops had trapped a group of partisan fighters here in Sorrento and gunned them down in the street outside the pastry shop. The bullet holes were still there in the wall. She shook her head and set to work, starting with stringing.

Stringing was a technique of wood-inlay that involved laying ribbons of contrasting veneer in a decorative design that was inset into a wooden object or piece of furniture. It was a process that Caterina particularly enjoyed. It took precision and a steady hand because the strings of veneer were fragile and could snap all too easily. She had selected a pale satinwood for the string on the lid of the jewellery box and took a sheet of it over to her workbench. She laid it tight against a fixed board to keep it stable and proceeded to cut a two-metre-long ribbon off the veneer using a slicing-gauge. She had just inserted the fine end of the ribbon into a thicknessing gauge to ensure the ribbon was a constant width and depth, when her concentration was suddenly broken.

Caterina felt a flicker of annoyance. The throaty growl of a motorcycle engine was making its way up the street towards her. Since American troops had taken over Sorrento's best hotels, the raucous noise of motorcycles and jeeps and huge Dodge trucks forever flooded the town, the soldiers spending freely in the cafés and shops. But they didn't often come all the way up this end of town and rarely this early in the morning.

The motorcycle was close and travelling slowly. It drew to a halt right outside her workshop. The door stood open a crack to let fresh air in and wood-dust out, so that a blade of sunlight had squeezed through on to the flagstone floor. The motorcycle gave one final harsh bark and lapsed into silence. Abruptly the blade of sunlight vanished and a tall figure in uniform stood in her doorway.

'*Buongiorno*, Signorina Lombardi.'

'*Buongiorno*, Major Parr.'

It was the American, the one who spoke Italian like an Italian, the one with dark eyes that looked as though he expected her to pull a gun on him and shoot him in the chest.

'This is rather early to come calling,' she pointed out.

'I knew you'd be an early bird.' He opened the door wider and gave her a polite smile that softened his strong features no more than a fraction. 'May I come in?'

He stood in the middle of the spotless floor and inspected the workshop for so long that Caterina gave up waiting for him to finish and went back to threading the string of satinwood through the thicknessing gauge. He was the kind of man who did things at his own pace. Well, that was fine with her as long as he didn't stop her working. She could, of course, ask him why he was here but she didn't. Stubbornness, her father would have called it, pig-headed stubbornness. But it was the same stubbornness that had made her the only female wood-inlay worker in a town where male wood-inlay workers were thick on the ground.

'No, Caterina, no, it's not a job that women ever do. It's just for men,' her mother had insisted with a dismissive flick of her fingers when Caterina asked to be trained into the family business. 'For God's sake, child, have some pride in yourself! Don't be a donkey all your life.'

A donkey.

Caterina balanced the satinwood strip in her hands and took a good look at the American studying her wall of tools. Why was he here? He wore no cap, his dark hair tangled by the motorbike ride, and his US officer's uniform sat easily on his broad frame, as if it paired well with something inside him. His eyes were more deep-set than she remembered, not as impatient as last time, as his gaze took in the regimented rows of tools. Each handle faced the same way, each blade was polished and sharpened to perfection. No dust. No rust.

Was he considering what kind of person she was?

She looked away from the wall. 'How did you find me?' she asked.

His mouth twitched briefly as though tempted to smile. 'I'm an Intelligence Officer, remember? I get paid to know how to find things.'

She gave a small laugh. 'War,' she commented, 'makes hunting dogs of men. They like to catch and kill.'

He glanced up quickly. 'I'm not hunting you, Signorina Lombardi.'

'Aren't you? It feels like it.'

'Of course not. In Naples you mentioned your mother's surname – Lombardi – and that you lived in Sorrento.' He shrugged, but there was nothing casual about it. 'It wasn't that hard to find you.'

'And why would you want to do that?' She faced him squarely. 'Not to admire my tools, I'm certain.'

'No.'

The sharpness of his answer increased her unease. She turned away and ran the ribbon of veneer through the thicknessing gauge, making several passes to shave off a millimetre of its width. Her experienced eye could judge when it was the exact measurement she required and the familiar rhythm of the action calmed her.

'I'm here to ask a few questions of your father,' he said.

Her hands didn't falter as they removed the string of veneer and picked up the lid of the box.

'Is Signor Lombardi here?' Major Parr pressed her. He looked expectantly towards the rear door that led into the tiny kitchenette.

So that was why he was here. Well, Major, you're in for a very long wait. She set about carving out a channel around the edge of the walnut lid, the teeth of the gouger cutting a straight line scarcely deeper than the satinwood string. It was delicate work but it came to her as naturally as breathing.

'Signorina?'

Caterina looked up. He had moved closer. She could see the dust that coated his black eyelashes despite the goggles he must have worn.

'Yes?'

'Is Signor Lombardi here? Yesterday you claimed that he made your boxes.'

'I lied.'

'Why would you lie about a thing like that?'

'If I'd told you the truth, that I made the boxes myself, not a master craftsman, you and your men would have thought less of them and paid less for them.' She saw his eyes widen with surprise. 'It's true, isn't it?'

He gave a brief nod. 'Yes, it's true.'

'But the boxes are good enough to be the work of a master craftsman. Admit that.'

He paused and for a moment she thought he would deny it, but he nodded again. 'You're right. The workmanship is beautiful.' His eyes lingered on her hands, but he switched his attention back to the door of the kitchenette once more, losing interest in her lies. 'Is he here?'

'Who?'

He frowned. 'Your father.'

'No.'

'Where can I find him?'

Caterina waved a hand towards a photograph in an ebony frame that hung on the wall right next to the scannella where she sat for hour after hour each day, cutting out the inlay sections.

'There. That's Papà.'

He strode over and pushed his face towards the picture in the frame. He studied the heavy-jawed laughing face closely.

'Where is he?'

His voice had an edge to it now, as sharp as her gouging blade.

'Papà is dead.'

Grief seeped into her words, despite all her efforts. She couldn't hold it back, couldn't stem its flow at the mention of the death of her father. It was private grief, not meant for this soldier's ears, so she turned quickly away and picked up an exactor. With rapid flicks of her wrist she started to clean out the channel, removing wood flakes to leave a crisp groove in which to inset the inlay strip. She reached for a large syringe of yellow fish glue.

'Signorina.'

Still she didn't look at him, but bent over her workbench and placed several beads of glue along the channel.

'I am sorry,' he said, 'for the loss of your father. How did Signor Lombardi die?'

'One of your American bombs, Major Parr. Two years ago.' She slid the satinwood string into the groove and snipped off the end with a chisel. She did not let her hands shake, not in front of this soldier. 'It fell on his workshop and he died in the explosion and the fire that followed.'

A silence seeped into the room and she could hear laboured breathing. She thought it was his, until she realised with shock that it was her own.

'What are you here for, Major? Why did you want to speak to my father?'

'Because I have some questions for him.'

'Then ask me. I now run the Lombardi business.'

'Very well, Signorina. The first question is this: is it true your father was a thief?'

His words stunned her. Her head whipped up. The American officer was watching her intently, everything about him alert, his eyes fixed on hers. She strode immediately to the door and yanked it wide open.

'Get out,' she ordered.

'First I would like us to talk about . . .'

'How dare you? My father was a good, honest and trust-worthy man all his life. He was respected in the community, elected on to councils, his word stood for something in this town. Antonio Lombardi was not a thief.'

Caterina could feel her blood pulsing in her cheeks and hear her voice rising in anger. She found the chisel still gripped in her hand and she pointed it straight at the soldier.

'Get out of here!'

He approached her slowly, the way he would a spooked horse, and stood unblinking in front of her, the buttons of his crisp buff shirt only a hand's breadth from the point of the chisel.

'Talk to me,' he said quietly.

'I will get my grandfather's gun to talk to you,' she hissed.

He gave her a joyless smile. 'It will make it easier for both of us in the long run if you listen to what I have to say.'

'There is nothing you have to say that I want to listen to, Major Intelligence Officer. How dare you barge in here and blacken my father's name? In America, maybe a good name counts for nothing, but let me tell you that here in Italy a man's good name means everything.' She stepped forward and jabbed the tip of the chisel against one of his buttons. 'Here in Campania, men have been killed for less.'

She heard his quick breath.

'When everything is stripped away,' she told him, 'a man's good name – or a woman's – is all that is left to them.'

'In which case, all the more reason for you to talk to me.'

'What do you mean?'

'I mean, if you are not willing to answer my questions about your father,' he gestured towards the street, 'I will have to go out there and speak to others who *are* prepared to answer them.'

It was said reasonably. Almost apologetically. It was not said as a threat, but still it sounded like one.

The kitchenette was too small for him. His voice rebounded off the walls and his words were too big to fit inside it. Major Parr had brought coffee, and he made a cup for each of them but she would not touch his thirty pieces of silver, not even when he placed the steaming cup in her hand and its aroma beguiled her starved senses.

He placed himself between her and the door, as though he feared she might bolt, but she had no intention of doing so. She might throw her coffee over his clean shirt but she wouldn't run. To remove temptation, she folded her arms across her thin body.

'What do you want?' she asked bluntly.

'I am stationed with my unit in Naples. If you wish to confirm that fact, you can speak to Colonel Quincy at . . .'

'What unit?'

'A special Intelligence Unit appointed by the government of my country in collaboration with your country and Britain. We are working together on this.'

'On what?'

'On tracking down artefacts stolen from the Museum of Naples and from the churches and the many old palazzos that were bombed or just abandoned when their owners fled.'

'Artefacts? You mean ancient marble statues?'

'Yes, among other things.'

'You've made a mistake,' Caterina said and unlocked her arms. 'My father had no interest at all in old statues.'

'Not statues, maybe.' He left a pause for her to leap into but she kept her mouth shut. 'Antique furniture perhaps?'

'You've made a mistake,' she repeated.

He was good at watching, this Major Parr. Good at listening. She saw in the faint tightening of the muscles around his dark eyes that he had heard the whisper of sudden uncertainty in her voice.

'My father was not a thief,' she declared. 'If you have heard otherwise, they are lies. What proof do you have?'

He smiled and it made her feel a whole lot worse.

'Well, there you have me, signorina. The truth is that proof is a bit thin on the ground. When I heard you say in Naples that your father was a master craftsman and that his name was Lombardi, I came out here to question him. To discover the truth. But . . .' his gaze drifted to her hands and she remembered the chisel she had pointed at him, 'I am too late.'

'His death is recorded in the town's register. Go take a look for yourself if you want proof.'

'I will.'

There was something about this man, about the stillness of him, about the straightness of him that made her unable to fathom what was going on behind his cool eyes. She looked briefly at her coffee growing cold but made herself ignore it.

'What makes you think my father was involved in those thefts?' Her tone was brisk now. She wanted him gone.

He leaned a shoulder against the wall and she knew what-ever he was going to say would be bad. Were all Milwaukee men like this, taciturn and watchful? And where on earth was

Milwaukee anyway? Somewhere in the middle of America, she thought, maybe somewhere cold where ice froze the heart.

'Antonio Lombardi's name kept cropping up in my investigations in Naples. The more people I questioned, the more I heard his name.'

Caterina shook her head vehemently. 'My father would never have been involved in theft. Believe me. I knew him, you didn't.'

For the first time since this American soldier had set foot in her workshop, stirring up her life, she saw a flicker of doubt in him, a faint fear that he may be wrong. It made him uneasy and his manner became stiffer, his eyes sharper.

'Did you ever see any antique furniture in his workshop, pieces that he was repairing perhaps?'

'No.'

'Did he go to Naples often?'

'No.'

'Did he talk about what might be happening to the priceless antiques in the great houses of Naples? Did he wonder what steps were being taken to protect them?'

'No. Major Parr, it may seem strange to an American, but here in Italy it was the lives being destroyed by your bombs that we worried about, not the furniture.'

He blinked. Taken by surprise. 'Of course. I didn't mean to imply otherwise.'

She stared at him long enough to be rude, but passed no comment. He put down his coffee cup and faced her squarely. His eyes looked weary.

'It was war,' he said. 'Italy and Mussolini sided with Germany, so your country brought the bombing on itself. I saw many of my friends and comrades killed during the fighting, terrible bloody deaths of fine young men who came all the way from America to free the people of Italy from the stranglehold of Fascists and Nazis. It was war,' he said again, his voice so quiet that the small room seemed to fit tighter around them and Caterina snatched a breath in case the air was sucked out.

'The war is over,' she reminded him. 'But still we are fighting to survive.'

'America is helping Italy to start again. So I'm asking you to help me, Signorina Lombardi.' He gave her something approaching a smile and it briefly touched his eyes. 'Where is your father's workshop, the one that was bombed?'

'In Via Caldoni. You can't miss it. It's still just a heap of rubble. You go past ...' She paused. Thought again. She couldn't let this American's boots trample over her father's workshop alone.

'I'll take you there,' she said.

CHAPTER SIX

Caterina couldn't look at it. Even now, two years later, she could not look at the broken remains of her childhood, because that's what the workshop had been to her – the place where she was happy. All the good things in her life had happened there and at the centre of them all was her father. Her father and his wood. She found herself a spot in a patch of shade out of the morning heat and leaned her back against the wall of the neighbouring building that had been damaged by the bomb but was still standing drunkenly.

She could hear Major Parr scrambling through the fire-blackened remains of the workshop, turning over stones with his boot, pushing aside weeds and raking through dirt. He was thorough. He took his time, but Caterina did not watch. She observed the street instead with its bustle and its noise and a woman waved to her from a window across the street, old Signora Addario with the glass eye. The Rocco brothers, two card-playing hard-drinking *amicos* of her father's, walked past with a rolled carpet over their shoulders. She didn't ask where it came from, but they kissed her warmly and invited her to join them for a coffee which she knew would be half sawdust. She thanked them, inhaled their familiar ferocious garlic odour and declined.

'I have to stand guard,' she told them.

They understood. The older brother made a rude gesture to the American officer whose back was turned and all three of them laughed, but even that didn't blunt the rasp of her father's saw in her ears or the echo of his deep bass voice carving a path through the *Te Deum* from *Tosca*. The brothers ambled off with their carpet and she continued her vigil alone in the shade.

'Tell me what happened that day.'

The American lit a cigarette, handed it to Caterina and lit one for himself. Her patch of shade had melted away by the time he had finished poking around among the broken stones and startled lizards. She accepted the cigarette and narrowed her eyes against the glare of the sun. His expression was sombre, and dirt coated his army trousers below the knee. His hands were filthy, large and muscular, and he had a smear of black soot streaked across his forehead where he had brushed back his hair with ... with what? With frustration? Impatience? Despair? Or was it anger?

She started to move away down the road, drawing him away from the workshop, knowing he would follow. She had not answered his question and he was not a man to let that pass. He fell into step beside her and they walked in silence for a while, keeping their cigarettes and their thoughts to themselves.

'Have you seen enough?' she asked.

They were walking past a section of the ancient town wall, built in the sixteenth century on top of the original Roman one that kept the Saracens at bay. The towering dark rows of tufo stones captured Major Parr's attention.

'I've seen enough of your father's workshop, if that's what you mean.'

'He's dead,' she said sharply. 'It's over. Leave him in peace.'

'It is only over for him, Signorina Lombardi. Not for me. Not for Naples.' He glanced sideways at her. 'And not for you.'

He paused in the street. A young woman in black was sitting on a chair in the doorway of her house that opened on to the road and on her lap lolled two babies, blond-haired and blue-eyed, and Caterina wondered if their father was German. In front of the woman's feet lay a basket of five oranges. She was selling them. The American bent over, tossed a handful of coins into the basket and took one orange. As he walked on, a torrent of blessings from the woman pursued him up the road.

'I was working that day,' she said abruptly.

'When the bomb fell?'

'Yes.'

'In the workshop?'

'No. I was put to work in a factory when the war started. I was sixteen. I made army uniforms.'

He looked at her, surprised. 'Quite a change from making boxes.'

'It wasn't so bad.'

She'd hated it. Hated the noise of the machines and the

constant chatter of the women and the shouts of the foreman, the quick slap of his hand if he was displeased with the speed of her work.

'The foreman summoned me to his office and told me what had happened to my father. I ran to the workshop. It was destroyed and on fire. That's all.'

So few words. To describe the worst day of her life. The acrid smoke. His flesh in flames.

'I am sorry, Signorina Lombardi. It must have been terrible.'

Caterina halted and turned to face him, the muscles of her face awkward and stiff. She could smell the orange in his hand. 'Sorry means nothing. What matters is that you must stop this. If you are sorry, leave my father his good name, don't drag him into your investigation. What is the point now he is dead?'

'The point is that it is my job.'

His words were quiet but had the sting of a slap. The sun was behind him, his face in shade, his shoulders pulled back as if he expected a slap in return.

'Are you the kind of person,' she demanded, 'who puts finding old cabinets ahead of all the good that a man has done in his life? Ahead of the beauty he has given to the world with his hands? Ahead of his reputation, ahead of *my* reputation as I carry the Lombardi name?'

He didn't move, not a muscle, but she felt him move back from her. The street was silent, no traffic, no children, no women on stools shelling peas in the sunshine. Just a breeze in a plane tree stirring its leaves, the way Major Parr was stirring her emotions. Just for the hell of it.

'Stay away from me, Major Parr. Stay away from me and stay away from my father. He is dead. Respect his name.'

She turned on her heel to march away but his voice, stripped of its professional politeness, pinned her to the spot.

'What about justice, Signorina Lombardi? Justice. What about men in this racket being knifed to death and others walking away with pockets packed with money while corruption warps people's minds? People are starving in Naples while these assets are being leeched from the city's coffers. Justice has to be brought back to Italy and corruption stamped out if this country is ever to climb back on its feet.'

She turned to face him. 'My father was not corrupt.'

But he had not finished. 'We're not talking a few bucks here or "a few old cabinets" as you put it. We're talking thousands of artefacts stolen and sold for millions of lire. Big, big money. And I believe your father was involved.'

'No.'

'Yes. He repaired the ones damaged by bombing.'

'No.'

'It's true.'

'No. Where is your proof?'

A woman stopped in the street and stared at them. Only then did Caterina realise she was shouting.

'There's a set of inlaid panels,' the American said in a harsh voice. 'Sixteenth century. Very valuable. Three different people have sworn your father worked on them.'

'They are lying. Do you hear me?' Half the street could hear her. 'They are lying to save their own skins.'

'You told me you were working at the factory all day.' Suddenly he reined himself in. He sounded reasonable. She was the one who sounded unreasonable. 'So you wouldn't have known,' he pointed out, 'what he was doing all day.'

'No, that's not true. Every evening I worked there. I knew every piece that passed through my father's workshop, I swear to you.' She struggled to keep her hands from snatching the orange from him and ramming it in his mouth to crush his words.

'Did he keep a list of the work he did, an order book?'

'Yes. But it was in the workshop. It burnt in the fire.'

'What was he making that day?'

'I have forgotten.'

'I've heard rumours about a table. A very special table that . . .'

'Enough of your lies!'

'Signorina Lombardi,' his hand touched hers, as reasonable as his voice, 'don't say . . .'

'Stay away from me.' She snatched her hand from his and scraped it down her skirt to rid it of his touch. 'And stay away from Sorrento.'

She turned her back on him and walked away, leaving him standing there.

Caterina had no intention of returning to her workshop. She veered off in the opposite direction, walking fast, arms swinging angrily at her sides, and she could feel a small spike of fear, sharp as a stiletto point at her throat.

What if this Major Parr was right?

But she crushed that thought. It was a betrayal of a good and honest man. She turned quickly into the narrow street that led to her house, grateful for its coolness on her burning cheeks, with no thought for the row of high arched doorways inset into the frontage of what had been a fine merchant's house three hundred years ago. She had to get home. She had to search for . . .

An arm came out of the shadows. Rough, bulky, choking. It wrapped around her throat from behind and jerked her into the blackness of the deep doorway. She fought like an alley cat, punching and kicking, but she was small and her attacker's other hand seized her wrists, wrenching them up behind her back, tearing her arm-sockets. Brutal and efficient. Panic raged through her and she opened her mouth to scream.

'Don't.'

A third hand clamped over her mouth. Stifling her. It belonged to a second man who slid out of the shadows, stinking of hair pomade. A pointed pock-marked face with cold narrow eyes leaned close.

'Don't make a sound or I shall hurt you. Show me you understand.'

She blinked.

He removed his hand but let it hover close. 'If you make a sound I don't like, my big friend behind you will break your arms. *Capisce?*'

She blinked.

'*Bene.*'

She couldn't swallow, couldn't breathe. Terror turned her knees soft and set her heart clamouring to escape.

'Now, signorina, what did the big American soldier want with you?'

She shook her head. Lights were flashing like forked lightning behind her eyelids. She couldn't speak. The arm wrapped around her throat was strangling her.

'*Stupido*! Don't kill her ...' she saw the other man's lips tighten. 'Not yet.'

The arm loosened and air whooped into her starving lungs. She tried to get a good look at the pock-marked face in the gloom. She could see a blaze of white in his dark hair at his temple like the brand of a knife wound, and a gold tooth was hiding behind a long moustache. Her eyes hurt, bloodshot and throbbing.

'What did the American want?'

'To see my father's workshop.'

'Why?'

'I don't know.'

The slap came hard and fast. Her head rocked back against the wall of muscle behind her.

'Don't lie to me.'

She spat at him, a sharp jet of spittle that slithered in a silvery ribbon down his cheek.

'It's true,' she said. 'I don't know.'

'What did he tell you?' He ignored the spittle.

'Nothing.'

He slapped her again. Harder this time, a stinging blow. Her teeth snapped together on her tongue and she tasted blood.

'It's true,' she said again.

'You argued in the street. What was that about?'

She swallowed painfully and tried to turn her head but it was like being in the grip of a python. She tried to think. Her mind had forgotten how. All she could feel was the terror.

'Let me go,' she whispered.

The narrow eyes loomed close to hers, black and cold as the sea at night. 'I am going to count to three. If you do not tell me what I want, Aldo here will break your neck.'

She dragged in air.

'One.'

'Who are you?'

'Two.'

The arm tightened.

'Three.'

'The American wanted to know what my father was working on when he died.'

'Did you tell him?'

'No. I didn't know.'

'Did he believe you?'

'*Si.*'

He nodded to her captor and the arm loosened a fraction.

'Tell me why he is here.'

His gold tooth flashed in the gloom. Was he smiling? What was so funny? Her pulse throbbed in her ears and she had to concentrate hard to hear his voice. Who was he? This man that the American had brought to her door and left her to fend off alone.

'He is looking for something,' she told him. 'I don't know

73

what, he didn't say. I couldn't help him. That's why we argued.'

She held her breath. The American's words whirled through her head. *A very special table*? How dare this man with the gold tooth value her life as less than a heap of furniture? Because she was quite certain he would kill her if it suited his purpose.

'Don't,' she whispered.

'Don't what?'

'Don't be fooled into thinking my father is involved. It's a smokescreen.'

He seized her chin in his hand and gripped it so hard she thought it would snap off. 'A smokescreen for what?'

'For whatever is really going on. Not here. Not in Sorrento. Go and break people's arms in Naples.' Her stomach heaved and she fought it down. 'That's where . . .'

'You have family, signorina. You don't want me to hurt them, do you?'

She vomited over his white shirt.

'*Merda*!' he screamed.

The arm released her. She bent double, shaking so hard she thought she would fall. When she finally stood straight, they were gone.

Caterina slammed her front door behind her, before anyone could even think of following her inside. She leaned her back against it. Breathed hard, and felt her blood trickle like ice through her veins. *You have family*. The pock-marked bastard was threatening Luca and her grandfather. Did he really know who she was – or was he just guessing that she had family? Was he bluffing?

He wasn't bluffing.

But his clinical gaze danced inside her eyelids, refusing to let her escape.

Who was he?

What was the American to him?

She stood there for a long time, eyes closed tight, back jammed against the door, ears alert for the slightest sound of a footstep in the street. A pulse was jumping in her throat. She wiped a hand across her mouth and forced herself to think straight.

How do I deal with this? With someone threatening to kill me? To *kill* me. Her teeth were clamped tight to stop them rattling in her head.

Do I go to the police?

She could picture their snide smiles. They would pick their teeth and look down their long noses. They wouldn't believe her. She had no proof. 'Why would anyone want to kill you? You're nobody.' Her cheeks flushed scarlet and she pushed herself away from the door. She had to speak to Major Parr.

But first she had to find the book.

Caterina yanked open drawers. Tipped them on the floor. She raked through cupboards, hurling everything in a jumble, to examine what lay at the back of them or stuck on the underside of drawers. She, who lived by order and neatness, created havoc and chaos.

She ransacked the desk that used to be her father's but which now mainly housed papers and her brother's collected hoard of bits and pieces. Oh Luca, you are such a magpie. Her hands rummaged through its contents, pushing aside strange-shaped rocks and a tin of glistening coloured stones, a seahorse skeleton, a carabinieri whistle and a gull's egg, blown and nestling inside one of her father's old gloves.

'Where, Papà? Where is it?'

She tore the cushions off her grandfather's chair. She lifted its upholstered seat and her fingers touched a knife. *A knife?* She found it jammed down the side, its blade so fine it could whisper between ribs and enter the heart before a man could open his mouth to cry for help.

Why? Why did her grandfather keep a blade at his side?

She hauled the sideboard away from the wall to look behind. She ripped lids from tins. She crouched down to search under the sink and climbed on a high stool to remove the top from the lavatory cistern.

Nothing. *Niente.*

Her mind was spinning. She forced herself to sit down in the silence and think.

CHAPTER SEVEN

Jake Parr liked Via Corso. It was the widest and longest boule-vard in Sorrento, so darn elegant in its ornate classical façades that he felt he should be sporting a velvet jacket and gliding along in one of those old barouche things with a lean wolf-hound padding at its wheel. That's the kind of place it was. It put strange thoughts in his head. To be walking where centu-rions from Ancient Rome once marched up and down made him look at his feet with new respect.

A young woman fell into step beside him and her gaze clung to the orange he was holding. Timidly she held out a cupped hand and he dropped the fruit into it, the aroma of its bruised skin scenting the air. She tried to scuttle off with a gaunt smile before he could ask more of her, but he gripped her wrist. It was like gripping a bunch of twigs.

'Tell me, *per favore*, signorina, where the police headquarters are in Sorrento?'

Her eyes grew flat and anxious. 'No, soldier, I don't know.'

He released her and she fled. He'd seen it before. That's what happened when you dropped the word *polizia* around here. Like pouring water into hot oil. It spat and hissed. Decades of existence under the shadow of Fascist police and the brutal Blackshirts had left this country nervous of strangers and frightened of uniforms.

He dipped into a maze of backstreets – they called them streets, but to Jake they were just ancient back-alleyways no more than the width of a car and some smelled of fish gone bad in the heat. The houses all rubbed shoulders, three or four storeys high, everyone knowing each other's business, and he eventually found his way to the police station, the *questura*. He'd been in too many of them since undertaking this work and they made his hackles rise. They were all hostile to him and his smart US officer's uniform, but he was used to that. Gloomy places, and this one had a distinct smell of its own. The air was thick with the stink of disinfectant, barely masking a lingering under-odour of mouse droppings. A drunk was still in the cells downstairs, judging by the banging noises that drifted through the open door at the back, but someone had stuck a pot of geraniums on the windowsill and it gave Jake hope. He walked over to the long wooden counter and touched his cap politely.

'*Buongiorno*, I am Major Parr,' he greeted the man in *polizia di stato* uniform behind the counter.

He was an *agenti* who had the kind of face that settled into comfortable folds as he took a drag on his cigarette and exhaled a thick smog into the room. Whatever muck he was smoking, it sure wasn't good old Virginia tobacco. Jake refrained from coughing but it took an effort.

'What can I do for you, Major Parr?'

'I'd like to speak to Commissari Balzano.'

'What about?'

'Tell him it's about a death here in Sorrento.'

The police officer raised a thick eyebrow. 'You killed somebody?'

Jake gave a thin smile. 'Not yet.'

The *agenti* chuckled. Jake took a pack of decent cigarettes from his pocket and slid it across the counter.

'I want to see him now.'

The policeman picked up the cigarettes. 'Sit down,' he said and marched out through the rear door.

Jake turned to find a seat. There was a row of hard chairs lined up along a side wall and on one sat a woman with a shiny yellow dress and a greedy smile. She patted the seat beside her and he saw a livid bruise on her arm.

'*Grazie*,' he said courteously but remained where he was.

'You got any nylons in those pockets of yours, soldier?'

'No.' But he drew out his last pack of cigarettes and tossed it to her. 'Don't smoke them all. You may need a few to get yourself out of this place.'

She laughed, a big Italian sound that set her bosom shaking and tore apart the gloom. It made Jake smile.

Commissari Balzano was like his office. Neat and sharp-edged. His shirt was starched, his trousers so crisp they looked as though they would snap if he sat down. His dark hair was brilliantined into a rigid quiff to distract from the fact it was receding at the temples, and his eyes were narrow and straight. They grew narrower and straighter as they regarded Jake.

'So, Major Parr, what is it you want?'

No preamble. No pleasantries about the beauty of Sorrento. Jake sensed this was yet another official with no taste for Americans, not even ones with cigarettes in their pockets. Jake looked at the desk where piles of paperwork were arranged in military formation and took a buff envelope containing Am-lire from his inside pocket. He laid it flat on the desk and then sat down in the chair in front of the desk without waiting to be asked.

Commissari Balzano moved with sudden energy to his own chair behind the desk, scooped up the envelope, glanced inside and tucked it away in his top drawer, which he proceeded to lock with a key. Only then did he take a seat.

'What can I do for you, Major?'

Jake liked that about Italians. They made no secret of the buff envelopes. It was the way things got done here and it made his job easier. In Milwaukee the envelopes were slid surreptitiously under the counter or tucked inside a newspaper before being handed over, but in Italy they were passed from hand to hand as freely and openly as a handshake.

When people had sidled into his Naples office with requests for Intelligence Office assistance in exchange for rumours about illegal hoarding or stashes of weapons by partisans, at first he had rejected the envelopes they offered. But he had learned better. It was offensive. Like a woman rejecting a gift of flowers. Not the way to loosen tongues. So now his bottom drawer was stuffed full of unopened buff envelopes and locals knew where to bring information to barter for an official stamp or a word in the right ear.

Balzano flicked a hand towards the window with all the elegance of a maestro conducting an orchestra. 'What is this nonsense about a death in Sorrento?'

'I am here to enquire about the death of Antonio Lombardi.'

'Ah! That was two years ago.'

'So I'm told. I want to know exactly what happened.'

'A stray bomb hit his workshop during an air-raid on Naples.' His eyes narrowed to slits. 'An American bomb. Why drop a bomb on Sorrento?'

Jake shrugged. 'A crippled B-24, I presume, jettisoning its last bomb so that it could limp back to base.' Jake was well aware that there had been over one hundred and eighty raids on Naples in 1943 alone, twenty-five thousand civilian casualties inflicted that year by the B-24's of the US 15th Air Force and the British Mitchells. Of course there were mistakes. The horror of war made people panic. He had smelt it. That stench of terror. 'But we are working together now, may I remind you?'

'*Si.*'

A stiff word that scarcely squeezed between his teeth.

'I understand there was a fire at the workshop after the bomb fell. Signor Lombardi was killed.'

Belzano nodded and crossed himself.

'Did you find his body?' Jake asked.

'Badly burned, of course.' He ran a hand over his eyes,

uncomfortable with the memory. 'We buried him in the cemetery and half the town was there. I wept at the funeral as if he were my own brother.' He struck his chest with his fist. 'My heart still weeps for him.'

It was one of the things Jake had grown used to in Italian men. They could say such things and not even blush. Back home in Milwaukee a guy would hammer nails through his tongue before he'd admit to weeping.

'Did you know Lombardi well?'

The police chief spread his arms wide in an expansive gesture. 'I know everyone in Sorrento well. It is my job.'

'He was in the wood-inlay business, wasn't he?'

'Yes. He was a great craftsman. There are many wood-inlay businesses in Sorrento; it is a speciality of this town. We even have a school for boys to learn the difficult techniques. The woodwork of Sorrento is famous throughout Italy for its beauty.'

'So I'm told. It must have been hit hard during the war. No customers, no tourists, no work for them, the young men called up into the army. Business must have been bad.'

'*Merda*! It was hard for everyone.'

Jake leaned forward and observed the police chief closely. 'Did Lombardi have enemies in Sorrento?'

There was a flicker of his eyelid. Like a cat closing its eyes in the sun. 'Why do you ask these questions, Major Parr?'

'Because I am interested in Antonio Lombardi.'

He offered no further explanation. The money in the envelope did his talking.

Belzano positioned a pen neatly across the desk in front of him like a miniature fortress wall between them. 'Lombardi was very successful before the war.' He eyed Jake shrewdly. 'So of course others were jealous.'

'Jealous enough to spread incriminating rumours about him?'

'It was not his work that caused the problems.'

'What caused the problems then?'

The police chief gave a slow lascivious smile. 'His wife.'

Caterina went quickly upstairs. On the first floor were her brother's bedroom and her grandfather's room. She searched Luca's room first but with no expectation of finding anything. It contained a bed, a wardrobe, an old pirate's chest her father had made, a wooden table and chair. Wardrobe first, then the chest.

Both smelled of the sea. There were thousands of shells in them, beautiful swathes of brittle pinks, greys, magentas and ginger-browns that swirled when she stirred them. There were twists of fishing rope and any number of model aircraft that Luca must have whittled from off-cuts of wood. She didn't know he'd done that. She turned to his bed. She stripped the mattress off it, and stared, surprised. Covering the metal springs were sheets of newspaper. Why had he put those there? She frowned, pushed back her long hair and snatched up one of the newspaper sheets. She wasn't sure what she expected to find under it. Comics maybe? What she saw were envelopes, small blue ones, each with Luca's childish handwriting scrawled across the front.

Caterina didn't touch them. She lifted another page of newspaper and then another. More envelopes in layers. Small rectangles of blue.

How many?

She counted them. Sixty-two. Carefully she picked one up, aware that she was trespassing where she had no right to trespass. She read the name on the outside of the envelope.

Signora Lucia Lombardi.

Her breath stopped as she stared down at the blue envelopes. Every one of them without exception had her mother's name on it but no address.

With a quick flick of her finger she opened the unsealed flap.

Mamma.

Where are you?

I miss you.

I know I tell you this each time. I don't remember you. I was too young when you went away. But I miss you. I have no pictures of you.

Come back.

Please come back.

Signora Ragone in the panettaria said Caterina looks like you, but her hair is dark and yours is blonde. So I stare and stare at my sister, making her into you.

I have made you a Christmas present, Mamma.

Please come home. I dream about you.

Your son.

Luca.

Caterina sat on the floor, dry-eyed, fighting back the sadness that swept through the room.

Oh Luca, Luca. You never speak about Mamma.

In this house Lucia Lombardi is dead. How could I not understand that a young boy needs to hear his mother's name?

She opened two other letters, no more. They were the same words but with no mention of a Christmas gift. One said he had received a swimming award at school that day and the other that he had caught a garfish for her dinner and had given it to Caterina to cook for her. Caterina bludgeoned her brain to recall that occasion, but the truth was that her brother often brought fish home and she could not separate the garfish from the others.

How long ago did he write it? She remembered the swimming award – when was it? A year ago, maybe eighteen months. Luca at ten years old could swim like a dolphin. The handwriting on some envelopes looked recent, but the writing on others looked very childish, wobbling across the blue surface and tumbling in odd directions. Her heart clenched but she didn't touch any more of them. If he'd wanted her to read them, he would not have hidden them.

She stood silent in the room and remembered the soft sound of his crying at night. She'd thought it was hunger, but now she was doubting herself. She had worked such long hours in the army uniform factory and then shut herself away in the workshop at night to earn extra money. What about Luca? Why hadn't she thought about her little brother at home in the care of an old blind man? What about the walking cane in Nonno's hand and the red marks on Luca's thin legs?

Quickly she replaced the letters on the sheet of newspaper, covered them up and pulled the mattress and bedding on top of them. Without a word she moved over to his pillow and ran her hand over it, as though expecting to find it wet with tears, but it was dry. She left the room and its shadows. She closed the door behind her, snapped it shut, but she could hear them still. The words. Seeping under the door in Luca's high young voice.

Please come home. I dream about you.

CHAPTER EIGHT

Jake entered Piazza Tasso, the sun beating down on the back of his neck, the morning traffic battling wheel to wheel for a pathway through the large square. On three sides rose an abundance of amber-tinted classical buildings, but on the fourth side the square ended abruptly in a thirty-metre drop to a steep gorge. An iron staircase clung to the cliff face and zigzagged down to the road below, where the marina lay. As Jake passed the parapet that divided the piazza from the drop, he could smell the tang of the sea but it was the prospect of a cold beer under one of the parasols on the far side of the square that drew Jake to Fauno's Bar. Two old men in dark suits were seated at a pavement table with a British army officer who had a strip of sunburn running down the bridge of his nose.

'Good morning to you, Captain,' Jake greeted the officer.

It was Harry Fielding. Jake gave no sign that he had arranged this meeting in Piazza Tasso, but he could always rely on Harry to be where he was meant to be. They had come here today to discover more about the Lombardi family.

'So you're working in Sorrento today too.' Harry shaded his eyes from the sun with his hand and smiled a welcome.

They shook hands and Jake sat down, nodding courteously to the elderly gentlemen at Harry's table. One was thin with a shock of white hair and a military bearing, his eyes obscured by dark glasses; the other was soft and fleshy, and when he smiled, his false teeth gave a little jump of surprise.

'Signore,' Harry said with easy charm to the Italians, 'let me introduce Major Parr. He's American, so he can afford to buy the drinks.' He laughed easily and the others joined in. 'Signor Lombardi,' he waved a hand towards the taller man, 'and Signor Verucchi were just discussing the likelihood of an election next year for a new government for Italy. What do you think, Jake?'

'Of course. After we've all gone,' Jake pointed out, 'an election will be essential. Once you're rid of the Allied Military Government and the Allied Commission, it will be time for Ivanhoe Bonomi to step down as prime minister of the interim government.'

'*Si,*' Lombardi, the one in the dark glasses, agreed with a stern nod at Jake, as if he were personally responsible for the American bombs on Naples. 'After you Allied soldiers sail back to your own country instead of occupying ours, we can start making our own decisions.'

'It was Allied troops who came to Italy's rescue and drove the Germans out of your country,' Harry pointed out mildly.

Jake noticed the way the old man's hand curled into a fist on the table, strong and muscular, the hand of a much younger man.

'Where were Allied rifles and Allied money when the partisans needed them in their fight against the Germans?' Lombardi demanded.

But Jake was not to be goaded into indiscretion and caught the eye of a cheerful waiter in a black shirt and white apron. 'Grappa?' he offered the two men.

The fleshy one nodded eagerly but the tall thin one shook his head. 'Prosecco, *per favore.*'

'Celebrating our retreat already?' Jake laughed.

'No, I am celebrating the fact that the partisans will win, come election time.'

'You sure of that?'

'*Sì*. Italy owes them that much.' He placed a hand on his heart. 'They were the ones who risked their lives to hound and harass first the Fascists, and then the Germans. Blowing up military trains and sabotaging equipment so that . . .'

'Ah, signor,' Harry interrupted, 'the trouble is that the partisans are hand in glove with the communists. The rumour is that Palmino Togliatti is confident that under his leadership the communist party will win a big majority in the new parliament.'

Jake shook his head. 'No, this new party of De Gasperi's is the one to watch, the Christian Democrats.'

But he didn't want to get into a political wrangle – sure as hell, that was not what he'd come for – so he pulled out his cigarettes and offered them round. Verucchi took two, lighting one of them for his blind friend and relaxing contentedly as he inhaled. In front of them in the piazza a donkey was ambling slowly in front of a military truck, indifferent to the hoots of its horn.

Yet Signor Lombardi was not willing to let the subject of the partisans lie. Something had agitated the old man, an anger lying just under his aged olive skin, waiting to be stirred into life. He snapped at Harry, 'The trouble is that you British have been bitten twice by partisan movements, first in Greece and then Yugoslavia. So you are running scared. Too frightened to back them here in Italy.' He drew hard on his cigarette.

'Our prime minister, Winston Churchill, does not want to see your King Victor Emmanuel removed,' Harry responded with an unaccustomed edge to his voice. 'That's what the communists plan to do. So he refuses to support them or the partisans.'

'Hah!' Verucchi snorted. 'Down here in the south we are royalist, so that will never happen, I promise you. We will never give up our monarchy, any more than you British will.'

'I hope you're right.'

Their drinks arrived, cool and inviting, dispersing the tension at the table.

Jake took the moment to ask, 'What jobs exist in the town, now that there are no tourists? It must be hard for the people here to earn a living.'

'They get by,' Lombardi said. 'They always have. We are strong people.'

'I am fortunate.' Verucchi patted his own ample stomach.

'My family are bakers.' He smiled kindly at Harry and Jake. 'You soldiers all like to feast on our bread and our pastries. We are grateful to you.' He gestured towards the other tables in the bar where groups of soldiers sat drinking coffee or beer, some with girls laughing at their sides. 'Our town needs you right now.'

'What about the wood craftsmen here?'

Verucchi laid a hand on his friend's shoulder. 'Skilled families like Giuseppe Lombardi's are the pride and joy of Sorrento. His granddaughter keeps telling us that once Italy is back on its feet, more tourists than ever will flock here.'

'Is that so?'

The rumble of the traffic and the urgent sound of the horns seemed to grow louder. The old man reached for his drink, guiding the glass with the tips of his fingers.

'My son,' Giuseppe Lombardi announced, 'was the finest craftsman in Sorrento, probably in all Italy. His skill was far superior to mine, long before I lost my eyes. But he died. One of your American bombs killed him in his workshop.'

'I'm sorry,' Jake said.

A silence slid on to the table.

'He suffered from TB as a child,' Lombardi stated, 'he had a bad lung. Other men's sons were marched off to face the guns of the Great War, but not mine. Not my Antonio. Let others spill their blood for Italy, but not my boy, who could make wood sing under his fingers.'

He took a final drag on his cigarette, tossed it to the ground and held out his hand to Jake for a handshake. Jake grasped it and they remained clasped together there, above the wooden table. What was it the old man was trying to say with his hand that he could no longer say with his useless eyes? Was he asking for friendship? Was he offering peace? Forgiveness to the American forces for having killed his son? Jake could only guess. But he could feel the heat of it, the pulse of blood through the hard muscle of his hand.

'What is it?' Jake asked in a low voice.

'It is retribution,' Lombardi said. 'Divine punishment because I did not want my son to fight for his country. I relished too much his safety in Sorrento. It was a sin, so God has punished me by taking my only son from me.'

'No, signor. You are mistaken. It was an accident, a random tragic occurrence of war. Nothing more.'

The old man snatched back his hand and rose to his feet, his mouth twisted in disgust. 'You are American. You know nothing about such things. In Italy we know all about retribution; it is in our blood.'

'Are you sure you don't mean vengeance?'

'Call it what you will.'

Signor Verucchi snapped his false teeth together and stood alongside his friend. 'Come, Giuseppe, let us take our walk.'

But Lombardi was standing rigidly in front of the table, gripping the head of his cane. A breeze from the sea tugged at his white hair and blew ash from the ashtray on to his dark suit but he was unaware of it.

'Signor Lombardi,' Jake said, concerned for the old man, 'don't forget that we each choose which battles we fight and which ones we retreat from. The bomb that landed on your son's workshop is not a battle worth fighting. For either of us.'

Lombardi's cane lashed out, and had Jake been half a metre closer it would have caught him. But it swung through nothing but air.

'Major, I fight what battles I choose. I need no advice from you. If you want to know about battles, go speak to the Cavaleri family. They will teach you what retribution means.'

He stalked off across Via Corsa, tapping his cane ahead of him and ignoring the irate blaring of horns, so that Verucchi had to scurry to keep up with him. Jake turned and saw Harry Fielding regarding him with a raised eyebrow.

'Well,' his friend said, lighting a cigarette, 'that went well.'

Caterina ran up the stairs to the next floor. Up here at the top of the house were her own bedroom and the one that used to be her father's. It was hot. The sun sprawled over the roof and raised the temperature of these upper rooms, so that sometimes at night it was impossible sleep, but she had always liked it here, high up, next to her father. She didn't bother with her own room. Instead she immediately opened the door to her father's bedroom, the handle warm to the touch as though he had been standing there with his hand on it. She forced herself to step inside.

Since Antonio Lombardi's death she only entered the room on the first day of each month to dust and fling the windows wide to air it. Always fast. In and out. Nothing had been touched or changed; it was exactly as her father left it the morning the bomb fell on his workshop, and she imagined she could still smell his hair oil, the leather of his boots, the wood-scent that always clung to his skin.

Caterina began her search, quick and methodical. It was the only room in the house that still possessed a profusion of objects. Elsewhere everything that was non-essential had been sold. But here there were silver-backed hair brushes, leather-bound books, gilt mirrors, photographs in tortoiseshell frames of Luca and herself, and on the walls hung numerous beautiful inlay pictures that her father had created himself. Caterina turned her back on them. She couldn't bear to look at his work. Instead she set about emptying the drawers of his dressing table, his bedside cabinet and the tallboy and searching through their contents. She found nothing.

She lifted the mattress. Nothing. She left opening the wardrobe till last because she knew what it would do to her. She rummaged through the clothes, turned over shoes, searching inside them, but there was nothing there that should not be there, not even when she shouldered the wardrobe away from the wall to look behind it. It was with relief that she finally left the room, closed the door behind her and rested her head against its warm oak.

'Papà,' she murmured. 'I know you. I am certain you would not have let it all burn.'

We think we know the people we love. But what if she were mistaken? What if the father she had loved all those years was not the man behind the bright laughing eyes and the easy way of smiling? What if she had got it all wrong?

She inhaled hard and her mind cleared. With clarity came anger. The anger was at the American soldier who felt he had the right to walk into a town and destroy a person's life without a second thought. Her father was a decent and honest man who would no more connive with thieves or steal what belonged to Italy than he would cut his daughter's throat.

How dare Major Parr make her doubt her father for even a heartbeat? She pushed herself away from the door and hurried down the stairs, the sound of her father's voice fading behind her.

Her grandfather's bedroom was next. It was on the same landing as her brother's but she'd left it till last because she was reluctant to put a foot over the threshold. She knew that Nonno permitted nobody inside. It was his private territory: the bolt hole of a proud blind man within an all-seeing world. He kept the window open and the shutters permanently closed, cleaned it himself and changed his bedding, seeing and feeling with his fingertips. Sometimes Caterina wondered exactly what he saw with them.

Did he see a grandson who missed his mother and father? Did he see a cane as his way to leave his mark on the world? Or was it that he had lost his only son two years ago and all his rage at that loss was hidden inside his cane, biding its time to strike?

Nonno was a good man. A family man. A loving grandfather who had taught her as a child how to hold a chisel and had taken her into the fields and up into the mountains to understand that wood was a living thing with branches and leaves, with sap that rose through its veins like its heart's blood. He had taught her to respect wood. It was her father who taught her to love it.

She felt like a thief in his room. She switched on the light and worked uneasily, barely touching things, glancing in drawers, sliding a hand under his mattress, kneeling to look under his bed. She found a small leather case of military medals she'd never seen before, and his Bodeo gun under his pillow. *Under his pillow*? She frowned as her fingers brushed its cold barrel. What was it he feared? A man with a pock-marked face and a gold tooth? Or was it the darkness? Did he fear the black world he inhabited each day?

Just the wardrobe left. A brief look inside and she'd be finished. But when Caterina opened its door, she was astonished. Alongside the shadowy shapes of suits and shirts and ancient silk waistcoats, tucked in amongst the old-man smells, were piles and piles of shoe-boxes. She felt her pulse quicken. Here she would find the proof she was seeking to push under the American's nose, the order book she needed to show him he was wrong. To make him apologise. Not to her, but to her father's good name. If she could drive the American away, then the gold tooth would go with him.

She lifted each box out of the wardrobe, all eighteen of them, and removed their lids. Her heart sank. Just shoes. Black, brown, tan, white, beige, cream, burgundy, so many shoes he never wore. Some were old and cracked. Others were highly polished and soft as butter, their smooth sheen catching the light. She covered them up again, confused by the profusion of them, aware of the fact that her grandfather wore the same black lace-ups day in, day out. Why all these?

She checked the bottom of the wardrobe and noticed something there. A small brass ring. Curious, she tried to pick it up but discovered it was attached to the baseboard. She gave it a tug. A section of the baseboard rose in her hand, revealing a compartment beneath, about the size of a roof tile. Inside it lay a book.

CHAPTER NINE

Caterina sat at the kitchen table, determined to find out the truth. The book lay in front of her and her hand rested on its surface. The cover was a rainbow of burgundy and black, the twin of the order book that had burned in the workshop fire, except that this one was smaller. She opened it to the first page.

There were columns, as she'd known there would be, and she scanned them with care. Names of clients on the right, ordered items on the left and their dates. In the middle there was one column for materials and one for costs. The words blurred as she stared at them, but her fingers lingered on the ink, sliding her skin over her father's neat small writing – an accountant's penmanship, it had always seemed to her. She could smell the tobacco from his pipe.

The rich aroma was an illusion, she knew that, but still she looked quickly around the kitchen and felt the bite of disappointment at not finding him there. It was a dreary kitchen. A few plain cupboards lined the walls and a pine shelf, all utilitarian. Gone were the handsome cabinets that Papà had lovingly crafted and decorated with inlay for her mother, sold to pay for repairing the roof last winter. Only the walnut table remained with its fine scrolled legs and intricately grained surface that bore the marks of her childhood imprinted on it.

She turned the page. And then another, her eyes greedy, and the memories came tumbling into her mind, crisp and colourful. A cabinet for Signor Lucente. A desk for Signor Vietti. A cigar box. A galleried tray. A pair of high-backed chairs. Wall panels. Tables of all shapes and sizes. A serving trolley. A coat stand. A set of library steps. And yes, the extraordinary birdcage for Madame Blanchard, the French dressmaker. All inlaid. All exquisite. Caterina remembered each one, the way you remember old friends.

A child's crib for Signora Marinelli.

A travelling chest for Dottore Trento.

The pages flicked past, faster now. She could feel the warmth of her father's breath on the back of her neck, the way she used to when he leaned over her shoulder, observing the manner in which she wielded a chisel or pressed the tip of a gouger to a channel.

'Patience, my daughter,' he would whisper. 'Have patience with your fingers. Have patience with the wood.'

1939. That was the year these orders were written into the book. It was the year before Italy entered the war in Europe, but already the tourists had dried to no more than a trickle. No one came to buy the musical boxes she was making then.

'Don't fret, Caterina,' her father had reassured her. 'The war will be over quickly and people will always want pretty things.'

But Papà was wrong. The next year everything changed. Italy entered the war, Mussolini sliding smoothly into Hitler's back pocket, and it was the end of business for the Lombardi family. Her father's TB lung meant he was not called up for military service but Caterina at sixteen had been required to work in the hated uniform factory. Suddenly the orders in the book dried up. The decoration of a piano in September. Nothing more till a small jewellery box at Christmas and then a firescreen and she remembered how hard it was for her to work mother-of-pearl for the first time, inlaying a white egret into the design. Papà had been patient. He was always patient.

Then nothing. The order book was blank for months. What had they lived on? What paid the bills? Certainly not her pittance of a wage. They must have lived off her father's savings, year after year.

No wonder all the money went. The bank manager had summoned her to his office after the funeral and informed her there was *Niente*. Nothing. He had lifted his hands in despair before replacing them on the snug cushion of his stomach. The account was overdrawn. With a drooping moustache, he declared there was not even enough to pay for the funeral. Caterina had sold everything she could lay her hands on, but as the years ticked past, they were slowly starving.

Now the guns had fallen silent. The screams had ceased, and the tears had stopped. The war was over and the soldiers were here. Whether they were English, American, Australian or French, Caterina didn't care, as long as they wanted to take one of her musical boxes back home to their loved ones.

'I made it, Papà. I got us through this accursed war after you'd gone. But I need you now.' She laid her palm flat on the page. 'I need you to help me, to tell me what today was all about. What were you doing, Papà? I am afraid.'

But she refused to allow a foreign soldier to blacken her father's name or threaten his family. She plucked out a serrated knife from the knife drawer and sliced its blade across the muscled pad of her thumb, let it taste her blood. A thin red ribbon emerged and she pressed down hard on the page of the order book.

'I promise to prove you are innocent, Papà. A blood promise.'

With sudden impatience she skipped to the last page of entries, and it was there. She found what she had been hoping for, as she read across the columns.

Table. Wedding gift. Bird's eye maple. And jewels. The cost column lay empty. In the right hand column was written the name *Count di Marco, Villa dei Cesari, Capri.*

She leapt to her feet, dizzy with fear. The American was right about the table.

Bird's eye maple. And jewels.

Jewels?

At that moment a loud knock on the front door rattled through the house, startling her. She snatched up the order book and thrust it into a kitchen cupboard, right at the back behind the stewpot, her limbs rigid as she walked to the door.

Caterina swung open the door. What she saw was an army uniform. All polished buttons, shoulder epaulettes and a heavy leather belt with a brass buckle that gleamed at her. He was back. She almost shut the door on him, but she blinked in time and realised that the uniform was British, not American, and the hair under the officer's cap was fair, not dark. The eyes were blue and friendly. It wasn't Major Parr.

'*Buongiorno*. I'm Harry Fielding.' The soldier's smile was respectful. 'We met yesterday.'

'I remember you.'

She didn't open the door any further.

'I know it's a bit of an intrusion, but I understand that you had a talk with Major Parr this morning.' He paused. She passed no comment. 'Is that right?'

'You know it's right.'

'Indeed.' He made a small gesture with his hand, apologetic. There was something gentle about this soldier, and about the set of his jaw. 'But I would like to have a chat with you myself in private, if I may?'

'What about?'

One of his blond eyebrows lifted. 'You know what it's about, Signorina Lombardi.'

She thought about saying no. This soldier was kinder than the American, more subtle in his approach, but he was here for the exact same purpose. Two women from the next street ambled past, swinging their hips, and eyed the handsome captain on her doorstep with interest, beaming at him when he touched his cap to them.

'Come in,' Caterina said sharply.

'*Grazie.*'

She permitted him into the tiled hallway, but she didn't want him nosing around her house or staring, as he was doing now, at the set of portraits on the wall.

'They're beautiful.'

'I doubt that Winston Churchill has ever been called beautiful before,' she responded.

He laughed, a soft refined chuckle that suited him. He had well-cut features and thick pale eyelashes. She couldn't imagine him firing a gun. The portraits on the wall were of the wartime leaders – Churchill, Roosevelt, Mussolini, Stalin, Emperor Hirohito and, in the shadowy corner, the fanatical face of Adolf Hitler himself. They were created out of fine fragments of wood, inlaid slivers of veneer using more than fifty different varieties of wood to give shape and shade and texture to each face.

'Your father was a true artist to do such fine work,' Captain Fielding said sincerely. 'You must be proud of him.'

Caterina turned away. She did not want this man in the house and certainly nowhere near the kitchen cupboards, so without a word she led him down the corridor to the back of the house. In her mind stretched the hundreds of hours she had spent creating those portraits herself. It was during the war, after her factory shift each day, when the bombers droned overhead and her emotions ran high.

They stepped out into a small courtyard that sat in the centre of the group of tall thin houses. There was a cobweb of iron stairs that zigzagged between floors, and slabs of black basalt underfoot that had soaked up the heat of the morning. A glossy-leafed lemon tree scented the air and a riot of magenta bougainvillea blooms sunned themselves in the triangle of light that slid over the roof.

'This is pretty,' Harry Fielding said with surprise.

Caterina steered him over to an oak table and chairs that stood in the shade.

'Please sit down.'

It was easier with him sitting down, not as much uniform to stare at. He removed his cap which left an indentation across his forehead and there were beads of sweat gleaming among the short blond hairs at his temples.

'What is it you want to *chat* about?'

'Major Parr informed me that he has spoken with you about your father.'

'Whatever it is that you and your Major Parr believe my father has done, you are wrong. He would never . . .'

'That's why I wanted to talk with you. You are Signor Lombardi's daughter, so you of all people are in the perfect position to clarify what was going on. We could be mistaken.'

He smiled and it was reassuring. This Captain Fielding was easy to like. His edges were smooth and his smile was warm. But she didn't want to like him.

We could be mistaken, he'd said.

It gave her hope.

'My father would never do anything so despicable.'

The Englishman nodded, as if he accepted her word. He

reached into a leather satchel at his side and took out a packet, which he placed on the table. It was coffee. He slid it across the table.

'For you.'

The rich heavy aroma that seeped from the packet made Caterina's stomach clench and sent a craving for caffeine fizzing through her blood. This was real coffee, not the bitter make-shift sawdust she bought yesterday. Firmly she pushed it back to his side of the table.

'No, thank you.'

He glanced from her to the coffee, surprised. 'I'm sorry,' he said, as if he had insulted her and he pushed the packet to one side.

'Why are you here?'

He smiled patiently. 'I told you. To listen to your side of the story. I'm not convinced by the accusations that I've been hearing from a bunch of thieves and crooks.'

'Major Parr is convinced.'

'I know. But these men who are pointing the finger at your father would sell their own sweet mother to save their blasted skins. Believe me.' He frowned. He seemed on edge. 'They'd hang if I had any say in it.'

It stunned her. The sudden brutality of the statement. Yet when she recalled the thick arm looped around her neck in the street doorway, she found herself nodding. Yes, hang them, if that's what it takes.

Captain Fielding was regarding her narrowly and only then did she realise she had spoken it aloud. Yes, hang them.

'Who are they?' she asked.

'Just small fry. Men involved in trading stolen ancient artefacts. Small links in the chain who panic when we haul them in and interrogate them. The big criminals stay in the shadows.'

'I can't help you.'

She shut her mouth tight before more words fell out. About a man with a white slash in his hair and a desire to kill in his eyes. She placed a hand over her lips to keep them closed because if the words tumbled out, it would be Nonno or Luca who suffered. He had made that clear. She clenched her teeth tight. Captain Harry Fielding was giving her a hard stare, as though he had heard something not quite right in her voice. He closed his hands together on the table and looked down at them.

'When I was fourteen,' he told her, 'I was at boarding school in Marlborough in England, a lovely ancient red-brick town. One afternoon my headmaster summoned me to his study to tell me that my father had shot himself.'

Caterina could not silence her gasp.

'It was 1929. Just after the Wall Street crash,' he continued in a flat tone. 'Pa had lost everything. Oh, my headmaster was kind and considerate, but nothing prepares you for the shock of losing your father.' He spoke softly. 'I know that.'

She wanted to say something to him, to offer sympathy, but found that tears were running down her cheeks.

'I'm sorry,' he said instantly, acutely embarrassed. 'I have intruded.' He rose to his feet. 'I must leave. I am keeping you from your work.' His words came out clipped and awkward.

Caterina wiped her face with the back of her hand, but could not bring herself to ask more about his father. 'How is it that you speak such good Italian?'

He seemed relieved at the change of subject. 'For the first fourteen years of my life my parents brought me to Italy for two months every spring. They adored Italy, especially Italian opera at La Scala.' He shrugged with a boyish smile, remembering. 'I always had an Italian nanny. My father was delighted when I could speak Italian better than he could.'

He looked ridiculously young suddenly. Too young for a soldier's uniform.

'Find out for me,' she said.

'Find out what?'

'Why someone is blaming my father.'

He gave her a brief nod. 'There is something else. Major Parr might not have told you, but I feel you have the right to know.'

She waited.

'A man's body was hauled out of the oily waters of Naples dockyard last week, but he didn't drown. His windpipe was crushed. He was a jeweller by the name of Orlando Bartoli. We were called in by the police to investigate because he had been caught with a stolen painting. When we interrogated others involved, your father's name kept popping up.'

Panic crawled up her throat.

'That means nothing,' she whispered.

'I agree. But Major Parr is convinced that the connection

means something.' He paused, studying her face. 'I apologise, Signorina Lombardi, if I have upset you.'

She shook her head. 'No.' Her movements and her words had grown jerky.

For a while they stood in the shade in silence, both aware that the conversation had changed things, both unable to find a way back on to solid ground. Then Caterina moved and led him back inside the house. She opened the front door for him and he stepped out into the narrow street, glancing up at the ribbon of blue sky above. Everything about him was awkward now. He lingered on the front step holding his cap and puffing out his cheeks as if he had more to say, but the words had lodged behind his teeth.

'Goodbye, Captain. Thank you for coming. For being honest.'

He looked directly at her, his blue eyes uncertain. 'There is a dance at the Santa Lucia Hotel in Naples tomorrow night. We hold one every week. I wondered if you would care to come. With me, I mean. I would fetch you and bring you back in the jeep.'

'No thank you.'

'Of course. Damn silly of me to presume.'

'I don't want to go to Naples or to attend a formal military event, but I'll share a pizza with you at Georgio's pizzeria round the corner from here, if you like. They are the best in Sorrento. Seven o'clock tomorrow night.'

He grinned at her. 'I'll be there.'

She closed the door and listened to his footsteps fade outside. Two soldiers in one morning. *Papà, they must want it badly, whatever it is they're after.* She had started to head back towards the kitchen cupboard, when she remembered that the coffee still lay on the courtyard table.

Every wood has its own voice when sawn. Its own fragrance when its flesh and veins are opened up. When Caterina walked into her brother's bedroom that evening she could smell yew. Luca was lying on his stomach on his bed with his schoolwork, but his smooth young cheeks were flushed. She wondered why. Had he been whittling something out of a piece of yew and pushed it under his bed when he heard her step on the stairs?

'I've brought you something.'

He looked up. Their father's eyes, round and dark as ancient oak. They brightened when they saw what she was holding. He sat up and she handed him a sfogliatella she had just baked.

'*Grazie.*'

He muttered the word through a mouthful of pastry, rolling his eyes with pleasure, but ended up, as he often did, staring at her hands, and she always had the feeling that he was trying to fathom why it was that she had inherited her father's talent with wood, but he hadn't.

'What are you studying?' she asked.

'Geography.'

Luca was not a keen scholar. He preferred to fish.

'Can I help? What are you learning?'

'The capitals of Europe.'

'Do you want me to test you?'

'If you like.'

He was grinning up at her just as he did when they played chess and he had her queen cornered. Their father had taught them the game and Luca had spent intense hours over the board with him. He was far better at it than Caterina.

She prodded a finger at the map in front of him. 'What is the capital of Portugal?'

'*Lisbona*.'

'*Bene*. And Finland?'

'Helsinki.'

'*Molto bene*.'

But now he was chewing at his thumbnail and staring at her with concern. 'What's wrong, Caterina?'

'Nothing.'

He shook his head. Her brother knew her too well. He was always quick to catch on to her mood.

She put a hand in her pocket to distract him. 'I have something for you, Luca.'

His eyes brightened, clearly hoping for another sfogliatella. She pulled out a postcard. It was yellowed with age and its edges soft and blurred. On the front was a black and white picture of the magnificent fourteenth-century Duomo of Florence. She held it out to him. He took it and glanced at the picture, but when he flipped it over to read it, his mouth dropped open. His finger traced the looped black writing.

'It's from Mamma,' Caterina said needlessly.

She knew the words by heart. *Having fun. Florence is party heaven. Your Mamma*. It was addressed to Caterina.

'She sent it to me when I was five. She went to Florence for her cousin's wedding.' She didn't add that her mother didn't come back for three weeks or that Papà didn't eat or sleep while she was gone. He even stopped shaving. When Mamma finally returned, she greeted her husband with a wrinkle of her nose in disgust and the comment, 'Antonio, you look like something a dog has chewed.'

Caterina didn't tell Luca that. Because he was smiling, not just with his mouth but with every part of himself.

'You can keep it,' she said.

His face was bent close to the card, and he said an eager 'Thank you', but didn't look up. So he didn't see what it cost her.

Caterina placed a glass of hot water and lemon at her grand-father's elbow. He had fallen asleep in his chair, his head at an awkward angle, and the stubbled folds of his face had slipped sideways.

'Time for bed, Nonno,' she said softly.

He jerked awake, his neck clicking audibly as he sat up straight, a legacy of the injuries of his fall years ago. He always sat straight. He constantly told Luca that slumping in a chair was not good for the brain.

'My water?' he asked.

'It's beside you.'

'*Grazie.*'

His long fingers searched for it, twitching like feelers. It was hard not to mollycoddle him, to place a drink safely in his hand, but if ever she did she was rewarded with a prod of his cane and a snort of disgust. She sat in the seat opposite him, sipping her own water, and waited for him to settle with his drink.

'Nonno, do you know someone called Count di Marco?'

'No.'

'Have you heard the name?'

'Yes, I have. I think he lives over on Capri.'

Her grandfather sipped his drink for a full minute in silence.

'Did Papà know him?'

His heavy white eyebrows swooped into a frown. 'What is this about?'

'I think he gave Papà an order for a table and I'm trying to find out a bit more about it.'

'Why? What does it matter now?' His voice was harsh. 'Your father is gone. No questions can bring him back.'

'I know that, Nonno.'

They drank quietly, her grandfather wary now, but Caterina had not finished.

'Nonno, was Papà involved in anything illegal? I know times were hard after the war started.'

'Wash those words from your tongue, girl. Don't you ever speak like that about your father.'

'Did he receive jewels from Count di Marco?'

'Would we have been starving if your father had jewels? Is that what you think?' His voice was rising. 'Stop this right now. Whatever you think you're doing, stop it. Your father was the finest man you'll ever know.' His hand was shaking. Water from his glass fell on his trousers. 'He was my son.'

'I know, Nonno. I know. I am not accusing him of anything.'

'You are his daughter, Caterina Lombardi. You should be loyal.'

'I am always loyal to Papà.'

Her grandfather discarded the glass on the table next to him, snatched up his cane and rose to his feet. He turned his sightless face in her direction and rapped the tip of his cane on the floor.

'Caterina, if you continue with this,' he waved his strong hand through the air to encompass *this*, as if it stretched, like the darkness in his head, beyond the room, 'I tell you, you do not deserve to be Antonio Lombardi's daughter.'

He made his way to the door and flung it open, his cane tapping like someone asking to come in. Caterina listened to his heavy footsteps on the stairs, but she continued to sit there. Remembering.

CHAPTER TEN

Caterina left the house with Luca the next morning, a smile on her face.

'You don't need to walk to school with me,' he moaned at her side. There was not much difference in their height these days. She was small and slight, while her brother was shooting up.

'I know, but I want to.'

'My friends will laugh at me.'

'Don't worry, I won't come as far as the school gate.' She ruffled his clipped hair.

To her surprise he didn't protest further and it occurred to her that he actually wanted her company.

'Luca, will you do something for me?'

There was something in her voice that wasn't meant to be there. Her brother heard it and looked at her instantly, his dark eyes bright with curiosity. He was wearing a sleeveless shirt that had been washed too many times, a scruffy pair of shorts and worn-out sandals, his limbs as lithe and brown as a colt's. He badly needed new clothes.

'What?' he asked suspiciously.

'I want you to come straight home after school instead of going down to the boats.'

'Why?'

'You spend too much time on the streets. I worry. So come straight home after school and we'll work on your school books together.'

He pulled a face but didn't say no. 'I wanted to catch you a big fish for dinner.' His eyes skimmed over her and he tutted softly in the way her father used to. 'You're too skinny, Caterina. Eat some of Nonno's chocolate.'

Such a small comment, but it meant a lot to Caterina. Her brother was growing up. But he was in that awkward stage where he was trying to learn to be a man, without a father to show him how. At the corner of the street where his school was, she stopped to let him go the rest of the way alone, but he stopped with her and faced her.

'What is going on, Caterina? Why are you so ...' he paused, searching for a word that came close, 'so unhappy?' he finished.

'I'm not unhappy, Luca.'

He frowned. 'I am your brother. Do you think I don't know by heart every expression on your face?'

He turned and set off towards the school.

'Don't forget, will you?' she called after him. 'To come straight home.'

He glanced back and grinned at her over his shoulder. 'Nor you. You forget the time when you're in your workshop.'

She wanted to run after him and wrap her arms around his bony frame and hold him close. But he wouldn't thank her for it.

The sea was still as glass, as if it had fallen asleep. Caterina stood in the queue to buy a ticket for the ferry to Capri and was staring up at the cliffs that soared above her. At the top of the vast slabs of pale limestone the town was bathed in the golden light of morning as it peered over the edge.

Nothing looked out of place. Nothing to set her heart hammering.

No unexpected figure gazing down from a balcony or terrace. No splash of sun from binoculars or the black gleam of a pair of sunglasses that was staring too long. Just the breeze ruffling the fronds of the lazy palms and a spiteful swirl of dust that lifted from the flowerbeds that adorned the town.

There was no reason for her to feel watched. None at all. But she didn't turn her back on it. Not for one second.

From the rail of the ferry that stank of diesel fumes, Caterina watched the waves roll and stretch and chase each other in an endless rhythm that soothed her mood, the way the moon did at night when it rose fat and powerful over the mountains. The great sweeping expanse of vivid blue water spread itself out around her and made the Sorrentine peninsula dwindle to nothing, to just a blur on the horizon, no more than a thumbprint. Her anger and her fear dwindled with it.

The isle of Capri rose from the Gulf of Naples in a great shoulder of rock, green and silvery grey, shimmering in the sun. A cornflower blue sky wrapped itself around the island and Caterina felt as if she were entering into an older world as she stepped off the ferry, a world where the imperious voices of emperors of Ancient Rome still whispered among their palatial villas and lavish gardens. Where lives were ended by the turn of a thumb.

She walked briskly along the marina, inspecting the sailing yachts as she did so, and the brightly coloured fishing boats that bobbed and tugged at their mooring ropes. She didn't know what she was looking for, but she was taking no chances. Alert for any sign of something unusual or any dark head with a white streak at the temple. But people were going about their business as usual, a smattering of military uniforms idling in the sunshine. A number of Capri's larger villas, including the one owned by the English singer, Gracie Fields, had been requisitioned as recuperation centres for wounded Allied soldiers, but there was nothing much to do on the island expect smoke and watch the crabs being hauled in.

Caterina had not taken the half-hour boat ride from Sorrento to Capri since before the war and she had forgotten how beautiful the island was – or perhaps she'd been too young to appreciate it – with its perpendicular limestone cliffs soaring out of the serene waters. She could smell the scent of its wild herbs and wooded slopes and see the rocky ridge of its back that ran across the island and up to the small town of Anacapri. In the Marina Grande she headed straight for the funicular railway and took a ride alongside a bunch of military uniforms up to La Piazzetta in the town of Capri.

'You live in this lovely place, signorina?' a shiny-faced sergeant asked politely as the funicular carriage eased itself to a stop.

Caterina shook her head. She had grown jumpy around uniforms. But she walked into the pretty pastel-painted square and immediately asked a local, who was selling strings of garlic from his bicycle, if he knew of the Villa dei Cesari. He pointed his cigarette to a headland further up the rugged cliff.

'Along there,' he said with a gap-toothed grin. 'But Count di Marco only hires male staff, signorina. Everyone knows that. He doesn't like women.'

It didn't bode well.

Caterina halted, sweat gathering in the hollows of her neck. The climb up from the town had been steep. She was standing in front of two bone-white marble pillars and a pair of iron gates, twice as tall as a person. She tried them. Locked. She inspected the stretch of road beyond them, a black tarmac driveway that seemed to bend and melt in the shimmering heat, but no house was visible. A dense tangle of juniper trees bordered the left side of the road, and on the right ran a white wall, chest-high. She couldn't see over it from here but knew that on the other side must lie a sheer drop to the rocks far below.

Villa dei Cesari. The words glinted in huge brass letters that straddled the pillars, big enough and bold enough to be seen from a hundred metres away. So this Count di Marco was a man who liked to protect his privacy, but enjoyed shouting out his importance to the world. She pressed the button on the intercom that was set into one of the pillars and immediately a female voice crackled out of it.

'*Buongiorno*, please state your name and your business.'

'I am Signorina Lombardi. I wish to speak to Count di Marco about a table he ordered from my father.'

'Wait one minute, please.'

One minute passed, followed by two more. After five minutes of standing in the hot sun, Caterina was just contemplating pressing the button again when there was a loud metallic buzzing and the voice said, 'Please enter.'

She pushed open the gate.

She was right about the sheer drop. It was there on the far side of the white wall, where seabirds skimmed the thermals rising up the cliffs from the sea, their wings like flashes of sunlight, their cries piercing. Caterina walked fast, past a row of statues that lined the left side of the road, arrogant life-size marble figures of Roman caesars in flowing white togas and wearing delicately carved ivy leaves on their heads to symbolise their power. Was that an indication of what mattered most to this Count di Marco? Power.

She turned her head and looked out to sea, dazzling to the eye, aware of the profusion of scarlet geraniums that trailed down the white wall like splashes of blood. It occurred to her that living here, high up among the ancient ruins, could easily turn a man's head and make him believe he was a Roman eagle.

Eventually the road abandoned the cliff edge and swung

inland through an avenue of elegant cypress trees. For the first time Caterina caught sight of the house and she felt a rush of excitement. It was a vast sprawling mansion, all soaring white columns and arcades of arches. A Roman villa fit for an emperor.

'*Buongiorno*, signorina.'

The great oak door swung open before Caterina had even finished climbing the wide semi-circular front steps, and an elegant woman wearing long silver earrings and a man's black suit and waistcoat stood ready to greet her.

'Good morning,' Caterina replied, conscious that her mother's blue dress was sticking to her legs and strands of her hair clung to her damp neck.

'It is warm today. Please enter.'

The woman stood back to allow Caterina to pass into a vast cool atrium with a high ceiling and an elaborate dolphin fountain in the centre. As Caterina came close to the woman she smelled a strong scent of verbena and felt the dark-eyed scrutiny taking in every detail of her appearance. Her hair needed a brush, her dusty sandals a clean before stepping into this pristine house, but she regarded the woman with interest.

She was tall, probably fifty, but with jet black hair, sleek as a seal, pulled back into a knot at the nape of her neck. She held herself very erect like a mannequin, and her strong features remained rigid, controlled into an unnatural stillness. Only her thick arched eyebrows lifted to show a ripple of surprise.

'You are young,' she said.

'I'm twenty-one.'

The dark crimson lips tightened, but nothing more.

'Count di Marco will see you now, but don't overtire him.'

'Is he unwell?'

'He is old.'

'I see.'

The woman in the man's suit flicked a glance at Caterina's face and held it there.

'I doubt that you do,' she murmured, and led the way down a corridor lined with ranks of marble female busts. The goddesses of Rome were out in force.

'Octavia, fetch the poor girl a drink, for God's sake. She looks . . .'

The man stretched out on a day-bed didn't finish the sentence. He didn't say what she looked like. His cool grey gaze was enough. Caterina stood in the centre of a graceful terrace, her blue dress the only splash of colour among a desert of white marble.

The woman in the black suit, the one he called Octavia, had stalked through the villa ahead of her without a glance over her shoulder, leading her through a room containing a white sunken pool surrounded by furniture that was elaborately gilded and protected from the fierce sunlight by fine white lace curtains. Beyond that lay the terrace where she was now standing in the midst of more bloodless statues of Roman beauties with a panoramic view of the Bay of Naples.

'Count di Marco.'

That was how the man had greeted her. With his own name, not hers.

'Thank you for agreeing to see me, Count.'

Caterina started to move towards him, curious to inspect him close up, but a sudden deepening of the creases on his forehead and an unease in his eyes made her halt. He was an extremely tall man with elongated restless limbs and a face dominated by a strong aquiline nose and a square clean-shaven jaw. The woman had said he was old but he didn't strike Caterina as so old, in his sixties, maybe seventy at most. His body was half hidden among an avalanche of snow-white cushions on a chaise longue and he was wearing some kind of flowing robe of bleached linen, almost a toga but not quite. Above his head stretched a pale canopy that shielded him from the sun's glare, his own personal island of shade.

'Excuse my not rising to greet you, signorina. My legs are not what they used to be.'

'I don't wish to disturb you. I just need to ask a few questions, if you have a moment.'

'Of course you are disturbing me, young lady.'

This was not a man who would welcome questions.

'I don't know if you are aware that my father died two years ago, when a . . .'

'I am aware of that. You are Antonio Lombardi's girl. That is the only reason I agreed to see you, otherwise you would not have been allowed past the gates.'

He said it brusquely, almost rudely, and yet a smile softened the harshness of it and he waved a hand towards a round table and chair which stood a few metres from him in a little patch of shade on its own. A parasol's fringe rippled above it. All white. All spotless despite the seabirds.

'Sit down, please, Signorina Lombardi.'

Caterina sat at the round table, her fingers caressing its surface. It was tulip wood but inlaid with a design of ivory and mother-of-pearl which turned it into a chess table, each square of inlay shadowed by carefully selected slivers of persimmon to give it a three-dimensional look. A fine hairline of ebony framed the board and a thread of spun gold was wrapped around the ebony. It was beautiful, so beautiful she could not take her hand from it. She had never seen the table before, but she knew it was her father's work as surely as if he had engraved his name across it.

'You like it?' the Count asked.

'Yes. It's lovely.'

'He made it for me before you were born.'

'That's why I've never seen it.'

'I am pleased you have finally come here, Signorina Lombardi.'

Caterina dragged her gaze from the table and concentrated on this strange man embalmed in white.

'Why is that?'

'Because your father told me about you.' The grey eyes studied her. Made her wait. 'He told me he admired your skill with wood. "My daughter could be as good as I am one day," he used to tell me, and when I asked, "Even better than you?" he would laugh, but he didn't deny it.'

The air on the terrace seemed to grow thin. She had not expected this, to be given such a gift. *As good as I am one day.* Her father had never said those words. Not to her.

'Thank you,' she murmured.

At that moment the woman in black appeared at her side and placed a tall glass of fresh lemonade with ice and mint on the table.

'*Grazie.*'

But she was gone, silent as a shadow on the marble.

'I am an old man now,' Count di Marco said softly, 'and not in the best of health. My life ...' he extended one long hairless arm from the folds of his robe and swept it in a curve that included the grandiose villa behind him and the splendour of the bay ahead of him, with Naples now no more than a dusky blur at the foot of Vesuvius. 'My life is quiet and simple now. I live vicariously through others. I watch the seabirds and in my mind I fly with them while my worthless body remains marooned on this island, on this great rock of ancient limestone.'

Caterina felt unexpected regret for this man who seemed to have given up on life.

'Your life isn't over yet,' she told him and smiled.

He frowned at her, his heavy brows swooping down, the nostrils of his hooked nose flaring in a sudden flash of anger. 'Don't pity me, Signorina Lombardi. One day you will be old and you will want no one's pity.'

'How can I pity you when you have all this? It is very beautiful here.'

'Beauty is not enough.'

Caterina sipped her drink, cool on her parched tongue, and rose to her feet. She picked up her white chair and carried it to a spot nearer his island of shade. She sat down on it in full sunshine, and leaned forward.

'Shall I tell you what happened to me yesterday?' she asked.

Instantly his eyes brightened. A twitch of anticipation stabbed at the corner of his mouth.

'Yes.'

'I was attacked.'

He pushed himself up on one elbow. 'Go on.'

'It happened in broad daylight in a street in Sorrento. Two men. One almost throttled me. The other threatened to kill me.'

'*Madonna santa*!'

'Fortunately I vomited over one of them and they ran off.'

'Ah, a girl as pretty as you can attract the wrong kind of . . .'

'It had nothing to do with my looks.'

The frown returned. 'What then?'

'They wanted information.'

'About what?'

She caught the whisper of his breathing, quick and sharp.

'About an American soldier who has been asking questions.'

'Why? What is this about?'

'I don't know.'

He looked at her hard, then smiled lazily and leaned back among his cushions. 'Thank you, signorina. That was most interesting. I don't even mind the lie at the end. Why should you tell an old man what is in your heart?'

But the heat seemed to gather around him, sheltering under his canopy, and he took out an ivory fan. He wafted it in front of his face, and she wondered if he was hiding from her, but abruptly he tossed it to one side.

'So, young lady, why have you come to Villa dei Cesari today?'

'To talk about the table.'

'Ah, yes. The table.'

CHAPTER ELEVEN

Caterina listened intently.

Count di Marco told her about the table with no apparent hesitation. He informed her that he had commissioned it from her father two years ago as a wedding gift for his granddaughter, Leonora, who was due to marry in May 1942, but everything conspired against the wedding and it was indefinitely postponed. He did not tell Caterina exactly why. But his face was like stone when he told her that he believed the destruction of the table in her father's workshop was an evil omen. The wedding was stopped.

'The odd thing is,' she said, 'that my father told me nothing about it. He never mentioned a table.'

'I ordered him to keep it secret.'

'Why?'

'Because it was to be a surprise.'

'Or because of the jewels?'

He stared at her blankly. 'What jewels?'

Either the old man was a good liar or there were no jewels.

Suddenly he started to laugh, a deep, boisterous sound that burst from his long chest and resounded across the marble. 'You mean the coloured glass?'

'Do I?'

'Your father designed a wonderful image to be inlaid into the bird's eye maple of the table. It was of Villa dei Cesari set up on the cliffs of Capri, surrounded by the blue sky and sea.'

'And he was using coloured glass?' she asked doubtfully.

'Yes. Intertwined with strings of gold and silver.'

'It would explain why nothing was found of it after the fire, of course.'

'Yes.'

Somewhere she could hear the excited bark of a dog. It seemed out of place in this carefully controlled setting.

After a moment's thought, Caterina stood up. The Count looked surprised. 'There is no point my staying any longer,' she said. '*Grazie*. Thank you for your time, but lies are no use to me.' She walked back towards the house, her shadow racing ahead of her as though eager to leave.

'Signorina Lombardi!' His tone was sharp.

She swung round. 'Do not insult me, Count di Marco. Or my father. He would never have worked with coloured glass. Nor would you have given your granddaughter such an object as a wedding gift. My father wrote the word "jewels" in his order book. He was not fool enough to mistake coloured glass for jewels. So don't . . .'

'What is going on here?' A young woman in a stylish

ice-white linen tunic and trousers strode out of the villa on to the terrace. 'Who are you?' she demanded of Caterina without a trace of civility.

At her side padded a white German Shepherd dog. Its ears lay flat against its head, its pale blue eyes fixed on Caterina. She could smell blood on its breath and there was a reddish stain on its muzzle. She took a step back.

'I am Caterina Lombardi. I came to speak to . . .'

But the young woman plunged past her and hurried with a fluttering of hands over to the Count on the chaise longue. He was looking displeased, his feet naked on the marble flooring.

'Nonno, are you all right? Is she upsetting you?'

'Of course I'm all right, Leonora.'

He lifted a hand and held it out to her. Gently the young woman took it between her own and kissed the mottled back of it. Her dark hair was cut in a sleek bob and her features were small and delicate, quite unlike those of her grandfather.

'Why are you discussing my wedding table again?' She laughed, a sound as brittle as glass. 'My fabled table. With a stranger.' Her hand drifted in Caterina's direction.

'She's not a stranger,' the Count said reprovingly. 'She is its creator's daughter.'

The glossy dark head turned to face Caterina for the first time, her arched eyebrows raised in surprise. 'Is that so? Did you ever see it?'

'Call off your dog.'

'What?'

'Your dog.'

The dark gaze slid to the German Shepherd. The animal was still standing in front of Caterina stiff-legged, head thrust forward, a silent snarl revealing long, blood-stained teeth. Caterina had not moved a muscle.

'Call off your dog.'

The Count's granddaughter snapped her fingers and the dog came instantly to heel. She caressed its white head and repeated a softer version of the laugh that wasn't a laugh.

'Behave yourself, Bianchezza,' she crooned. 'You mustn't frighten Nonno's guest.'

'Damn that animal,' the Count muttered with irritation. 'It scares us all, Signorina Lombardi. Take the creature away, Leonora. It has blood on its face.' He made a retching sound. 'You know the sight of blood makes me sick.'

Leonora di Marco's eyes met Caterina's and gave a fleeting smile, before she flounced off the terrace with the dog like a second skin at her side. It occurred to Caterina to wonder whether the young woman had brought the dog on to the terrace with its muzzle bloodied on purpose, yet she had appeared genuinely affectionate to her grandfather. It struck Caterina as odd.

The moment Leonora was gone, Caterina crossed the terrace to be at the old man's side before they were interrupted again. He was staring at the glass door through which his granddaughter had vanished and his fingers stripped threads from the hem of his robe with impatience. A breeze from the seas carried the scent of the lemon trees that grew on the slopes, as Caterina sat herself next to him. His head jerked around and he scowled at her.

'Remove yourself.'

'Count di Marco,' she kept her voice low, away from inquisitive ears in the house, 'if there had been coloured glass in the table it would have melted in the fire in my father's workshop. If there had been jewels, they would have been lying there among the ashes. They weren't. I scoured the burnt remains for anything that could be salvaged.'

The Count placed a hand on her shoulder. She felt the bite of it, the full weight of him bearing down on her bone as he used it to push himself to his feet to stand upright in front of her. Behind the shapeless toga and the relentless shell of whiteness, she could see the sharp edges of the man picked out by the sunlight.

'So where,' he demanded, 'are my jewels?'

'I don't know. Tell me about them.'

His grip on her shoulder tightened. 'Emeralds from India that would break your heart with their beauty. They were for the depiction of the island. The sky and sea were to be of sapphires and diamonds. Pearls for the villa, sheets of gold for the sun on the water. Before the war I was an international dealer in precious stones and I know from experience that they can steal a man's soul.'

'Or a woman's.'

Caterina eased herself from under his hand and stood up. She was far shorter than the Count. When he spoke of the jewels, a softness came into his voice and relaxed his fingers which were long and spidery. He treated her to a half-smile.

'Yes, you are right there, even yours maybe?'

'So it seems that we cannot help each other. Neither of us knows anything.'

Her words unlocked something in him, and he gave her a brief bitter glare.

'Octavia!' he called.

The black shadow slid into place at his elbow.

'Yes, I'm here.'

'Tell Leonora to drive our visitor back to the ferry at once.'

There was laughter in the car. Caterina had not expected that. It was a sedan, sleek and smooth, the creamy colour of buttermilk. The laughter came from Leonora di Marco, but unlike the brittle version of it on her grandfather's terrace, here it was effortless. She was laughing fondly at her dog on the back seat as it hung its big white head out of the open window, its silky fur and ears buffeted by the wind. Ever since speeding through the gates on to the dusty road, Caterina felt as if she were sitting next to a different person. Younger and more pliant, her voice less guarded, and she noticed there was no gold band on her finger. No wedding then. With or without the table.

As the car plunged downhill, Caterina gripped her seat. The road was narrow and swept through switchbacks and hairpins as it zigzagged down the flank of the mountain. A forest of pine trees and steeply terraced olive and lemon groves clung to bare rock in a dizzying feat of tenacity, as the ground fell away on one side, while on the other side rose the grey shoulder of the island mountain itself. Rough and jagged, not something to argue with. Leonora drove fast, taking the lethal bends with confidence, demonstrating a familiarity with them that was reassuring, but every now and again Caterina felt a back wheel skid on a loose patch of gravel and her grip tightened.

'Well?' Leonora asked without preamble. 'What did you think?'

'Of what?'

'Of the villa. Of my grandfather.'

Caterina regarded her warily. The girl was probably younger than herself, her sleek bob tucked behind one ear to show off her elegant profile, her focus on the road. Caterina decided not to lie to her.

'It must be like living on an iceberg.'

Leonora's head snapped round to stare at her. 'Exactly,' she said. 'That is exactly it.'

A tree trunk was suddenly racing towards them.

'Watch the road!'

Leonora swung the wheel as they entered the next hairpin, just in time to avoid flying off the mountain edge into the void that reached out to the blue waters of the bay far below. She grinned and the dog gave a yip of excitement.

'Did you ever see my father's table?' Caterina asked.

'No. It was to be a surprise, but I'm not sure it ever really existed. That's why I call it the fabled table.' She laughed.

'It existed, I'm sure. It was in my father's order book.'

'As it turned out, it didn't matter.' The white tunic shrugged. 'No wedding.'

Caterina couldn't tell whether it was regret or relief that lay behind the words, but it was clear Leonora didn't wish to discuss it further. She stamped on the brake as they hit another bend.

'I was told,' Caterina said, 'that your grandfather only employs male staff, but I only saw Octavia.'

Again the easy laugh.

'Octavia isn't staff. She's his niece. My aunt.'

'His niece? He doesn't treat her like a niece.'

'She lives there as his housekeeper.'

The loud blare of a car horn behind them shattered her sentence. The dog yanked its head in with a sharp bark.

'Damn fool,' Leonora snapped. 'He can't overtake here.' She put her foot down and they leapt forward at increased speed, but the horn blared again.

'Slow down, Leonora. Pull over. Let him go by.'

'*Stupido!*' Leonora blasted out her own horn.

Caterina twisted in her seat. Looming behind them was a large black Buick, right on their bumper, the big man in the driving seat stern-faced. He hooted again.

'What the hell . . .?'

Trying to pass here was suicidal.

Leonora accelerated and for a split second the black car was left behind, but it quickly caught up and hitched itself to their bumper again. Caterina rolled her window down and leaned out.

'You maniac,' she shouted. 'Pull back!'

'Get off my tail,' Leonora screamed.

The car slammed into their rear. The crunch from behind snapped their heads back and catapulted their vehicle forward.

Leonora's hands were slick with sweat on the wheel and for a second she lost her grip. She stamped on the brake, but the car behind was too heavy, its momentum too great, the slope of the road too steep. They slowed a fraction, skidding forward, wheels locked.

We're going to die, thought Caterina.

Time seemed to unravel and thoughts scrambled in her head. Luca, she had promised to pick up Luca from school. She could smell the bruised orange in the American army major's hand. Or was it the scent of the terraced lemon groves directly below her. Twenty, thirty, forty metres below her. She was going to die on the next bend.

She reached across and seized one side of the steering wheel, preparing to swing the car on to the wrong side of the road. Only then did her ears register Leonora's low keening sound.

'I don't want my *bella* Bianchezza to die.'

'We have to stop the car.' Caterina's words came jerkily. 'Crash it against the rocks.'

'No!' Leonora started to scream. 'No!'

'Not over the cliff.' Caterina tried to turn the steering wheel but Leonora fought her.

As if the black car could read her mind, it veered onto the opposite side of the road between them and the wall of rock. If any car came round the bend, they would all be dead.

'Brake! Now! Now!'

But the other car was abreast of them and when Caterina looked across to Leonora she was staring straight into the driver's face. Fierce eyes. A wide, mocking grin. A mountain of a man in a dark suit and with a heavy moustache. Thick muscular arms.

Her heart clawed at her lungs. She knew what was coming. She knew this was the end. The black Buick swerved and body-slammed their sedan with ferocious force. Grinding metal shrieked. Leonora's door buckled. The steering wheel jerked free from her grip, and the car crashed through the flimsy barrier of undergrowth at the edge of the road.

No ground beneath them. No sound. As if the world had died.

CHAPTER TWELVE

The world came back. Not with a whisper. Not with the soft sigh of death. It came back to Caterina with Leonora being tossed across the car as it spun in a wild arc through the air. It came with a tortured shriek of steel and an explosion of glass. A mangled ripping of metal and an unexpected howling that she couldn't place.

The car smacked to earth with an impact that jolted her spine, but her hands were fused to her seat with a grim grip. That's what saved her when the car smashed its way down the steep terraces in an uncontrolled race to the sea.

It stopped. Quite suddenly. A sickening crunch. Then nothing. The car lay still. Nothing moved. Every bone in her body ached and something was wrong with her eyes because a spectacular light-show danced at the edge of her vision. A tree seemed to have sprouted out of the bonnet of their car and it took her a moment to make sense of it. The car was jammed against the trunk of a stunted umbrella pine that had put an abrupt halt to their descent.

'Leonora?'

No reply. Caterina twisted round. Hands shaking. Her companion's slender body lay face down, slumped between the seats, half in the front and half in the rear. It had a crumpled look to it and wasn't moving. Caterina touched her back, her neck, her shoulder, calling her name, but no answer came. Glass sparkled like diamonds in her hair and a thin line of scarlet threaded through the white silk of her tunic.

Caterina knew she had to get them both out. Fast. She could smell petrol. She tried the door handle. It worked but the door didn't budge. She hurled her shoulder against it but it was jammed, so she lay back on the seat and jack-knifed her feet against the buckled metal. With a sound like a gunshot it burst open and she tumbled out on to the stony ground, relief shuddering through her despite the precipitous slope of the mountainside on which she was sprawled. She scrambled to her feet, skidding in the dirt, and leaned inside the car.

The stench of petrol was growing stronger.

She wanted to run. To charge up the slope on all fours, to escape back to reality.

How could this be real?

The cream bodywork of the car had buckled, the front wing caved in, and it was now balanced precariously against the tree that had proved to be their saviour. Quickly Caterina reached in, grasped the inert body of Leonora and started to haul her from the car. One foot was caught between the seats. Caterina clambered inside to dislodge it, but as she did so she felt the vehicle shift and there was a groan from Leonora.

'Leonora! Help me. Quickly.'

The young woman's eyes rolled open but she could do nothing to help. Another jolt and the scraping sound of metal moving against metal sent the strength of fear surging through Caterina and she put both hands under Leonora's armpits and yanked hard. They both spilled on to the ground. A trail of blood snaked from Leonora's forehead on to the front of her tunic but Caterina knew she couldn't stop to deal with it now. She knelt down and draped one of Leonora's arms over her shoulder to lift her up and that was when she heard the snarl. She froze.

From under the car slunk a shadow, eyes intent on Caterina's face, fangs bared to tear flesh from bone.

'No,' Caterina said, fighting to keep her voice calm, 'no, no Bianchezza. I'm helping her, not hurting her.'

The dog's belly skimmed the ground as it crept closer, each broad paw placed in front of the other with intent, its fierce gaze never leaving Caterina. A slash of blood swept down over its white coat from the point where a shard of glass was embedded in its neck, and all the time the blood-chilling snarl rose from its throat.

'No! Get back.'

She could sense panic in herself, smell the petrol fumes, feel the limp weight of the wounded woman she was struggling to drag uphill.

Leonora moaned.

It was all the animal needed. It launched itself at Caterina.

The dog went for her throat.

Thirty-five kilos of solid muscle. Caterina could see strings of saliva as it flew at her, its black lips drawn back, its pale eyes consumed with fury.

She released Leonora. Instinctively her arms shot out to ward off the attack but she had not bargained on the weight of the animal. The impact sent her sprawling backwards on the ground and its jaws closed on the forearm she had raised to protect her throat. Pain ripped through her flesh and tore a scream from her throat. In desperation she slammed her other fist into the side of the animal's head but it didn't even blink. Its jaws closed tighter.

'Down, Bianchezza!'

Leonora's voice was weak but in an instant the attack ceased. The jaws released their hold. The dog backed off, its long tongue removing blood from its lips with fast efficient flicks.

'I'm sorry,' Leonora whispered in horror. 'She was protecting me.'

Caterina's arm felt on fire, but she forced herself to her feet. 'Quickly, we have to get out of here.'

Using her good arm and with one eye still on the dog, she lifted the young woman to her feet, supporting her, and started up the slope towards the road.

'Bianchezza is hurt,' Leonora wailed when she saw blood oozing in thick rivulets from the dagger of glass embedded in the animal's neck.

Right then Caterina wished the dog dead and buried, but she propped Leonora on her feet and bent to extract the piece of glass.

That was the moment the car exploded.

*

'Caterina.'

The voice came from so far away that Caterina had to squint to find the person speaking somewhere on the horizon, but all she saw was sky. Thin and brittle. So bright it hurt. She had an odd feeling it was about to crack and fall down on her.

'Caterina Lombardi.'

That voice. Again. She'd heard it before. But where?

'Can you hear me?'

Yes, I can hear you.

'It's all right, you're safe. We're going to move you up to the house.'

The house? Which house?

A hand touched her face. Wiped her cheek. 'Don't cry.'

She wasn't crying. Of course she wasn't crying. Why would she cry? She was in her workshop, wasn't she? She had a jewellery box to finish with . . .

With what?

She couldn't remember. She could feel her teeth chattering and clamped them shut.

'A doctor is coming.'

The voice. Again. But this time a face came with it. A voice and a face she knew, but she had no idea to whom they belonged. The face loomed closer. A woman with smooth black hair tied back, long silver earrings and a smear of blood on her chin, lips that were moving and saying words that slid away from Caterina's grasp and tumbled down the mountainside.

Mountainside? Why was she lying on a mountainside? She tried to sit up.

'Don't move, Caterina.'

The sky cracked. Fragments of its bright blue shell fell down on her.

Caterina opened her eyes. Blinked. Opened them again. Where was she?

On a sofa.

She sat up and every muscle in her body groaned, stiff and sore, her arm throbbing as if one of the American Sherman tanks had driven over it. She looked down and found it neatly bandaged. What the hell had happened to it?

She glanced around her, swaying slightly, and noticed everything in the room was white. Realisation trickled back into her mind.

The car.

The dog.

Leonora.

How did she end up here, back in the ice palace?

'You're awake.'

The woman was there, a black shadow in one corner. She approached on silent feet, brisk and efficient.

'How are you feeling?'

'Sore. How is Leonora?'

'She's in bed. She has a gash on her head but the doctor has seen her. Nothing broken. You are both lucky it wasn't much worse.' Her cool gaze skimmed Caterina from head to toe. 'Young bones,' she murmured and there was a skin of envy to her words.

'Someone forced us off the road,' Caterina said, angered by the calmness of this woman. 'Tried to kill us. How the hell could it be worse?'

Octavia di Marco narrowed her eyes and something close to a dart of amusement softened her mouth. 'He could have succeeded.'

Caterina was questioned by a policeman who drove up to the Villa dei Cesari, a sallow man with bad skin, who tried unsuccessfully to hide the fact that he was overawed by his surroundings. The doctor had given her something for the pain in her arm, but it was her head that pounded relentlessly while she described again and again the man in the black car – big and swarthy, a felt hat and a moustache like a walrus. Only on the fourth time of telling did she dredge up the image of his beefy hand on the steering wheel with a hefty chunk of gold on his finger.

'*Grazie*, signorina,' the police officer said and finally snapped his notebook closed with a small sigh of relief. 'I do not recognise the man from your description of your attacker in the car but I will look through our file of photographs. I will contact you if I find any that match it.' He rose and said with genuine concern. 'I wish you a speedy recovery.'

'Surely you must be able to find that black car. It has to be badly damaged and this is a tiny island.' She wanted to shake the small nervous smile off his face.

He tucked his cap under his arm and spread his hands helplessly. 'It has vanished.'

*

'Octavia, fetch the box.'

The tall woman regarded Count di Marco with unease.

'Are you sure?' she asked grudgingly.

'Yes, I am.'

'It won't work.'

A thin smile spread across his lips. 'It always works.'

Caterina watched her turn and walk stiffly into the villa, leaving behind her a pool of silence that Caterina felt no urge to disturb. They were back on the terrace, the Count still reclining on his bed of cushions, Caterina isolated once more on her small island of shade, as though he feared contamination. She wanted to say, 'Go and sit by your granddaughter's bedside, hold her hand, tell her you are glad she didn't die.'

What was this box that the Count required? Her thoughts were fragmented, disconnecting from each other. She shook her head to clear it and felt a bolt of pain hit the back of her eyes.

'Signorina?'

Caterina's head twitched round. The two di Marco pairs of eyes were scrutinising her. She realised they had been speaking to her.

'Be quick,' the woman in black said to the Count. 'She is not looking good.'

'What is it you wish to say, Count?' Caterina asked.

'First, I want to thank you, Signorina Lombardi. You saved my granddaughter's life. I am grateful, of course. She is the one destined to carry the di Marco name to the next generation.' He frowned at her from under his canopy. 'I am sorry you are upset.'

'Upset?' she hissed at him. 'I have been questioned by American and British Intelligence Officers, my father's name is being blackened, I have been attacked in a Sorrento street, my family has been threatened and now I have been forced off the road down a cliff in your granddaughter's car and savaged by a dog. So yes, Count di Marco, you could say I am upset.'

He showed his teeth and she could not tell if it was a smile or a grimace.

'Octavia, the box.'

The woman placed a box on the table beside his day-bed and as she did so Caterina recognised the similarity between them, the same high forehead, the same arrogant manner, the same ice in their veins. But it was the box that seized her attention. She wanted to snatch it from them.

'Recognise it?' he asked.

She nodded.

It was made of the palest sun-streaked sycamore. On its lid was a design of Romulus and Remus with the she-wolf, inset with tortoiseshell.

He reached out and unlocked it with a brass key, but it was facing him, turned away from her, so she could not view its contents. Octavia stood just outside the reach of his canopy, her face blank, but her fingers betrayed her as they gripped a button on her waistcoat and twisted the life out of it.

'Your father made it,' the Count reminded her.

'I remember.'

It had been the year her mother left. Eleven years ago.

'This is for you, Signorina Lombardi.'

145

The Count removed an envelope from the box, buff and bulky, and held it out to his disapproving niece who placed it on the chess table next to Caterina. She snatched it up, hoping it would contain a message from her father. She flicked open the envelope.

Stupido!

Inside lay money. A thick wedge of banknotes that Caterina didn't even touch. She replaced the envelope on the table.

'I am not for sale.'

'It is a thank-you.'

'The only thank-you I want is the truth about what my father was doing.'

'I have told you everything I know, signorina. The table was a commission for my daughter's wedding.'

'Why would someone want to push your granddaughter off a cliff?'

'As I told the policeman, I have no idea and neither does she.' He was observing her carefully, his face watchful. The breeze that rose up the cliff-face crept across the white marble to lift the hem of his robe. 'Regard it as a fee.'

'A fee for what?'

'To find the table – if it still exists.'

She stood up. Too fast. The floor tilted under her feet. She picked up the buff envelope and tossed it on to the Count's cushions.

'Hire yourself a proper detective,' she told him.

'A detective will get nowhere, we both know that. This is southern Italy, not Rome. An outsider – like your Intelligence

Officers – will get nowhere. We are close-lipped down here with strangers and we protect our own. If I am ever to see my jewelled table again, I need you to . . .'

'No, Count Di Marco, I am going to clear my father's name. If I find your table in the process, you will be the first to know.'

'Don't expect me to wait, young woman. Your father owed me those jewels when he died. The debt is a debt of honour. Don't you forget that.'

The dog was lying on the white bed cover beside its mistress and lifted its heads with a flash of teeth and a low-throated growl of warning. The room was another ice chamber, without colour or soul.

'I've come to say goodbye and to see how you are,' Caterina said softly.

The face on the pillow was pale and delicate, fragile as lace. There was a bandage on Leonora's head but she smiled and held out an unsteady hand.

'Thank you, Caterina Lombardi. Thank you for . . .'

'How are you feeling?' Caterina interrupted. She hadn't come here for thanks.

'Sore. And you?'

Caterina laughed grimly. 'Battered.' She paused, aware of the muddy bruises under Leonora's dark eyes. 'Did you recognise the man in the black Buick?'

'No. Did you?'

'No.'

'Come here, please.'

Caterina took a step forward, while Octavia hovered in the doorway. The dog snarled, soft and sibilant, but still a snarl.

'Give me your hand,' Leonora said.

She took Caterina's hand in hers, raised it to her lips and placed a kiss on the back of it, just as she had done when greeting her grandfather on the terrace. It embarrassed Caterina, but Leonora would not release her hand and pulled it over towards the dog. The animal's fur had been shaved on its neck where the glass had penetrated and wore a bandage over the area, so that they looked a matching pair, dog and mistress.

'Here, Bianchezza,' Leonora commanded. 'Thank Signorina Lombardi.'

For a fleeting second the pupils of the animal's blue eyes grew huge as if remembering the taste of Caterina's blood and she almost snatched her hand away, but then its muzzle pushed forward and nudged the two hands. Its soft sinuous tongue gently licked Caterina's fingers and it became an oddly emotional and intimate gesture.

'I apologise for the bite,' Leonora said with sincere regret. 'But I can't be cross with her. She'll never bite you again now.'

'Not if I see her coming first,' Caterina laughed, and withdrew her hand. Their eyes met and held for a long moment. 'Don't worry about it. Just get well.'

She turned to leave the room and heard Leonora di Marco burst out in an unexpected ripple of laughter. 'Oh God, you look a horrible mess. The back of your dress is scorched brown and your hair is all singed into a frazzle.' She waved an imperious hand towards the shadow in the doorway. 'Octavia, do something about it.'

Caterina unlocked her front door, stepped quickly inside and locked it again. She had run up through the town, her head spinning, her pulse jumping at every shift of a shadow in a doorway.

'Nonno!' she called.

But the house lay quiet and unresponsive around her, dust motes spiralling in a shaft of sunlight from the glass above the door, the only sound the catch of her breath. It was early afternoon already and the heat shrouded the town in a sleepy haze that discouraged activity. Her grandfather would be dozing in his chair in the courtyard, a cup of the Englishman's coffee at his side, no doubt, his fingers whittling a length of wood even as he dozed.

Caterina dragged herself upstairs and threw herself on her bed fully clothed. The thickness of the walls barred the worst of the heat from the room and the closed shutters kept it dim and secretive, the way she needed it right now. Her body ached and her mind felt as if it had been flayed. From her pocket she took a small white tablet that the doctor had left for her at the Villa dei Cesari and swallowed it dry.

She drew her bed cover into her arms, reached out for its vivid blues and yellows and soft amethyst and wrapped it around her shoulders, spread it over her chest like armour against the ice palace. She lay back on her pillow and let her eyes fall shut, but they were scoured by sharp images of a cliff sliding away beneath her to rocks far below, of murder written in a man's eyes, of death's beckoning finger.

But it was sleep that claimed her. Not death.

When the night rolled in from the mountains, it brought with it the scent of pine forests and the eerie shrieks of bats swooping from the duomo bell tower. As the hours crawled past, Caterina paced in the darkness of her room, heels snapping down on the boards, arms rigid at her sides.

Today. It was a day she could not take back. Couldn't change. Couldn't erase and redraw, even though it was a day that had torn off the doors of her life and let in the storm that was now battering her.

Someone tried to kill me. Not threatened to kill me. *Tried* to kill me.

Terror is a word that doesn't belong in normal daily life. It is the preserve of frontline battle troops. For most people the word has no real meaning. A terror of spiders. Of rats. Of childbirth. Of heights.

That isn't terror. That is fear.

Caterina knew the difference now. Terror is when someone tries to wrench your life from your grasp. Terror is when a car forces you over a cliff and you know you would be dead instead of pacing on bare feet across the floor of your room, if it weren't for one small determined umbrella pine tree that decided today was not your day to die.

Caterina stared into the heart of it and knew that nothing would ever be the same after today. Her life had changed.

CHAPTER THIRTEEN

Jake Parr was back in Sorrento. He was smoking a cigarette on the terrace of the Hotel Vittoria, his eyes feasting on a view so extravagantly beautiful that it could almost rinse from his mind the images of the squalor of Naples and the naked misery in its street.

Here in Sorrento lay a world of enchantment. It captured his soul in a way he was not prepared for. Jake didn't regard himself as a sentimental guy. He left that to the raw young army Joes who sauntered around, hands in pockets, open-mouthed and astonished at the effortless display of elegance and artistry in the towns of Italy, as well as at the hip-swinging stride of the dark-eyed signorinas. No, Jake was a police officer to his core, trained and tested, despite the army major uniform. He liked facts, he liked logic, he liked to take hold of a tangled thread and inch by inch unwind it until he found what the dirty end was looped around. He was here to investigate a crime. Not to be seduced by this stealing of his senses.

'*La bella Italia* will beguile you, my Jacko,' his Italian grandmother had whispered to him in the final minutes when he
was packing his kitbag to leave behind the windy chill of
Milwaukee. 'It is a country that will break your heart,' she
warned, 'with its beauty. And with its pain.'

She tucked a greaseproof package of her home-baked ang-
inetti into his pocket and reached up to cradle his face in her
strong hands. Her skin against his cheek was as dry as apple
peel that has been left out in the sun too long.

'No, Nonna,' he had smiled. 'I have a job to do over there.
No sight-seeing or . . .'

'That's what you think now,' she had said simply. 'You wait.'

He had laughed. He was that stupid. He regretted it now. He
should have learned long ago to listen to her words. Here he
was sitting in the sun, knocking back a slug of morning coffee
with the Bay of Naples stretched out before him like blue silk
and that strange volcanic cone of Vesuvius glowering across the
water, biding its time. It was like Italy itself – you never knew
when the whole damn thing would blow.

It was Bomber Harris who had lit the touch paper in 1943,
the British Air Chief Marshal. A no-holds-barred kind of
guy. He believed in area bombing, not the daytime precision
bombing that the Americans carried out. Jake had to admit
that Winston Churchill was right when he stated that British
night-time raids did not lend themselves to accurate bombing
and so could not be confined to military targets. But even so.

It jarred. Grated bone on bone inside Jake. Italians were the
enemy at the time, he reminded himself, they had sided with

Nazi Germany in fighting the Allies. So destruction of houses and utilities was an acceptable weapon of war. It caused fear. Lowered morale. It broke a nation's spirit and therefore shortened hostilities. That was the theory. But Italy was not like other countries. It was unique. Because it was the cradle of human civilisation and the riches of that civilisation lay directly in the path of war. The first Allied bombs were dropped in July 1943 on the industrial north of Italy – on Milan and Turin and Genoa. That was just the start.

Jake had seen Milan. He'd clambered over the blackened rubble and it had choked something in him. Okay, the Breda armaments factory and the train stations were legitimate targets – but the centre of Milan had also been brutally punished by bombs, as well as incendiaries, all manner of hell let loose. And in that hell had burned the paintings in the Breda Gallery and the Ambrosiana Gallery, paintings of breathless beauty that were part of mankind's heritage. By Leonardo da Vinci. Blackened to ash. By Raphael. By Mantegna. By Caravaggio. All destroyed because of men greedy for power.

'Works of art are not diamonds,' Jake muttered aloud. 'They can never be replaced.'

He lit a cigarette, his anger heavy in his chest. He did not possess an artistic bone in his own body, could not draw a picture to save his life, but he was in awe of those who could and was passionate about restoring to their rightful owners those paintings and artefacts that remained of Italy's heritage. His grandmother was right. *It is a country that will break your heart.*

He glanced at his watch. Not long now. He stubbed out his cigarette.

The war in Europe had been over less than a month and the Allied military now found itself struggling to fix a country that was well and truly broken. They had come to bring liberation but now they were wielding shovels and pick-axes, and it was their military muscle that was starting to shift the mountains of brick and stone rubble that the bombs had left behind, to fix the telephone wires and the water mains. The Supreme Commander of Allied Forces in Italy was General Mark Clark, billeted at this hotel, but it was General Eisenhower who had established the Intelligence Unit on orders from President Roosevelt himself.

He had pulled together an elite force of American and British officers, each with specialist knowledge and skills to undertake the task of saving Italy's works of art. Jake was proud to be a part of it under the command of Colonel Royce Quincy. As an ex-cop, he was here to use his policing skills, to help lift Italy up onto its feet again and to move it forward to a future free from the corruption and destruction that was choking it to death. He would not permit thieves to strip Italy of its heritage. Not while it was on its knees, bleeding into the dirt.

The meeting with Colonel Quincy was at ten. He pushed back his chair and made his way inside the hotel.

Colonel Royce Quincy was studying the Manila folder on his desk. His forefinger tapped it with disfavour.

'Is this your report?'

'Yessir.'

'Not much to it.'

Jake couldn't argue with that. He wasn't one for paperwork, it got in the way of doing the job, but he couldn't persuade the army to take the same view.

'I'm working on the new lead I mentioned, sir,' he assured his senior officer.

Colonel Quincy was efficient at running the unit but he could be hot-tempered with subordinates, as fiery as his frizzy ginger hair, and he possessed an unswerving belief in his personal superiority over the rest of mankind. As far as Jake could make out, this seemed to be based firstly on the fact that he was English and educated at Eton, secondly on the knowledge that he was taller than the rest of the world and therefore nearer to God. And thirdly because he knew more about Italian Renaissance artworks than was humanly possible.

The Colonel made a note on a pad in front of him with a sleek black fountain pen and asked without looking up, 'Do you think the young woman is important?'

'I do, sir.'

'Bring her in then, this Caterina Lombardi. We'll question her thoroughly.' He closed his notebook with a snap. 'If she knows something, you'll get it out of her.' His gaze settled once more on Jake with grim satisfaction. 'After all, that's what you American policemen are good at, isn't it? That's why you're in my unit.'

Jake was far too smart to let the comment rile him. He and Colonel Quincy had reached an understanding, a way of working together that suited them both. They tolerated each other, but that was all. The Colonel was an academic. He had been drafted into this unlikely line of work because of his specialist knowledge of art but he didn't care to dip his fingers into what he regarded as the murky world of criminals that Jake inhabited. And he didn't like working with Yanks. But right now, they had need of each other's skills to get the job done.

Jake shifted his weight on the fragile hotel chair and its spindly legs creaked. The room was all soft blues, fringed tapestry drapes and ornate gilded mirrors, like a goddamn New Orleans brothel. Except classier. It sure as hell didn't feel like a military debrief office.

'I have locked up a suspect who is kicking his heels in the interrogation room in Naples,' Jake informed Quincy. 'His name is Sal Sardo. We picked him up in a raid on the basement of one of the abandoned houses. My information links him to the Giotto painting of St Francis that was stolen from the museum, though at the moment all we've got on him is that he seemed to be guarding a bunch of stolen artefacts in the basement.'

'Then why in God's name aren't you back there putting the thumbscrews on him?'

'I'm letting him stew, sir. No lawyer. No contact. On his own. Alone with his fear. He'll be sweating right now. And Captain Fielding is watching him, so everything is under control.'

'How much does this Sardo know?'

Jake shrugged one shoulder. 'That's what I intend to find out, sir.' He carefully banished all disrespect from the final word.

'Make sure you do.'

'Sir, Captain Keller and Major Gardner have left Naples,' Jake informed him. 'They have transferred north to continue identifying and cataloguing the retrieved works of art in Rome and in Florence, alongside Lieutenant Hartt.

'I am aware of that. We are now trying to evaluate all the monuments and art collections throughout every conquered town and city in Italy. It's a huge task.'

'But here in Naples our team is now dismally small. We are struggling, to be honest, sir. We badly need more personnel.'

'There are never enough men for the job, Parr.' Quincy dragged a despairing hand through his hair and started pacing the room. 'Barbarism,' he muttered. 'Damned barbarism. How could the Germans do such a thing? Stripping Naples like that. What they couldn't cart away, they set on fire – like the archives of the university. And now, Major, on top of that, our own troops are looting and carving their initials on historic monu-ments. This vandalism has to be stopped. The worst culprit is that damn Nazi thief, Reichsmarschall Göring – he transported Naples' masterpieces to his estate at Carinhall in Germany. But we've learnt that they are now hidden in a saltmine in Austria, so there is hope for retrieving them, thank God.'

'In the meantime I am still searching for further caches in Naples itself,' Jake said, 'but I badly need more men.'

Colonel Quincy frowned. 'Very well. I'll try to assign you more personnel.'

'Thank you, sir.'

Quincy stared thoughtfully at a map of Italy that hung on the wall, its regions speckled with different coloured pens to indicate the distribution of Allied army divisions.

'We'll be decamping any day now,' he announced solemnly. 'It is essential that we get this country into shape before we leave.' He released an irritated sigh. 'We've liberated Italians from oppression, yet still they want to retain that treacherous old king of theirs. Even Prime Minister Bonomi is committed to keeping King Victor Emmanuel on the throne. Christ Almighty, don't they ever learn?'

'Sir, you underestimate the Italian people,' said Jake.

'Meaning?' Quincy asked tersely.

'They believe in vengeance. The King will be made to pay, along with his son, Umberto. Italians have long memories. When they're asked to vote in a referendum next year on whether or not to dump their monarchy, they'll stick the knife in where it hurts most. They will get rid of him.'

'I hope you're right, Parr.' He looked at his watch. 'Now, that young woman you were talking about. What's her name?'

'Caterina Lombardi.'

'Make sure you bring her in for questioning. Find out what she knows.'

'With respect, sir, I don't think that's the best way to extract information from her.'

The Colonel sat down with a sigh of displeasure. 'Bring her in. That's an order, Major Parr.'

Jake let ten seconds tick past. 'Yessir.'

CHAPTER FOURTEEN

As Jake crossed the hotel terrace, a hand descended on his shoulder.

'Jake, where you been hiding yourself, buddy?' A lazy Texan drawl.

Jake broke into a smile. 'Chester!'

Chester Fowles was a short wiry terrier of a soldier who had fought alongside him in the skin-flaying sands of Egypt, but they had lost touch after the bloody slaughter that followed the landings at Anzio. That was at the start of 1944 when over a hundred thousand Allied troops had scrambled on to the Italian mainland and been pinned down on the beachhead by the panzer divisions of Generalfeldmarschall Kesselring's Tenth Army for three months.

Bonds of friendship were too often formed and then broken as divisions were moved around on the chessboard of war, but it was good to see his comrade safe and sound of limb. Allied troops were spread throughout Sorrento, some billeted at the elegant Tremontano Hotel, while the RAF were at the Minerva, but it was the Hotel Vittoria that had the edge, with its frescoed dining room and impressive cliff-top terrace. A bit heavy on the marble statuary for Jake's liking.

He steered his friend towards a terrace table and summoned coffee. It came black and thick enough to polish boots. Chester, who was now a Civil Affairs Officer, moaned at the inefficiency of the distribution of food to the starving inhabitants of Italy, despite the issue of ration coupons. But as they sipped their coffee, a waiter with slick brilliantined hair and a slick brilliantined smile appeared at his elbow.

'What is it?'

'Someone to see you, Major Parr.'

As far as Jake was aware, no one other than Quincy knew he was here today. 'Who is it?'

'A young lady.'

'Bring her over.' To Chester he said, 'It'll be another of the prostitutes keen to sell me information. God only knows how they track me down; their jungle drums are second to none. That's the trouble with being an Intelligence Officer. Everyone reckons they have a secret I'll want to buy.'

'You lucky bastard. Pursued throughout Italy by ravishing signorinas of the night.'

'As I recall, my friend, you were the one in Cairo who had the joys of a dancer shaking her belly-button in your face in that bar where we . . .'

His words dried. He forgot the smoky bar in Egypt. Out of the shadows of the doorway walked a young woman and every eye on the terrace turned to stare. It was Caterina Lombardi. But it was Caterina Lombardi looking very different from yesterday. She was still small and slight, but her dense dark hair was chopped short in an elfin style with a feathery fringe, and instead of the cinnamon work clothes of yesterday, she was wearing a sleeveless silk dress of ice-cream white with a cinched-in waist and a skirt of razor-sharp pleats that swayed around her slender hips with every step. But as she wove her way towards him, he couldn't miss the stiffness in her walk, as though she were hurting, and the hard edge to her eyes beneath the thick lashes, accusing him of something, though he had no idea what.

'Signorina Lombardi,' he said, rising to his feet and holding out his hand, 'this is an unexpected pleasure.'

'Is it?' She didn't take his hand.

'Let me introduce Captain Chester Fowles.'

'Pleased to meet you, ma'am.'

She didn't even look at him. In the unforgiving blaze of the sun Jake saw the greyish purple shadows circling her eyes, the raw graze in her hairline, the tension in the tendons of her long neck. Her mouth was set hard and a veil of something untouchable cut her off from the world. Her arm was bandaged above the wrist of her left hand.

'What is it?' he asked quickly.

'I wish to speak to you.' For the first time she switched her gaze to Chester. 'In private.'

They could have been lovers: heads close together, voices secretive, lingering in the shade under the abundant orange trees while a pair of wood warblers serenaded them from a jacaranda tree. Jake led Caterina through the lush sub-tropical gardens of the Hotel Vittoria. The scent of citrus was warm and sweet in the air and the thick rubbery leaves of the spiky heliconias twisted in the sea breeze. There was a softness here, a gentle beauty that he thought would help soothe her. But he was mistaken. As she walked at his side he could feel a new hardness in her, a sharp bright edge. The elegance of her ice-cream dress and the delicacy of her different hairstyle hid none of her anger.

'Tell me,' he said, 'what happened.'

'There's something I need you to do, Major. It will help us both.'

'What is that?'

'There is a family in Sorrento who may have information about my father that would be useful. I can't go to them myself because they will not talk to me.'

'Why not?'

'Because there is bad blood between our families.' A flush rose up her pale throat.

'The Cavaleris?'

She turned to face him. 'How do you know about the Cavaleris?'

'It is my job to know.'

She stared at him far too long and then moved deeper into the cool shade, as though to escape from him.

'Tell me what happened to your arm?' he said.

'A dog bit me.'

'I'm sorry. But I have a feeling there was more to it than that.'

'What makes you say so? And don't tell me it's your job to know.'

'You are walking stiffly. You can hardly turn your head. Your shoulder looks swollen and there is a scrape on your forehead. Have you been in an accident?'

For the first time today the corners of her mouth softened a fraction. 'You are good, Major Parr. Sharp eyes. It is no wonder you are an Intelligence investigator.'

'I used to be a police officer in Milwaukee back before the war.'

She studied him, nodded and turned away. Sunlight edged between the leaves of the orange trees and dappled her cheek, highlighting the tension in the muscles under her skin. Why the hell did he tell her about being a police officer? Usually he kept that private. But he wanted her to trust him.

'How did the accident happen?'

'I was forced off the road in Capri. A man in a black Buick slammed into the car I was riding in and sent us skidding down the cliff.'

'And you blame me?'

'Yes.'

'Why?'

'Because one day you questioned me in the street and the next I am attacked. They made it clear that they are going to kill me.'

She again moved away from him, this time to a circular bed of sugar-pink roses that were lazing in the sun. He let her stand there alone for a moment, the fingers of her right hand cradling one of the velvety blooms before he went to stand at her side.

'I intend to find these people,' he promised her. 'But I will need your help.'

She nodded, but did not look away from the flower in her hand. He laid a hand gently on her bandaged arm.

'Tell me what happened, all of it. We will need to work together.'

So she told him. About the commission in her father's order book for the jewelled table, about her trip out to Capri and the Villa dei Cesari, about the sterile whiteness of it, the disturbing strangeness of Count di Marco and the fragility of the girl with the dog. She spoke quietly and calmly and if he didn't already know her better he might have thought she was talking about someone else. Someone she scarcely knew.

'We left the villa in Leonora di Marco's car and as we were driving down the mountain a black car pulled alongside us and deliberately rammed us. We crashed over the edge and ended up jammed against a tree. It gave us a brief moment to escape before the car blew up.' She shivered.

'The dog bite?' he prompted.

'The animal turned on me when I was hauling Leonora out of the car. It was trying to protect her. I can't be angry with it. It is a loyal creature.'

Loyalty was something she prized, he could hear it in her voice. She made little fuss of the crash but Jake had seen in her eyes today what it had done to her.

'Did you contact the *polizia*?'

'Yes. A policeman came to the villa and took a statement from us.'

'The di Marco girl?'

'She survived.'

'The black car?'

'Disappeared, apparently.'

'It's a small island.'

She uttered a small angry sound. 'That's what I said.'

'But no luck finding it?'

'No.'

'What about the person in the other car? Did you get a look at the driver?'

She ripped the head off the rose and threw it on the earth. 'He was big and muscular. He filled the side window, a huge shoulder in a black suit, menacing and . . .' She grew silent as she stared down at the ruined rose.

'And frightening?' he finished for her.

'Yes.'

'Can you describe his face?'

She shook her head, her forehead creased with effort. 'Not really, it happened too fast. I had the impression of a thick moustache and heavy features. There was a ring on his finger on the steering wheel, a large chunk of gold on his right hand.'

He could sense her frustration. It matched his own, but he changed the subject, knowing from experience of questioning witnesses that more details would come if she stopped pulling and prodding at it. He drew out his cigarettes and she accepted one with a nod, watching him as he lit them both with a match struck by his thumbnail.

He inhaled a lungful of smoke. 'What made you think I'd be here at the Hotel Vittoria?'

She ruffled a hand through the unfamiliar strands of her cropped hair. 'I called on the off-chance.' She observed him from head to toe, taking in his crisp army shirt and mohair tie tucked between the second and third buttons according to regulations, his shoes buffed to a glassy sheen, but above all the bar of military awards above the left pocket of his jacket. She spread her arm to encompass the sumptuous hotel.

'It's the kind of place you Americans would go,' she said and laughed. It was a small private laugh that stung Jake more than it should have.

'So,' he adopted a police officer's official tone, 'you came to ask me about the Cavaleri family.'

'Yes. They are the ones who have reason to blacken my father's name.'

'Why is that?'

'Because . . .' her brown eyes became blank, blocking him out, 'because eleven years ago my mother ran off to Rome with Roberto Cavaleri, the head of their family. It nearly destroyed their business and brought shame on us all.'

She didn't look away. Jake knew she wanted to but she kept her eyes fixed on his, despite the colour that flooded her cheeks. He was acutely aware of what shame meant to an Italian.

'That must have been tough,' he said.

He saw her stiffen. She didn't want his pity.

He continued briskly, 'So it's just as well that I have an appointment to see Signor Stefano Cavaleri this morning, isn't it?'

Her eyes widened with surprise and the cigarette burned unheeded in her hand, but at last she gave him a real smile.

CHAPTER FIFTEEN

The house sat back off the road at the edge of town, keeping itself to itself. It was a fine single-storey stuccoed building, long and elegant, the kind of place Jake wouldn't mind living in himself. Its terracotta tiles gleamed golden in the sunlight and the courtyard at the front was a blaze of colour with bougainvillea scaling the honey-coloured walls and scarlet geraniums climbing out of stone troughs. But as Jake approached, he became aware of the air of neglect that hung around it. The walls and shutters were cracked and peeling, crying out for a coat of paint, but that was nothing unusual in a country where paint had become a luxury item that could only be bought on the illegal black market. And then only for a king's ransom.

But the neglect ran deeper. Weeds had colonised the courtyard cobbles and in one corner an ancient fig tree was collapsing drunkenly to the ground. Dusky lizards flitted among its branches and the sweet scent of figs lingered in the air. A skinny goat huddled in a patch of shade near a water barrel, its droppings baked iron-hard by the sun. Jake arrived bearing cassata-filled pastries in one hand and his identity card in the other, but not for one moment did he anticipate a warm welcome.

As he entered the courtyard a mongrel that was draped across the threshold, announced his arrival to the household, startling the goat. A man was quick to appear in the doorway. Mid-forties, thin-bellied and with thickly bristled jowls, he looked the kind of man who kept a shotgun behind the door. He was wearing a wine-stained vest and a workman's dusty blue trousers, patched at the knee.

'Major Parr?'

'That's me.'

Jake held out his identity card and the man snatched it from him. 'I am Stefano Cavaleri.'

So this was the brother of the man who ran away with Caterina's mother.

'Good morning, Signor Cavaleri. I would like a few words if I may.'

He presented the pastries plus two packs of the American cigarettes that servicemen received free and the man's heavy features broke into a greedy smile.

'*Benvenuto*, Major. Come inside.'

'*Grazie.*'

They walked into a spacious hallway that was cool and dim after the glare outside, with a high vaulted ceiling, but bare of furniture. Signor Cavaleri continued to inspect Jake's card.

'Monuments, Fine Arts and Archives Officer attached to the

Allied Military Government,' he read aloud. 'What in God's name does all that mean?'

'It means I'm here to ask you some questions.'

They entered a pleasant room with tall windows overlooking the emerald slopes of the hills and a mosaic floor of turquoise tesserae. The upper layer of the walls was nicotine-stained and the leather of the chairs was as wrinkled as an old man's skin. Another dog sprawled on one of them. Jake was not invited to sit down.

His host stood in the centre of the room and scratched his armpit thoughtfully. 'What kind of questions?'

'Questions about Antonio Lombardi.'

Cavaleri reacted as if Jake had given him a shot of bourbon. The sag of his shoulders vanished. He became as alert as a gundog.

'What about him?'

'I'm here to find out about his wood-inlaying business.'

The man sneered. 'The bastard is dead.'

'I am aware of that.'

'So what is Lombardi to the United States Army? Why the interest in him?'

'It's like this, Signor Cavaleri. Certain valuable items of antique furniture have gone missing.' He paused. Let that sink in. 'I am making enquiries among cabinet-makers, wood-workers and restorers in this area because Sorrento is a famous centre for wood skills. I wish to learn if any of them have been approached by people looking to use those skills to make repairs to bomb-damaged valuable pieces.'

He watched Cavaleri closely. Jake was quick at spotting lies; at picking out the tightening of the eyes, fine threads of deceit at their corners, the downward twitch at the sides of the mouth, the slight stiffening of the fingers. That was one reason he was good at his job.

'Do you know of anyone,' he asked, 'who is going round these parts with requests for restoration work on antiques?'

'No.'

Liar.

'Has anyone approached you to do this kind of work?'

'No.'

Liar.

'Do you know whether Lombardi was involved in such activities before he died?'

'I heard rumours.'

'What kind of rumours?'

Cavaleri shrugged. He opened up one of the white packs of Lucky Strike and flicked out a cigarette. He didn't waste one on Jake, who waited with a show of patience, hands in his trouser pockets, watching his man buy time for his next lie. Cavaleri struck a match on the rough wall and touched the flame to the tip.

'The rumour is that he was into dirty business. Maybe even working with the Camorra,' he said.

Jake breathed out heavily. The Camorra was bad news. It was the name of Naples' own personal mafia, in control of drugs, whores, gambling, protection money, kidnap, stealing of medicines from the Allied hospital and every other dirty violent racket that he could think of. It was the rotten underbelly of the city. The jeweller with the crushed windpipe, whose white and bloated corpse had been hauled out of Naples' filthy harbour three days earlier, bore the marks of a Camorra killing, with cement blocks fixed to his ankles. But Jake had learned the hard way that you could never be sure. People imitated their methods. To divert attention. To hide tracks.

'Tell me about the Lombardi family,' he said quietly.

'Lombardi?' Cavaleri said the name as if it tasted sour on his tongue.

'I'm told there is bad blood between your family and the Lombardis.'

'Who told you that?'

'Everybody.'

'People should stay out of my business.'

'Somebody has been spreading those bad rumours about Antonio Lombardi. Accusing him of being involved in crime.'

'Is that so?'

'Was it you?'

Cavaleri grinned, revealing good teeth. 'No.'

A lie? The grin made it hard to spot.

'Okay, tell me about Lucia Lombardi instead.'

It was like dropping water into a pan of hot oil. It spat everywhere.

The thin Italian seized a dog's enamel water bowl that lay on the floor and hurled it at Jake's head. He sidestepped it with ease but water sprayed his neck and the dog leaped off the seat, growling.

'Get out!' Cavaleri bellowed, his cheeks the colour of the wine stains on his vest. 'Get out of my house or I'll . . .'

From the back of his waistband he whipped out a knife. It had the look of a butcher's knife, long-bladed and honed to a razor edge. Jake felt a torrent of adrenaline hit his system at the sight of death coming at him.

'Calm down,' he said evenly, stretching one hand out flat towards the oncoming Italian, his other hand leaping to the gun-holster at his hip. He had shot men before. But never this close, never when he could smell their breath and hear their fingers chafing on the bone handle of the blade.

'Put it down,' he ordered, 'before I . . .'

'Stefano! *Bastardo*. Stop that at once.'

Stefano Cavaleri froze. Eyes full of rage. Yet the blade paused in mid-air, suspended inches from Jake's clean buff shirt, and the owner of the voice stepped into the room.

'Don't be a gutter-brained fool, my son.'

Jake allowed his head to turn a fraction. Out of the corner of his eye he saw a woman clothed in black to her ankles, grey hair hidden in a black beaded net, taller than her son and her back as straight and stiff as a rifle barrel. But what struck Jake was her face. It was the face of a warrior.

'A glass of Marsala, Major Parr?'

'*Grazie*.' Jake hated the sweet liquor. He smiled.

The bottle that Signora Cavaleri produced was dusty, as if it usually sat at the back of a cupboard, only seeing the light of day on rare occasions. Times were hard.

'You must excuse my son,' she said. 'He has the manners of an ox. But he is right. We do not speak the name of that woman in this house.'

'My apologies, signora. I did not mean to offend.'

They were seated in the wrinkled armchairs and Stefano regarded him with ill-temper through a haze of cigarette smoke while his elderly mother poured their guest a drink. She had the hands and the skin of a woman in her late seventies who had lived and worked in a hot country all her life, but she possessed the vigour and demeanour of a much younger woman. Her features were mannish, large and strong with a heavy brow, though her voice was deliberately soft. But Jake wasn't fooled by her courteous tones. Her face revealed who she was. There were deep lines of determination scored down her cheeks and a broad silvery scar ran right across her forehead, for all the world like the mark of a sabre.

'So you want to know about the Lombardi family, Major.'

Her son opened his mouth to say something but she gave him a hard look that silenced him at once.

'Major?' She waited for Jake's response.

'Yes. I am enquiring whether anyone has been approaching local wood craftsmen to work on damaged antique furniture. Your business is respected in Sorrento.'

'Our business *was* respected in Sorrento. No longer.'

She showed no emotion. Just a slide of her tongue over her teeth, as though the words stuck there.

Jake turned to Stefano Cavaleri. 'You are now the chief craftsman of the Cavaleri business, I am told.'

'Go to hell, you Yankee *bastardo*.'

'Stefano!' his mother hissed. She inclined her head a fraction towards her visitor. 'When my eldest son, Roberto, ran our business we were one of the finest producers of inlaid wood in Sorrento. Roberto was an inspired craftsman.' A smile of maternal pride softened the harsh lines of her face and Jake caught a glimpse of the person she might once have been.

'Was he a friend of Antonio Lombardi?'

'Oh yes. They were friends. And rivals.' She laughed with bitterness.

'What happened?'

'That bitch, Antonio Lombardi's wife, happened. She seduced and bewitched my son, God curse her. They ran off to Rome eleven years ago and I have not seen my son since. His wife hanged herself the same day.'

'You still have me, Mamma,' her other son pointed out in a surly voice.

Signora Cavaleri regarded her middle-aged son for a full half-minute in a silence that chilled the room. 'You will never be the man Roberto was,' she stated finally. 'We both know that.'

Stefano lunged to his feet, snatched a glass from a cupboard and filled it to the brim with Marsala. He threw the liquid down his throat in one gulp, wiped his mouth with the back of his hand and stormed out of the house, slamming the front door.

The dog trembled on its chair, but Signora Cavaleri did not even flutter an eyelid. There was a frozen stillness to her that was as unnerving as it was unnatural. Where was the Italian mamma with the torrent of words, the hands flying around her head and the emotions knocking holes in the wall? Isn't that what Italian mammas did, for Christ's sake? Did her eldest son steal that from her when he left, leaving only a shell behind for his brother? Jake felt a shudder pass through him and knocked back his own drink.

'You are hard on your son,' he told her.

Her eyes narrowed. 'It is none of your Yankee business, Major.'

'It is my business if you drive Stefano to try to prove his worth to you.'

'How?'

'By working on stolen artefacts himself.'

'I would not permit that.'

'He is a grown man. He does not need your permission. Any more than he needs your permission to stick a knife in my chest.'

Her dark eyes glared at him. 'You take liberties in my house, signore.'

He noticed the demotion from major to signore.

'It is my job to discover the truth,' he responded.

He stood in front of her, crowding her in her chair. 'Have a word with Stefano, Signora Cavaleri. Instruct him to give me the information I need. It is for the good of Italy. Get him to tell me what he knows about the people involved in this criminal racket, because I feel sure he must know something.'

Anger rippled across her face, but whether at him or at Stefano,

Jake couldn't tell. She pushed down hard on the arms of the chair to raise herself to her feet and the physical effort required was obvious. He wanted to put out a hand to help her up, but he knew she would despise such a gesture. He stepped back.

'Why should I do that?' she demanded. 'Why should I have this *word* with Stefano?'

'Because if you don't, I will.' He paused to inspect her stern eyes. 'At the police station.'

'Leave us in peace, Major.'

'Maybe it is your other son, Roberto, I should be talking to.'

Jake saw her suck in air like a drowning person, heard it rasp at the back of her throat.

'Roberto is dead,' she stated baldly. 'Shot in Rome by a German bullet.'

Caterina waited outside Sorrento railway station, exactly as agreed. But she didn't want to be there. Instead she wanted to be inside Jake Parr's pocket, eavesdropping on what the Cavaleri family had to say. She hadn't set foot inside their house for eleven years, despite young Carlo Cavaleri being her friend, but she occasionally saw the old grandmother at market, still as upright as ever, still unbroken by sorrow, though garbed in black from head to toe. Years ago Caterina had made the mistake of greeting her when they came face to face among the melons and the purple aubergines, but Signora Cavaleri looked straight through her as if she did not exist.

She paced back and forth, ducking into the shade of a wall, while a steady flow of travellers passed in and out of the station.

That's why she had chosen it as the place to meet with Major Parr after he'd finished with the Cavaleris. She avoided empty spaces now. Steered clear of dark streets. In the canvas bag slung over her shoulder, spoiling the line of Leonora's elegant white dress, lay her grandfather's old Bodeo revolver. This time she would be prepared.

A couple of American jeeps, hot and dusty, were parked on the short hill up to the station, surrounded by a huddle of street children in ragged shorts, fingering the headlamps and the utility spade on the side of the vehicle. Anything that wasn't bolted down would surely vanish. The sudden growl of a motorcycle drew their bright eyes when it peeled off the main road and accelerated up the hill, the raucous sound of it ricocheting off the station walls as it approached. The grinning urchins crowded round when it swung to a halt, spitting gravel.

'Hey there!'

It was Major Parr on a Harley Davidson motorcycle, US Army issue, revving the engine and smiling at her.

'Hop on,' he said. 'I have something to show you.'

Caterina didn't hesitate. She hitched up her wide pleated skirt and swung a leg over the pillion seat fixed above the luggage rack. The bike's leather saddlebags lay snug against her calf.

'Ready?' he called above the roar of the engine.

'I'm ready,' she said.

Caterina's hands were on his waist. It was not unpleasant, gripping tight to the muscular frame of him under the olive drab material of his US Army officer's jacket, but she was well aware of the inappropriate intimacy of it. How could she even think of holding on to a man she scarcely knew? One who was accusing her father of unthinkable crimes?

It felt like betrayal.

The wind snatched at her short hair, fraying the edges of her thoughts, as the motorcycle roared through the streets to the edge of town. She had never ridden one before and each bump in the road rattled her bones, pummelling the air in her chest, but the freedom of movement, the joy as it swayed and swerved, seduced her. The onrush of air robbed her of breath, but she ducked her head behind the broad shoulders in front of her and she leaned when he leaned, trusting him, even when the roadway came leaping up at her.

Why trust him – this man with the guarded eyes and the words that had brought a hornet's nest to her door? What possible reason did she have to trust him?

She unfastened her good hand from his jacket and tapped his shoulder.

'Stop,' she shouted against the noise of the engine.

'What?'

But he'd heard. She knew he'd heard. She caught a glimpse of his profile, the fine nose and firm jawline, and she knew that manipulating this man would never be easy.

'Stop.'

She tapped his shoulder again. Harder.

Major Parr pulled over at once and Caterina swung herself off the motorbike before he could offer her a hand. They were on a tiny patch of sandy scrubland just where the last straggling houses of Sorrento gave way to lemon groves that were wrapped in an armour of netting and tall poles. The American didn't dismount. He remained astride the motorbike, the engine idling.

'Is something wrong?' he asked warily.

'Yes. Everything is wrong.'

She strode in a circle around the khaki Harley Davidson until she came to a halt in front of him once more. He removed his sunglasses.

'What is it?' he asked.

'You and I want the same thing,' she stated flatly. 'To find the people who are committing these crimes. Isn't that true, Major Parr?'

'Yes, it's true.'

'Then why is it,' she demanded, 'that you expect me to tell you everything that I know but you tell me nothing. I want to know who these people are who are trying to kill me. I want the names of the people who accuse my father. You owe me that much.'

The muscles of his face tightened under his skin. For a second she thought he was going to rev the engine of the motorcycle, ride off and leave her standing there among the lizards.

Instead he said, 'We are here to help each other find out what we need. Don't be impatient. We have to proceed step by step.'

'Before or after I'm killed?'

He shook his head. 'I am taking you to Naples to . . .'

'Naples?' That caught her by surprise.

'Sure. To see something that might clarify whether or not your father was involved.'

'He wasn't.'

'So let's prove it.'

She hesitated, uncertain how far to trust him. 'Give me one name,' she said. 'One name. In exchange for my help.'

An American Army truck swept past on its way to Naples, kicking up a cloud of dust that swirled between them, and the driver raised a hand in greeting, but Major Parr's attention was fixed on Caterina. On her bandaged arm.

'In an interrogation room at headquarters,' he said, 'I have incarcerated a man right now who was caught guarding a secret stash of stolen artefacts, including an early Tintoretto sketch of Belshazzar.' His voice had sunk low, hissing between his teeth, barely audible above the sound of the engine.

'What's his name?'

A full ten seconds passed before he answered, 'Sal Sardo.'

'*Grazie.*'

It was what she'd wanted. Somewhere to start. A name, but it wasn't a name she had expected. In one smooth movement she swung herself back on to the motorbike behind him.

'Satisfied?' he asked drily.

'For now.'

'Okay, let's go.'

'Tell me,' she said, 'what happened at the Cavaleris' place?'

He gave a sour laugh. 'Other than Stefano Cavaleri holding a knife to my throat and the old woman wanting to silence my tongue with her foul Marsala, do you mean?'

Caterina remained silent.

He sighed and took off his jacket. 'Stefano Cavaleri claimed there were rumours that your father was deep into it all.' He turned to face her. 'Do you know anywhere that the Cavaleri family themselves might hide stolen artefacts?'

'Really? You think they're caught up in this?'

'It's possible.'

But his eyes gave him away. It was obvious to her that he thought it was more than just possible. She considered for a moment and nodded.

'Stefano and Roberto have a younger brother, Vito, who was not interested in joining the family business of intarsia work.' She glanced ahead where the road doglegged up to the cliff-edge route. 'He runs a garage just this side of Naples. There is storage there.'

'What are we waiting for?' He flicked his jacket over her shoulders. 'You'll need this. I don't want you getting chilly and falling off.'

'No, I don't need it. No.'

But he had already turned away. Reluctantly she slipped her bare arms into the sleeves and became aware of the scent of him wrapped around her, fresh and male in the weave of the material. She could smell his American cigarettes.

He gunned the engine. She gripped his waist.

'One thing,' he added without glancing round. 'The old woman told me that her eldest son, Roberto, was shot dead by Germans in Rome.'

Caterina had opened her mouth to urge *'Avanti'* but his words stopped her cold.

'Mamma, oh Mamma,' she murmured.

But it was lost in the roar of the engine and in the thud of her pulse as they rode north.

The cliff edge hurtled towards them. Far below, the sea climbed higher up the rocks, as though it had caught the scent of them, but each time on the tight bends they swept around with a squeal of rubber, their right knees almost grazing the limestone cliff wall. Caterina didn't even bother to breathe as she saw the next switchback already charging towards them.

The coastal road between Sorrento and Naples was like no other. It had been hacked out of the flank of the cliff, hundreds of metres above the glistening blue Bay of Naples and at each twist and turn a new vista opened up, offering breathtaking views. Even Caterina, who had lived there all her life, could not resist the exhilaration that came with racing round the corkscrew bends and through the small villages of white-painted cottages where lush gardens of flowering shrubs flashed by in a blur.

She felt no fear. Her heart was hammering with excitement, and as her fingers clung to the soldier in front of her, she wondered if his was hammering too.

Did he always drive so fast, pushing himself and the bike to the limit?

She saw the bunching of his back muscles under his shirt, the way he leaned and swayed as if he were part of the machinery. She saw the rush of air whipping his hair into a tangle and how every now and again he lifted his head to face the world that was hurtling towards him.

Right now he had forgotten she even existed.

*

'What the hell are *you* doing here?'

'Good morning to you too, Vito Cavaleri,' Caterina responded with a dry edge to her voice. 'Not exactly busy, I see.'

The Harley Davidson had pulled off the highway to roll up on the Cavaleri garage forecourt. There was no shade and the sun beat fiercely on the metal roof of the work shed, which stood open. There was one car inside, a big burly Lancia, its bonnet up, but Vito was not working on it. He was lounging in a wicker chair near the pumps, reading a newspaper, a rough-rolled cigarette dangling from one corner of his mouth. He didn't bother rising to his feet.

Vito was the youngest of the three brothers. He had wild black hair and was wearing oily dungarees with no shirt underneath. On his bare shoulder a tattoo was clearly visible, snaking down onto his arm – the words in italic script, *Prima la Famiglia*. Family first.

'Get your Lombardi arse off my property,' he said bluntly. '*Pronto*.'

Major Parr ambled over to the chair, an easy rolling stride, and stood over the smaller man, his tall shadow with the gun holster on its hip, hunkering down on top of Vito.

'That's no way to talk to a lady, signore.'

It wasn't the voice of the man who had said 'Hop on' so invitingly. It was the voice of the police officer he used to be – hard, street-tough, the kind of voice that could have you face-down in the dirt before you even blinked. Vito Cavaleri spat out his cigarette and jumped to his feet. He was a head shorter than Jake Parr.

'Hey, Major,' Vito said placatingly, 'I meant no harm.' He shrugged and backed off a step, scratching the hairs on his forearm. 'You got trouble with that?' He nodded in the direction of the Harley.

Jake Parr draped a heavy arm around the man's shoulders, switching from hostile to friendly so fast it made Vito's eyes roll. 'Come take a look at it, *amico mio*.' He steered Vito towards the bike. 'It was misfiring all the way down the mountain.'

At the prospect of American dollars, Vito's face broke into a broad smile.

The American bumped the big motorbike off its stand and started to wheel it towards the workshop shed, with Vito scuttling alongside.

'It could be the spark plugs,' Caterina heard Vito suggest. 'Or the carburettor . . .'

They vanished inside the shed, the Italian still talking. The major had done his job well. Caterina drifted casually to the side of the rough wooden wall of the building, but the moment she was out of sight, she hurried. Through the thin timber wall she could hear the murmur of male voices and then the Harley's engine kicked into life and died again. She felt sweat gather in the crook of her elbow where the major's jacket still hung over her arm.

She turned the corner and came to a halt. The old brick building she had been heading for was gone. Where there had once been a beautiful old building that used to be a small mill for glove-making, there was now nothing but a heap of twisted rubble.

'It's gone.'

Caterina swung around. Young Carlo Cavaleri was standing at the back of the work shed, watching her. He was wearing dungarees like his uncle, his swarthy skin even darker in the shade, his usual easy smile of greeting missing.

'What happened?' she asked.

'What do you think? An American bomb dropped off target.'

Caterina sighed. 'We had good times there, you and I.'

She and Carlo used to play among the old car parts and dismantled engines, days of innocence, long gone. Rheumatic fever at the age of ten had damaged Carlo's heart and kept him out of the army. It had dented his macho image but had ironically kept him alive.

'Well,' Carlo whistled softly, 'look at you, signora.' She heard the admiration in his voice. 'All dressed up and nowhere to go.'

'I do have somewhere to go.'

'You've changed, Caterina.' He shook his black curls in dismay. 'Not just your hair and your fancy dress.'

'We all change, Carlo.' She smiled fondly at him. 'It's what life does to us.'

She glanced at the gleaming vehicle parked behind him, as black as a beetle and even Caterina, who knew nothing about cars, couldn't fail to recognise the mascot with its flying wings on the long elegant bonnet. A Rolls-Royce. She looked down at the polishing cloth in Carlo's hand.

'You work for your Uncle Vito now?'

'Some days.'

Keeping it casual, she asked, 'Where does he store all his junk now that the millhouse has gone?'

'Just throws it at the back of the shed. He's an untidy bastard.'

Just then an engine kicked into life somewhere behind the wooden wall. It shattered the sunny stillness and sent a crow lifting up from the roof, spiralling lazily into the sky and trailing its shadow across the citrus groves below. Carlo regarded Caterina with a frown.

'So where are you going?'

'Naples.'

He jerked his head towards the shed. 'On a motorbike?'

'I'm with someone.'

The frown became a scowl. 'A soldier someone?'

Only soldiers could get hold of petrol these days.

'Yes.'

Abruptly the scowl vanished and a look of concern replaced it. 'Take care, Caterina.'

She was touched. The tension in her aching body slipped down a notch. 'Thank you, Carlo.' She smiled at him. 'Don't get into trouble yourself.'

They both heard the engine slide into gear. She leaned forward and kissed his cheek, then set off back the way she had come. As she turned the corner of the building, Carlo's voice, urgent and worried, chased after her.

'Take care, Caterina. Or you'll turn into your mother.'

CHAPTER SIXTEEN

Naples swallowed them up. It sucked them into the noisy world of blaring trucks and impatient crowds. Stone walls came crashing down as bombed buildings were torn into mountains of masonry that were obscene to the eye, while clouds of dust swirled through the streets. Major Parr was quick and decisive, swinging the bike first one way and then another when the street was blocked or the road was ripped up for repairs to damaged gas and water mains. He knew far better than Caterina the tangled maze of backways and alleys, the narrow crowded *vico* that would skip around the blockage.

It was as they were riding down Vico Noce that they saw the fight. A British Army sergeant-major was pounding heavy fists into the kidneys of an American GI Joe, a tall gangling youth whose eyes were rolling in his head and whose mouth hung open in shock and pain. Blood zigzagged down his chin.

It was a miserable street. It stank of sewers and unwashed bodies. Water was in short supply because of broken water mains, and the houses were crammed on top of each other, four storeys high, but a splash of coral fuschias still managed to cling to life in one of the window boxes. It struck Caterina as strange that a queue of a dozen soldiers stood outside the door where the fight was taking place and watched the fracas in silence.

The Harley Davidson skidded to a halt on the cobbles and both Caterina and Major Parr leapt off. Major Parr wasted no time in jamming an elbow forcibly into the side of the British soldier's head and at the same time yanked the GI from his meaty grasp.

'What the fuck . . .?' the sergeant started to say, while pulling back a fist to land a blow on his attacker's face, but he spotted the major's insignia in the nick of time. They all knew the punishment for striking a senior officer. He pulled himself together and saluted half-heartedly.

'Sir,' he snapped out.

'What the hell is going on here?' Major Parr demanded.

'That son of a putrid whore stole my tin of bully beef,' the sergeant-major growled. His cheeks were puffing, as hard as if he'd been running.

Caterina looked at the soldiers in the queue outside the house, a mix of American and British. Each one carried a can of tinned food in his hand. What was going on here? None of the men in the queue would look her in the eye. They shuffled nearer the open door.

Curious, she left Major Parr to sort out the brawlers and she walked quickly towards the door. She stepped into a dingy passageway with cracked brown paint on the wall. It led into a living room on the left and at the sight of her the five soldiers clustered around the doorway to the room pulled back. Again the awkwardness. Again a tin of bully beef in each soldier's hand.

'Caterina Lombardi!'

She heard her name called from outside. Jake Parr was looking for her. But she remained where she was, unable to turn and walk out. Four women, neither old nor young, sat on a row of hard chairs in the room facing the door and beside each one stood a small pile of tinned food. They were ordinary women, all of them thin, in dull worn-out dresses, their cheekbones etched into fleshless ridges, their eyes as blank as a doll's.

A British Tommy infantryman stepped smartly around Caterina, placed his tin on the floor next to the one with blonde hair and lifeless blue eyes. The woman stood and walked without a word behind a flimsy curtain that was stretched on a string across the back of the room, creating a ripple of murmurs in the waiting soldiers. Another stepped forward. Grinning. He placed his tin on the floor beside a woman with long dark hair and for a split second she closed her eyes tight. Then she too walked with bowed shoulders, as if trying to hide from herself, followed by the soldier.

The ends of two old mattresses on the floor stuck out beyond the curtain and Caterina could hear a flurry of suppressed sounds, a man's stifled moan. It was brief. Over in a couple of minutes flat. A wave of sadness for these desperate women flooded through Caterina, and she turned and stared at the men behind her.

'This ain't no place for you, love,' one said, but not unkindly. 'Clear off.'

'Leave them,' she said in stiff English. 'Leave the women. All of you. Give them food and go.' She swept her hand towards the street in an attempt to brush them from the room. From the house. From Italy.

'Look, love,' a cocky young corporal smiled at her, 'you don't understand . . .'

'Caterina, come out of there at once.'

It was Major Parr, his tone sharp as he shouldered his way to her side, but Caterina swept past him and out into the street, the sadness of it devouring her.

'Count yourself lucky,' he said, 'that your father gave you your skill with wood. Or you could be in that room yourself.'

They climbed on the motorcycle without a word and rode away from that street.

Major Parr had brought her to what he called his headquarters. She looked about her. Only a flat-hearted foreigner could term this a *headquarters*. It was an ancient Neapolitan palazzo, gently crumbling, but still beautiful. Its rococo plasterwork with elaborate curves and complex scrolls was chipped and broken now, hanging off the walls in places, as tired as Naples itself. In the huge marbled reception hall in which she was standing, she could see tell-tale marks on the walls where paintings had been removed, but the massive mirrors remained in place with their ornate gilded frames and crazed glass. Despite the heat outside, it was pleasantly cool inside and dust motes drifted lazily through the air.

'This way,' Major Parr said.

She followed him smartly across the marble mosaic floor and past the two desks of khaki-painted metal that looked ridiculous in the middle of the opulence of the seventeenth-century hall. Behind the desks sat two army officers in uniform, one American, one British. Major Parr came to a halt in front of the US lieutenant.

'Hi, Forester, anything new?'

'No, sir. All quiet on the western front.' He grinned, his blue eyes bright with interest as he took in Caterina nearby. 'But Captain Fielding has been down there with him.'

'Is that so?'

'Yessir.'

'Okay, get me the keys.' Jake unhooked a key from a chain on his belt and handed it over.

'At once, sir.'

The young lieutenant shot to his feet, clearly delighted to have something to do to relieve his boredom. He took a key from his desk drawer and vanished down a corridor at the back of the hall. Two minutes later he returned clutching three heavy iron keys of the kind that opened Venetian prisons.

'Please follow me, Signorina Lombardi,' Major Parr said.

The awkwardness still hung between them. She followed. She watched his shiny black boots snap down on the floor, crisp, assured, determined. Why had he brought her here? His earlier words leapt into her mind: *To see something that might clarify whether or not your father was involved.*

But was it true?

Or was that just the bait?

Her hand slipped to the bag that hung from her shoulder and she fingered the bulk of the weapon inside it.

Using the first key, Major Parr unlocked a door. It seemed innocent enough, painted a pale jade and its panels picked out with richly decorated scrollwork. It wasn't the kind of door that hid nightmares, so she didn't turn and run when he opened it. He looked back to check on her, with quick, intelligent eyes. Caterina liked that about him and yet at the same time didn't like that about him, because it made her wonder how much he saw.

'Ready?' he asked.

'Yes.'

'Then let's get those wagons rolling.'

What wagons? What was he talking about?

He stepped through the doorway into a short stubby corridor, but she remained where she was. He looked round, surprised.

'Major Parr, where are you taking me?'

'I told you, I have something to show you.' He smiled. 'What's the matter? Don't you trust me?'

'No.'

He broke into an easy laugh. 'Well, that's telling me straight.'

The laugh lingered on his mouth and it was hard not to smile.

'Make sure you stay in front of me,' she said, 'where I can see you.'

'Signorina Lombardi, I am sorry that my investigations have brought trouble into your life. But *I* am not the danger.'

Caterina waited for him to move further down the corridor before she walked forward.

The second key, as large as a meat fork, unlocked the second door. This one possessed no scrollwork or colourful paint. It was bare oak, as ancient as the palazzo itself, knotted and cracked, and the lock was a massive clunky iron contraption. Immediately her nervousness turned to curiosity.

What lay behind it?

The American hauled open the door. It should have creaked on its great metal hinges, but it didn't, so Caterina knew instantly that it was well-oiled and well-used, but when she caught site of what lay on the other side she blinked with surprise. It was yet another door. But this one was made of heavy black metal and it looked brand new.

As he reached for the third key, Caterina muttered, 'This had better be good, Major.'

His smile softened the tense line of his jaw. 'I think you'll like it.'

She didn't like it. Not one bit. She positively disliked it. The metal door swung open to reveal a bare flight of stone steps leading down into the blackness of an unlit basement. Caterina's heart took a leap into her throat and the fine hairs rose on her forearm.

'No,' she said.

He took her wrist. She yanked it away.

'I am not your captive. You cannot lock me away.'

'What? Don't be . . .' He flicked a switch. 'Look.'

Some days when Caterina was intent on creating her intarsia

designs in wood within her workshop, it was as if a crack opened up in her mind and she fell into it. Her hands and her eyes no longer belonged to her body; they belonged to the wood. When that happened, she seemed to be no longer part of a world peopled with human flesh but instead constructed of burr-walnut, finely polished maple and purpleheart, the silky sheen of creamy white basswood, and the intense fires in the heartwood of teak and butternut. When she looked at her arms, they would have the glowing grain of red oak and she would lift them to her nose to inhale the scent of them.

It was like that now.

She descended the stone steps into a world of wood.

Caterina stood in front of a Madonna whose cloak-folds were so skilfully conceived they enraptured her, while three life-size mahogany saints stood beside her in a row, regarding her with expressions of grief. Slowly she released her breath. In silence she started to prowl among the objects heaped in the basement, touching, caressing, feeling the rich life of them.

'So many,' she murmured. 'All stolen?'

'Every one of them. We have recovered these. But there are still many more out there that we are tracking.'

Caterina could see nicks and scratches in a number of the artefacts, damage to the wood, as though they had at some time been crammed together in a truck, no better than oranges in a crate. She could see where the lid of a mahogany box had cracked open. It sent a shudder through her. Yet even in the dim light she could admire the cross-framed Dante chairs and carved strapwork chests. In the centre, four tall ornate candle-holders stood sentinel around a cardinal's magnificent gilded throne and Caterina recognised the ancient lion of Venice carved into its clawed feet.

There was so much here that her hands yearned to touch, but a hot anger rose within her at the realisation of how close all this had come to being lost to Italy forever. But when she turned to voice her thanks to this American who was helping Italy, her eye fell on a cedarwood triptych that was propped up on a cabinet and the words grew silent in her throat.

She had seen it before. It came from the church of San Giuseppe dei Ruffi in Naples. Carved with the finest inlay-work after the style of Raphael, it depicted three of the Stations of the Cross and had been ripped from an altar. It dated back to the early sixteenth century at a time when Michelangelo was painting the Sistine Chapel. Her eyes struggled to find the repair she knew was there, but it was so skilfully done, she couldn't detect it.

'That is beautiful,' the major commented.

Caterina had forgotten he was there. She nodded and moved deeper into the basement, inspecting a giltwood curule seat, scanning the hundreds of objects but trying not to betray her aim – to seek out anything familiar. The second time she saw a piece she recognised, a delicate marquetry screen, she felt the same jolt of shock, but the third time was not as fierce.

Oh, Papà. What were you doing?

The next time she didn't even blink. She just kept weaving her way between the narrow aisles, but her mouth was dry, her tongue unwieldy. She took her time circling back to the door where Major Parr awaited her.

'Thank you,' she said. 'For bringing me here.'

'Colonel Quincy is the expert whose job it is to catalogue it all. The guy is a genius at it,' he added. She heard the admiration in his voice.

'The atmosphere is dry and cool here. I can see that someone cares. There is no dust.'

They were speaking softly. Respectful. Aware of what they were viewing.

'There is another basement area for storage of marble and stone statuary. Another for paintings.'

He told her this as though she had a right to know and she wondered why. Was it because she was Lombardi's daughter? Or was there something else? His gaze was fixed on her, not on the works of art, and she felt an urge to peel off the hard sheen on his eyes, to look behind it and find out how much they had seen.

She gestured to the priceless collection around them. 'Were these all taken from churches and museums?'

'Yes. All are stolen items. From the old palazzos too.

'So many. It's hard to believe.'

'This is only the tip of the iceberg. They ship them out at night in trucks, often for export to the highest bidder. Many have been destroyed already, maltreated and defaced. The thieves are . . .'

But he offered no word to describe them.

'I need your help,' he told her instead. 'To identify who did the repairs.'

She took a step back. 'I'm no expert.'

He took a step forward. 'But your father was.'

A chill spilled through her veins. The American had tricked her. He had laid a trap and she had walked straight into it. She had betrayed her father.

Without a word she headed for the door and yanked it open.

'How many pieces did you recognise?'

'What makes you think,' Caterina asked coolly, 'that I recognised any of them?'

He didn't argue, but she heard his soft sigh. They headed back into the marble hall with the khaki desk and the crazed mirrors that reflected a softer speckled world. Jake Parr pulled out his cigarettes and to her surprise lit one for her and one for himself. It seemed the fact that she had ridden on his motorcycle gave him that right. She accepted the cigarette and exhaled a thick skein of smoke to veil the dismay in her eyes.

'Signorina Lombardi,' he said. It wasn't the police officer's voice this time. It was looser, the American accent seeping more strongly into his Italian words, giving them an odd lilt. 'I do not have your skill to create art, but nothing is going to keep me from saving this country's art from men hell-bent on stealing it. I lost my heart to Italy long before I ever stepped on its soil, entranced by my Italian grandmother's stories of her life here in *Napoli*. Saving Naples' treasures and its priceless relics is my personal mission. The sooner you understand that, the better.' He drew hard on his cigarette. 'I wish to find the truth,' he added. 'Just as you do.'

'Be careful what you wish for, *Americano*.'

He regarded her steadily. 'How many pieces in that basement did you recognise from your father's workshop?'

Caterina could hear the ghost-whisper of a groove-cutter in her father's hand as it sliced through the wood of the triptych, but she couldn't bring herself to look at the soldier. A number slipped uninvited into her mind.

Twelve.

She had counted twelve pieces. But there could be more. She had stopped counting at twelve. How many, Papà? Fifteen? Twenty? More, if she dared look?

'Three,' she said softly. 'Three pieces. The triptych, a screen and an inlaid wood panel.' She raised her eyes to his. 'Satisfied?'

But before he could reply there was a flurry of khaki beside them and it was with relief that she saw Captain Harry Fielding's figure materialise at Major Parr's elbow.

'Hello, Jake,' he said in English. 'What took you so long?'

The breeziness of his greeting did not quite disguise his impatience. This was not the Harry Fielding who had sat so easily in her courtyard in Sorrento. Here in his headquarters there was a sharper edge to the Englishman. His blond eyebrows were gathered in a tense line, but his eyes took in Caterina's new hair and her dress, and he smiled.

'It's good to see you again, Signorina Lombardi. I didn't expect to find you here.'

'She has been viewing some of the beauties in the basement.'

'Really?' Fielding frowned. 'Is that wise?'

'Don't you trust me?' Caterina asked.

'It might be dangerous for you, that's all I meant.'

'It's too late for that, Captain Fielding,' she said. 'Who am I in danger from this time?'

But Jake Parr cut in. 'Do you have Sal Sardo locked up safe in the cells?' he asked Fielding.

'Yes. The man's a damn weasel.' He grimaced with distaste. 'He gives one answer to every question. "*I know nothing. Niente*".'

Jake Parr turned to Caterina. 'Would you mind waiting here, Signorina Lombardi, while I question this man?'

'No, Major. I won't wait.'

The edges of his mouth tightened.

'I won't wait, Major. I will come with you. I want to see whether I recognise this prisoner of yours, if he is one of the thieves. Let me see if I can identify him.'

'No.' The word was flat. Absolute.

'Jake, she might be right,' Harry Fielding pointed out reasonably. 'Think about it. She could help us.'

'No.'

'Why not?'

'I don't want her there.'

As if she were a stranger to him, as if he had not felt the warmth of her hands on his hips or put his lips on her cigarette.

'Major.' Caterina's voice was quiet. 'It is the price I ask for my co-operation.'

A silence fell, as abrupt as a door clicking shut.

CHAPTER SEVENTEEN

Jake saw no glimmer of recognition when Caterina Lombardi set eyes on Sal Sardo for the first time on the other side of the grille. Just a brief shake of her head.

'*Niente! Niente!*' The words came from the interrogation room.

Harry Fielding was questioning the prisoner, but using the soft touch. To lower his guard. Sal Sardo was forty-two, thin and twitchy, his bones restless inside his skin. with chestnut-brown hair in need of a brush and a face that looked as though it had been squeezed to a point from peering through too many keyholes. Jake had known wastrels like this back in Milwaukee, stoolies who turned police informer or were runners for some two-bit criminal.

'Nice and easy, Harry,' he murmured under his breath, as he peered through the metal grille that divided the dark observation cubicle from the harshly lit interrogation room.

Beside Jake, Caterina Lombardi's small frame was perched on

a seat, her knee almost touching his own. He had motioned her to silence when they entered the cramped cubicle, but he was never sure with her. She was clever, he had to admit that. The way she'd manoeuvred him into compliance with her request to sit in on the interview. It both impressed and annoyed him.

'So, Sal,' Harry was asking for the tenth time, 'what were you up to in that basement with all those stolen items?'

'*Madonna mia*,' Sal Sardo whined, scrunching a greasy black cap between his fingers. 'I told you already. I have nowhere to sleep. I break into people's basements for the night or into empty houses, but I do no harm, I tell you. It was dark. I had no idea what was in the stinking rat-infested hole. I would never have gone near it if I'd known what was there.' He shot Harry a look of hostility. 'How the hell was I to know your lot would come charging in at dawn?'

'Ruined your beauty sleep, did they?'

Sardo scowled. 'You got nothing on me. *Niente.*'

Harry gave a patient half-smile and sat back in his chair. 'Well, Sal, I don't see it like that. What I want to know is why you were carrying a knife?'

'Why do you think? It's fucking dangerous out there on the streets.'

'The house was deserted. The owner died in the war. How long had you been staying there?'

'One night, that's all.'

'Is that so?'

'*Si.*'

'And how did you get in?'

Sardo sighed with exaggeration and abandoned the cap. His fingers started on the buttons of his fraying blue shirt. 'I told you all this stuff already. It was through an air vent. I kicked in the cover and crawled inside. I couldn't see nothing in the dark.'

'You had a torch in your pocket.'

'*Si*, but I was scared to use it. In case anyone saw.'

'So you knew you were breaking the law,' Harry said sharply. The smile had gone.

'Come on, Captain. I needed somewhere to sleep.'

'Who told you about it?'

'No one. I found the place myself.'

'Very convenient. A bedroom for you with thousands of pounds' worth of treasure in Renaissance artefacts.'

Sal slumped further in his chair. 'I told you, I didn't know it was there.'

'Who paid you to guard it?'

'No one.'

'Lies, Sal. All lies.' Harry rose to his feet dismissively.

'No, it's the truth, I swear.'

Harry let a dusty silence settle in the room.

'Last chance, Sal,' he said. 'Give me some names.'

'I know nothing, Captain.'

Harry strode to the door, but paused to glance back over his shoulder.

'Tell me this, Sal. What do you know about the jeweller, Bartoli, the one whose body was dragged out of Naples harbour the other day?'

'Never heard of him.'

'You're a fool, Sal Sardo,' Henry said through tight lips. 'And very soon, without our protection, you'll be a dead fool.'

Jake walked into the bare and comfortless interrogation room. It smelled. Not of unwashed bodies or fear or even the usual disinfectant. To him it smelled of sadness and it was emanating from the black rectangle of the grille on the wall. He was acutely aware of Caterina Lombardi's invisible presence behind it. He wanted her involved. That's why he'd brought her here today, because he was certain there were things in her head that he needed to know, a key that would unlock a door in his investigations.

But he didn't trust himself not to want her involved for other reasons as well, reasons that he didn't care to examine too closely. He pushed the thought aside and took a seat at the small table. He inspected Sal Sardo opposite him, aware of his bad breath, and it flitted through his mind to wonder if the tremor on Sardo's lips was actually a prayer.

'Name?' Jake demanded.

'I've already told . . .'

'Name?'

'Salvatore Sardo.'

His neck sank down between his shoulders, looking more tortoise than weasel.

'Address?'

'No address. I live on the street.'

His voice was surly. Jake liked that. When a suspect passes through the early frightened and defensive stage to the angry and resentful stage, he is liable to lose his temper and make mistakes.

'So you slept in that basement overnight.'

'*Si.*'

'By chance.'

'*Si.*'

'With a host of holy religious treasures from the churches of Naples.'

A sigh. '*Si.*'

'Look at me, Sardo.'

Sardo had been gazing at his own grimy fingers on the edge of the table but now he looked up, quick and furtive.

'My name is Major Parr. Do I look like a fool to you?'

'No, Major Parr. No, no, of course not.'

'So pay attention. You were in that basement as a watchman for someone, a useless watchman, but a watchman nonetheless.'

Sardo was shaking his head.

'I want,' Jake continued, 'the name of the man who employed you to be there.'

'I know nothing. *Niente.*'

Jake's hand slapped down hard on the table, making the prisoner jump out of his skin and a strange wailing sound whooped from his mouth before being swiftly silenced.

'Listen to me, you piece of gutter garbage,' Jake snapped, 'I will throw you in a cell and toss the key in the harbour if you don't give me some straight answers. Who set you up to do it?'

'No one.'

'I am going to charge you with being in possession of the stolen property hoarded in that basement – gold candlesticks, a marble statue of Christ and the Madonna, six silver crosses, three carved ...'

'No!' Sardo's fingers started to drum on the edge of the table but he seemed unaware of them. 'I am innocent,' he wailed.

'How did you transport the marble statue? Who helped? Give me a name.'

The head-shaking and shoulder-twitching started up again. 'You have no right to keep me here.'

'I have every right to detain thieves.'

'I am not a thief. I know ...'

'*Niente.* So you keep saying.' Jake abruptly leaned back in his chair, easing the pressure on the man opposite him. He considered providing a cigarette but decided against it. 'So you used to be a carter, hauling goods around Naples.'

The drumming stopped instantly. Sardo regarded his inquisitor through narrow eyes. 'How do you know that?'

'It is my job to know things. It is your job to answer my questions. I say again, you had a horse and cart and used to make deliveries. Right?'

'Yes.'

'Just in Naples?'

'No. To the villages as well. To Messigno and Starza Vecchia.'

'To Sorrento?'

Sardo pushed his hands between his knees as if he didn't trust them not to run wild. 'Sometimes.'

'It's a long way.'

Sardo shrugged, the sharp bones of his shoulders jabbing the thin material of his jacket. 'My Vulcan was strong, a big powerful horse who could pull all day. Muscles like boulders and brown eyes that would melt even your stony heart, Major. He was my ...' He stuttered, swallowed hard, and tried again. 'He was my good friend.'

Jake saw the man's face change. Its hard angular points softened, his lips grew loose, his grey eyes blurred.

'Tell me,' Jake said, matching his tone to his prisoner's, 'what did you deliver?'

'Machinery, furniture, shop goods, crates of oranges, anything that was wanted. Vulcan could haul it up the mountain as easy as one of your American Sherman tanks.'

Jake nodded. Seemingly in no hurry. 'Did you deliver to Antonio Lombardi in Sorrento?'

Bull's eye.

The man's hands started dancing all over the table. 'Never heard of him.'

'Or to the Cavaleri place?'

'I don't recall that name.'

'What happened to the horse?'

To his horror, Sardo's small eyes filled with tears. 'When the war came, I couldn't feed him any more. We were starving, both Vulcan and me. Not even grass to eat.' He dragged in a whistling breath. 'So I ate him.'

Sardo dropped his face in his hands and sobbed like a baby. Jake realised he would get nothing more out of his prisoner today and after smoking another cigarette in silence, he decided Sardo would be of more use to him back out on the streets.

*

Jake opened the door to the observation cubicle. Adrenaline was still charging through his veins like a boxer after a bout. It was always the same after an interrogation. He could smell Sardo's guilt the way he could smell shit on his shoe.

In the dim light he could make out Harry Fielding in his seat, bent over a notebook and writing furiously. It was hot and airless in the small space and a line of sweat had gathered at the base of Fielding's neck – or was that adrenaline too? Jake knew he was lucky to have the English guy on his team, watching his back.

But when he looked around for the white figure of Caterina Lombardi, as though she might be hiding in one of the dark corners, she was gone.

Caterina was patient. She waited. She watched. Wreathed in shadow. Traffic was grinding past in a plume of grit and fumes, and the heat was turning the bandage on her arm grey with sweat.

Finally the man came scurrying down the front steps of the old palazzo. The pavement was busy with military uniforms, flashing epaulettes and polished brass, but he dodged between them, head down, scuffed sandals held together with string. The cap that he had been scrunching in his fist was now on his head. He did not see her step out into his path until her arm slid through his and steered him into a grubby alleyway that stank of last night's vomit.

'Sal,' Caterina said softly, '*come stai*? How are things?'

Sal Sardo squealed. His eyes grew wide and his nostrils flared with panic as he tried to dislodge her arm from its grip on him, but it wasn't going anywhere.

'Caterina, what in the sweet name of Jesus are you doing here?'

His eyes were jumping in his head, darting to everything except her face.

'I want a word, Sal.'

'What about?'

She smiled. She waited until he looked directly at her, then she jingled a few coins in her hand. 'Let me buy you a beer.'

He grinned.

The bar was in Camorra territory. They both knew that, but neither of them mentioned the strangeness of his choice or the danger of trespassing where you were not wanted. Maybe it was because Sal knew that neither the army nor the police liked to venture into this violent area of Naples where the rules were Camorra rules. They sat in a corner, backs to a grimy wall, one eye on the door at all times. The Naples mafia would know they were there. If it chose to tolerate them, it was for a reason. That thought made Caterina uneasy. Spread out through the bar were six other men, two of them playing briscola, but all of them made a point of keeping their gaze off the two strangers at the back.

'I'm sorry about your father,' Sal said as soon as the beer was set in front of him.

Caterina swirled her coffee, trying to drown his words in it.

'I'm sorry about Vulcan,' she said and raised her cup. 'To Papà and Vulcan. May they be in a special heaven for big-hearted woodworkers and horses.'

Sal sniffed loudly and knocked back half his beer. 'So, Caterina Lombardi. What's this about?'

'Why did they let you go?'

'Who? Those fucking army bastards?'

'Yes.'

'They had nothing on me. I didn't do nothing.' His eyes screwed into narrow slits. 'What do you know about it?'

'They're questioning me too. About Papà.'

His hands grabbed the lip of the table, scarred by cigarette burns, and for a moment she feared he would bolt. She would never find him again in this shattered city.

'This is me you're talking to, Sal. Not Major Parr. You used to give me rides on Vulcan's broad back, remember?'

But Sal was all over the place and suddenly started pulling at the skin at the sides of his fingernails, tearing off strips till they were raw.

'Don't, Sal.'

Caterina laid a hand on one of his to calm him, and a flood of words came pouring from him, but in a dialect she didn't understand. Before Italy was united into one country in 1861 most Italians didn't speak Italian because the citizens of every major city – Rome, Venice, Florence, Milan – had their own language. Even now it could cause confusion when someone reverted to their local dialect instead of using the Tuscan language that was generally adopted as the Italian language.

'Sal,' Caterina whispered. 'I told them nothing. I didn't mention your name.'

Sal picked up his beer and lapsed into silence. His eyebrows kept on the move as if chasing his thoughts.

'I believed my father was a decent honourable man,' Caterina said in a low voice, 'I looked up to him all my life, but now . . .'

'He *was* a decent man. And he loved you even more than he loved his wood.' A rare smile flashed across Sal's bony face. 'And that says a lot.'

Caterina couldn't find an answering smile. 'All those years that you were delivering the veneers that he imported into Naples, you were bringing stolen antiques for him to work on as well, weren't you?' She shook her head in disbelief. 'I often asked him why he didn't have the veneers brought to Sorrento by boat from Naples – it would have been easier. What a blind stupid fool I was. Papà always said he wanted to give you the work, rather than anybody else.' A tremor spilled through her hands. 'Now I know why.'

'Don't despise him, Caterina.'

'Why not?'

'He was your father. He deserves respect. He was a good man.'

'He was robbing Italy.'

Sal ran a hand across his mouth and stared at his empty glass. 'We all have to survive in our own way,' he muttered.

'Who employed you? Who paid you to cart these valuable wooden antiques to my father? Was it the Camorra? Tell me that much, Sal, and I'll buy you a brandy to go with your beer. If you . . .'

Her glance flicked to the door. A man had entered, wearing shabby blue overalls and a greasy cap. Nothing remarkable in that. But from the moment he stepped through the doorway he ignored everyone in the gloomy room except Sal and Caterina, whom he was regarding with open interest. He slouched over to the bar's counter and a beer was placed in front of him without any words passing. Unlike the other scrawny customers, this man's face was well-rounded and his stomach curved like a ripe pumpkin. Caterina took it as a bad sign. Honest Italians went hungry these days.

She lowered her voice to an urgent whisper. 'Who paid you, Sal?'

Sal's restlessness was growing. She could feel the tension in him twisting to snapping point and his eyes looked into hers with a pained expression.

'You ask too many questions, Caterina.'

'Who arranged where you should pick up and deliver?'

'A man, Caterina. Just a man. And no, I don't know his name.'

'Was he one of the Camorra or . . .?'

'I don't ask questions,' he hissed at her. 'I do what I am paid to do and take my money.'

'Is that what my father did?'

'Don't disrespect your father. There was more to it than that for him.' His hands were leaping up and down his glass.

'What do you mean, "more to it"?' She frowned as she tried to make sense of his words. 'What—?'

'Enough, Caterina. Where's the brandy you promised me?'

His gaze shifted to the bar with a narrow smile but it froze on his face at the sight of the man standing there in overalls, beer in hand. Sal leapt to his feet, knocking over his glass, which rolled with a crash to the floor.

'*Andiamo*,' he said in a rush. 'Let's go.' Without waiting for Caterina, he raced for the door.

She was on her feet and following him when the man with the well-fed face reached out and gripped her arm, right on the bandage, squeezing hard.

'Wait,' he snapped.

She tried to pull away but the softness of his face belied the steel strength in his hands.

'Let go of me,' she shouted.

The men in the bar watched with impassive expressions, only pausing in the game of cards, but no one lifted a finger to help. With her free hand she snatched at the canvas bag that hung heavily against her hip and slammed it against the side of the plump man's head. The skin at his temple split wide open and blood spurted down his nose and over his lips, as his knees buckled. Caterina was out of the door before he hit the floor.

Fear is like acid. It burns away parts of you and leaves you scarred. Caterina could feel it stripping her raw inside every time her foot hit the pavement as she raced after Sal Sardo. He was some distance ahead of her, hurtling down the bustling street, his limbs whirling in crazy arcs, knocking aside a woman with a child and perambulator as if they had no existence in his world of white-hot panic.

He was fast and agile, accustomed to fleeing, and quickly widened the gap, but Caterina kept her eyes fixed on the back of his bobbing head. Blindly she pushed past people in her way, afraid to lose him, so she had full view of the moment when he jerked to a halt, stared transfixed at something for no more than two seconds, and then veered off down a side-street.

Caterina paused, dragging air into her burning lungs, and looked straight ahead where Sal had stared. Searching for the something. Except it wasn't *something*, it was *somebody*. A man. Waiting at the next corner of the narrow street was a man dressed in black, a slight figure with a moustache and dark hair with a blaze of white at the temple. He started moving towards her fast.

A blaze of white. Like the brand of a knife wound.

Rage shook her. Rage at this man who in a Sorrento back-street had threatened to break her arms and hurt her family, rage that drove her to leap forward, gripping the weight of the Bodeo in the bag at her side. This time there was nobody to hold her captive. This time he was alone. This time she would be the one to . . .

He vanished. The white blaze and the black suit with lapels like elephant's ears were suddenly nowhere to be seen. Caterina blinked, confused. Her gaze scoured the people ahead of her. It swept over the headscarves and the caps gathered around the makeshift stalls selling lemons and second-hand bootlaces, but there was no sign of the man. It was only when she reached the spot where he had been standing that she found an ancient brick passageway between tumbledown houses, running parallel to the side-street Sal Sardo had taken.

It wasn't her he wanted. It was Sal.

Caterina didn't find them. She hunted in doorways and under arches, she searched through dismal courtyards and ran under strings of washing that hung over her head like ghosts waiting for release. When finally she was forced to admit defeat, beads of sweat and despair chilled her skin and her hope of finding out more from Sal was abandoned in the gutter along with the garbage and the flies.

She had to get away from here.

She had no idea how long she'd been running wildly through these backstreets of Naples. Time felt uncertain. She must leave. If only Jake Parr were here with his Harley Davidson. Calm down. Her chest felt too full of air, as if she were breathing for Sal too and that frightened her. She wanted him breathing for himself. But as she stepped into one of the wider vicos and tried to get her bearings, a sight halted her in her tracks. At the opposite end of the filthy little street with its layers of wretched apartments piled on top of each other stood the figure of a large and powerful man. He was outlined in a shaft of sunlight at the far end.

Aldo.

Caterina knew him at once, no need to go a step closer. The image of him was imprinted on her retinas for all time. He wore a black hat that put his eyes in shade, but as he caught sight of her his thick lips stretched into a hard, hostile smile. His muscles seemed to expand, straining the seams of his expensive suit, filling every scrap of space in the noisy street.

A stillness swept into Caterina's head. A clarity that outlined each thought as crisply as she would outline a flower that she was inlaying in wood. She could pull out the gun right now and shoot him. That's what her fingers itched to do. That's

215

what the Bodeo was here for. To stick in his face, this Aldo who had almost throttled her, this bastard who had tried to push her off a cliff.

With a movement that was heavy and cumbersome to begin with, he started towards her, picking up speed fast, massive arms swinging dangerously at his sides. Caterina's fingers plunged into the bag and seized the gun. She stood her ground for all of ten seconds, visualising the gory mess a bullet would make of his face, seeing blood on the black flagstones and hearing people screaming. Then she whipped round and ran.

He came after her. She didn't think he would be fast but she was wrong. The man moved like a tank and just kept coming. He knew this maze of streets better than she did and took shortcuts to head her off, but she doubled back time and again to evade him, startling inhabitants as she scampered over walls and dodged through backyards.

Twice she hid in deep-set doorways, breathing hard, and twice she was betrayed by gaunt-faced locals for the toss of a coin. Poverty makes people cruel. She didn't hate them for it. But she hated him and hated the sound of his running feet, thumping on the basalt slabs like an ugly echo of her own heartbeat. And she hated the raw cough that exploded from him each time he stopped to draw breath, but she never looked back, never turned to face her pursuer, because she knew that if she did, she would take out the gun and shoot him.

She hated him for that too. For turning her into a killer inside her head. So she kept running and dodging and darting and swerving, but it was like having a bloodhound on her heels, and gradually as her brain grew starved of oxygen, she began to think that one of them would have to die. It was the only way to make this stop. When she ducked into a shoe shop in the hope that he would keep running past, his shadow came to the door and she was forced to make her escape through a back entrance.

Her lungs burned. Her bruised muscles ached. But the only thought that rose to the surface of her mind again and again was: *Where was Sal?*

Sal Sardo could move faster than a jackrabbit. He'd be tucked away by now, hiding somewhere safe. She crashed deliberately into a man pushing a wheelbarrow of baby chicks under netting. They scattered everywhere, spilling out speckled fluffballs that brought hungry hands swooping down on them from all directions. The street filled with noise and chaos.

Now. She dived under a dim archway. A series of courtyards opened up behind it, gloomy and stifling with heat. Even the flies were too heavy to take wing in the airless yards and spread like smears of oil over the windowsills. Tenements five storeys high towered over them and metal stairways zigzagged up the walls. Caterina shot through to the furthest yard, deep in shadow, and clambered behind a huge overflowing garbage bin jammed against a wall. She squeezed herself into the narrow gap between the protruding metal lip of the bin and the cracked stucco.

The stench was appalling. A rat squatted on its haunches and regarded her with interest, while cockroaches marched in formation along the base of the wall. She didn't move. But she listened hard. The muscles of her face were taut and adrenaline was pumping fiercely in her chest as she heard feet come pounding into the courtyard.

'Bitch! Where are you, bitch?'

High up on one of the metal staircases a woman's lascivious voice shouted something that Caterina didn't hear and then laughed insultingly when he growled something back at her.

'You're here, bitch. I know you're here!'

Caterina closed her eyes, so tight she felt a tiny blood vessel burst under her eyelid. She pictured the sea as she'd seen it today from the motorcycle, a lapis lazuli sheet of blue that seemed to swallow the sky. She conjured it up and let it wash away the dirt and the filth and heard its gentle waves replace the roaring inside her own head.

She opened her eyes. How long had they been closed? She didn't know. What she did know was that there was total silence in the courtyard and a cockroach was sitting immobile on her shin, waving its antennae at her. She remained there until the sound of voices of two women entering the yard made her jump, and the cockroach leapt to the ground. She waited till she heard their footsteps climb the metal stairs and a door bang, then she moved crab-wise and emerged from her hiding place. The gun was in her hand.

No one.

The yard was empty. She set off for the street. This time she didn't run.

The body lay on a bombsite. Caterina would have missed it if she had stuck to her plan of following Via dei Tribunali up towards Garibaldi Station. There were crowds of Neapolitans going about their business and no one chasing anybody else. But a wedding parade crowded the pavement, the young bride relishing her dazzling moment in the sun among her friends and flowers, and Caterina could not bear all the laughter, so she veered off down Vico dei Panettieri.

That was when she saw the body.

The street was busy. An old soldier, whose legs had been amputated, had abandoned his begging and was scooting along the pavement on a board on wheels to take a closer look. Then Caterina saw the police car, the ambulance and the stern faces of authority keeping back the crowd that had gathered. She elbowed her way through the onlookers, heedless of stares or sharp words. Voices buzzed in her ears and people's faces came and went at the edge of her vision, but all she could see was the body sprawled like a spider at the very top of a heap of bleached rubble that must once have been an apartment block.

'Stay back, signorina.'

Polizia. Of course. The policeman's arm crossed her path. Two men in white medical uniforms were crouched by the body, which lay on its back, eyes wide open and swimming in blood. Flies came, thick and fast. Four crows perched on the broken chimney pots, waiting for their chance. The body was male. Under his chin a gaping wound curved like a smile from one side of his throat to the other and his blue shirt glistened purple as it soaked up the blood.

It was Sal Sardo.

Air wouldn't go into Caterina's lungs. Noises crackled in her head. Vaguely she was aware of the policeman talking to her but when she stared at his lips she could make no sense of his words. When he started to move away she gripped his arm.

'Is he dead?' she asked. Her lips stumbled on the words.

'*Sì.*'

'Did you catch the killer?'

He shook his head. He was a middle-aged police sergeant who looked hot and sad, doing his job as best he could. 'No. He was gone by the time the body was reported.' He glanced reluctantly back at the thin limbs that lay lifeless in the sun. 'Poor dead bastard,' he muttered.

'Poor dead bastard,' Caterina echoed in a whisper.

He would have been a poor *live* bastard if she had not invited him to have a drink with her.

The train was full. No empty seats. Caterina found a spot by the door to stand, hemmed in by the crush of passengers, as the Circumvesuviana carriages shook and wheezed their way across the plain of Naples for the half-hour journey up into the mountains.

From the train the city of Naples looked white and innocent. It shimmered in the sunlight and nestled against the base of Vesuvius. You couldn't see the blood that ran in the streets. Not from here. No more than you could see the thousands of dead who lay under the rich black soil around the volcano. Caterina fought to curb the emotions that threatened to spiral out of control within her. This was a place of death.

Not just of death, but of cataclysmic death. This was the

bloodland. Vesuvius was one of the most dangerous volcanoes in the world, tearing the heart out of communities with a relentless indifference every few years throughout the centuries. Not just in AD 79 when it stole Pompeii's sixteen thousand lives. Or in 1631 when it took thousands more. But even last year, in 1944, the eruption of lava flow caught everyone by surprise.

Caterina remembered it vividly, the way the burning basalt lit up the night sky for weeks around the Bay of Naples. Seen as far away as Anzio, they said. It spewed from the vents and engulfed the villages of Massa and San Sebastiano, reaching out its greedy fingers for more than a kilometre. It even snatched Air Force planes from under the noses of the military at Terzigno, east of the mountain.

Yet no one seemed to learn. They kept coming back to the bloodlands. They kept building new houses, planting new crops after every eruption, like children drawn to play with fire. They were locked into a terrible trade with the volcano. They risked its wrath and in return it covered the land with a precious ash that made the earth fertile and the grapes grow lush and abundant.

To convince themselves it was a trade worth making, they called the slopes of Vesuvius the *Campania felix* – the Happy Land. Caterina felt herself sway with disbelief as the flourishing vineyards flicked past the train window. She knew better.

This was not the happy land. She had seen Sal's scarlet eyes on the mountain of rubble. She knew this was the bloodland.

CHAPTER EIGHTEEN

Caterina arrived at the school. Hot and sticky, breathing hard. It usually took twenty minutes to walk from Sorrento railway station to her brother's school but she'd made it in ten. Lessons at Scuola San Giovanni normally ended at one o'clock but today the pupils were working until three o'clock to complete a project before the end of term next week.

She would take Luca home. Lock the door. Open it to no one. Not let him out. Ever.

She gripped the gate, waiting for the children to emerge. It was a single-storey stuccoed building surrounded by a concrete yard, with a small jaunty bell-turret at one end of its terracotta roof.

'What on earth happened to you, Caterina?'

Caterina turned to the young woman speaking at her side. 'Hello, Albertina.'

'You look terrible.'

'Thanks.'

Albertina Donati was a quietly spoken friend and her face

was creased with concern. She was working four jobs with fourteen-hour days to keep food on her family's table since the death of her father at the Battle of Stalingrad in 1942.

She touched Caterina's elbow. 'What happened? Look at you.'

For the first time Caterina looked. Her white silk dress was no longer white. It was covered in dirt and greasy yellow stains, and it smelled bad. Her bandaged arm was weeping blood. She could feel something encrusted on her cheek.

'I was in an accident,' she said.

'Let me take you home and fix your ...'

At that moment the schoolchildren came flooding out with shrieks of pleasure and laughter. The project they'd been working on was about the life of a Roman gladiator and most of them were dressed in costume of some sort. Caterina had sat up at night creating a convincing *retiarius* costume with cardboard tasset straps and buckles, while her grandfather had whittled a fearsome three-pronged trident for him out of wood and a short dagger called a *pugio*. Luca himself had made a *rete*, a weighted net, from a length of old netting that he had begged from one of the fishermen. He had been eager to show it off today.

The gladiators streamed past her and Albertina's young brother, Paolo, brandishing a wooden sword, charged over to his sister and ran her through with it.

'Where's Luca?' Caterina asked at once. Paola giggled as his sister pretended to die. 'I walked him to the school gate this morning with his *retiarius* costume.'

'He wasn't at school today.' Paolo shook his shaggy head and vanished into the brawl of swords and shields, now that the long arm of the teacher lay on the other side of the fence.

'Caterina, don't look like that,' Albertina said. 'Paolo was probably mistaken. Luca will be . . .'

But Caterina was already hurrying into the school.

Paolo was right. Luca had not been at school. His teacher was adamant. Caterina set off at a run for the small fishing harbour at the base of the cliff on which Sorrento perched.

He had skipped school.

That's all.

Don't panic.

It wasn't the first time. It wouldn't be the last.

Don't panic.

He'd gone out with the fishing boats. That's what he'd done.

He loved the sea. More than he loved gladiator costumes.

He'd be in the marina. Mending nets. Listening to tall stories. Smoking a cigarette.

Don't panic.

Her feet pounded back along the streets and she switched to the shortcut through Piazza Tasso and down the steep staircase with the iron railing that clung to the side of the deep gorge. She plunged downward, shoes drumming on the hundred steps, down to the road that led finally to the narrow grey beach below.

Brightly coloured boats bobbed on the water, while others had been hauled up on to the beach and fishermen lazed in the shade of the hulls, repairing nets and smoking pipes in companionable groups. A dark-haired boy of around Luca's age was playing on a penny-whistle and for a moment Caterina willed herself to believe it was her brother. But it wasn't. Of course it wasn't. She scrambled along the beach to question every single fisherman, but none had seen Luca all day.

'Don't worry, the lad will turn up,' a bearded skipper assured her with a chuckle.

As though Luca were a coin from her pocket that she had misplaced.

Caterina entered her house and the air struck cool on her skin after the scorching heat outside. She kicked off her dusty sandals and convinced herself that Luca must be with the soldiers again, chewing their gum and riding their jeeps. She clung to that idea. But her thoughts had become jerky and disjointed. She wanted to lie down on the cool tiles and close her eyes.

'Is that you, Caterina?'

'Yes, Nonno, it's me.'

'Come here.'

She walked quickly to the living room, preparing to explain to him that his grandson had gone missing, that if Luca were not back soon – very soon – they must inform the police. She did not relish the prospect of the policemen's laughter – boys of Luca's age wander off all the time, they'd insist, and she mustn't worry her pretty head about it. She stood in the doorway of the room.

Her grandfather was seated in his usual armchair, wearing his customary spotless white shirt and polished black shoes, and his head was up, alert and listening hard. The smile on his face made Caterina realise how rarely he had smiled since his son's death. Beside him a wireless in a scratched oak case was playing big band music at low volume and he was whittling a piece of honey-coloured beechwood in time to the rhythm of it.

Our wireless was sold two years ago, thought Caterina. She stared open-mouthed at the chair opposite him, at the long khaki legs and the smart buff shirt, the cap on the lap, and the lazy smile that greeted her.

'Signorina Lombardi, a pleasure to see you again.'

It was Captain Harry Fielding. More importantly, at his side on a low stool sat Luca, his head bent over a military map that he was studying with keen interest.

'Luca!'

Her brother looked up reluctantly, guilt already woven into his glance, but at the sight of her he uttered a cry and leapt to his feet.

'What?' his grandfather demanded, his blind eyes scanning the room in vain. 'What is it?'

'It's Caterina. She's bleeding.'

All three of them were on their feet suddenly, fussing and questioning until she swatted them away with her good hand. 'Stop it. I'm fine. I took a tumble and the dog-bite opened up again. It's nothing.'

'I'll fetch water to bathe it,' Luca offered, but as he tried to scamper from the room she seized his shoulder.

'Why weren't you at school today?' Her brother lowered his eyes, his cheeks flushing scarlet.

'I got a lift in a truck going to Naples.'

'An army truck?'

He nodded.

Caterina wanted to shake him. To seize both shoulders and shake her brother's skinny frame until some sense rattled into his head, but it was all she could do to stop herself wrapping her arms around him and smothering his grubby cheeks with kisses. Relief ran like honey in her mouth. He was safe. He was not lying on a bombsite with blood in his eyes.

She looked at Captain Harry Fielding, remembering his performance in the interrogation room, and wondered if he knew Sal Sardo was dead. 'And you, Captain Fielding, what are you doing here? Is this your fault?'

He laughed kindly. 'No,' he said, 'I was about to drive to Sorrento for a meeting with Colonel Quincy and I found this young monkey outside the Palazzo Umberto – that's our Forces Club in Naples – begging for a lift from anyone going up into the hills. He mentioned you and your music boxes, so,' the captain opened up his hands in a gesture of appeasement, 'I brought him here.'

'Thank you.' She turned to her brother. 'Luca, what were you thinking? You can't skip school whenever you feel like it. Education is important. I won't have you running wild, you hear me? What were you doing in Naples?'

'Swapping my comics, that's all.'

'For what? More gum to chew? More chocolate to eat? And who did you swap these comics with?'

'Just boys,' he muttered. He wouldn't look at her.

'Boys? You mean the street kids, the *scugnizzi*? Luca, they are thieves and scavengers. They will get you into real trouble.'

Suddenly her brother was looking at her directly with her father's eyes. 'It's all right, Caterina, don't worry.' He said it gently, the way her father would. 'I can look after myself.'

This time she did shake him. 'No, you can't, Luca.'

'Caterina, stop this at once.'

Her grandfather's deep growl was followed by a smack of his cane-tip on the floor and his hand landed squarely on Luca's other shoulder. As if they would tear him apart between them.

'Leave the boy alone, Caterina. Are you going to keep him on a leash like a dog forever? So he missed a day of school. So what? It's time he learned about being a man.' The deep furrows at the sides of his mouth softened. 'You can't keep him tied to your apron-strings all his life, Caterina. Look what Luca brought me, look.'

'The wireless? Luca got you the wireless?'

'Yes, he did.'

'Luca, how could you afford it?' she asked uneasily.

'I didn't steal it,' he said before she could accuse him. 'I asked around on the streets.' He shrugged. 'I found a boy who had one to sell and I traded my comics for it.' He looked up at his grandfather, a smile sneaking to his lips and turning him into a child again. 'For Nonno.'

'It must be stolen goods,' Caterina pointed out angrily. 'You shouldn't . . .'

'Signorina Lombardi,' the English captain interrupted sooth-ingly, 'the whole of Italy functions on bartered goods right now, no questions asked.' He laughed easily, and the tension in the room unwound a notch. 'Let's all sit down and let me see if I can fix up that arm of yours.'

He reached out to take her elbow but she backed off.

'I can do it myself. I'll go and wash.'

She walked out of the room, away from all the words. But she didn't enter the bathroom. Instead she made straight for her bedroom, shut the door behind her and lay down on her bed exactly as she was, dirt, blood and all. She forced her eyes closed and wanted the day to end.

Twilight slipped into the room, robbing it of colour. Caterina lay on her bed, eyes wide, and watched her world slowly lose its sharp edges. Objects blurred. Their greyness was soothing. In her mind she examined each minute of her day and every one of them was as sharp as broken glass. She touched them with care.

She didn't recognise her own life any more. It was as if she had fallen into someone else's and she needed a new map to find her way around it. She was running down blind alleyways and into dead ends. She knew that what she needed was to return to her workshop, to hold on to something solid, something real, something unspoilt. The chisels would steady her hand. A sheet of satinwood under her fingers or the flame curls of a mahogany inlay would slow her heartbeat, and the scent of them would clear the foul stench from her nostrils.

Her father was corrupt.

She pressed a hand over her mouth, to stop herself denying it. She had seen the triptych, seen it with her own eyes in the dim Naples basement crammed with the glorious treasures of Italy, the exact same triptych she remembered her father working on only weeks before he died, but he had told her the church had commissioned him to do so. Yet it was not listed in his order book, no mention of it. She had forgotten it until she saw once more the carved figure of Christ bearing the cross, the crown of thorns on His head. It had all come rushing back to her. She had been working at the factory making uniforms for the military, her ears thrumming with the racket of the machines. That day, one of the porterage trolleys had snapped a wheel fixing, spun out of control and slammed into her back.

She had exaggerated the injury. Of course she did. She wanted the afternoon off so that she could spend it at her father's workshop, and that was when she caught him. He was at work on the beautiful triptych, repairing damage to one of the three hinged panels. She had managed to see that much but no more, because in an instant he had thrown a length of sacking over it and set her to work on a galleried tray he was inlaying with burr walnut.

At the time she had thought nothing of it. But when she looked up, the triptych had vanished and her father was instead slicing a strip of white pine veneer into narrow strings. Now that Caterina thought back to that day two years ago, she remembered his unease, his dark round eyes narrowing as he glanced in her direction. She had thought he was concerned about her back injury, but now she realised she had thought wrong.

She sat upright too fast and the bedroom rolled around her. Is this what the American wanted from her? Her memories? Memories that she didn't even know she had. A dull ache throbbed in her chest and she rubbed her knuckles over it, as though it could be dislodged, but she knew it wouldn't move. It was there to stay.

Her father had deceived her. And the American had trapped her. She slid her legs off the bed and let the floor steady beneath her feet, a sibilant moan escaping from her lips. She listened hard. It was one word, over and over.

Sal, Sal, Sal.

She knew now she would have to protect her family herself.

'Well?'

'Well what, Nonno?'

Caterina had entered the room and seen the Englishman's open packet of Players cigarettes lying on the table, but of Captain Fielding himself there was no sign. She could feel the contentment he had left behind him, her brother stretched out on the floor, nose in a map, while her grandfather was relaxing in his chair, legs outstretched. Their faces swivelled towards her with a crease forming on both their foreheads, as if she had come to take that contentment away from them.

'Well,' her grandfather repeated, 'are you going or not, young lady?'

Giuseppe Lombardi was listening to his wireless, to a discussion about Prime Minister Ivanhoe Bonomi's latest decision to increase rationing, one hand unconsciously stroking the warm grain of its oak casing the way other people fondled the ears of their dog.

'Going where?' Caterina asked.

'To meet the English captain.'

'What?'

Luca was grinning up at her. 'Captain Fielding said he has

a date with you this evening. At Georgio's pizzeria at seven o'clock. You should go, Caterina. He's nice.'

She had forgotten.

'So?' her grandfather asked.

'No,' she said flatly.

'Why not?'

'I feel . . .'

Battered. Battered and bruised.

'I feel tired,' she said.

She had washed the dirt off herself and the stains off the white dress, torn strips off a clean sheet to rebind her arm and changed into her cinnamon work-dress. But no amount of scrubbing was going to wash away the dirt inside her head.

'Luca,' she said, crouching down on the floor beside him. 'What are you doing with Captain Fielding's map?'

Her brother's eyes shone. He bore no ill-will for her earlier sharpness. 'He was showing me where the Allied Forces landed. Here, at Salerno.' His finger traced a trail from Sicily. 'They got stuck on the beachhead at Anzio.' He peered closely at the spot as if he could conjure up a glimpse of the soldiers on the beach. 'Captain Fielding said it was because the terrain is too difficult for tanks. Look at these mountains, Caterina.'

'The Apennines.'

'Captain Fielding calls them the spine of Italy.' He dragged his finger down the map, gazing transfixed at the long peninsula that was his country. 'A hundred and eighty thousand.' He whistled softly through his pearly white teeth. 'That's how many Allied troops landed on our mainland, Captain Fielding says.'

'Luca, I don't want to hear any more of . . .'

But Caterina could see he was alight with the excitement of it now that he had a map. 'Look at this. This is the Gustav Line. It's where Field Marshall Kesselring built Germany's line of defence right across Italy.' His finger landed on a point halfway between Naples and Rome, and she was sure his young ears were hearing the guns and the bombs. 'And then the Gothic Line was . . .'

'Enough, Luca,' Caterina broke in. 'The war is over.'

A rumble of disagreement came from the old man's chair. 'The war is never over.'

Caterina looked across at him. What did he mean?

'It's seven o'clock,' her grandfather announced. 'Isn't it time for you to meet Captain Fielding?'

But she shook her head. Talking to one soldier in public in a Sorrento street had brought catastrophe galloping into her life and she wasn't going to risk it a second time.

'Luca,' she said, 'leave your map for a minute, please, and run down to the pizzeria to tell Captain Fielding that I can't come tonight. But if he wishes to talk, he can come and sit in our courtyard with me instead. It's cool there now.'

And private.

Luca leapt for the door and it dawned on her that he wanted to see his sister happy.

'And tell him,' she called after him, 'to bring wine.'

*

The wine seeped into Caterina's blood and she felt her limbs grow loose and pain-free. Captain Fielding was describing a polo match played on camels in the deserts of Egypt, a game so crazy it set her laughing and the sound surprised her. She emptied her glass and smiled at him.

'You miss England, don't you?' she murmured in the darkness that lay warm on her skin.

'Yes, I admit I miss England, I miss Marlow, my home town, but,' he spread his long arms expansively, 'I have all the glories of Italy to enjoy instead.'

They were sitting in the courtyard with their chairs propped against a wall, away from the ears in the other houses that backed on to it. They had been there for over an hour, moths darting blindly at the lantern, but neither had mentioned Naples or Sal Sardo or anything concerning stolen works of art, and she liked it that way.

But that wasn't why she'd asked him here.

'Thank you,' she said, 'for giving Luca the map. He is loving re-enacting the campaign that your armies waged through Italy.'

'It's important he should know. It's his country.'

'Of course, but it's too . . .'

'Too soon?'

She nodded. 'It's all still so raw.' She lifted her glass for him to refill and said, 'Tell me about the jeweller who was pulled out of the harbour.'

Even in the dim light she saw his frown. 'Do you really want to know?'

'Yes.'

He poured more red wine into her glass and she noted with surprise that they were well into the second bottle.

'His name was Orlando Bartoli. He owned a jeweller's shop in Naples.'

'Where in Naples?' she asked.

The captain hesitated.

'Where?' she asked again.

'On Via Medina.'

'Tell me how this Signor Bartoli ended up in the harbour?'

'A chap whom we arrested for trying to sell a Giorgione sketch on an open market stall squealed on Bartoli in exchange for leniency. It seemed that he'd been going around purchasing any artworks he could find on the black market. Paying a fraction of their worth, of course. We marched into Bartoli's shop at dawn and obliged him to open his safe. He wasn't keen on the idea.'

'What was in it?'

'A small painting, Madonna and child. By Tintoretto.'

Caterina whistled softly.

'Unfortunately,' Fielding regarded her speculatively, 'he had also had a gun in his safe. He shot and wounded the arresting officer and escaped.'

'He'd have done better to sit it out in one of your cells.'

'You're right. Bartoli turned up in the harbour three days later with a concrete block chained to his ankles.'

Caterina sipped her drink and she thought about Orlando Bartoli. And about what it means to be afraid. What damage it does to you.

'Caterina?'

The Englishman was offering her a cigarette. She shook her head. She studied his face in the flare of his lighter flame as he touched it to the tip of his own cigarette. It was a good face. The kind of face that stays calm when everyone else is screaming.

'Captain Fielding . . .'

'Call me Harry.'

'Harry,' she leaned closer, 'are you afraid?'

He made a sound. But it was not an answer.

'Your work is dangerous, Harry. Do you wake in the night afraid?'

Somewhat startled, he pulled back, merging with the blackness beyond the lantern's reach. She could feel his embarrassment.

'No, I am accustomed to it,' he said. 'Accustomed to danger, I mean.'

An Englishman, she realised, does not admit to fear.

'And Major Parr?' she asked.

Harry Fielding laughed good-naturedly. 'He says the whole of Italy scares him shitless – if you'll excuse the language.'

She drank the last of her wine and rose to her feet, walking past the velvety brown moths that fluttered like lost souls around the lantern.

'Harry, do you know a man with a blaze of white in his black hair? At his temple. He also has a moustache and a gold tooth. Involved somehow in this . . .'

The Englishman jumped from his seat as if she'd kicked him. 'What the hell do you know about that man?'

'I saw him chase after Sal Sardo in Naples yesterday.'

'Stay away from him. He is evil.'

'What is his name?'

'No, Caterina. This is not for you. Forget all about that man.'

He reached out to remove his officer's cap from the table, suddenly eager to leave, but Caterina seized his wrist.

'His name, Harry? I have a right to know.'

'No. He's dangerous.'

'He tried to have me killed.' She drew the Englishman closer to her. 'He threatened my family, all because you and Major Parr came here accusing my father of stealing treasures from Italy.' She kept her voice reasonable and persuasive. 'Listen to me, Harry. I need to know that man's name.'

But Harry Fielding was having none of it, the line of his mouth unyielding. A light leapt on in a window of one of the upstairs apartments, casting an amber rectangle over them both below, trapping them inside it. The Englishman replaced his cap on his head and tried to move away, but Caterina stood rooted to the spot, her hand holding on.

'His name?' she persisted.

He said nothing. She was tempted to stick her hand down his throat and yank out the words he was hiding. The thought must have been written on her face because he uttered a low sound of protest.

'Caterina, your father worked with him. They were partners in crime.'

His words were as shocking as the sudden taste of blood in her mouth as her teeth clamped down on her tongue.

'His name?' she demanded relentlessly. 'Tell me his name.'

'Drago Vincelli.'

'Drago Vincelli,' she echoed. 'Is he Camorra? One of the mafia?'

'No, Caterina, Vincelli works only for himself. But I want you to forget his name. Forget you ever heard it.' He removed her hand from his wrist. 'Before you have reason to regret it.'

He made a move to leave.

'Wait, Harry. At least tell me this. If you know so much about Vincelli and his illegal activities, why on earth don't you arrest him?'

'Hah, I wish we could, but we have no proof to convict him. We were hoping to find a connection through your father, both of them involved in this trade of stolen artefacts, both thieves, but now ...'

There was a movement in the shadows close to the house, a rustle. A harsh cry of anger. Caterina and Harry Fielding swung round. Harry's hand was ready on the Enfield .38 on his hip, but it froze when a pale young face emerged from the darkness. It was Luca.

'My father,' the boy shouted, 'was not a thief.'

He rushed back into the house and slammed the door on them.

Luca.

Her brother's name reverberated in Caterina's head. She was sitting on the edge of his bed, listening to his breathing, slow and regular. For half an hour she had sat wrapped in the silence of his bedroom, with the rumbling creaks and sighs of the old house for company as it cooled after the heat of the day. The stub of a candle in a pewter holder glowed on the windowsill where she had placed it, but its light scarcely reached as far as the bed. Her brother lay with his back to her, his face firmly to the wall, and only his dark head on the pale pillow had any substance.

'Luca,' she said, 'I apologise. I have let you down.'

His shadowy outline didn't move a muscle, but not for a moment did she believe he was asleep.

'Luca,' she continued, her voice soft, 'I have been treating you like a child when it's obvious to anyone with eyes in their head that you have grown into a young man. To me, eleven years old seems so young. But I should have recognised that the misery of war and the death of Papà have stripped away your childhood, Luca, I see that now. Forgive me for being so blind.'

Caterina could feel the heat of the wine in her stomach.

'This isn't how I wanted it for you, I swear it isn't,' she told him. 'But it's the way it is and we have to live with it, you and I. What you overheard in the courtyard tonight about Papà is true. I know you're angry. Oh Luca, so am I. I realise now I should have trusted you.'

Her hand slid across the bedcover and nestled against his back.

'Now,' she announced in the gloom, 'I will give you the facts. So you will be prepared for whatever happens.'

Caterina told Luca everything. She spared him nothing. Starting with the first visit from Major Parr, then on to the white-blaze man's threat in the doorway, the finding of the order book and the crash on Capri. The Naples' basement. Sal Sardo sprawled on the rubble. The chase through the back-streets of Naples. It all came out and it was like lancing a boil. Just the bare bones. Nothing more. No details. No emotions. No mention of pain or fear or blood. She could have jotted the facts down on the back of a cigarette pack, they were so slender.

'That's it,' she said matter-of-factly at the end. 'I'm only telling you now so that knowledge of what is hiding out there will save your skin. If a man steps into your path, you turn and run like your shoes are on fire. Got that?'

No sound. No breathing.

'In future you stay off the streets. When the school term is finished, you can spend your days helping me in the workshop.'

Not a flicker of movement from him.

'Or you can try to earn money by going out with the fisher-men, or . . .' she sighed, 'you can hang around sometimes with the troops, I suppose. But Luca, I need to know where you are at all times and you *must* stay off the streets. It's too dangerous.'

Her head swam gently round the room as the effects of the wine started to blur the edges. 'I love you, my Luca,' she murmured, 'and I intend to keep you safe.'

She slid down, lying on her back beside her brother, her head sharing his pillow, her arm touching his sharp shoulder blade. The wine lay heavy on her eyelids but they wouldn't close. Sal Sardo's pointed face was floating up on the ceiling, staring down at her. If she had not offered him that drink . . .

Caterina felt movement next to her, nervous and hesitant. Luca turned slowly to face her, the expression in his eyes obscured by the folds of night, but she could feel the heat of his breath, sense the speed of his young heart.

'What about Nonno?' he whispered.

'Don't worry, we'll take care of him too, you and I. The Lombardis together.'

For a long time after that neither spoke. The night air seemed to stretch taut in the room and somewhere an accordion was playing Italian love songs.

'What now?' Luca asked uncertainly. 'I want to help, Caterina. I don't want you to be alone. I can do things with you.'

She kissed his hair. Held him close.

'We find the person who can put a stop to this,' she said.

'Captain Fielding?'

'No. I wish it were that easy. It seems to me that the military are no match for these men.'

'The police?'

'No. That would get us killed.'

'Who then?'

'Drago Vincelli, the man who murdered Sal Sardo. We will find him.'

CHAPTER NINETEEN

The heavy carved doors of the great banqueting chamber within Palazzo Rudolfo swung shut and the ancient iron key was inserted into the lock and turned. It was the signal that the meeting could begin.

The chairman, Drago Vincelli, raised a hand for silence and the ten men seated around the eighteenth century table that once had belonged to King Ferdinand IV of Naples turned to him respectfully. Each one was wearing evening dress, each one was nursing a glass of fifty-year old cognac in his hand and each one had a silent fear gnawing at his guts.

They stood, pushing back their chairs, and raised their glasses in unison.

'To King Victor Emmanuel,' the chairman declared. 'King of all Italy.'

They drank together, wetting their lips in the amber liquid with satisfaction, and resumed their seats. The chairman observed each man through narrowed eyes, assessing where the danger lay tonight. Which one had already drunk too much? Who had fucked his mistress this evening and so believed he had balls of iron? Whose bank manager was threatening to foreclose? Whose wife was demanding a grander apartment? Who had been to confession and felt his conscience was clear as driven snow?

It was the chairman's job to know these things. To have eyes that saw into the hearts that gathered around the table here tonight and to recognise the ones who would cut each other's throats given half a chance. He smiled to himself and let them settle. Made them wait.

His carefully manicured hands smoothed the papers laid out on the finely polished walnut surface in front of him and he knew their eyes watched his movements, wondering what was in these papers. What accusations? What lies? What secrets?

Let them wonder.

Let them wonder and piss themselves.

He smiled benignly and saw them relax. Saw the tendons in their necks loosen and their well-filled bellies grow slack. Their first mistake.

There would be others.

'Good evening, gentlemen,' he began smoothly. 'Tonight we will discuss the fact that one of our number is missing.'

He paused. Someone would fill the gap. They always did.

'It's Orlando Bartoli, poor bastard,' muttered the bald man on his right, the one who thought no one knew he was fucking his young wife's mother.

'Hauled out of the harbour,' added another. 'God rest his soul.'

Three of them crossed themselves. The chairman noted which ones.

'So,' he said quietly, 'let us discuss the reason why Signor Bartoli, the jeweller, ended up as fish food.'

He could smell the fear then. Sweeter than cognac.

CHAPTER TWENTY

For four days Caterina did nothing, nothing out of the ordinary. She stuck to a strict routine. Early each morning she walked Luca to school, except on Sunday, exchanged a few words with her friend Albertina at the school gate and then hurried to her workshop. If anyone was watching, she didn't spot them. Though God knows, she tried.

She worked on her music boxes all morning, replenishing her stock and relishing the contact with the wood again. She had missed it. In the afternoon she picked up Luca from school and checked on her grandfather at home, before continuing to work in her workshop with Luca at her side until the evening. He didn't complain. Not once. Didn't ask to run down to the boats or kick a ball in the street with his friends. He remained as close to her side as her shadow and learned the technique of using a router plane and how to master sand-shading by scorching the edge of a veneer to create a shadow. He was trying to please her.

They talked while they worked and a closeness grew between

them, an intimacy that they hadn't shared since the death of their father two years ago, when Caterina had been obliged to step into the role of parent. She made herself talk to him about her mother, and found that once she started she couldn't stop. The words crept out from some dark place inside her, slow at first, too heavy to rush, but faster and faster as the hours slid past.

She told him things about Lucia Lombardi that she had made herself forget. How she used to sing as she worked. Kneading dough, scrubbing a floor or changing her son's nappy, she would let the music flow out of her in a rich contralto voice that used to stop Caterina's heart with pure joy. Tendrils of her long silky hair, which she dyed a golden blonde, would stray around her face and caress her cheeks in a way that Caterina's fingers itched to do.

Caterina told Luca about the white rabbit costume their mother had sewn for him for the Easter flower festival and about her passion for dancing around the kitchen table in a shaft of shimmering sunlight, as if it were a spotlight. But no word passed Caterina's lips about the stinging slaps from her pale elegant hands or the string of impatient curses that used to burst forth from between her full red lips.

And especially she made no mention of the time when she disappeared for a whole weekend, no one knowing where she had gone, when Luca was only a couple of months old and sick with croup. His cough was like a dog-bark and scared the ten-year-old Caterina. She had sat up all night laying hot flannels on her brother's small white chest, while her father waded to the bottom of a bottle of whisky. Lucia Lombardi had breezed in on Monday morning with the black pupils of her eyes as huge as craters and a new softness to her mouth that made Caterina want to hide in her room, though she didn't know why.

Luca listened to her stories enraptured and in the small confines of the workshop that smelled of varnish and the sweet scent of olive veneer, time slowed to an easy pace that they could both manage. Whatever danger it was that lay outside these four walls seemed to recede into a distant haze. When he asked, 'Did she love me?' Caterina almost choked on tears.

'Of course she loved you, Luca. You were her beautiful boy, always her favourite. I was the one she didn't like.'

He looked at her with bewildered eyes. 'Why didn't Mamma like you?'

'I don't know. Papà said it was because I looked like her. She saw too much of herself in me, that's what he said. But maybe it was because I spent too much time with Papà in his workshop. Or because . . .' the scorper in her hand sliced a groove far too deep in the piece of satin wood on the worktable and she swore at herself, 'because I was a girl. She never liked her own sex. You see, Luca, our mother was one of those women who come alive in the company of men.'

Luca's mouth hung open and his chest was pumping hard. 'What do you mean?'

'She would light up inside.' Caterina laughed softly. 'She always said that her favourite smell was the aroma of cigars and brandy.'

Caterina's reward was the smile that blossomed on her brother's young face.

*

Caterina reached behind the *casseruola*, the stewpot, and drew out of the cupboard the package wrapped in old newspaper. Sometimes she just stood and held it. That was enough. To stand in the kitchen and feel her father's presence inside the package in her hands.

But not today. Today she needed more. She sat down at the kitchen table, swiftly peeled away the layers of newspaper and smiled as the burgundy and black book-cover spread itself before her. She started at the beginning and turned over each page of the order book, studying in detail yet again every word of her father's neat script, and when she reached the end she closed it, drew in a deep breath and started again at the first page.

Nothing had changed. Nothing was different. Still the desk, the galleried tray, the high-backed chairs and the fantastical birdcage for the French dressmaker.

Patience, my daughter. Have patience with the wood.

Those words of her father's had been whispered into her ear a thousand times, but now she was struggling with patience for her father. She had trusted him. Believed in him. But everything shouted that she'd been wrong, been too trusting, too believing.

When she came to the page with the smeared thumbprint of her blood promise to her father, she skipped over it fast and turned to the final page of writing. She scoured the columns again. *Table. Wedding gift. Bird's eye maple. And jewels.* The cost column lay empty. Then the client: *Count di Marco, Villa dei Cesari, Capri.* She flicked through the final pages. *Niente.* Nothing. All blank. But something hard and tight inside her wouldn't let go. She ran the flat of her hand over the last page as if by force of will she could make it give up its secrets, and she felt something under her palm. Something so small it was almost nothing.

The slightest indentation.

A faint ripple in the smooth surface of the paper.

She lifted the book. Angled it towards the light. More ripples.

'*Grazie*, Papà,' she whispered and seized a pencil from the drawer.

Slowly, carefully, she began to shade in the whole page with light sideways strokes. It was dimpled and uneven, threaded through by lines and curves where the ripples lay. A twist of excitement made her push out a whistle of surprise as the lines came together and coalesced into something.

That something was the outline of a table. And under it were two words scribbled across the corner, as if as an afterthought. She studied them closely and could just make out what looked like *Caesar Club*.

Faint and blurred. But there.

It seemed that her father had sketched a drawing of a table on the previous page and its imprint had remained on the next one. She ran her finger along the seam of the open book and, sure enough, she could feel the rough edge where one page had been torn out.

This was it. This was the jewelled table.

She shut the book with a snap before the grey grainy image could escape. Now she knew what it looked like.

*

Caterina knew she could hide no longer. She rose early, but Luca insisted on sitting her down and re-dressing the wretched dog-bite with gentle hands. So she was late. In a rush she threw a grey cardigan over her shoulders, picked up her two canvas bags and ran for the ferry.

The boat was crowded. Boisterous male laughter and a smog of Lucky Strike cigarette smoke vied with the rumble of the old marine engines and the stink of diesel fumes as the early morning ferry made its way to the Isle of Capri.

Clouds had rolled in overnight, as grey and relentless as the German army, turning the water of the bay to steel, and the wind off the sea flung spume in her face as she stood at the rails. The United States Army Air Force boys were on board, crowding the deck and flashing their brass buttons and buckles. Their good-natured banter made the deck noisy as Caterina eased her way among them, squeezing between their broad backs till they created a khaki wall around her. It seemed they were a group of pilots and crews from the 780th Squadron taking up their billets for rest and recuperation on Capri.

'Hell and damnation,' a gawky sandy-haired youth in uniform called out as the green mountains of the island of Capri slid gracefully into view. 'Damn me if that ain't one shit-hot slice of paradise we got for ourselves, fly-boys.'

'Mason, watch your mouth. Ladies present.'

The curt reprimand came from a raw-boned airman at Caterina's side. 'My apologies for my friend's language, ma'am.' He tipped his cap to her. 'He don't know no better than to cuss in front of a lady.'

She smiled, accepting his apology.

'You fly bomb airplanes?' she asked in halting English.

'We sure do, ma'am.'

'You bomb Naples?'

'We don't bomb nobody now,' he pointed out quietly and added, 'thank the Lord.'

'But you bomb Naples before?' She pointed back over her own shoulder to indicate the past.

'Yep.'

That was all. Just 'Yep'. But she saw his fingers creep up to the silver insignia on his short jacket, a pair of wings with a propeller at its heart, as though to remind himself why he did it.

'Flight Engineer Chas Lennox,' he said, 'that's me. It was my job, ma'am, me and my crew, to bomb Naples. Many times. We were at war.'

She nodded. 'I understand.'

But 'understand' was a big word. With many meanings. Too many for a brief boat ride.

'You drop bombs on Sorrento?' she asked.

'No, Sorrento had no military significance.'

She didn't understand the English words. But the 'No' and the shake of his head made his meaning clear.

'My father was killed in bomb. In Sorrento,' she told him.

The big man's face crumpled for a second. 'I'm real sorry to hear that, ma'am. Sorrento was never a designated military target. If it caught a stray, that would be from a crippled kite. They would jettison any remaining bombs to enable the plane to gain height, you see.' He raised a hand up in the air to demonstrate. 'To go upward.'

'Was it you?'

'No, ma'am, it wasn't me.'

Of course it wasn't. A crazy thought. With a wide smile for the airman, she reached into the larger of her canvas bags and drew out a musical box. Its intarsia scene of the bay and Vesuvius gleamed under the layers of varnish that Luca had spent hours perfecting.

'Flight Engineer Chas Lennox,' Caterina said, 'you look to me like a man whose mother would like a memento from Sorrento.'

The slate-grey ridge of cloud and its skirts of mist tried to hide the beauty of the island but failed. After riding the funicular from the marina up to Capri's busy central Piazzetta, Caterina struck out along the twisting narrow road that climbed Capri's wooded mountain slopes. At every turn her eyes fixed on the view across the Bay to Naples.

Except Naples wasn't there.

The mist had stolen the city. In its place lay a grey striated blur, the colour of tears. She tried hard to conjure up the city out of the dense murk because she needed Naples. She knew beyond doubt that the answers to whatever her father had been doing were hidden somewhere in that ancient city that had once ruled over its own kingdom.

Was Major Jake Parr there? Was he laughing to himself now that she had given him what he wanted, now that she had betrayed her father in that crowded basement? Was that why she had not heard from him since?

She felt a stab of dismay. Had he sent Harry Fielding to her to test her out? Had Harry reported back and told him to steer clear?

Spied on. Hunted. Trapped.

She quickened her pace.

'You're back.'

'Yes, I'm back.'

The expression on Octavia di Marco's austere face was not quite a smile but it came close. 'Are you feeling better, Signorina Lombardi?'

'Yes, *grazie*.' Caterina unconsciously ran her fingers along the edge of her chopped hair. 'Thank you for your help. And for the haircut.'

'You are welcome.'

The tall woman stood in the grand entrance of the white villa, again a striking figure in her man's black suit and intricate long jet earrings, vivid against skin that was too pale.

'The Count is engaged at the moment,' she announced.

'I'm here to see Leonora.'

She followed Octavia di Marco through a maze of pale marble corridors, but as they approached a closed door at the far end, Caterina lengthened her stride and came alongside the Count's niece.

'I'm not here to hurt her.' Caterina spoke softly, 'I'm here to help her.'

Octavia di Marco's eyes raked her from head to foot. 'Liar,' she said and knocked on the door.

A voice inside called, 'Enter,' and Caterina walked in.

The shutters were open, the blinds raised. The French windows stood ajar and a warm wind snaked through the room. It stirred the scent of citrus that hung heavily in the air. A lemon tree grew almost to the ceiling.

'Welcome to my playroom, Caterina.'

Leonora di Marco's greeting was warm, despite the fact that she was performing a headstand in the middle of the room. An upside-down smile spread across her face and she lifted one hand briefly off the floor to wave. She was wearing a white tunic and shorts.

Caterina glanced around the room. Virgin-white, of course; she had come to expect that in this bleached household. At the far end stood a trampoline, and a skipping rope lay abandoned on the floor. Along the length of the room a row of rubber hand-rings hung suspended from the ceiling about three metres from the floor. It took Caterina a moment to realise what they were for and she almost laughed out loud at the mental image of this young slip of a girl swinging from one to the other like Tarzan. It demonstrated a bravery that surprised her.

Leonora flipped easily on to her feet and Caterina advanced towards her, but before she had taken more than two steps the white dog materialised from nowhere and stood stiff-legged between them.

'Bianchezza,' Leonora spoke sternly.

The German Shepherd flattened its ears, silently bared its teeth.

'I thought we were friends,' Caterina murmured and held out her fingers.

The dog sniffed at them, its leathery black nostrils flared, and its pale eyes relaxed, but its irises remained huge.

'Bianchezza!' Leonora scolded. 'Stop that.' She ruffled a hand through her dog's milky white fur and earned a quick flash of its tongue. 'Behave.'

Caterina straightened up. But there was a strange atmosphere in the room. The dog could sense it too, its hackles not quite flat. The feeling seemed to rise from an awareness between the two young women, an awareness that what had occurred in the car on the steep mountainside had fused them together in a way that was oddly intimate, despite the fact that they were strangers.

'How are you?' she asked Leonora.

'Much better.'

There was a pause. The wind snatched at one of the hanging rings and set it swaying.

'And you?' Leonora asked. 'How is the bite?'

'Healing well.'

'I'm glad.'

'And Bianchezza?'

Leonora laughed, that brittle sound, painful on the ear. 'As you can see, she has recovered.'

The white fur around the dog's neck-wound had been shaved away, revealing a vulnerable slash of pink skin around a jagged scab. They both looked at it. Images of the mountainside at an odd angle rose inside Caterina's head, and to banish them she drew out a brown paper package from her shoulder bag. It was the white dress, laundered and pressed, but Leonora refused it point blank.

'Keep it,' she said. 'It looks better on you.'

Her smile was generous.

Caterina extracted another brown paper package. She presented it to Leonora who unwrapped it. It was a box. Not a musical box. They were gone. She had sold all six of them to the battle-weary AAF troops on the ferry. No, this was something special for Leonora. It was a jewellery box, lined with pure white parachute silk that she had got hold of on the black market in Via San Antonio for a cupful of the excellent coffee that Captain Fielding had brought her.

Inlaid on the wooden lid was the profile of the head of a German Shepherd dog. She had devised it in the creamiest of satinwood, with the tufts of fur and its ears picked out in slivers of ivory and mother-of-pearl that she had cannibalised from an old tray she had made as a child for her mother. There was no point keeping that tray under her bed. Not any more.

'It's beautiful,' Leonora declared, astounded. 'Thank you. I've been waiting for you to come. To thank you for saving my life.'

Caterina held out a hand. She intended to shake hands, to formalise their friendship, but the moment their palms touched, the unstable barrier between them collapsed. She found herself wrapped in Leonora's embrace, the dark threads of their hair mingling together, and she could not but inhale the scent of loneliness on her new friend's pale skin.

'Tell me, Leonora,' she asked in a careful tone, 'why would anyone want to kill you?'

Leonora glanced pointedly at the closed door and cupped her hand to her ear to indicate eavesdroppers. 'Let's take a walk.'

Together they slipped out through the French windows.

Leonora knew the paths, the tracks, the faintest of animal trails through the forested slopes of Capri better than Caterina knew the streets of Sorrento.

Caterina watched the girl's bare legs flash in their white shorts, scampering ahead beneath the arching canopy of the umbrella pines whose cones and needles lay under her feet, the undergrowth scented with wild oregano. Fearlessly she leapt on to limestone crags that threatened to tumble her into the sea far below. In the dips and hollows lay drifts of purple bee-orchids and ox-eyed daisies, and always there was the breath of the sea at their shoulder.

Caterina padded along at Leonora's heels as silent as the dog, and waited for this onrush of wild energy to end. Finally Leonora clambered to the top of a cliff and ducked under its rocky overhang.

'Welcome to my castle,' she grinned.

It *was* a castle. Of sorts. A jumble of limestone boulders and weathered rocks carved out by the wind and the rain, a natural fortress with a small knoll at its centre covered in a cushion of moss campion for them to sit on. In front of them stretched a vast unruly grey sky that sucked the warmth from the day. They sat down together and there was an easiness to their companionship that surprised Caterina.

'Guard!' Leonora commanded her dog with a flick of her hand and the animal immediately picked its way out of the castle on to the slope behind. 'Bianchezza will warn us,' she confided, 'if anyone comes.'

They talked quietly and frankly, the heartless cry of gulls the only sound to puncture their private world.

Caterina asked once again the question she had put to Leonora in the villa. 'Why would anyone want to kill you?'

Leonora shook her head, bewildered. 'I have asked myself that a thousand times. Why would anyone want to kill me? There was *no* reason. It doesn't make sense.'

Caterina laid it out clearly and simply. If the big man called Aldo had been trying to kill her, rather than Leonora, then he must have followed her from the mainland. In which case he would not have had a car. So where had the big bull-nosed Buick come from? The fact that he had access to the car, which then disappeared, indicated that someone on the island was helping him.

Or employing him.

'No.' Leonora was adamant. 'I know what you're thinking and you are wrong. Totally wrong. My grandfather would never try to kill me. I am the only one to carry our name on to the next generation. No, Nonno is no killer, I swear to you. It's not him.' Her small fingers clung to each other in her lap. 'Maybe the driver was just a drunk who was playing a game, pushing us off the road, and has now gone back under the rock he crawled out from.'

'No, Leonora. He hasn't disappeared.'

Caterina told her about the chase, the one through the old city of Naples, the one that made her skin sweat and her limbs tremble even now. She turned her face away from Leonora and fixed her eyes on three black shearwaters that were circling on thermals like burnt scraps of paper. She let the wind scythe across her face, scouring away any trace of fear. But she was glad of the solid rock at her back.

Leonora was happy to talk about her family. Count di Marco had made his fortune as a dealer in South African gold and diamonds, but now never left the villa, and his niece rarely left the island, though Leonora didn't know why. Neither was keen on communication, it seemed. The Count and his niece had frequent rows and liked to outmanoeuvre each other at chess, and though they occasionally entertained visitors, Leonora had never seen any guests who looked remotely like the massive Aldo or had a white blaze in his hair.

There was nothing of use to Caterina, despite all the prodding and pushing and teasing out of answers. She thought of Jake Parr, the soldier with a police officer's eyes. He would know what questions she should ask to find answers. She thought for a moment and started to question Leonora about her life.

'My parents died on Vesuvius in August 1928 when I was two,' the girl told her.

That made her nineteen. She looked younger.

'There was an eruption that summer,' Leonora elaborated. 'My father was taking photographs of the lava spouts and he and my mother got caught by one.' A forlorn smile pulled her mouth out of shape. 'My father was a crazy risk-taker apparently.'

'I'm sorry.'

'I was brought up by Nonno and Octavia.'

No wonder she needed the dog. Something to love her.

'I'm also sorry about the loss of your fiancé two years ago,' Caterina added, 'it must have been—'

'Don't go feeling sorry for me about that.' Leonora clicked her fingers and within half a second there was a flash of white and the dog was at her side. She pressed her small dark head against the animal's flank. 'Because I'm not.'

'Didn't you love him? Your fiancé?'

'No.'

'Then why on earth did you agree to marry him?'

Leonora grinned at her. 'Because I want to be a racing driver.'

Caterina's jaw dropped open. 'What?'

The girl laughed, and this time it was that joyous unfettered sound that only seemed to exist away from the house. 'That's why I keep myself fit. I've always wanted to be a racing driver. To drive the Mille Miglia for Alfa Romeo, like Tazio Nuvolari. But they won't take women. *Bastardi*! But there's a circuit in England called Brooklands, that's where I intend to go. They hold women's races all the time, but I need a car of my own. Caterina, can you imagine it?'

Her hands were spinning an imaginary steering wheel with excitement and Caterina remembered the drive down the mountainside. Fast and furious. Brakes squealing. Dust flying. The thrill on Leonora's face. Her dark eyes were shining now. Yes, she could imagine it all right.

Leonora scooted forward on her bottom to the cliff edge, dangling her feet over the sheer drop and proceeded to tell Caterina that as her grandfather had refused to give her money for a car, she had decided to marry instead.

'For your husband's money?' Caterina's fingers itched to seize the girl's hair and drag her back to the safety of the knoll.

'Holy Mother, no. I just wanted my wedding gift from Nonno.' She glanced over her shoulder at Caterina, her eyes mischievous, her full lips open, showing hungry white teeth. 'The fabled jewelled table that your father was making! I never saw it but I would have sold it to finance a racing car.' She held out a hand to Caterina. 'Help me, help me find it.'

'I have already told your grandfather that I'm not interested.'

A foolhardy brown lizard with eyes as yellow as a celandine scuttled across the stones of their fortress, and the dog snatched it up with a loud click of its jaws. The updraft from the cliff swept into Leonora's tunic, puffing it out at the back, making her look bigger.

'Come here, Caterina. I have something to show you.'

Caterina took two steps forward. Enough. No more.

'Look down there.' The girl pointed down to the foot of the cliff far below where there was a tiny cove and a few metres of bleached sand.

'See?' Leonora pressed her. 'The grey smears at the cliff base. They are caves. All around Capri. Most people don't know about them. Few tourists go beyond the Azura Grotto cave, the Blue Pool.'

'So?'

'So I walk the cliffs all the time. I see things. Boats pull in. At dawn. At dusk.'

Was this girl offering her an exchange?

'One evening I watched four men dismantle an army Jeep on the beach,' Leonora continued casually, giving Caterina time to consider. 'At the end they loaded the parts on to a fishing boat and shipped them back to the mainland to sell.' She chuckled.

'And crates?'

'Sometimes. Yes, I've seen crates come in.'

Caterina was trying to make sense of this. Her mind was sluggish, the back of her neck ached. What was it about this family that could wrong-foot her so readily? Did Leonora really believe that the dowry table was hidden somewhere on the island? Or was that just her way of holding out a carrot to the donkey? It was obvious that Leonora was a crazy risk-taker too, like her father. What other risks did she seize blindly with both hands, other than balancing on a limestone cliff edge, that is? The wind was picking up. One good puff and the girl would be gone.

Caterina took another step forward and the precipice jumped closer. She rested a hand on the girl's shoulder with a steadying grip, aware of the muscles underneath the white silk tensing and un-tensing.

'Leonora.' She kept her tone light. 'Have you ever heard of the Caesar Club?'

'Yes, of course.'

Caterina inhaled a quick breath. Tasted the salt air on her tongue. She had asked on impulse and expected nothing.

Yes, of course.

'Why do you say 'of course'?' she asked.

'Because my ex-fiancé's brother is a member. Giulio Macchione.'

Everything entwined. Strings that wound in and out of each other. Caterina couldn't make sense of it, but she could feel the strings tightening.

'I'd like to meet this Giulio Macchione.'

Leonora shrugged, irritated by the change of subject from racing cars, and she plucked a tiny golden beetle from the front of her tunic. A green stain remained to mar the pristine whiteness of the silk.

'That's no problem. He's always at Pompeii's.' She rolled her eyes skywards when she saw Caterina's blank expression. 'For heaven's sake, that's a nightclub in Naples. On Via Toledo.'

'Will he be there tonight?'

'Probably. You want to go to Pompeii's tonight?'

'Yes.'

An amused smile spread across the girl's delicate features as her gaze skimmed over Caterina from head to toe. 'You wouldn't get in even as a kitchen skivvy in that dress, but . . .'

The dog's head whipped round. Its ice-blue stare fixed on the overhanging rock at the entrance to the castle and it stood still, legs rigid, but uttered no growl. Caterina grasped Leonora's tunic and yanked her to her feet on safe ground. An expression of excitement crossed Leonora's face, but Caterina gestured to her to remain silent. Her hand slid into the canvas bag still on her shoulder, felt for the gun, and flicked off the safety catch. She had practised this.

She rounded the shoulder of rock first. A figure stood there, tall and clad in a suit and Caterina's trigger finger tightened ready to shoot right through the bag. Except there was no white blaze. No arms of solid muscle, nor gold glinting on knuckles. Instead a jacket was slung over a shoulder and a coal-black shirt was stuck with sweat to narrow ribs.

It was Octavia di Marco.

Caterina exhaled sharply.

'Octavia,' Leonora laughed with relief behind Caterina, 'what are you doing up here? You scared us.'

The woman's intent gaze shifted from Caterina to her niece and back again. 'I came to watch over you, *bella*,' she said to Leonora in her usual quiet voice, though her eyes were fixed firmly on Caterina. 'To make sure you were safe.'

But a dangerous thought skidded into Caterina's head. What if the dog had not been there? What if they had been alone on the edge of the cliff? Would this tall masculine woman have silently pushed them both over the precipice?

CHAPTER TWENTY-ONE

Jake Parr was in a foul mood. He was propping up a bar. It was at the back of the grand ballroom of the Palazzo Vanucci, a Baroque over-ornamented mansion that had been turned into a noisy, vibrating nightclub, the Pompeii Club. Jake's attention was only half on the band on stage, who wore stiff white jackets and the smiles of men doing what they loved best. He envied them that. In one hand he nursed the dog-end of a Lucky Strike and in the other a straight bourbon. It was his third. It would not be his last. Jake had had almost no sleep this week, working long nights as well as days. He was only here now because that bastard Colonel Quincy had ordered it.

'Be there,' his senior officer had bellowed down the telephone.

The line crackled, breaking up. The repairs to the Naples telephone exchange were far from complete. It was a never-ending task for the British Army Royal Engineers and the wires were constantly being cut, stolen from the telegraph poles to sell on the black market alongside the army blankets and army petrol.

'I want a SITREP,' Quincy had informed him. A situation report. 'Are you hearing me on this blasted line?' Jake winced as Quincy banged the receiver on something hard to try to clear the disturbance. 'I'll see you there tonight, Major.'

Jake had abandoned the receiver and continued to trawl through a long list of names supplied to him by the Office of Housing and Relocation. It had been set up to deal with the homeless. But it was depressing. The office was swamped. Hell, half of the inhabitants of this benighted city were homeless, bedding down alongside the rats in mounds of rubble or huddled in the dirt in doorways, but right now, that wasn't Jake's problem, thank God. He already had enough of his own.

He was searching for a name. Sal Sardo's to be exact. Okay, the guy was dead, but that wasn't the point here. Sal had claimed to be one of the homeless, but if Jake could pinpoint him to an address – even an old one – he could maybe discover more about his previous whereabouts and which guys he did business with. It was a long shot.

That's why the bourbon was firmly in his grip now in the nightclub and his expectations were way down deep in his boots. But that wasn't his only gripe. The Lombardi girl had walked out on him. Without a word. Just like that. She'd upped and left while he was grilling Sal Sardo in the interrogation room, as if she'd lost interest in the whole sordid business, and he couldn't blame her. Except for one thing. Her father. Where exactly did Papà Lombardi fit into this darn mess?

He'd seen her face, the way it fell apart when she set eyes on the triptych in the basement. It was obvious that she had recognised her father's work instantly. She knew what it meant, and it was like watching a snared rabbit have its guts torn out. Not a sound escaped her lips. But it did something bad to Jake's insides to see what he'd done to her.

He was a fool. Hadn't he learned his lesson? Once before, he'd felt sorry for an Italian woman getting the shit beaten out of her in the street and he'd ended up with a thumping great bullet-hole in his chest, courtesy of the woman herself.

Don't get involved, Jake reminded himself. Stay objective. The first rule of any good cop. But it was too late, he was already involved, dammit, each time he pictured that new elfin fringe fluttering on her forehead or recalled the warmth and weight of those strong hands of hers tight on his hips. Constantly he heard in his head the echo of her voice, sad and empty, when she said to him, '*I want their names. These people who accuse my father. You owe me that much.*'

He downed the last of his drink and felt it hit where it was needed. He stubbed out the cigarette butt in a pool of beer inside an ashtray and heard it hiss. He let the Big Band music that whipped through the room melt some of the tension that was making his bones feel as though they were held together by red-hot metal screws. It was a Benny Goodman number – *Sing, Sing, Sing* – and it suited his mood. All discordant trumpets and pounding of jungle rhythms on the drums. They blurred the smoky air, took the edge off the sharp bursts of laughter at the tables, as the room seemed to sway and a clarinet set out on its lonely sultry solo.

Jake stared at the glass in his hand. Half full again. When did that get there? Faces came and went, but the one he wanted to see wasn't here. Dimly he was aware of holding conversations with other men in uniform, the place was stuffed with them, a handful of female officers parading on their arms. But he was sick of khaki. In all its shades. With all it pips and stars and fancy medals. Sick to his stomach of war.

He concentrated instead on the glamorous couples on the dance floor, the ones in slinky shimmering gowns and glossy black evening-dress. The ones who looked clean. Untouched. As though they didn't even know the meaning of the word *war*, as though they had never smelled the foul rancid stench of it or seen their diamonds dulled by blood in the air. To those, he raised his glass.

'Major Parr! There you are.'

Colonel Quincy was advancing through the crowd. To hell with him. That wasn't the face Jake wanted to see.

The brilliantine on Quincy's ginger hair shone like firelight under the chandelier, and Jake could smell the woody scent of his cologne from three yards away. It made him wonder who his senior officer was meeting later and whether his wife back in the States knew about it.

They had moved away from the grand ballroom to what had clearly once been the palazzo's music room. A choir of angels graced the ceiling and the vast black carapace of a grand piano gleamed in the centre of the oak floor. On the walls hung portraits of Italy's great composers − Vivaldi, Rossini, Verdi and Puccini − a stern-faced audience to their conversation.

'Get on with it, Parr. Let's hear your report. I'm having dinner with some top brass tonight and they'll want to know the latest from this unit. Make it good, man.'

'Yessir.'

Quincy had chosen for himself the grandest chair in the room but it looked uncomfortable, his long limbs not settling. In one hand he cradled a brandy glass large enough to swan-dive into, and Jake noticed the way he swirled the amber liquid relentlessly round the curve of the glass, his own private tidal wave, the only sign of his impatience. Jake had parked himself on the piano stool. He had not been able to resist lifting the lid and allowing his fingers to caress the ivory soundlessly. It had been a long time, too long, since he had played. A war had come and inserted itself between his fingers and the silky feel of piano keys, thrusting a Colt .45 into his hand instead. He turned his back on them now and gave the British Army colonel his full attention.

Jake kept the debrief short. He'd save the details for the written report – whenever the hell he got around to it, but for now he just stuck to the main facts. He proceeded to inform Quincy of the storm that had broken out since Sal Sardo was murdered. People were scared. Informants were panicking, running for cover. Jake was having to increase the sweeteners on offer to entice them back into his office.

He had heard a rumour. There were always rumours whipping through the city, as elusive as smoke, sending him off on wild-goose chases that got nowhere, but this one came from a usually reliable source and Jake's cop-nose could smell the meat in it. It ended up with Jake and one of the new recruits to his team staked out beside an old disused brick-making factory night after night. The painting they were on the hunt for was one of Mary Magdalene weeping at Christ's tomb.

'By some artist called Bronzino,' he informed Quincy. 'Or that's what they say. Ever heard of the guy?'

Instantly the colonel leaned forward, green eyes glinting through narrowed lids, the brandy still spinning like a dervish in his glass.

'Bronzino is one of the Florentine Mannerist painters, you ignoramus,' Quincy said with the slow intonation of someone talking to a child. 'Sixteenth century. Mixed styles of High Renaissance into the early Baroque period. Not a favourite of mine. Portraits too icy. Too aloof. But he worked on a magnificent series of frescoes at the Certosa di Galuzzo monastery with his master, Pontormo, in 1522. The great Duke of Tuscany, Cosimo de Medici . . .' he paused, his mouth a scornful line. 'Even a philistine like you, Parr, will have heard of *him*, I presume.' But he didn't wait for a reply. 'Cosimo de Medici became Bronzino's patron. Died in 1572 at the Florence home of his pupil, Allori.'

Jake laughed out loud. 'You never cease to amaze me, Colonel. That is impressive.'

Jake never got used to it. This intimate knowledge. However obscure or however famous the name of a painter, Quincy could reel off facts and dates the way other people recite nursery rhymes. But a flush was rising up over the sandy skin on Quincy's throat and darkening the freckles on his cheeks. Warning signs.

'Where the blazes is the painting now?' he bellowed. The force of it made the piano hum.

'It's safe, sir. In our paintings depository. Securely under lock and key. I put it there myself this evening.'

The brandy ceased its dance. 'And the men involved? At the factory. Did you arrest them?'

'No, sir. Unfortunately the two men guarding the painting at night attacked us and I was forced to defend myself. They are both dead.'

There. It was said. The reason for his foul mood. The reason for the red mist in his mind. They say if you put a bullet directly into a man's heart, there is not so much blood. But they say wrong.

'What happened?' Quincy growled.

'They got wind of us. Attacked our position.'

That's what came of working with a raw rookie, one who didn't know the meaning of the order "Maintain silence".'

A stillness took root in the music room, but it could not erase from Jake's ears the wet sound of those two bullets finding their targets. He'd expected a dressing-down from Quincy, but instead the Englishman was grinning like a ginger Cheshire cat.

'I'll take a look at the Bronzino first thing in the morning,' the Colonel announced and snatched a healthy swig of his drink, the liquid glistening like oil on his lips. 'By the way, Major, I have a task for you.'

'What's that, sir?'

'I had a drink earlier this evening with Signor Palmiro

Togliatti. You know, the leader of the Italian Communist party. His politics may be dangerous claptrap, but he is becoming a powerful figure and it looks as though he could be head of the new government after the election. So we are obliged to work with the man.'

Jake studied him warily. Where was this going?

'You know what his nickname is among his followers?' Quincy demanded. 'It's *Il Migliore*. The Best.' He grimaced. 'Not a bad chap really, and he does seem to be dragging his fragmented party to the right. He is even disarming the Garibaldi Brigades, those bloody resistance fighters of his. I tell you, there is hope for Italy.'

He paused. Jake did not like the pause.

'Anyway,' the colonel rubbed a hand over his freshly shaven jaw, as though seeking a smooth path for his next words, 'you must be aware that Togliatti's Communist party consists largely of those partisan resistance factions who bore arms against Fascism. First against Mussolini and then against the Germans.'

Another pause. Wherever this was going, Jake knew it was nowhere he wanted to be.

'They may be a bunch of misguided riffraff, brainwashed by Stalin,' Quincy conceded, 'but they are also fierce patriots. And more to the point, they have their ear very close to the ground.' He waved his glass through the air, setting the brandy in motion again.

'So, Togliatti and I have agreed a mutual exchange of information. His sources believe that a cache of artwork is hidden somewhere in the village of Sant'Agata up in the hills on the Sorrentine peninsula. They don't know exactly where. So I want you to take your whole unit tomorrow and do a clean sweep of the location. House to house. Got that?'

'Yessir.'

'Good man.' Quincy unravelled his spidery limbs and leapt to his feet. 'You deserve a drink, Major.'

Jake wasn't going to argue with that.

Jake spotted the arrival of the two young women in white gowns, elegant in their simplicity. Short stylish dark hair. No jewellery. Just their skins for ornamentation, as smooth and gleaming as satin. The one who walked in front was Caterina Lombardi.

What the hell was she doing here? And who was the girl with her?

Jake watched Caterina scan the room, eyes dark and suspicious, her chin held high in that way she had. Scenting the air.

What was she here for?

The moment her gaze found him, she carved a path through the drinkers and the dancers, through the smoke and the smiles, straight towards him. He was absurdly pleased to see her. He smiled a welcome and wrapped his hands around his glass to stop him wrapping them around her.

'Major Parr,' she said without preamble, 'I am surprised to find you here. I thought you'd be out chasing artworks.'

Her hostility came at him like she'd stuck the muzzle of that prehistoric Bodeo pistol of hers right in his face.

'Good evening to you, Caterina,' he drawled amiably. 'No, I'm just chasing a glass of good whisky tonight.'

'So I see.'

'And what is it that brings you to Naples this evening?'

She didn't reply. Instead she glanced at her friend whom she did not introduce and they exchanged a look. Her friend flicked a beautifully arched eyebrow in the direction of a huddle of young Italian bucks in evening garb over by the bar and she shrugged one glossy naked shoulder. Impatient to join them. Jake was sorely tempted to ask her to move away, because he wanted Caterina to stay right here. There was something about her that was different, something he couldn't quite pin down, but it raised goose-bumps on his skin and he examined her appearance, seeking it out.

Not the grainy new shadows under her eyes. Nor the lack of a bandage on her forearm. Nor the jut of her hip bones through the thin skin of silk of the beautiful gown that he was certain was not her own. Yet the difference in her struck him forcibly. It lay in the boldness of her manner. That had not been there before. There was a firmness to her chin that he did not recognise and a faint narrowing of her eyelids as she regarded the world around her, as though assessing the threat it posed.

He wondered what had happened to her. To change her. And he tried to work out what was making her so all-fired angry at him.

'Caterina, I . . .'

'Well, well, signorinas.' It was the smooth tones of Colonel Quincy at his side, bending from his great height to greet them.

'What a pleasure this is. Our army boys will be delighted to have you here.'

He shook hands with both, enveloping their small fingers in his mighty paw. Caterina nodded politely at him, taking in his oiled hair and the expensively tailored jacket and the brandy flush at the base of his throat. She switched on a smile.

'I am not here for the delight of your "boys", Colonel,' she said in English. 'Do you chase paintings also?'

'No, my dear, I leave the chasing to Major Parr and his unit. My work is to collate, identify, and then find the rightful owners.'

She gave no sign as to whether she understood. 'Do you know someone called Drago Vincelli?' she asked.

'No. No, I most certainly do not.'

'I think you do,' she said. That boldness again.

With no further word she vanished into the crowd, her friend following. To Jake's astonishment, Quincy roared with laughter and thumped Jake's back between the shoulder blades, spilling his drink over his fingers.

'Damn fine fillies, what? These Italian signorinas really were worth starting this bloody war for, don't you agree, Major?'

Jake didn't agree. He marched over to the bar and ordered two Jack Daniels. One for himself. One for the person he used to be.

'Will you dance, Caterina?'

She was standing there quietly, not talking, not drinking, a point of stillness in a ballroom bursting at the seams with noise

275

and movement. One of the young bucks was standing beside her, an arrogant face with blond corkscrew curls and his hand hooked in the crook of her elbow. He could not take his eyes off her.

There was a new intensity to her, like a spotlight shining inside her. When Jake stepped close, he could feel the heat of it.

'Will you dance?' he asked again.

She detached herself from Signor Curly Hair and walked on to the dance floor.

Jake watched Caterina stare at the bar of service ribbons on the left side of his chest. At the way his thumb rested against hers as they danced. At the band-player thrumming his double bass as if it held the strings of his soul. Anywhere but at Jake's face. She danced well, thistledown in his arms, and he steered her small figure through the crush of dancers, letting her keep her silence until they reached a spot on the edge of the floor where the press of warm bodies grew less.

'Why did you run away, Caterina? When you left my interrogation room, where did you go?'

He felt her back stiffen under his palm, a tightening of tendons.

'I didn't run away. I had something to do.'

'It looked like running away to me.'

'Then you should get yourself spectacles.'

He took that one on the chin. She was observing a string of smoke that hung like a grey snake above one of the tables where a man was smoking a cigar. Her face was closed and tight.

'Why are you so angry at me?' Jake made his voice soft, so she had to lean closer to hear.

For the first time since stepping on to the dance floor she looked directly at him, her eyes so unhappy that he wanted to pull her close and fold his arms tight around her. He wondered again what had happened to her since he last saw her to turn her nerves into taut wires, and to bring her here, dressed like that. Surely not the young man with the blond curls that reached down to his collar like a girl's and the face full of sheep smiles. His expensive evening wear did not quite hide that he was carrying a little too much weight on his well-fed cheeks, so that to Jake he looked soft and shapeless. Like butter left out in the sun.

Jake had stood at the bar and watched Caterina dance with Signor Curly Hair not once, but three times. The man's soft hands had caressed the gleaming skin of her naked shoulders, his loose lips had bent and kissed the mulberry line of scabs along her forearm. The wound gave her an air of danger that was beguiling, as though she were the kind of person who had fought off a lion. Jake considered breaking one of Curly's fingers.

The warm seductive rhythm of Duke Ellington's *Take the 'A' Train* swung through the nightclub, but instead of thawing the ice-sheet between them and drawing them together in a slow mirroring of steps, it left her still staring angrily at him.

'Why did you let Sal Sardo go?' she demanded.

'Pardon me?'

'You should have kept him in a cell and you know it. No,

don't deny it. You had the power to keep him locked up but you chose not to. If you had done your job properly he would still be alive. Not dead. Not . . .'

'Wait!' His voice was sharp. 'Where the hell has this come from? I released Sal Sardo because I had extracted all I could from him and have enough riffraff clogging my cells.'

'Liar.'

She didn't raise her voice. The word was no more than a whisper, a small stiletto gliding between his ribs.

'You released Sal because you were using him as bait to catch a bigger fish. He was a tadpole to you. Throw him back in and see who looms up to eat him. It's true, isn't it?'

Jake didn't deny it.

'Why this sudden interest in one of the dog-end dregs of the criminal world, Caterina?'

Her thumb lifted away very deliberately from his where he held her hand as they danced. A gesture of silent rejection.

'Nor did you contact me afterwards,' she continued, as if he had not spoken. 'For days I wondered where my so-called protection was and here I find it swimming in the bottom of your whisky glass.' For a brief moment she removed her hand from its place on his shoulder and snapped her fingers together. 'That's what your promises are worth.'

He had no defence.

'I was working.'

It was all he said. No mention of the blood, spilled like red wine over the shirt fronts of the two men he'd been stalking at the factory. Or of the two empty chambers in his gun. Nor did he mention the dreams that spiked his nights, but she must have caught a faint trace of something in his voice because she looked at him oddly and fixed her gaze on his chest for a long time, as though she could hear something cracking inside it. A thick barrier of silence rose between them, though their bodies continued to dance in perfect harmony.

'Tell me,' Jake asked to break down the barrier, 'how you know about the man called Drago Vincelli?' He heard her breath quicken. 'Caterina, Drago Vincelli is not a name you tout around in public so blithely, if you want to hang on to your . . .'

'Who is he?' she asked.

'He is a greedy, ruthless killer, one of the scourges of Naples who is making a corrupt fortune while the city is on its knees. You must stay away from him, Caterina.'

He saw shadows gather in the hollows of her face, but all she said was, 'Why don't you arrest him?'

He guided her smoothly past a couple of dancers who had more enthusiasm than skill on the floor. 'Two reasons. He keeps himself squeaky clean. No dirt on his fingers. No blood. We have not a shred of proof against him, and no one dares speak against him if they want to keep a tongue in their head. Secondly, Drago Vincelli is always on the move, he is never in one place longer than a heartbeat. He has bolt-holes all over Naples and as soon as we track him down, he's gone.' He could hear anger grating in his voice and pushed it away. 'What do you know about this killer?'

'He is the one who threatened me. Threatened my family. In Sorrento.'

He drew her slender body closer to his, whether she wanted it or not. The saxophones wailed in his ears.

'Tell me more,' she said.

'Drago Vincelli is a bomb expert and a brigand,' he continued. 'A highly dangerous and ruthlessly successful one. He keeps a close team around him and has gained control in many areas of this city. He brushes up against the Camorra at times, but also he chooses to work with them when it suits him. When this stinking war hit Italy, it was jackpot time for him – he started to deal in stolen firearms and in pharmaceutical drugs stolen from the Germans at first and then from the Allied stores. Nothing is out of this guy's reach, it seems. Nothing. Now it is stolen artworks that he . . .'

'Enough,' she whispered. A dry exhausted sound. 'Enough.'

She leaned her slight body against his as they glided across the dance floor, her cheek an inch from his. He inhaled the scent of pine trees in her hair. On his shoulder her hand rested with a feather-light touch, but while they danced he became aware of her fingers slowly tightening. The insistent rhythm of the music swelled around them, and with every step he felt her gripping the khaki material harder. He wanted to tell her that he would not run. That she could hold on as long as she liked, that he would find Vincelli for her, but it would take time and she must keep out of sight and out of Naples till then.

'How is your arm, Caterina?'

'Much better, thank you.'

'And the dog. Did it survive?'

One corner of her mouth lifted in a half-smile. He was

tempted to kiss that tilted corner, so close to his, but he knew that it was the whisky doing the thinking, so he put the brakes on that notion.

'Who is your friend?' he asked.

'You mean Leonora di Marco?'

They both knew he meant Signor Curly Hair. She twisted her head round, but whether she was seeking the girl in white or the arm-kissing Curly Hair, he couldn't tell. The music paused. A slinky blonde female singer swept out on to the stage and the band struck up the opening bars of *You Always Hurt the One you Love*, slow and achingly sad.

'Caterina, it strikes me that Drago Vincelli must believe you know something crucial.' She was staring blindly at the band, not at him. 'Crucial enough to make him want to keep you alive.'

He saw her mouth fall open. Registered the infinitesimal flicker of anguish before she clamped down on it and blanked any expression from her face. A pulse ticked at the base of her throat. She detached herself from him, sliding her fingers from his, and stepped to one side of the dance floor where she stood immobile. Still the steady throb in her throat. Jake slowly scanned the ballroom, but could spot nothing to set alarm bells ringing.

'*You always hurt the one you love, the one you shouldn't hurt at all*,' crooned the singer.

She possessed a rich sultry voice, the kind that knew how to slide inside you, smoky and seductive, drawing her audience close. A spotlight caressed her silky blonde hair that fell in a curtain across one cheek, and she wore a figure-hugging gown of crimson with sequins. A raw slash of scarlet for a mouth and eyes that could peel the skin off you.

Though Caterina's face was turned towards the singer and the band, Jake doubted that she was seeing them. He decided it was time to leave, to get her away from here. He could drive her home.

'*You always take the sweetest rose and crush it till the petals fall.*'

As the final words of the torch-song breathed their last, wild applause broke out as men at the front tables rose to their feet. But Jake was more interested in the sight of the white elfin figure of Caterina's young friend sidling off the dance-floor, moving fast between couples and heading straight for the gilded door at the far end. He swung round, tracking her flight, and he murmured to Caterina that her friend was leaving but she didn't respond.

He touched her arm. It was cold.

At the corner of his eye there was a flash of red and a skein of cigarette smoke was exhaled in his direction.

'Ah, my *bella* Caterina, what in hell's name are you doing in a place like this?'

It was the singer. She was standing with one hand on her curvaceous hip, a cigarette-holder poised in the other, a tight smile flashing fine white teeth right in Caterina's face. Full-breasted and older than she had appeared on stage, her challenging stare whisked over to Jake and skimmed appreciatively from his head to his toes, taking in his rank and his ribbons.

'Are you going to introduce me, sweetheart?' The singer's voice came out low and provocative.

Caterina turned her rigid face to Jake, a small jerky movement. 'Major Parr, this is my mamma.'

Jake should have known. Should have seen. The mirror-image, the same but different.

If anything, the mother was the more beautiful. Her features were subtly finer, her eyes a more startling blue, but it was the same delicate oval shape to her face, the same angle to the jaw-line and razor-edge cheekbones, the same wide forehead. The same, yet glaringly different. The lines were harder, steel mesh under the satin-soft skin, and the full scarlet mouth possessed a sensual twist that was not her daughter's.

'Sweetheart,' she said with an attractive chuckle in her voice, 'what's the matter? Lost your tongue? Aren't you going to give your mother a kiss?'

'No.'

The air between them seemed to ignite, suddenly too hot to breathe.

Caterina's lips were chalk-white, but her eyes dark with rage. She raised a hand, palm flat towards her mother, warding off any approach, but Jake saw the tips of her fingers curl. Wanting something. To rip her mother's eyes out? Or to cling to her mother's neck. It was impossible to tell.

'Go away,' Caterina said. Short spiky words. 'Don't come near me. Don't come near Luca. You have done enough damage to our family. No word from you for eleven years.'

It did not dislodge the scarlet smile. Her mother spread her elegant bare arms in a wide generous gesture and said, 'All the more reason to celebrate being together this evening, don't you think?'

Nothing from Caterina.

Signora Lombardi continued with a small shrug, 'All right, darling, I admit I should have sent you a postcard.'

It was a joke. A bad joke. She laughed at it herself but no one else did. 'Anyway, what are you doing here in a nightclub? And what have you done to your beautiful hair, though I must say your gown is divine, my angel.' She turned to Jake and kept up the flow of words, as though nervous of silences. 'You soldier boys know how to pick all the best girls. Don't you think she looks lovely in it, Major?'

'Divine,' he said.

Caterina's eyes jumped to him. For a second he thought she would laugh but she didn't, so he slipped her arm through his own. 'If you'll excuse us, Signora Lombardi, it's interesting to meet you but I was just about to drive Caterina home. Goodnight. Enjoy the rest of your evening.'

He felt Caterina's small arm tighten on his, and her shoulder tuck in close, but she made no attempt to leave. Her mother's blue eyes registered the uncertainty in her daughter and she brushed her hand along Jake's sleeve.

'Be a sweetheart, Major, and get me a drink, would you? Singing is thirsty work. A vodka for me to drink my girl's health would be perfect.'

She laughed up at him, but Jake paid no heed to her practised charm. This was not the time to play at being a gentleman. He had to get Caterina out of here.

'Mama, what are you doing here?' Her words came out stiffly, each one separate from the next.

'Singing for my supper, of course. You always liked my singing when you were young, remember?'

'I mean, what are you doing here in Naples?'

'Oh, I'd had enough of Rome.' She gave a dismissive toss of her head, setting her long earrings swaying. 'All those parties.' She drew on her cigarette so hard it burned almost to her fingers. 'So tedious.'

'Go back to Rome, Mamma.'

'Don't be unkind. I've come all this way to see you. And little Luca too, of course.'

The mention of her brother's name was like a wasp sting. Caterina jerked herself free of Jake and took a sudden determined step towards her mother. Lucia Lombardi was the taller of the two but she backed off, her eyes suddenly wary.

'Now, Caterina, I . . .' she began.

'Stay away from Luca.' Caterina pushed her face close to her mother's. Jake saw it again, the strength mirrored in each face, but Caterina could not quite hide the anguish behind her anger. 'I'm telling you to stay away from Luca. You hurt him by leaving us once. I will not allow you to hurt him again.'

Her mother relaxed, sensing first blood, and she gave another small shrug. Her smile this time was harder.

'Or what, my bella Caterina? What will you do to me if I go near my son? Push me off a cliff?'

For a fraction of a second, Jake thought Caterina was going to slap the cool mocking face. But instead she said in an icy tone, 'Eleven long years, Mamma. I do not want you in my life now.'

Then Caterina was gone. Her pale figure vanished into the crowd. The band launched into Glenn Miller's *In the Mood*.

CHAPTER TWENTY-TWO

Lucia Lombardi stood immobile, her face a frozen mask.

The whisky had done its job well on Jake. The treacherous amber road to oblivion. Jake cursed it. It had dulled his reactions. He would have been right on Caterina's heels if not for the whisky, but he missed his chance. He was too slow, caught off guard. He started after her and called, 'Caterina, I'll drive you home,' but a hand gripped his arm. He looked down to where red-painted nails had sunk their tips into the weave of his khaki sleeve.

'Wait!' Lucia Lombardi said. 'I wish to talk to you about my daughter. If you care for her at all – and I can see you do – help me to become her friend again.'

'Why would I do that, signora?'

He removed her fingers from his arm.

'Because,' she held his gaze, 'you and I both know she needs me. You saw it. Here. Tonight. As plain as day.' She looked over towards the bar. 'Now buy me a drink, soldier, and let's talk.'

Her smile was intimate. As if they shared something important. And he wondered how often she practised it in the mirror.

'With respect, signora, I do not think you are the expert on what your daughter needs. But you are right, I do care for her, which is why I am going to find her now and take her safely home.' He nodded curtly. 'Good evening to you.'

He pushed his way through the crowd. Frustrated by the delay. Disturbed that this woman had thrown herself back into Caterina Lombardi's life with the force of a hand grenade. He had to find her. He sidestepped a couple of soldiers who were weaving drunkenly towards him and carved a path to the door with no sighting of a white dress. He hurried out into the marble-columned reception hall, but still no Caterina.

He cursed himself.

Sweetheart.

The word had lingered on the glossy scarlet lips like cigarette smoke.

My bella Caterina. That's what her mother had dared to say.

Caterina turned her face and spat out the words on to the wet slippery pavement. As if *sweetheart* could kill her.

When she ran out of the Pompeii Club into the dark night, it was raining. The odours of the city were more pungent in the rain and she could smell its stale breath. Her own breath came in shuddering bursts as she looked up and down the street in search of Leonora's retreating figure, but the girl was nowhere in sight. The road was a main thoroughfare lined with fine tall buildings, its surface black as wet ink in the rain, but it was empty at this hour. Some of its street lamps were surprisingly still working, tossing buttery yellow pools on the ground and in one of them two alley-cats were yowling in a stand-off.

She hurried down the club's front steps and turned to her right, ducking her head against the rain. It slithered down her neck, along her bare arms, and she was shivering but it wasn't from the cold. How could her mother think she could waltz back into their lives and tuck her feet under their table once more? She had forfeited that right long ago.

Sweetheart.

The word crawled inside her brain. She quickened her pace to outrun it, and wished Jake was at her side, walking with her, talking with her, bringing his calm strength to the turmoil of her mind. She should have waited for him but she couldn't make herself go back in there. She turned quickly down a side alley to be less conspicuous in the street, but her head was still full of a red dress and blue eyes that wanted something.

So she heard nothing.

Saw nothing.

Hands came at her out of the darkness. She tried to scream but one stinking of fish clamped over her mouth. A sack was dragged down over her head, reeking of onions, but she lashed out with fists and feet. Too many hands, too much sacking jammed between her lips to silence her. She felt a sharp stinging prick in one arm. It wasn't the rain, however much she told herself it was. Silence came first, warm and silky as the sea in summer, and then, bit by bit, came the darkness.

But even in the darkness one word continued to pulse inside her head: *sweetheart*.

Where was she?

Jake stood on the nightclub steps in the rain. He scanned the street. No sign of Caterina. Where the hell was she?

On the other side of the road a boy in rags crouched in a doorway, presumably sheltering from the rain, and Jake darted across to him. The kid huddled deeper into his corner.

'Did you see a young woman in a white dress leave that building just now?'

The boy shook his head. He was wearing a cap, his eyes invisible beneath it. Jake dangled a cigarette, just out of reach.

'Are you sure?'

A small hand stretched up for it, palm open. 'She got in a car.'

'Going in which direction?'

The hand pointed to the right. Jake stared up the wet road.

'What kind of car?'

'An American car. Black.'

Jake dropped the cigarette on the palm and it disappeared. He headed quickly back towards the steps but a chill swept through his veins.

A car?

Why would she get in a car? Whose car? The image of the black Buick on Capri and the big brute driving it churned in his head and he hung on to the thought that she could still be somewhere inside the club.

That the boy was lying.

'Signora Lombardi.'

The mother was at the bar, a vodka in her hand and a smug-looking naval officer at her side. Jake didn't blame the guy for being smug. She looked stunning, arranged gracefully with one elbow casually on the bar, one elegant leg crossed over the other under the scarlet dress. A cigarette holder in her other hand.

'You're back, soldier.' She raised one carefully arched eyebrow at him. 'Didn't she want to climb on your white horse?' She laughed teasingly.

He had no time for her tricks. 'She has disappeared. I need your help to find her. Right now.'

She did not take offence at his brusque manner. She put down her glass.

'Push off, buddy,' the naval officer advanced towards him. 'This lady is taken.'

Jake gave him a look that halted him in his tracks.

'What do you want me to do?' Lucia Lombardi asked.

'I want you to go and take a look in the ladies' powder room for me. Check out that she isn't in there.'

'And what are you going to be doing?'

'Searching other rooms.'

'You think she's hiding?' She batted her long eyelashes at him in mock horror. 'From me?'

'I wouldn't blame her,' he said sternly and taking her arm, steered her across the room.

That was the moment the explosion hit.

A massive roar ripped through the room, tearing it apart. It punched the breath out of Jake.

Debris hurtled at the dancers. Scything through limbs. Shredding skin. A great wall of sound blasted over the screams and the air became a living thing that shuddered and convulsed and sucked the breath from lungs. It battered Jake's and something hard crashed against his ribs. Most of the lights were out. He was choking on dust and grit, fighting for breath, a zigzag of sparks flashing behind his eyelids.

A bomb.

God knows, he'd heard enough of them to recognise the sound.

Beside him Lucia Lombardi had let loose a high-pitched wail of terror, and she was clinging to him with both hands. Swaying on her feet. He dragged off his jacket and threw it over her bare shoulders to protect them from the sharp edges of masonry flying around.

People were panicked. Screaming and stampeding to the doors. Bodies lay strewn where they fell, the floor slick with blood. The remaining few lamps flickered like dying heartbeats.

Jake bent down and hoisted a table off a man in evening dress whose cheek was sliced open and hanging in a crimson flap. An older woman was groping blindly, a torrent of blood streaming down her face. Jake seized her hand and, with the other arm gripping Lucia Lombardi, he forced a path away from that spot towards the door, just as the lights went out and the immense chandelier directly overhead plunged down on those below.

Shrieks pierced the darkness. The stink of blood and faeces was strong as Jake propelled the two women forward, but only one thought was thudding through his mind: Caterina. Where was she? Had she come back into this room? An image of her lying injured and bleeding leapt into his head. Trampled. Broken. It crushed something inside him.

In the suffocating darkness he bellowed her name. 'Caterina!'

He listened for her voice. But if it was there, it was lost among the cries of pain and fear. He had just reached the door with the women when there was a sudden deafening crack. A shuddering of the room. With a roar the ornate ceiling collapsed. A violent blow to Jake's shoulders sent him stumbling to his knees, losing his hold on the two women, and he tasted blood and plaster in his mouth. He fought to regain his footing but could see nothing and felt something soft and human under his feet.

Not this way. Don't let it end this way.

A mule kick to the back of his head sent him spinning down to the floor. Screams lodged in his ears and blackness rose from the floor to sink its teeth into him.

CHAPTER TWENTY-THREE

How much darkness can there be?

Caterina could feel the weight of it pressing against her skin. A wild pulse kicked into life in her throat.

Where was she?

Twice she forced up her eyelids, but all she saw was more unyielding darkness, solid enough to touch. It crammed itself into her head. Stifling. Shutting down her thoughts. Her heart drummed in her ears.

Where had all this darkness come from?

Who had put her here?

Her mind struggled in vain to make sense of it. Dimly in some distant shadowy world, she recalled the street outside the Pompeii Club. Empty. Vague. Blurred. As though the image was many years old, curling at its edges. Surely that was where she should be, inside that yellowing old picture. Not here. Not hunched on a damp floor in blackness. She was shivering.

Abruptly she recalled the stinging pain in her arm and the

realisation of what it meant rolled over her. The grey fog in her mind. The blank space in her head where the memory of how she got here should be. They had to be the result of a needle plunged under her skin by hands that would be coming back for her. A low moan seeped out of her mouth.

Panic threatened to stalk the darkness. Breathe. Breathe. In and out. Slowly, breathe slowly. Her chin slumped on her chest and at last the moaning stopped. The relief from it cleared a small corner at the back of her skull where thoughts could gather.

Concentrate, she told herself. Concentrate.

One by one she started to ask herself questions.

Why are you here?

Because someone dumped me here in this dark hole.

Why aren't you dead?

That one sent a flicker of hope skimming through her. Because I am more valuable alive.

Why can't I move?

The question cut through the fog in her brain. How could it have taken her so long to work that out? She couldn't move. *She couldn't move.*

With a scream she yanked at her hands but they remained firmly behind her back. Only then did it dawn on her that she was lying on her side on a concrete floor, tethered like a goat to a metal stake in the ground. The scream ripped out into the darkness, tearing it to shreds, but there was no one to hear.

Don't, don't, don't. Please don't.

But the scream kept coming. It stampeded over her.

To make it stop she jammed her face in the dirt. Her body bucked and shuddered but it stopped the noise. The sudden silence was deafening, but in the brittle emptiness that now lay within the darkness, she started to think.

To concentrate.

Thin fingers of dawn slid under the door. Caterina focused her gaze on their approach, faint threads of grey reaching out into the layers of blackness and she felt a quickening within herself. Whoever was responsible for this would come when it was daylight. She was convinced. And when they walked through the door that she could now dimly make out, she stood a chance. Faint perhaps, but still a chance. Tethered alone in a black hole, she stood none.

She was in a shed. At least she could make out that much. A stone storage shed, it seemed. No windows. Where the darkness edged into greyness around the door, there stood what looked to Caterina like a stack of slatted wooden boxes, fish boxes, judging by the stink. She peered hard through the gloom, blinking away the wisps of fog that kept drifting through her mind, and saw dark humps huddled on the cold floor.

Her mouth went dry. People. Surely they looked like people. Asleep. In her shed. Soundless and unmoving. Black shapeless humps that changed everything. She froze. Earlier she had examined the stake to which she was tethered, but the ropes on her wrists were knotted as tight as wire. She had pulled and yanked at them, tearing her skin. She'd cursed like a trooper.

Yet there had been no movement from the invisible humps on the floor, no answer to her scream.

Who were they?

Thoughts came at her in pieces. Guards? Had Drago Vincelli abducted her and placed guards around her? Was that who they were? But why so many? And why the silence? It made no sense. There were six black humps that she could see, some larger, some smaller, all of them terrifying.

Yet she was still alive.

That had to mean something.

But what?

She narrowed her eyes in an effort to bring the indistinct humps into sharper focus, and tried to think logically, but her mind was skittering all over the place. She needed to ask the right questions. Think like a policeman. Think like Jake Parr.

Find me, Jake.

With your stern eyes and your unrelenting mind, come and find me.

But she knew that if anyone was going to get her out of this filthy hell-hole, it would have to be herself. She turned her head and saw that the thread of dawn was creeping closer, nudging up against one of the black mounds. Who were these people?

Time to find out.

As quietly as possible she wriggled her body as far down as she could towards the shapes. Her hip-bone scraped across the concrete as she stretched out, elongating her limbs, wrenching up her arms behind her back. She cursed the rope and the stake, and ignored the twisting of her shoulder sockets. With her head raised a fraction, she took aim and jerked her leg in a savage kick. The tip of her shoe caught the nearest hump, connected with something hard. It felt like a head.

A shriek rang out. The noise of it rattled through the shed. In the dark the hump reared up and a fist slammed against her offending foot.

'You bitch! You gutter-whore bitch! Stay away from me.'

It was the voice of a child.

A candle flared into life, sending shadows scuttling into the corners of the shed and painting pools of yellow on the silent figures. Six nervous faces. Staring uneasily at Caterina, as if she had two heads. She stared back at them, aghast. They were all children.

Small and ragged, thin as sticks, hair spiked with dirt. Some were standing, wrapped in filthy sacks, others crouched on their knees. Even in the gloomy shadows she could see they were all boys, three of them little sprats of no more than six or seven. The other three were rangier, all feet and sharp elbows, nearer ten or twelve years old, but all possessed the tense stillness of feral creatures. She could smell the wildness on them.

They were *scugnizzi*. A pack of street kids.

She felt her pulse climb down and the air find its way into her lungs again.

But why here? And why her?

Using her elbows, she manoeuvred herself up into a sitting position, arms tight behind her back, and asked, 'Who the hell are you?'

'We're Vanni's wolves.'

It was one of the younger ones who piped up with the

answer, the kid whose lice-ridden head she had kicked. He puffed out his chest.

'Vanni?'

Caterina switched to the older boy who lit the candle. He was standing, one hip thrust forward, his scruffy head angled so that it was half turned away from her, ignoring her. An army shirt with its sleeves ripped out hung down to his knees.

Something clicked in her brain.

Vanni.

He was the one on the bombsite. The one with the knife. The boy with the eyes of a man, the boy who'd wanted to snatch her sack of music boxes from her and swap them for a blade in her ribs. That Vanni.

'Hello, Vanni.'

He didn't recognise her. Not with her hair cut short and the white gown bestowing a classy opulence. Of course he didn't. He was too busy working out how much trouble she was going to be to him.

'Well now, Vanni,' she said calmly, 'this is a strange situation, isn't it?'

His mouth turned down in a sneer that he'd copied from someone a lot older and it didn't yet sit right on his young features. But he didn't bother to answer her.

'You've got the wrong person,' Caterina continued. A quick frown puckered the boy's swarthy forehead. 'Vanni, my family has no money. They can pay no ransom for me. This is borrowed finery I'm wearing, so there is no point keeping me tied up like this.'

She even smiled at him, a rocky smile but still a smile. These were kids. It was hard to be afraid of children who were scarcely older than her brother. Suddenly she kicked off her shoes. They were white satin slippers with tiny pearls sewn across the tip.

'Here,' she said, 'take these. Go and sell them. Bring me back an ordinary work-dress – it can be an old one, I won't mind – and you can keep the rest of the shoe money as payment for letting me go.' She laughed, carefully watching them, and saw the younger boys break into grins. 'And then you can have this dress too. It is silk. A deal?'

Vanni crouched down on all fours, his eyes level with hers, and a shiver slid down her aching spine. In the semi-darkness she had the impression of a young wolf, hollow-cheeked and grey skinned. She wondered when he'd last eaten. He smelled of hunger.

'What's to stop me,' he whispered menacingly, 'taking that dress off you anyway? Why should I waste good lire on buying another?'

Caterina didn't blink. She recalled his knife flicking from hand to hand, the sunlight dancing on its blade. No gun at her side this time.

'Because I say so,' she stated. 'You are not laying a finger on this gown until I am wearing another dress.'

He moved closer. 'Maybe I'll take it now.'

She stared into his pale eyes. 'Really? You think so? Just try, Vanni. Try that.'

One of the others sniggered.

Vanni snapped his head round and silenced the child with

a look. 'Meo, take the shoes,' he ordered. The boy, slightly younger but with a stoop to one shoulder and a submissive manner, scooped up the shoes. 'Sell them,' Vanni told him, 'in one of the street markets.'

'It's too early,' the boy grumbled, 'it's only just getting light and ...'

Vanni raised one dark eyebrow. That was all. And the boy was gone. There was a rustle in the dim fish-tainted air as the children settled back to sit on their sacks once more, expectant. Except for Vanni. He chose to remain standing, leaning one shoulder against the wall, and for the first time she glimpsed the outline of the knife under his army shirt.

'Vanni,' Caterina said firmly in the kind of tone she used with Luca when he walked filthy footprints through the house, 'now tell me why I am here.'

'*Puttana!*'

Vanni insulted her. But when he'd got that out of his system, he started to talk. Short, sharp sentences. It surprised Caterina at first, but under his flat bald words glowed the hot embers of pride. He wanted her to know. Wanted her to admire him. For kidnapping her. She didn't laugh in his face but came close.

He described his wolves as scavengers.

'We feed on people,' he said. 'On their scraps.'

'Thieves,' she said.

He laughed. Not a childish sound. 'We use rumours and whispers.'

A chill lifted the hairs on Caterina's neck. 'What whispers?'

And then it came, the reason for her being hog-tied with a

301

bunch of urchins in a stinking hovel. He'd heard that a certain someone in Naples wanted her, wanted Caterina Lombardi badly. So he reckoned that if he and his wolves could track her down and drag her off to their den, they could do an exchange. Her for a car. A straight swap.

A car? Was he insane? What use was a car without petrol and everyone knew petrol was as scarce as smiles in Naples. Anyway they were too young. The candlelight gilded the raw bones of their faces, the scabs on their arms, the dirt under their fingernails. Maybe it gilded their dreams too.

'I can get you a bicycle,' she lied, 'if you let me go.'

But Vanni wasn't having it. No, he didn't trust her. He spat disdainfully on the floor. Instead he told her of Meo's skill with a syringe because his father had been a veterinary surgeon before getting himself shot out of the skies in his Centauro aeroplane in the Italian Air Force during the war. They brought her here in a handcart shrouded in fish boxes.

She listened to each word, trying to find the boy inside them, a boy she could talk to, but he wasn't there. Only the hard shell of a grown man who enjoyed inflicting pain. Yet all the time while he talked, one of the youngest kids edged closer to her, until he could place his small hand on her leg. It was young Tino, the other child from the bombsite, with the wide shy smile and the hedgehog hair she remembered. He had torn strips off his sacking bed and started to bind up her feet with quick neat movements, creating shoes of a basic kind. She wanted to kiss his grubby cheek. It struck her that if they were giving her shoes, they weren't going to kill her.

By the time Vanni had finished his boasting and linked his arms with satisfaction across his chest, a ribbon of bright daylight was sliding on its belly under the door and the candle was down to a stub.

No name. Vanni had offered no name for the person who would be the recipient of the swap. Her for a car.

The door burst open. With relief Caterina inhaled the clean air that swept in and caught a glimpse of rubble outside, a scrap of blue sky and the smell of fresh bread, before the door was slammed shut again. The candle flickered and threatened to die. For one brief heartbeat Caterina's hopes had rocketed but were instantly shattered into broken glass in the pit of her stomach. It wasn't Jake Parr.

It was Meo, clutching two loaves of bread under one arm and a bundle of grey cloth under the other. He threw the bundle at Caterina, though she had no hands to catch it, and the children descended on him with the excited cries of gulls as he tore the bread into chunks for them.

'Vanni,' Caterina said quietly to the youth who stood aloof from the feeding frenzy. He did not have to fight for his lion's share. It was his by right. 'Who is the person who you say is interested in me?'

Vanni stepped up close to her, his thin body leaning over her in the gloom and drew his knife.

'Whoever this person is,' she said sharply, 'he won't want damaged merchandise.'

She looked away and focused instead on the dirty hands that were cramming bread into moist pink mouths, on the relief painted all over the children's gaunt faces as food hit their stomachs. The knife swept towards her and Vanni laughed in her ear, a soft indecent sound, relishing the tremor that ran down her neck. With an expert twist of the blade he sliced through the rope behind her. Her wrists parted, her shoulder joints uncramped as she straightened up and pushed herself stiffly to her feet.

'Is it Drago Vincelli?' she asked.

His eyes widened. The other children stopped chewing, mouths open.

'Take me to him,' she said and slipped the dress that Meo had provided over her head. It was grey and shapeless and too big for her, but it had a piece of string threaded through the loops at the waist to act as a belt. She slid the silk straps of the white gown off each arm and let it slither down under the cotton dress to the ground. Vanni snatched it up and sniffed it.

'Take me to him,' Caterina repeated, 'and I will get you that car you want.'

'Liar,' he hissed in her face, but in the dim light, his eyes glittered. He wanted to believe her.

'Take me to him,' she said for the third time.

It was all he needed.

They ran through the streets of Naples, three of them in single file: Vanni in the lead with a loping wolf stride, his skeletal legs pounding out a relentless pace, Caterina at his heels while behind her, Meo had breath to whistle as he ran and it occurred to her that these *scugnizzi* must spend a lot of their day on the run.

Streets flashed past, streets she didn't know. Cramped rows of unkempt houses and tall crumbling tenements where police didn't venture. It was still early, the sun skimming the roof tops, gilding the chimney pots, but the city of Naples was already coming to life and donning its gaudy colours. Street markets, vibrant with fresh-picked oranges, lemons and artichokes, were already crowded and full of noise and bustle. Vanni's hand snatched an apple without breaking stride as he shot past one stall, but it was Meo who caught the slap on his ear from the irate stallholder.

How much further?

Caterina's lungs were heaving. Beads of sweat clung to her skin, pasting the grey dress to her back, but she concentrated on placing one foot in front of the other, pushing all else from her mind. Yet the name Drago seemed to echo back up at her each time her sacking shoe hit the pavement.

Drago Vincelli.

She grieved for the lack of the Bodeo banging against her hip as she ran.

Each time they passed a church, however mean or however grand, Vanni paused for two seconds, bowed the knee and crossed himself, and it struck Caterina as a gesture of hope on his part, a reaching out for a miracle. She was tempted to join him, but miracles were thin on the ground in Naples, so she kept running instead. At any time she could have stopped, could have thrown herself at a passing Allied soldier on patrol or a police officer directing traffic and begged for help. She could have rid herself of these vagabond *scugnizzi* who wished her harm.

305

But she didn't. She needed them, these homeless street-rats. Especially their volatile pack leader with his absurd dream of a car. She would use him, just as he was using her. Her hand wanted to slide under his filthy army shirt and snatch his knife, but she stuck to the running, purposeful at his heels.

When Vanni halted this time she almost crashed into him. It wasn't just the usual two seconds in front of a church but a full minute, repeatedly crossing himself, lips moving in silent prayer. When he finally turned, he gave her a smile and there was something savage about it.

'Inside,' he said and took the steps with one bound.

The church of Santa Maria smelled of God and of damp. The vaulted nave soared above Caterina and rustled with the whispers of forgotten prayers that had lodged there. Naples was riddled with churches and even those in the poorest districts like this one abounded with superb sixteenth-century frescoes and wonders of Renaissance statuary by the likes of Tommaso Malavito and Caccavello. Standing obediently next to a statue of the Virgin Mary, Caterina couldn't stop her thoughts veering towards her own mother. Was she in some hotel room? Lying among white goose-down pillows? Painting her nails a shimmering poppy red and waiting for breakfast to arrive on a tray.

The thoughts lunged at her and she parried them by training her eyes on Vanni on the far side of the ancient oak pews beside the confessional box. He looked smaller here, no danger at all. A child in need of a blessing. What on earth had she been afraid of? A shaft of blue light fell on him through the stained-glass window and gave him the ethereal skin of an angel. Caterina looked away. Vanni was no angel.

An old woman swaddled in black garments was moving around, feet shuffling on the moss-coloured tiles, a pannier of potatoes strapped to her bent back. She started stroking the feet of a statue of San Sebastian and holding a quiet conversation with him, but when she saw Caterina, she shambled over. Her face looked like rumpled brown paper.

'You want to buy a potato?' she whispered and held one out to Caterina.

'In a church?'

'Why not? The good Lord knows we have to eat.'

'No. I have no money.'

'Something to barter?'

'I have nothing.'

The woman stared at Caterina's sacking shoes and murmured a Hail Mary. She wrapped her crow's fingers around Caterina's hand and forced the potato into it, before lurching away back to her stone-hearted saint.

The kindness of strangers wasn't something Caterina was used to in Naples and she took it as a good omen. This church of Santa Maria harboured kindness. Even Drago Vincelli was human. His greed may boil over like the molten lava of Vesuvius, but somewhere under it all must still lie a human heart. With a mother, a sister, a daughter. Why else would he choose this place to meet?

She was relying on it.

Her gaze turned back to the confessional.

As tempting as it was to put a fist through the delicate wooden latticework of the grille, Caterina refrained. She took her seat in the tiny wooden confessional box and waited, but she couldn't resist running the flat of her hand over the ancient oak of the walls with their dark patina of age and the feel of it soothed her taut nerves. It had a strange odour. It took her a moment to place it. It was guilt, she decided, the currency of confessionals. The coarse-grained wood reeked of it.

She could hear him breathing. He was there on the other side of the grille in the section where the priest would sit to listen to the whispered words of sinners. 'Bless me, Father, for I have sinned,' they would murmur into the grille.

I have sinned.

She stared hard at the latticework and wanted to shout through it, '*You* have sinned.'

Ask Sal Sardo with the scarlet smile across his throat. Ask Sal who has sinned.

'Caterina Lombardi.'

Drago Vincelli's voice sparked a fire in her chest, this man who had dared threaten her family. All she could see of him was a shadowy profile, sliced into squares by the lattice. She felt safe inside this gloomy box in the church of Santa Maria, but she knew it was an illusion.

'What is it you want, Caterina Lombardi?'

'I have two questions to ask you.'

She heard his harsh exhalation, an expression of annoyance. Had he expected her to beg?

There followed a full minute of silence but she could

out-wait him. Out-silence him. Her hands squeezed the potato hard enough to strangle it.

'Understand this, daughter of Antonio Lombardi. I am a busy man,' he said at last.

'Busy stealing from Italy.'

Silence again. Longer this time. This man used silences the way other men used words.

'My business is none of your affair,' he said softly.

'You made it my affair.'

He continued as though she hadn't spoken. 'First, I have two questions for you to answer. In detail. Remember that.'

She remembered an arm around her throat.

'How much does the Intelligence Officer know?' His words whispered through the grille, squeezing through the holes, bringing a chill into her box. 'The big American. He is a thorn in my flesh, that one. He killed one of my brotherhood this week and had to pay for it.' He uttered a low, sour laugh, swallowed by the shadows. 'He must learn that retribution is the Italian way.'

Had to pay for it . . .

Jake. What has he done to you?

If she opened her mouth now, the wrong words were going to come racing out, so she removed her gaze from the grille. She couldn't bear to look at him, not even his shadow.

'The American does not tell me what he knows,' she stated.

'Then why does he spend time with you?' He paused. 'Dances with you.'

He knew even that.

'Major Parr asks me questions.'

'And what do you tell him?'

'Nothing.'

'They must be short conversations then.' He made an odd sound and at first she thought it was some kind of laugh, but decided it was a grunt of frustration.

'Your second question?' she asked. She could not talk about Jake. A dull kind of panic fluttered inside her. 'What is it?'

She saw the profile turn to face her. The heavy black moustache and the blaze of white in his hair drew close to the oak lattice, and instinctively she drew back.

'Where is the table?' he demanded.

'What table?'

He put a hand to the grille and for a moment she thought he would tear it down. 'I will ask you one more time, Caterina Lombardi, and then I will get Aldo to ask you. He can be very persuasive. Where is the table?'

'I don't know anything about the table or even whether it ever existed. Only recently did I hear about it. I swear I never saw it in my father's workshop. Believe me, someone is lying.'

'Is that someone you?'

'No.'

The word burst out of her too loud and she lowered her voice to a more conciliatory tone. 'Signor Vincelli, if the table were real and if the jewels were real, they would have been destroyed when the bomb landed on my father's workshop. But I think it is a myth.'

'What do you mean?'

310

'Someone has made up this story of a jewelled table. I don't know why.'

She could feel his hesitation, sense the seed of doubt. He ran a hand over the pock-marks on his cheek and pressed his black eyes tight against the wooden grille, so that he was looking straight through the holes directly at her. She kept her gaze on him and thought about slamming the potato in his eyes.

'I do not like,' he said in a guttural voice, 'to be taken for a fool.'

'I do not take you for a fool, Signor Vincelli.'

'Look what happened to the di Marco girl when someone else made that mistake. She fell off a cliff.'

Caterina caught the note of triumph in his voice. Suddenly the shadow of the di Marcos seemed to have slipped between them, and she flicked her head to rid herself of it, but the thought of the man in white robes playing caesar on the clifftop did not vanish so easily.

Had he taken *her* for a fool?

To be duped with lies and beguiled by the sight of her father's exquisite work on the terrace of his bloodless world of marble. The confessional box abruptly became too small, claustrophobic and clammy. She felt cocooned in a smoky grey web that was binding her to the man on the other side of the grille.

Did you kill Sal Sardo? she wanted to ask, but now was not the time. Instead she narrowed her eyelids, so that she saw nothing but Drago Vincelli's pointed face, squeezed into squares by the lattice, and asked, 'Did my father work for you?'

'Yes.'

'Did he repair the damage to valuable antique pieces that were stolen?'

'Yes.'

'Does the Cavaleri family now do this work for you?'

A pause. It silenced any doubts she had.

'That is not your business.'

'I am better than Stefano Cavaleri. Ask anyone and they will tell you it's true. My work with wood is as fine as my father's, so let me work for you instead.'

This time the pause stretched so long it seemed about to snap and then there came the grating sound of a soft chesty chuckle on the other side of the grille.

'Yes,' he said at last. 'Yes, Caterina Lombardi, you may work for me. Just like your father.'

'One more thing.'

'What's that?' His tone was impatient. He was done with questions.

'The boy wants a car.'

'He is not worth a car.'

'But I am.'

Drago Vincelli leaned back in his seat and became a blur. He frightened her more like that. He let a silence build between them, and Caterina matched it, brick for brick. From inside her dim claustrophobic box she heard footsteps approach and stop outside, Aldo's heavy footsteps, and she heard a groan from the wood as he leaned against the confessional. The box became a coffin, the silence a shroud.

He had been fooling her, this Drago Vincelli. And she had

been fooling herself into believing that she could sidestep his threats. It was all ending right here. Right now.

'So, Caterina Lombardi, this is my decision. If you go to the police, you will die and your family will die. I promise you that.'

Drago's words barely penetrated, but the sound of Aldo's lumbering breath rumbled in through the cracks.

'You have a week,' Drago announced. 'One week. To find the table.'

A week. One more week of life. Her hand steadied itself by gliding along the surface of the wood.

'Find the table,' he said, 'and you can work for me.'

'And if I don't find the table?'

'You will have to discuss that with Aldo. You and your brother.'

CHAPTER TWENTY-FOUR

'Sit down, Major.'

Feeling underdressed in his dressing gown, Jake perched on the very edge of his military hospital bed in concession to his senior officer. His shoulder felt as if an elephant had him in an armlock.

'You're not walking out of here yet, so don't even think about it,' Colonel Quincy rapped. 'That's an order.'

'Sir, there is work that needs to be done. I have to . . .'

'Captain Fielding will deal with it. You say yourself he's a good man.'

'He is. A first-class investigator. But after last night's explosion, we will need every man we have on the ground to . . .'

'I mean it, Major. You remain here for the next forty-eight hours.'

'Really, sir. That is not necessary.'

The colonel's ginger eyebrows rose dangerously and he released a snort of irritation. 'Are you defying my orders, Major?'

'No, sir.' Jake looked down the ward at the regimented rows of metal beds with their grey blankets and their grey-faced occupants in need of serious care. 'I feel a fraud here. Some other poor bastard can have my bed.'

'Don't talk nonsense, man. Get well first. Don't want you keeling over on me.' Quincy glanced uneasily at the other patients. Earlier he had walked the ward, exchanging a few words with each man. 'I was one of the lucky ones,' he muttered and his jaw clicked audibly. 'I had left for my appointment by the time ...' He exhaled heavily and left the sentence incomplete.

Jake prised himself off the bed. It hurt more to sit there doing nothing about the carnage of last night than it did to force his battered limbs into action. As he straightened up, the floor tilted wildly and the walls did a dance, but he wrestled them back into position and attempted something close to a correct military stance. The dressing gown did not help.

'Have they confirmed that it was a bomb, sir?'

Colonel Quincy gave a curt nod. 'They have.' He ran a hand over his head, slowly, as if the thoughts inside it hurt. 'The perpetrators of this atrocity will be found and punished.'

'Have they any clue who laid the bomb?'

'Not yet.'

'Sir, this could be connected to our investigation into ...'

'Major Parr, not everything that goes on in Naples is centred on your investigations. I suggest you remember that.'

He spoke sharply and Jake wondered what toes he had just stepped on to set his senior officer off like that. But Colonel

Quincy did not hang about any longer. He gathered himself together, replaced his cap on his head, adjusted it to the desired angle and prepared to leave.

'Sir,' Jake stripped his voice of the frustration that threatened to boil over, 'I am requesting permission to discharge myself from hospital immediately.'

'Request denied, Major.'

A pretty army nurse came bustling over in her brown and white striped seersucker uniform and cap. She was smiling brightly but her eyes looked tired. 'Back into bed with you at once, Major Parr. We don't want you taking a turn for the worse, do we?' She flapped her hands at him with a dainty laugh.

'Indeed we don't,' Quincy mumbled and took the opportunity to depart. 'Get well, Parr,' he threw out gruffly, already heading for the swing door.

The moment the colonel was out of sight, Jake shooed away the nurse and her thermometer, and persuaded his legs to take him to the office of the Ward Sister. It was woefully slow progress and the wall became his new friend each time he leaned on it for support, fighting off the grey mist behind his eyes, but he made it to the office and requested use of the telephone.

'Harry?' he said into the mouthpiece. 'Get over here. Fast.'

'Good God, old chap, you look like death warmed up. Shouldn't you be in bed or something?'

'Don't you start, Harry. I've had a gutful of Florence Nightingales today.'

Harry Fielding chuckled, reached into his pocket with a careful glance around and extracted a slim silver hip-flask.

'Here,' Harry passed it across, 'this will buck you up.'

Jake took a swig and felt a shot of vintage brandy glide its way to where it was needed, but there was a touch of awkwardness between them as they sat down on the edge of the bed. Maybe it was the dressing gown. It made a man vulnerable. A uniform gave you power and right now Jake needed all the power he could get, but his own uniform had been reduced to tatters last night. He took another swig of brandy and hung on to the flask.

'What are they saying, Harry? Who are they dumping the blame on?'

'They are saying it was an unexploded German bomb that went off. That's the public story anyway.'

'What?'

Jake considered the possibility. Everyone knew that when the Germans withdrew from Naples in the face of the Allied advance, they had attempted a scorched earth policy. Destroying archives, torching government buildings, ransacking the museum and art galleries with a thoroughness that turned Jake's stomach. Ships were scuttled in the harbour to foul up access for the Allied fleet and, worst of all, time-bombs were planted in buildings throughout the city, hidden in offices, in palazzos, in factories, in rail stations, with the sole purpose of terrorising the populace. It succeeded.

'Unexploded bombs do detonate with distressing regularity, it's true,' he admitted, 'but it could also be because we are getting too close to someone.'

'Or it could be the work of rival political factions. Or warring clans within the Camorra. Or a revenge attack on the military. We don't know, Jake. It doesn't have to be connected with our investigation, you know it doesn't.'

But Jake knew no such thing.

He rose to his feet. Black spots like fingerprints danced in front of his eyes. He downed another mouthful of brandy and held out his hand. 'Did you bring the list?'

Harry extracted a sheet of paper from his inner pocket. 'It took some pulling of strings to get my hands on this, I can tell you.'

Jake nodded, waited for the spots to settle back into place, then inspected the paper. It was a list of sixty-three names. The letters on the page wouldn't stand still.

'Is she on it?' he demanded.

'No.'

Thank God. Jake offered up a *grazie* to San Gennaro, the patron saint of Naples. It was a list of the names of those killed or injured in the nightclub last night.

'Get me some clothes, Harry.'

'Jake, I don't advise it.'

'A uniform, quickly. Any uniform.'

He tossed the hipflask back to his friend. She was safe. Caterina was safe.

CHAPTER TWENTY-FIVE

Caterina waited for the pretty young American nurse to finish scanning the list of names of the dead. It struck Caterina as indecent, this nurse so alive, blonde curls fighting to escape from her cap, cheeks pink and well-fed, while the names in her hand were so grey and so dead.

'No Lucia Lombardi,' the nurse announced. 'And no Major Jake Parr or Leonora di Marco.' She beamed, as though personally responsible for the good news.

Caterina's grip on the desk slackened and for a moment the blonde's features blurred, so that she had to blink them back into focus.

'Thank you,' she said in English.

'Are you all right?'

'Yes.'

'You don't look it.'

Caterina was in the 300th General Hospital, an American military hospital with two thousand beds in a modern six-storey building, two wings of it used as a tuberculosis sanatorium. The place was staffed by army nurses and doctors. Caterina had come here because she trusted their lists.

'Is Major Jake Parr here as a patient?'

He was an American soldier. This is where he'd be if he was wounded. She couldn't imagine him swathed in bandages or one of his long limbs in plaster, vulnerable under an army blanket. He wasn't that kind of man.

'Please,' she added urgently. 'Is he here?'

'I'll check for you, ma'am.' After opening a new Manila folder and examining its contents with a thoroughness that Caterina appreciated, she shook her head. 'Yes, Major Parr was here, but he's not here now. He discharged himself this morning.'

'Thank you. I . . .' But the words grew foggy in her mind and she couldn't quite find their shape. She kept seeing Drago Vincelli's face sliced into shadowy squares.

'Are you all right, ma'am?'

Caterina nodded, but suddenly a seat was placed behind her, gentle hands eased her down onto it, concerned faces fussed over her in a dim blur. The blonde nurse was kneeling in front of her. How did that happen?

'When did you last eat, ma'am? You don't look good.'

Eat? Not today. Did she eat yesterday? She doubted it.

'I am okay.' She used their American word. 'Please, don't . . .'

'Let me look at your wrists.' So full of concern.

Her wrists? She looked down at them. The skin was ragged and torn. The rope damage. She hid them behind her back.

'I am okay,' she insisted. 'I had a bad night, that's all.'

A biscuit was suddenly in one hand, a cup of sweet tea in the other. She bit into the biscuit, drank the tea, and submitted to the swabbing of her wrists with antiseptic. She thanked the nurse profusely and then she hurried towards the exit, but before leaving she looked back to where the young army nurse was already tending to another. These foreign liberators had brought kindness with them to Italy, as well as chocolate and chewing gum.

Caterina entered Jake Parr's office and the grandeur of it took her by surprise. He hadn't torn down the tattered silk wall-hangings and the crumbling curlicues of the gilt ceiling mouldings, nor had he removed the dishevelled Italianness from the room and reshaped it into a proper office with American efficiency. It touched her that he had chosen not to.

He was seated behind a sumptuous desk of carved satinwood. A large round scorch-mark marred its surface where someone had placed something hot on it, which offended Caterina, but right now she only had eyes for the man behind it. Jake Parr was studying a large-scale map of southern Italy, but he was holding his head at an odd angle as though something hurt, and his skin was grey. She felt a lurch of alarm. He raised his head. At the sight of her, his mouth opened but no sound came out. He gave her a hard stare, abruptly abandoned the map and came from behind the desk, striding across the room to her. There was no shaking of hands. No 'Hello, how are you?'. Just anguish on his face.

Did she look that bad?

She tried to put on a smile but it seemed to break before it reached her face. She was suddenly conscious of the filthy sacking looped around her feet, trailing grit and blood on his army-polished floor. He gathered her in his arms, drew her to him and held her there. A soft sound came from him, and his cheek was pressed against her hair.

Caterina started to shake, great wrenching tremors that left her chilled to the bone, as if a poison were working its way through her system. The poison of Drago Vincelli's words, thick and toxic. And all the time, Jake held her steady until the storm had passed and she was breathing again. Her cheek rested against his shoulder, the wetness of tears on the material of his shirt.

Was she crying? She should have been embarrassed, but she wasn't. She had a sense of the layers of skin and of US Army cotton between them ceasing to exist and her blood pulsed in time with his, and she could so easily have let the world stay like that, but she took a deep breath and lifted her head from his shoulder. She wasn't broken. She didn't want him to think she was broken.

She smiled at him. 'Hello.'

His gaze was dark with concern, moving from her eyes to her mouth to her chin and up to her brow, tiny shifts of focus, as if putting her face back together in his mind.

'You're here. In one piece,' he said. 'That's what matters.' She could hear the relief.

His forehead had a dozen small nicks across it and a purple

bruise spilled from the corner of his jaw, down the side of his neck and crawled under the clean collar of his shirt. Caterina lifted her hands and gently clasped his freshly shaven jaw between them.

'We're both here, both in one piece,' she responded and raised herself on her toes within the cradle of his arms. She brushed her lips over his. 'Both alive,' she murmured.

One week. To be alive. She could feel the pulse of her blood strong in her veins. In her ears. At her throat. In her ragged wrists. A sense of being alive, so intense that it bubbled out of her in a laugh, and each breath tasted good.

'Breakfast?' she queried.

He smiled and kissed her forehead. The gesture was light, gone in a second, but the intimacy of it lingered on her skin.

One week. To be alive.

He sat her down and fed her coffee and almond biscotti, and then a brandy. It set her insides on fire but the grey fog inside her head lifted so she could think clearly.

'Are you all right, Major? Not injured?' she asked.

'Nothing much. The odd knock, that's all.' His face grew still, images from last night crowding his eyes, but he blinked them away and said, 'Call me Jake.'

'At the hospital they told me it was a bomb in the nightclub. My mother's name wasn't on the casualty list. Do you have any idea what happened to her? Was she hurt?'

'I'm sorry, I don't know.'

To her bewilderment he knelt down on the hard marble floor

in front of her chair. He lifted one of her feet and rested it on the palm of his hand.

'Your mother was with me when the bomb went off, and unhurt. But I don't know what happened to her after the ceiling collapsed. I have checked all the hospitals,' he said. 'No Lucia Lombardi on any of their lists of patients.' With crisp military efficiency his fingers worked loose the tangled knot that held the sacking shoe in place and began to unwind the filth-encrusted strips. They stank. 'I checked hotels too, but there was no trace of her. The owner of the nightclub has no address for her either – he paid her cash for her performance. So I'm afraid I haven't been able to trace her.'

He wasn't looking at her. His attention was on her foot, removing the sacking, layer by layer, so he didn't have sight of her face. Didn't see what it meant to her.

'You searched for her? For my mother?'

His eyes shot to her face and whatever he saw there, it made his voice soften, the military edge peeling off it. 'Tell me, Caterina,' he said gently, 'why are you wearing shreds of old sacks on your feet?'

She told him, piece by piece, what happened last night. The *scugnizzi*, the prick in the arm, clawing back to consciousness in the shed. She told him the facts. That was enough, he didn't need more. She hid the rage. More than anything she concealed the fear, buried it under a detailed description of the leader of the pack and the run through the backstreets of Naples.

Jake said little, reacting with only an occasional question or an intense look that scoured her face. At times a frown or a long breath. When she told him of her decision to run with the street kids, he gave a tight shake of his head but made no comment and she was grateful to him. All the time she talked, his hands worked on her feet. When her first foot was freed from its rags, he cradled it carefully and studied the state of its chafed sole, running his fingertips over the patches of red and raw skin.

'Jake,' she murmured, 'who do you think planted the bomb?'

'They are saying it was one left behind by the Germans.'

He placed her foot on the floor and started on the second mess of sacking. This one was worse.

'But who do *you* think it was?'

'I think it was intended as a warning to our Intelligence Unit,' he replied, 'to keep our noses out of the business of searching for stolen artefacts.' He paused, staring down at the dirt under her toenails. Oddly she felt no embarrassment.

He glanced up and saw her watching his hands. A smile touched his eyes and he added, 'I have no proof of that, needless to say. It's my gut feeling.' He resumed the unwinding of the filthy strips and found them welded to her heel with blood.

'Do you think Drago Vincelli is behind it?' she asked.

'Yes, I do. He is a known bomb specialist.'

'Arrest him.'

'On what charge?'

'Any charge. Just throw him in prison and chuck away the key.' She said it quietly because she wanted him to understand she meant it.

He looked up at her, eyes serious, while the warmth of

his hand was wrapped around her foot. 'This is no longer Mussolini's Fascist state, Caterina. There are laws to respect.'

He took a pristine white handkerchief from his pocket and a carafe of water from his desk. While she told him about entering the church of Santa Maria, he dipped the handkerchief into the water and, one patch at a time, he soaked the sacking so that it peeled away from her heel and she could flex it with relief. Jake proceeded to bathe both her feet, each toe, each bone, each curve, soothing them with the water, removing the grit.

Caterina didn't want him to stop.

His dark head was bowed as he worked, so that she couldn't see his face, and she knew that was how he wanted it, keeping his emotions from her, letting her talk herself out. Only his hands spoke to her with a gentle eloquence. All she could see of him was his dark hair, thick and wavy. Italian hair. She wanted to sink her fingers into the springy depths of it and to rummage round among his thoughts, but instead she kept her hands wrapped around her brandy glass.

He left the room, but returned only minutes later with a pair of black canvas plimsolls dangling from one hand and a knife in the other. He fitted the shoes on to her feet. They were far too long, like clown shoes on her, so he removed them, sliced the toe off each, and replaced them, winding the laces under the sole before knotting them on top. They looked odd but were surprisingly comfortable.

'Thank you, Jake,' she said and touched his khaki shoulder as he sat on his heels in front of her, checking his handiwork. His shirt felt warm, his muscles tense, the bruise breathing out its own heat, and she wondered what he'd say if she undid his buttons and laid her hand on the damaged area, keeping it safe from the day's slings and arrows.

'I went into the confessional,' she told him.

He regarded her with surprise. It struck her that he had the face of an expert listener. Inquisitive but receptive. Easy to talk to.

When had this happened? How had it changed? She had moved from seeing this American soldier as her enemy to viewing him as her friend without being aware of the steps in between. It was about trust, she realised. She trusted this dedicated police officer. So she said it again.

'I went into the confessional.'

'Why was that?' he asked. 'What sins were you admitting to?' His dark eyes smiled at the corners, as if he thought she might have a whole pocketful of sins she wasn't admitting to.

'To speak to Drago Vincelli.'

The police officer in him did not allow the shock to show, but he rose to his feet and stood over her, very still.

'He was there? In the confessional box?'

'Nearer to me than you are.'

She didn't wait for more questions. She sat there in her cut-down shoes, knowing that the minutes of her life were counting down, and related her conversation with Drago Vincelli. She described the sight of him through the grille, the shadowy squares of his pointed jaw and his dark-etched profile. The flash of gold in his mouth.

He leaned close. 'Is that everything?'

She considered, remembering the satisfied laugh when Drago Vincelli believed he had hooked her to take her father's place, though she only intended to find incriminating evidence against Vincelli. And then there was the threat at the end.

'Yes,' she said, returning his gaze. 'Everything.'

It was hard to lie to Jake; his scrutiny was so intense. He straightened up and became brisk and professional.

'I'll order a unit together,' he said at once. 'Right away. We'll move in on the church of Santa Maria before they . . .'

'No. He has gone.'

'We'll drag the priest in for questioning. And the street kid as well, the one who led you there for the meeting. Vanni, you said his name was.'

'He'll have vanished.'

'I'll inform the Italian police that . . .'

'No, Jake, no. He threatened my family if I go to the police.'

An uncomfortable silence spread through the room. Caterina prodded her wrist, jabbing at the ragged skin to bring back the rage because she needed rage, not fear, needed to feel it break through her skin.

'Why so many "No's", Caterina?' Jake's tone was quiet. 'Why all these "No's" to stop me going there? What are you keeping from me?'

She wanted to reach out to him, to make him understand the clarity of her decision to do this without the Naples police, where tongues were loose and money passed from hand to hand. Her brother's life was at stake. She could take no risks.

'Jake, please don't go barging in there with heavy military

boots. If Vincelli believes you are involved, he could change his mind about doing a deal with me.'

'A deal? You've struck a deal with him?'

She had to tell him.

'Yes. He has given me one week to find the jewelled table.'

'Caterina, are you mad? The table may not even exist any more. Does he realise that?'

'Yes.'

'But still you made the deal?'

'Yes.'

He did not ask her why. He knew. He knew what was at stake. He had seen dead people walking before. He shook himself, ridding himself of some emotion she could only guess at, and moved quickly to his desk where he picked up the telephone. 'I'll fetch a car to drive you home.'

Before she could refuse, a knock sounded on the door.

'Not now,' Jake shouted.

But the door opened and into the room walked Harry Fielding.

'I've come to inform you, Jake, that Colonel Quincy has ordered me to lead our unit up into the mountains today to do a sweep on the village of Sant'Agata. He thinks you are still in your hospital bed.' He grinned. 'I didn't disabuse him of the notion.'

Jake nodded. 'Thank you, Harry.' He said no more.

Harry's gaze travelled from the American to Caterina, taking in her ill-fitting dress and unconventional footwear, before commenting, 'I'm glad to see you safe, Caterina. But for God's sake get some rest, both of you. You're not looking good.'

'Thank you for that advice, Captain,' Jake said.

Harry headed for the door, brisk and businesslike, but Jake stopped him.

'Good luck, Harry. Take care. Watch your back.'

Harry gave an elegant salute and left. Jake stared at the door for a long moment, then poured himself a brandy and drank it straight down.

'Now,' he announced, 'I'll drive you home.'

'If you lend me the fare, I can catch a train.'

He sighed. 'Don't be difficult, Caterina.'

'I have to go somewhere first. Here in Naples.'

He frowned. 'Please, Caterina. It is dangerous for you to go running round the streets of this city like one of those urchins. Last night showed that.'

Caterina shook her head and watched the room and its bookshelves spin. 'No, Jake.' She laughed and was pleased it sounded real. 'I've been granted a week. For one week I am not in danger, so I must use it well. I will accept your offer of a lift, thank you, but I have to see someone first. I'll come back here and meet you outside in an hour.'

'Who are you meeting?'

But she was already out the door and running for the streets.

Caterina watched the shop from across the road for ten minutes but during that time no one went in, and no one came out. Lights shimmered inside but a metal mesh was fitted on the outside of the window, so it was next to impossible to see what was on display unless you were right outside.

Caterina had to restrain herself, make herself wait and watch. But she didn't have long and didn't want a customer to intrude on the scene and spoil her chances.

Customer?

She gave a shake of her head. No one had money for the likes of these goods. This was a smart street with elegant buildings boasting what must have been smart shops before the war. Couturier fashion houses, beauty salons, perfumeries and posh little emporia for grooming pampered poodles, but now the shelves were mostly bare and dusty, pockets were empty and poodles eaten. A sense of desolation trickled through the gutters of Naples alongside the cigarette butts and the lost dreams.

The name in bold gold lettering above the shop told Caterina all she needed to know. *Orlando Bartoli. Jeweller.* The one whose corpse Harry Fielding told her had been dragged out of the harbour. She entered the shop.

The girl behind the counter was sharp-eyed and had a look of Mussolini about her. Big square head and a jutting jaw, though she had more hair. It was long and straight and very black. She could be no more than fourteen but was confident behind the counter, as if she'd been standing there for years, guarding the smattering of jewellery on display in the cabinet in front of her, a few brooches, a pendant, a tray of antique rings. Caterina had no doubt that a gun lay somewhere within reach but safely out of sight.

'Buongiorno,' Caterina greeted her in a friendly manner. 'Are you Signorina Bartoli?'

'I am.'

The girl spread her hands to include the shop, implying that she and the jewels came as a package. The place must once have been impressive, when the walls glittered with polished cabinets of precious gems, gold and silverware, the badges of the wealthy elite of Naples. Now all but one showcase held shoes, brand new, soft shiny leather that soaked up the light. New shoes were like gold-dust in this stricken city.

'Could I speak with your mother, signorina?'

The girl's gaze raked up and down Caterina's shabby grey dress and landed on her shoes. 'Mamma,' she called out, without shifting her eyes from her customer.

A door at the back opened and a woman stepped into the shop, fair where her daughter was dark, and small-featured. Both were clad in the dense black of mourning. She welcomed Caterina with a surprised smile, as though unused to customers.

'How can I help you, signorina?' She had a kind face and was quietly spoken, sadness etched into the lines around her mouth.

'My condolences, Signora Bartoli, on the loss of your husband.'

The woman pulled the black scarf tighter around her head. 'Who are you?'

'I am Caterina Lombardi.'

The woman's eyes widened and her hands flew to her mouth to silence the sound that struggled from her lips.

'You're his daughter,' she whispered.

'I am Antonio Lombardi's daughter, yes, it's true.'

Signora Bartoli's soft hazel eyes filled with tears as she

reached out and clasped Caterina to her ample bosom. 'Poor little kitten,' she crooned.

An intense wave of this woman's emotions broke over Caterina's head. To be held like this by a pair of strong caring arms in a way that her own mother never held her, was almost too much, and to her horror a single sob shuddered its way up through her chest.

'Mamma,' the girl sounded cautious, 'she may be dangerous. Here to spy on us.'

'Let her spy as much as she wants. There's nothing to find.'

Gently Caterina extricated herself from the folds of the pillowy bosom. 'I am not a danger to you, Signora Bartoli.'

The woman touched Caterina's cheek. 'I know you're not, *bella*.'

'I'm here to ask about the table that my father made.'

'You'll have to stand in the queue then.'

'Who else is questioning you?'

'The police. And others.' She spat the final word.

'Which others? The Camorra? Or a man with a streak of white in his black hair?'

'Forget them,' the jeweller's wife shrugged. 'I am sorry about the loss of your father. He was a good man. He had a warm heart.' The woman's fist thumped her own heart. 'Like my own Orlando. They were friends. Both good men.'

'Thank you, signora. I always believed my father was a good man. But now I am wondering how well I knew him.'

'Believe your heart, child,' she said firmly. 'Always believe your heart.'

'What did you tell the men who came to question you?'

'Nothing. I know nothing. My daughter Delfina knows nothing. My son Edmondo,' she waved a hand towards the rear door, 'knows nothing.'

'That's what you told the police?'

'Yes.'

'The Army Intelligence Officers?'

The woman's eyebrows rose. 'Yes. You know about them too?'

Caterina would not be put off a second time. 'The man with the streak of white in his hair and the heavyweight one at his side. Did they come?'

The woman shuddered theatrically and her daughter came to stand beside her, sliding her arm around her mother's thick waist. The easy familiarity of the movement touched Caterina. *Sweetheart, lost your tongue? Aren't you going to give your mother a kiss?*

'Is it true that you know nothing?' Caterina asked.

The woman casually kissed the side of her daughter's head. 'Of course not.'

From behind the counter a glass of Marsala materialised for each of them. Caterina felt it mingle with the earlier brandy and slow her pulse to a more manageable rate. The three of them sat on stools in a triangle with their drinks and Caterina coaxed out of Signora Bartoli what had happened to her husband. It had started with a police knock on the door in the middle of the night. They had forced Bartoli to open his safe – because of a tip-off they said they had received – and they spotted a small unframed painting of the Madonna and Child hidden there, but not before the jeweller snatched out a gun from inside the safe and pumped two bullets into the chest of the chief of police.

Signora Bartoli wept. Her daughter refilled her glass.

'He ran,' Delfina said angrily. 'He ran with the painting and vanished, leaving us with a wounded policeman in our house. Oh Papà, oh Papà ...'

Caterina put her arms around the girl and for a while the only sound in the shop was the soft whisper of weeping and murmurs of comfort from Caterina. It was strange, this intimacy with two women she scarcely knew, but something was binding them together, she could feel the strands of it cutting into her flesh. Something strong.

'What made your husband shoot the policeman, Signora? Why would he do such a thing?'

The jeweller's wife brushed a hand across her face, wiping away the sorrow. 'Orlando was hiding the stolen Tintoretto painting for someone. I don't know who, so don't bother asking. He didn't tell me. But he knew he was a dead man if he lost that valuable painting.'

A handkerchief came out of a pocket and more silent tears flowed down the woman's cheeks.

'Papà was afraid,' Delfina explained. 'And he was right to be afraid. We don't know who killed him but it must have been because they were frightened he would betray them if the police took him in for questioning. So he was dumped in the harbour.'

Signora Bartoli suddenly eyed Caterina carefully. 'Is that why you are here? Have they come for you?'

Caterina nodded. 'But I don't intend to be dumped in the harbour.'

Jake was stuck in an argument that was going nowhere. The US Army sergeant had the kind of solid face that reminded Jake of a barn door that had been firmly bolted. Nothing was getting in or out.

'I'm sorry, sir, but that's not possible.'

'I require a car,' Jake informed him yet again. 'A civilian vehicle.'

'Sir, you can sign out a jeep or one of our motorbikes. But no civilian vehicles. It's against regulations.'

'Soldier, in that shed behind you are at least twenty civilian cars belonging to no one and doing nothing but sitting there gathering dust. Open up at once.'

The soldier was standing to attention, gaze fixed somewhere around the tip of Jake's left ear, but with a mutinous hitch to his shoulders he marched across to the vast corrugated shed that sprawled in the burning sunshine. He unlocked the double doors and slid one open. It squealed in protest, and Jake strode inside where an array of assorted cars was huddled together under layers of dust. Some were big bulky machines, others were small and sad, shoved into corners.

Jake prowled among them and could not resist a smile. He spotted a 1936 Chrysler Airflow, like the one he used to drive at home in Milwaukee a lifetime ago. He stroked its stream-lined nose and patted its sloping backside, remembering a day when he'd driven a girl he was dating out onto the edge of the woodland, so she could fly her hawk. The bird reminded him of Caterina. The way she turned her head, the focus she possessed. He recalled the way the hawk's yellow talons gripped the brown cloth of the seat-back and he suspected that Caterina's grip would be just as sharp.

It was tempting to slide behind the three-spoke steering wheel once more, to go back in time to the person he was then. These cars were ones that had been plucked off the streets of Naples, their owners fled or dead. It was stifling in the shed, the metal bodies radiating heat. The interior was dim, but a bright shaft of sunlight fell through the open door and caught the fender of a humble Italian automobile. Jake wandered over. Its headlamp was cracked and its paintwork scratched.

'I'll take that one,' he announced.

'Tell me about the jewels,' Caterina said.

She noticed a look pass between the two Bartoli women.

'The ones,' Caterina added, 'for the table my father was commissioned to make.'

Still no response.

'Where did they come from?'

'From Count di Marco.'

That came as no surprise.

'My Orlando went across to Capri, fool that he was, and returned with a box wrapped in a goatskin. It was full of emeralds and sapphires and diamonds so big they could poke your eye out.' She paused and dragged a hand across her mouth, then wiped the back of it on her black skirt as if the words tasted sour. 'The diamonds had dried blood on them. None of the jewels was new. I washed each one of them with my own hands to remove the dirt, and the water turned red.' She stared at her fingers accusingly.

'Have you any idea where the table is now?'

'No.'

'Signora, why do you tell me all this? I am a stranger to you.'

A look of surprise crossed the woman's lined face, but it was Delfina, her daughter, who answered.

'Because they were blood brothers, your papà and my papà. That makes you family.'

'Blood brothers?'

She pictured them, two Italian men, each drawing a knife across his palm, blood slithering to the stone floor. Clasping hands, mingling their blood. A blood brother was held closer than family.

But why? What made them do it?

A thought slid into her head. 'Have you heard of the Caesar Club?' she asked.

Again it was the young girl who answered. 'Yes, of course. Papà and your father both belonged to it. Its members meet in Naples.'

'What do they do?'

The mother gave a snort of indulgence, her heavy bosom rising alarmingly. 'They drink and talk men's talk, and they think they make the world turn around their little fingers.'

'Why do they think that?'

'Because they are men, and men are fools.'

'Are all the members of the club blood brothers?'

But at that precise moment the door at the rear of the shop swung open and a tall young man walked in, head held at an arrogant angle, slender hips leading the way. He was clearly the brother of the girl. He possessed the same face, but on him it looked good, with the same intelligent eyes. He wore a coarse brown apron and held a half-finished black shoe dangling from one hand, the smell of oil on his fingers.

'Mamma, I . . .'

But it was not the young cobbler who attracted Caterina's attention, it was the other person inside the back room. He was seated at a table, surrounded by leather skins, his head turned to look into the interior of the shop. At the sight of Caterina, his mouth fell open.

'Carlo!' she exclaimed.

She felt the small hairs on her bare arms rise in shock. It was Carlo Cavaleri, her childhood friend and a flush was rising up his handsome cheeks, a curved cobbler's blade in his hand.

'What are you doing here?' Caterina asked.

'I work here.'

'I thought you worked at your uncle's garage.'

Carlo nodded. 'You thought right. But I hate engines and grease and being yelled at by Uncle Vito. So on my days off, I come here to learn a new trade.'

Signora Bartoli bundled her son back into the workroom and shut the door on them.

'They are good boys, those two,' she said. 'Fine cobblers.'

She walked over to one of the shelves where their handiwork

was on display and selected a pair of ladies' shoes that were the colour of ripe figs, not black, but not quite purple. 'These should fit,' she said and thrust them into Caterina's arms. 'Put them on.'

'No,' Caterina protested. 'They are too valuable to give away.'

The woman gave a gentle tap to Caterina's cheek. 'Do as you're told. You are family.'

'Then tell me,' Caterina said, 'about Drago Vincelli.'

'Drago,' the signora snapped. 'Stay away from that evil man. Years ago he used to be a good man. He fought against Mussolini alongside your father and my Orlando. But he got greedy. He turned bad and now that the war is over, he is turning others bad too. Stay away from him, I tell you. Enough death in this city. No need for more.'

Was that true?

Caterina thought not. One more. There needed to be one more death.

'Where can I find him?' she asked.

The woman looked away, mopped her eyes with her handkerchief and cast a quick glance at her daughter who gave the smallest shake of her head.

'I don't know,' Signora Bartoli stated.

Caterina stepped forward and entwined a finger into the black sleeve. 'He is going to kill me if I don't find him first. Just like he killed your Orlando.'

'Caterina Lombardi, I don't want you to die.'

'So tell me. For my father's sake.'

'If you go up against Drago Vincelli, you will end up with

your throat cut for certain and I won't permit that. He has men behind him. Powerful men. They will not want you spoiling their plans.' Signora Bartoli's expression was tearful, but her mouth hardened. 'So no, I don't know where to find Drago Vincelli.'

It was a lie. They all knew it.

'What men?' Caterina asked quietly. 'What plans?'

'Enough Caterina. Your papà always said you asked too many questions.' She shook her head in sorrow at the mention of her father.

But Caterina refused to let go. 'Who are these powerful men? And what is it they do? Do they organise the stealing and selling of artefacts? Without getting their own fingers dirty?'

Signora Bartoli turned again to her daughter, but Caterina stepped between them. 'Is that it, signora? Tell me. Is that what they do? Is that what your Orlando and my papà did?'

A nod, so faint it was scarcely a nod.

'And is that group of men,' Caterina continued relentlessly, 'the Caesar Club?'

Signora Bartoli wrapped her arms around Caterina's neck and kissed her cheek.

'Go now,' the jeweller's wife whispered. 'You know too much.'

But Caterina was certain there was more to know.

Caterina kicked open the door. She entered the shed.

She expected nerves to come barrelling at her, but they

didn't. She was calm. No panic. But she had forgotten not one moment of last night, of being hog-tied and humiliated in this filthy scrap of shelter, forced to bargain with her shoes and to lie still among the stench of fish while one boy strutted.

She pretended she had come back here to find the *scugnizzi,* pretended even to herself. Not that she really expected them to be here. Their sleeping sacks were gone. They had flown and like wild birds they left no trace of themselves. By daylight she saw the empty fish boxes and discarded ends of tarred rope that lay in the corner. Her hands were steady as she squatted down and tipped a small stone jar of kerosene oil over the boxes, oil for which she had swapped her cut-down US Army plimsolls. It smelled strongly, burning her nostrils. Outside, the harsh cry of seagulls, like voices of the dead, increased her sense of isolation and quickened her pulse.

She drew out a box of matches from the pocket of the ragged grey dress, removed one match, and struck it. She watched its flame consume the sliver of wood, then threw it.

The match arced through the air, flaring as it sucked in more oxygen, a firefly in the gloom. By the time it hit the oil and uttered a roar of pleasure, Caterina had gone.

CHAPTER TWENTY-SIX

Jake saw Caterina flying up the street towards him, speeding past pedestrians, wings on her heels. She was late, but she looked unstoppable in her too-big grey dress that billowed out behind her. He adjusted the muscles of his face to hide the rush of relief he felt that she had returned to him in one piece and opened the car door for her.

'Nice shoes,' he commented.

'I didn't steal them.'

She didn't enter the car immediately but instead stood on its running-board, inspecting him slowly from head to foot and then the small vehicle. He was wearing no uniform, just a soft white shirt, sleeves rolled up, cream slacks and canvas shoes, and the vehicle was a black Lancia Aprilia that had seen better days. She nodded approval.

'Nice camouflage,' she said with a smile, and slid into the passenger seat.

He had brought trouble into her life ten days ago when he

marched into her Sorrento workshop in his uniform, and he had no intention of doing so again this time, so he had discarded the khaki. He drove rapidly through Naples, aware of the extra *polizia* on street corners and military boots patrolling the piazzas. They were jumpy, nervous of another bomb. He didn't point them out to Caterina but knew she would notice. Her sharp eyes missed little.

A jagged wall from a bombed building had collapsed in Via Foriaso, which meant he had to do a detour through the backstreets behind the pedimented National Museum, but after that he put his foot down. The Lancia wheezed its way up the hills, rattling its windows in their sockets, and as they climbed, the wind off the blue waters of the bay snaked into the car, ruffling Caterina's short hair and bringing the smell of wide horizons to them, instead of the stink of the city.

They had just squeezed their way through the narrow streets of the flower-strewn village of Sant'Agnello when Jake asked outright, 'Who was the curly-haired sheep you danced with last night at the nightclub?'

'No one,' she replied, staring ahead.

'Does this *no one* have a name and a purpose?'

'No.'

Jake sighed. 'His name is Giulio Macchione and he works for his father in the wine export business. More to the point, he is the brother of the ex-fiancé of your friend on Capri, Leonora di Marco.'

He paused. It was a risk. This display. She might open the car door and leap out, or draw around her an armour of silence. He couldn't predict. His gaze was fixed on the tight switchbacks that made the road feel alive, but out of the corner of his eye he saw Caterina turn her head to stare at him. She said nothing. Just stared. He could feel the heat of it on his cheek.

'Okay,' he admitted. 'I checked the guy out.'

She laughed, a real laugh that brightened the dowdy car.

'Have you heard of the Caesar Club?' she asked.

'No.' He slid a glance at her. 'What is it?'

'It seems it might be involved in all this. Giulio Macchione is a member and claims it is nothing more than a Naples drinking club. You might see what more you can dig up on it, Mr Police Officer.' Her damaged arm reached out and lightly her fingers touched the bare expanse of his forearm. They felt like feathers. Warm feathers on his skin.

'I will make enquiries,' he told her.

'Discreetly.'

'Of course.'

Her fingers vanished. He became businesslike.

'I will take you home first and then meet you at the bell tower. We should discuss what could have happened to the jewelled table if it did manage to survive the explosion in the workshop.'

She wound down the window and let the sage-scented air buffet her face. 'If it was ever there in the first place,' she said softly and turned to him. 'Are you all right? Should you be in hospital?'

'Of course not.' He shot a scowl at her. 'Don't I look all right to you?'

She was smiling. 'No. No, you don't.'

*

345

Caterina let Jake drop her at her house. At the end of the dusty street, to be exact. She wasn't going to risk him getting her grandfather's machete in his face for keeping her out all night. The heat was intense despite the shadows that packed the narrow space, and she looked forward to tearing off the heavy grey dress that had welded itself to her back. But she had scarcely laid her hand on the front door when it swung open and her grandfather's firm grip dragged her inside the house. Instantly his fingers were on her face, feeling its curves and planes, scouring the surface of her skin with his calluses.

'Where are the tears?' he bellowed at her. 'Where are the tears of remorse?'

His breath smelled of too many cigarettes, she noticed, even while he rocked her head from side to side, as if to tear it off.

'Where are the cries for forgiveness, Caterina Lombardi, for dancing your decency away in a nightclub in Naples, for letting grown men paw you?' He shook her harder. 'For staying out all night while your grandfather wept with shame for your honour.'

Caterina placed her hands over his and pulled them from her face. Her cheeks were scarlet. He would know, despite his empty eyes, he would know by the heat of her skin.

'Nonno, what do you know about my being in a nightclub in Naples?'

He said nothing, but Caterina jerked free and swung towards the doorway of the living room. She could smell her. Even before she saw her, she could smell her. Her lies. Her perfume.

'Hello, Mamma.'

The air in the room was thick with a grey shroud of cigarette smoke. Her mother must have been there for some hours.

Go away. That's what Caterina wanted to say. Go away, Lucia Lombardi, before you rip my heart up through my throat and leave it bleeding in the dirt like you did eleven years ago.

'What do you want?' she demanded.

'Is that the way to greet your Mamma, my precious *bella*?'

Her mother's full scarlet lips were set into a gentle smile, her voice smooth and silky as she rose from her seat and held out her arms.

Don't. Inside her head Caterina shouted the word at herself. *Don't move.* Remain here in the doorway. Where she cannot touch you. Cannot blind you to her lies, cannot lay a trail of honey. There were tears glistening in her mother's eyes as she stood poised, unmoving, her arms extended to her daughter in entreaty. No, Caterina thought, you do not trick me so easily. But her feet betrayed her and stepped forward.

She had no recollection of crossing the distance between them. She stepped forward and felt her mother's arms enfold her in the embrace she had dreamed of ten thousand times at night with only her pillow as witness. Her mother's skin felt like gossamer against her cheek, softer than she had remembered, and her caress sent treacherous shivers of pleasure rippling through Caterina.

'It's such a shame that you've ruined your lovely long hair,' her mother murmured.

Carefully Caterina removed that stiletto from her heart and stepped back. Her mother had twisted her hair up into a sleek knot at the back of her head, her eyebrows were blonde and

347

plucked to a thin line but her long eyelashes were dark. She wore a black dress, stylish and Rome-cut, with elegant cap sleeves and a dropped waist that skimmed her hips. She was slender but not thin. No hollows in her cheeks, no shortage of meat or cheese in her firm flesh. Caterina knew she was forty-one, but she looked younger, except for her eyes. There was nothing girlish about those steel-blue eyes.

'You've seen her,' her grandfather growled at Lucia Lombardi from the doorway. 'Now get out.'

'No,' her mother said quickly. 'Don't be so cruel.'

'Signora, you betrayed my son. You dragged the Lombardi name through the dirt. You deserted your children.' His voice was rising, strung tight with rage. 'Get out of my house and never come back.'

She turned a sad smile on Caterina. 'Is that what you want too, my darling daughter?' She put out a hand, palm up in gentle entreaty. 'Forgive me.'

Forgive me?

This time Caterina's feet didn't let her down but did exactly what they were told. They walked over to her grandfather and she stood beside him shoulder to shoulder, and all the words inside her head remained locked there. They couldn't escape.

'Get out,' Nonno said once more.

Her mother's smile faltered, struggled to remain on her lips, but failed.

Why was she wearing black? The question slipped into Caterina's head. In mourning for her dead husband? Her dead Cavaleri lover? Her dead German general lover? Or someone else? A thousand someone elses, for all Caterina knew, and she held on to that thought like armour to ward off the blue eyes.

'My son,' Lucia Lombardi said suddenly, her tone bright and determined. 'Luca. Where is my son, Luca?'

'Out on the fishing boats.'

'When will he be back?'

'This evening.'

'Then I shall return.'

'No,' Nonno raged, rapping his cane on the floor like a gun-shot. 'You will not return, Lucia Lombardi. Stay away from this house. You bring nothing but pain and misery to this family. Your son does not need you.' His muscles were clenching and unclenching under the loose folds of skin on his face.

'Nonno, Luca has a right to see his mother.'

'No! Never!'

'You are a cantankerous pig-headed bastard,' Lucia Lombardi hissed and strode past him to the front door.

'Where will you stay?'

'Ah, my Caterina, I hoped to stay here. So who knows?' She gave a crooked smile. 'Perhaps I will sleep in the gutter.'

The door slammed behind her.

Jake observed the mother as she emerged from the house and strutted towards the far end of the street. Judging by the speed with which her black high heels were clicking on the paving slabs, things hadn't gone well. He stubbed out his cigarette and fell into step beside her.

'Hello again, Signora Lombardi.'

She flashed a glance of irritation at him, clearly not welcoming the intrusion. 'Go away.'

'Did you leave your daughter in one piece?'

'Go to hell.' She said it easily. As if she said it often.

'Not yet. I have some questions to ask first.'

She stopped walking and stared straight at him, hands on hips. 'I remember you, soldier, even without your fancy uniform. You are the lover boy who kept my daughter out all night.'

'I brought her home, that's all.' He considered adding, 'I'm the one who saved your life last night,' but he rethought that. Instead he asked in a casual way, 'Tell me, Signora Lombardi, did your husband ever confide in you where he kept the antiques he was restoring? A secret storeroom somewhere?'

Her hand lashed out and would have slammed into his left cheek, but he caught it, his fingers tight on her wrist. Anger made her eyes flat and colourless. Before he could start to release his hold on her, her other hand shot up and smacked his right cheek. Hard. The jagged pieces still loose inside his head from last night's explosion crashed together and stabbed into the back of his eyeballs. Her laugh was quick, light and stiletto sharp. Her arm coiled itself through his, her face turned up to him appealingly, her mouth soft.

'Soldier boy,' she said, 'you don't get anything in this tawdry life for nothing. There is always a price to pay. You deserved the slap for sticking your nose in where it doesn't belong.' She paused and stroked his battered cheek. She ruffled her shoulder against him in a good imitation of contentment. 'Let's get a drink, soldier.'

'The question is, signora, do you have anything worth selling?'

She laughed. Threw her head back and laughed with a freedom that was infectious, so that Jake was smiling as they walked down the street, her arm still through his. He heard a sound behind him. He glanced over his shoulder and caught sight of the figure of Caterina standing in her doorway, her face as grey as her dress. She was watching him.

Lucia Lombardi led him to a bar. Not in Piazza Tasso for everyone to see. No, this was tucked out of sight in the shadow of Sorrento's ancient town wall, a tiny dark room with four rickety metal chairs outside jammed against the crumbling stucco for shade. Inside, two men in work clothes stained by cigarettes and sweat were hunched over beers at a counter and a half-bald goat on a tether lay in a blade of sunlight that sliced through the shutters. Lucia perched in a corner on a high stool which showed off her fine legs and drew the gaze of the bar owner when he brought the drinks.

While her hands were occupied – an espresso in one and a grappa in the other – Jake risked the question again but he was all prepared to duck if the coffee came his way. 'Did your husband have a secret storeroom?'

'No.' She downed her coffee, and the shot glass of grappa followed on its heels. She licked her lips. It was hard not to watch, she did it so expertly. 'No, he didn't.'

The expression on her face was relaxed, with a professional friendliness to it that made Jake wonder what she'd been up to since the Germans pulled out. But there was tension in the hair-line creases around her eyes, a tautness that betrayed her. He could spot the lie before it came.

'It was the Cavaleri family who had all the secrets,' she said in a voice low enough to force him to move closer. 'Not the Lombardis.'

'What do you mean?'

'I mean that black-hearted old witch, Signora Augusta Cavaleri. It's no wonder her son's wife committed suicide. I would too if I had to live with that evil old crone. She is a gaoler to her sons.'

'Signora, as I understand it,' he pointed out, 'Roberto Cavaleri's wife took her own life because you ran off to Rome with her husband.'

She smiled, wide and nonchalant. 'Yes, there was that too, I suppose.'

She sat straight-backed on her stool, composed in her elegant black frock. He offered her a cigarette and lit it for her. The awful thing was that he found himself liking her, even though he didn't want to like her, this woman who had deserted her children.

'What secrets,' he queried, 'did the Cavaleri family have?'

'You'll have to ask the Cavaleri witch herself.'

'I'm asking you.'

She shrugged. 'If I knew them, they wouldn't be secrets any more, I promise you that.'

Quietly in the dim smoky bar, he questioned her about her husband, Antonio Lombardi, and to his surprise, she answered.

Crisp and precise. Antonio's business was intarsia, a form of wood-inlay, and to her astonishment he had become renowned, with customers coming from all over Italy, all over the world. Americans were passionate about his work. He'd spent his life scouring through catalogues for rare veneers. Yes, parcels came and went, but no, she never enquired about them, and she detested his workshop. Never went there. A place for donkeys, for people who thought with their hands instead of their heads.

But when he mentioned the daughter, it was a different matter. That subject ruffled her smooth feathers and she withdrew another cigarette from his pack on the table, shrugging her shapely shoulders again.

'Antonio was an idealist,' she remarked, using the term as an insult. 'Not a realist. He hated Mussolini and his Fascists with a fury that would summon the demons from hell. It's why that daughter of mine idolised her father. They both believed that all the world's ills could be cured.'

'What drew you to come back here now?' he asked.

She snapped her fingers at the barman and another grappa materialised in front of her which she drank down. 'My daughter and son, of course.' She narrowed her cool blue eyes at him. 'I miss them.'

'Is that so?'

'I need a job,' she stated. 'The Pompeii Club is closed for repairs because of that filthy bomb.'

So that was it.

'A body has to eat.' She glanced at the empty glass on the table. 'And drink.' Her scarlet lips spread in a teasing smile.

'You Yanks hold this country's purse-strings now.' She slid her fingers over his hand.

Jake rose to his feet, brushing off her touch.

'I will see if I can find you work,' he promised.

'Not donkey work. Something decent. In Naples.'

He nodded. 'Where are you staying?'

'You can leave a message for me at the Pompeii nightclub.' She flashed her tongue across her lips.

'Have you heard of the Caesar Club?'

She frowned, making one beautifully arched brow swoop down. 'No, I haven't.'

She was lying. Exquisitely done.

'Does the name Drago Vincelli mean anything to you?' he asked.

This time it was as though he'd slapped her pale cheek. Her head rocked back and her elegant black dress seemed to grow limp, a loose strand of blonde hair trailing down her cheek. The sheen was all a disguise, he realised. A good disguise, but still a disguise. Underneath it Jake now caught a glimpse of someone else, someone who wanted to put her head on the table and weep.

'What is it?' He took her hand and it lay curled in a tight ball, the scarlet nails sunk into his palm. 'What did Drago Vincelli do?'

Time slowed. Stretched. Each blink of her eye took an age.

'Drago Vincelli,' Lucia Lombardi spat a silvery jet of scorn on the grubby tiles of the floor, 'is the reason I left Sorrento.'

*

Caterina was there, waiting for him. As he sprinted up Corso Italia he spotted her standing at the base of the Byzantine bell tower. It rose above her like an elaborate red and yellow wedding cake, tiers and arches piled on top of each other, dwarfing her small figure in the plain cinnamon dress. She looked tense and angry. She knew he was late because he had spent so long with her mother and that was something, he suspected, she was not in a hurry to forgive.

He stepped out of the harsh glare of the sun and joined her in the shady archway.

'Okay,' he said briskly, 'we have work to do. Let's go.'

She didn't move, her face still as stone. 'You don't have to help me, Jake. You can go and join Harry Fielding and your unit up in the hills at Sant'Agata.' She was speaking softly, staring out at a child on the street struggling to carry a watermelon bigger than her head. 'That's where you're meant to be, isn't it?'

'Don't,' he said sharply.

Her gaze jumped to his face.

'Don't act,' he continued, 'as if we're not in this together. We have six more days. On the seventh day I don't want to scoop you out of the harbour in a net, so I am here doing the job I'm good at. And if that means questioning your mother – or your brother or your grandfather – then that's what I do. Understand?'

She nodded. 'I'm sorry.'

She came forward and for a brief moment she leaned her forehead against his shoulder. He felt the weight of it, the heat of it through his white shirt.

He took her hand. 'Let's go.'

*

A priest moved down the aisle in his black robe. In his hands he was carrying a vase of lilies and humming quietly to himself. Jake recognised the piece at once. It was Haydn's *The Creation* and it made his fingers itch for the feel of piano ivory. He had ducked into Sorrento cathedral with Caterina to avoid a crowd of rowdy GIs who were approaching along Corsa Italia, several of whom he recognised. Colonel Quincy believed him to be still in the military hospital, so he had no wish to advertise his presence here in Sorrento.

The cathedral was a plain boxy building from the outside, no great architectural enticement, but its interior was a glorious display of marble arches, intarsia panels and Renaissance frescoes.

'Did my mother tell you why she came?' Caterina asked.

'Yes, she did. She said she had come here to see you. And your brother. She says she was missing you.'

He thought she would be happy at that, and might even allow herself a flicker of pleasure that her mother, after all these years, wanted to spend time with her and Luca, but he was wrong. She snatched away her hand. Disgust settled in her eyes.

'She is lying,' Caterina announced. 'But you can't see it. She has snared you, like she snares every man.'

She turned her head away and wouldn't look at him.

They were polite to each other. That was the best that could be said. Caterina felt the politeness like ice on her skin and she wanted to take a blowtorch to it. They were in her workshop, seated on stools on opposite sides of her worktable, and as they discussed a plan of action, each word was dipped in politeness before being handed across the table. Jake had a pen and small pad in front of him and jotted down notes. It looked efficient and professional, a routine he must have done a thousand times before, and it gave Caterina confidence.

'Thank you for your help, Jake,' she said politely. But she meant it.

He looked up from his pad, surprised. His eyes were blood-shot and there were white patches around his mouth as if the blood was slowly draining out of him. Caterina felt a lurch of alarm and threw down her pencil.

'Go home, Jake. Go to bed.'

'Not yet.'

They had set out the plan, starting at the beginning with Antonio Lombardi's workshop again. Jake had drawn the short straw for that task, to revisit it and make enquiries of its neighbours and to put in a request to view the police report on it. But Caterina understood that right now what Jake needed was rest. She walked round the table, removed the pen from his hand, tucked it in his breast-pocket with a gentle tap, and closed his pad.

'Jake, go home.' She touched his springy hair. 'You're no use like this. We'll start again tomorrow.'

'Every hour counts.'

She took his stubborn face between her hands and kissed his lips, tasted coffee and exhaustion on them.

'I don't want you here,' she whispered. 'Go home.'

*

Caterina jerked awake. Her hand had gripped a chisel even before her eyelids opened. The banging on the door had wrenched her off the cliff-face she was climbing in her dreams, and her mouth was dry, her limbs tense. She realised she was in her workshop, slumped over the work-table, the scent of linseed oil in her nostrils.

She sat up and the banging came again. She advanced towards the door on silent feet in her soft new shoes, chisel-point out in front of her. It was almost dark outside, the last rays of the sun sliding through the high slatted window. The door was locked and bolted, and she stepped to the hinge side of it, so that she would be behind any assailant who burst in. She listened hard.

'Are you there, Caterina?'

It was Jake.

She unbolted the door and threw it open. He was there in the doorway. His dark hair tousled by the wind.

'Jake! What are you doing back here?'

There was an air of exhilaration about him. He was still out of uniform, smiling at her and when he saw the weapons in her hands, the smile stretched into a broad grin.

'Expecting me, were you?' he laughed.

She threw them on the table. 'So why are you back here? I ordered you to bed.'

'So you did. And I obeyed.' She could see his eyes were clearer and his skin less grey. 'But the only medicine I need is right here, Caterina.'

For one fleeting moment she forgot the struggle to protect her family, she forgot the white blaze in black hair, she forgot her mother's hard eyes and Sal Sardo's indecent scarlet smile. All she could think of was the way he said her name. As if it belonged there on his tongue. As if he would devour it.

He was standing still, just staring at her and the heat of it warmed a locked placed inside her that had been cold ever since the day eleven years ago when she had searched for her grandfather in the rain.

'Jake, I'm sorry I was rude in the church earlier. I would take the words back if I could.'

'You can make it up to me.'

She gave him a slow smile. 'What do you have in mind, Major Parr?'

'I thought you might like to come out for a meal tonight. I found a great eating place up in one of the mountain villages and ...' He was talking too fast. He stopped and said more formally, 'I'd be delighted if you would come to dinner with me, Caterina.'

She thought about it for no more than half a second. 'Thank you, Jake. I'd like that. But first I need to change my dress.'

His eyes studied her carefully from head to toe. 'No,' he said, 'you look perfect to me.'

Caterina raised her glass and felt the knots loosen at the back of her neck. There were movements out there in the darkness and each one quickened her heartbeat, but it was the rustling of the leaves, she told herself. A bat flitting through the olive grove. An owl. Nothing more.

'Jake, tell me something you did as a child that was bad.'

He laughed easily.

'That's a long list you're asking for there.'

'Just one will do.'

'Well, there was the time I went skating on the ice on the lake when I'd been told not to. It was too thin.'

Her eyes widened. 'And?'

'The ice broke and I crashed through. I tell you, those waters of Lake Michigan are damn freezing in the winter.' He laughed again and drank a mouthful of the local smoky gragnano wine. 'I lived to tell the tale though.'

'Not so bad then, after all.'

'Except I took my kid brother with me. He nearly drowned.' He smiled fondly. 'Little rascal never stopped reminding me of that fact afterwards whenever he wanted something.'

She liked that he had a brother. Someone close.

There was a small hesitation, not much, but enough, and suddenly she cursed herself for asking.

'He died at the Battle of Aachen in Germany last year.'

'Oh Jake, I'm so sorry.'

'It's war, Caterina. It happens.'

That was all. But he knocked back the rest of his wine and signalled to the proprietress for another bottle. They were seated on a terrace high up on a mountainside, the silvery olive groves rolling away down into the darkness of the valley floor. Lemon trees, rich and glossy, spread a latticework of fruit and branches over their heads in the cheerful little trattoria, scenting the air and keeping the evening mosquitoes at bay. A candle shimmered on the table between them.

She had relished the meal of *cannelloni ai funghi porcini* and their easy flow of conversation about anything that had absolutely nothing to do with Sorrento or Naples. He informed her that the Kentucky Derby had just been won by Eddie Arcaro on Hoop Jr which made him a few bucks and she discovered that he liked Frank Sinatra songs and Ingrid Bergman films. But now, with the coffee, the darkness seemed to draw nearer.

It was when they were alone on the terrace, and he leaned over to light her cigarette, his dark head close to hers, that he said in a low voice, 'I dug up some stuff on the Caesar Club.'

She exhaled a skein of smoke. 'Tell me.'

'They meet in the Palazzo Rudolfo. A drinking club, by all accounts.'

She frowned. Shook her head.

'But listen to this,' he added quickly. 'It was set up in 1922.'

She waited. She could feel his excitement, see his breath on the candle flame.

'What else happened in 1922?' he prompted.

'Mussolini and his Fascists came to power.'

'Exactly.'

'There's a connection?'

'There could be.'

'But what?'

'There's more.'

She put out a hand and wrapped it tight around his on the table.

'Caterina, I trawled through all the Naples police records I could lay my hands on, going back to 1922.' He rolled his dark eyes with impatience. 'They are in total chaos but I found the recorded thefts of antiquities from churches and museums. Guess what?'

'They rose after 1922.'

'Bull's eye.'

'That's quite a connection you're making there.' She could feel his hand clench.

He treated her to a cool police officer's smile. 'Let's see where this takes us.' He drew on his cigarette, focused on the thoughts in his head. 'What if this group of men could see from the start that Mussolini would destroy Italy's economy, so they started building a nest egg for themselves, organising the stealing and selling of priceless works of art. Against the day when the country was bankrupt and their businesses collapsed.'

Caterina nodded slowly. 'Yes, you could be right. They didn't know a war would come and make everything even easier for them, with bombed churches and palazzos. You could stroll along a Naples street and pocket a Renaissance silver candlestick, if you had a mind to.'

'And then *we* came. The Allied Forces.'

She smiled at him, touched his cheek, and ran a finger along the line of his jaw. 'I'm glad you came,' she murmured.

'To spoil it for them.'

She raised her glass. 'To spoiling it for them.'

He touched his glass to hers. She knew what was coming next, but she didn't want to hear the words on his lips. Not now. With the cicadas and tree frogs singing their love songs in the soft night air and her hand wrapped around his.

'Your father,' he said.

She put down her glass.

'Let's talk about your father.'

She shook her head.

'Caterina.'

She looked out at the night. Somewhere a fox barked. 'He belonged to the Caesar Club,' she said flatly. 'So did Roberto Cavaleri and Orlando Bartoli, the jeweller.'

She heard Jake's intake of breath. He hadn't known about Bartoli's membership.

'All dead,' she said.

'The only death that could be connected to the club is Orlando Bartoli's.'

'But if my father was hiding a fortune away somewhere, I haven't seen it.'

The weight of her admission that her father was the thief that Jake believed him to be crushed something in her. She could taste the betrayal like acid on her tongue and she drank her wine, all of it, swilling the bitterness from her mouth.

'He was selfish,' she said. 'Without honour.'

'Have you asked your grandfather about what happened?'

She shook her head. 'He refuses to talk about it. But I will try again.'

Jake refilled her glass but she pushed her chair back and stood up, taking the few paces to the rail at the edge of the terrace, moving closer to the darkness.

With her back to Jake, she whispered, 'Beware of me, Jake. I have a father who was a traitor, robbing his country of its treasures, and a mother who destroyed a family. Not just mine. The Cavaleri family. It is because of her that a woman committed suicide and their business was ruined.'

She heard his step behind her, felt his arms wrap around her, his broad chest warm against her back. He kissed her hair. 'I'll take my chances,' he said.

'Beware of me. I mean it, Jake. There are things in me that I didn't know were there. Things I am capable of doing to protect my family.'

'Caterina,' he said softly, 'we are all capable of things we never dream of. But I am here with you.' She turned to face him within the circle of his embrace, her lips finding his as he murmured, 'Whatever needs to be done, we will do it together.'

Caterina waited. Despite the late hour, the room was stifling. A wind had blown up straight from the heart of Africa, hot as the devil's breath, and was rattling the shutters. She was waiting for Luca to go to bed and for her grandfather to finish listening to the wireless. For the right small space of time to open up.

Or was she waiting because she did not want to ask the question?

She couldn't tell.

'Nonno.'

The white head lifted to her voice, his lined face turned towards her, just as it used to in the days when his eyes were not covered with a milky white film.

'Nonno, what do you know about Drago Vincelli and Papà working together?'

The old man flinched as though she had hit him with his stick and the glass of warm lemon-water that he was drinking spilled over his shirt-front, but he didn't shout, didn't even raise his voice. Instead he held out his hand.

'Caterina, come here.'

She left her seat and crouched down on her heels in front of her grandfather in his carved armchair. His gnarled hands reached out and stroked her spiky hair, smoothing it flat as though to quieten her thoughts, while the other hand touched her face. His fingertips felt for the knots under her skin, between her brows, under her eyes, at the corners of her mouth. Reading her face. His fingers saw better than most people's eyes and after a minute of silence he leaned forward and kissed her forehead. The gentleness of it touched her. She wrapped her hands firmly around his and lifted them to her lips.

'Nonno, help me. This family is in danger. I need to know more about what happened back then.'

But his hands broke free from hers. One came down firmly over her mouth, silencing her, the other rested on her eyes, holding them shut.

'Don't, little one. Silence. See with your mind, not your eyes.'

She made a sound of protest behind his broad fingers.

'Silence,' he whispered, 'is the only answer.'

CHAPTER TWENTY-SEVEN

Hell and damnation!

The chairman did not expect *her*.

Not *her*.

He could still see her in his mind as he locked the door of the banqueting chamber. As he uttered the toast to the king who no longer deserved to be King of Italy. As he lifted the cognac to his lips, she swam in the glass and his anger swayed his judgement.

He made the men at the table take risks.

He blamed everything on the bomb.

He clutched at his silences the way other men clutch at whores. Today her daughter had sat as close to him as the wealthy funeral director on his left, the one who will bury a man alive for the right fee.

And he didn't break her bones.

Or carve her throat into smiles.

He gave her a chance.

He narrowed his eyes and narrowed his thoughts and let the men around the table argue where the next shipment would go. To Paris? To London? To New York? But he had already chosen. To Calcutta, where a maharajah with rubies the size of pheasant eggs was building himself a palace greater than all others and he needed the treasures of the ancients to glorify it.

The deal was done.

He was silent. Let them argue. Let fear goad them. Let greed guide them.

Acquiring the goods was easy. In these days of chaos and confusion, they fell from the trees like autumn leaves in a storm. Storing them was hard, the searches coming always closer. Shipping them was harder still. The military controlled ships. He nodded at the uniform at the bottom of the table. So he would know that the deal was done.

'The bomb in the nightclub was a disgrace,' declared the dentist with a lisp and a weakness for injecting chemicals into his veins. 'I accept no responsibility for it. We should have been warned.'

'He's right. I was there only minutes before it exploded.'

'Christ, that was close.'

Others muttered. And murmured. And whined.

The chairman held up a hand. Silence fell.

Let them shift their sins on to him. Let them shrive their blackened souls. Hell was big enough for them all.

'Gentlemen,' he said, calming them. 'Let us not talk of blame. Let us talk of profit.'

Their pricks rose. Their smiles came. They had no time

for the problems of shipping permits. He pushed them. Into danger.

And all the time *she* was there in his cognac. Laughing at them.

CHAPTER TWENTY-EIGHT

Sleep didn't come to Caterina. She lay in bed, tangled in the hot sheet, but her mind would not let go. Piece by piece, it took apart her grandfather's refusal to help her. She could feel the weight of his hand forcing her eyes closed, sealing her lips shut.

Why?

Why would Nonno do that? What was he frightened that she would see? That she would say? She didn't doubt for a minute that he loved her, but why silence her? Her thoughts were occupying her mind, so that she almost missed the faint noise in the silence of the Sorrento night. There were no cats or dogs in the streets, all devoured long ago, and this noise was something that didn't belong here. Her mind leapt instantly to Aldo.

Hairs rose on her arms and silently she rolled out of bed. She snatched the carving knife from under her pillow, gripped its bone handle and felt safer as she made for the door, blind in the darkness. She turned the doorknob. On the landing she listened intently but she heard no further sound, so had she imagined it? Was her mind so fearful that it was filling in the gaps?

She waited in the blackness, the night air moist and heavy, the house closing in around her while the minutes ticked past. A snore rumbled out from her grandfather's room, but from downstairs came a rustle of papers, faint but distinct. A mouse shredding Nonno's newspaper? Mice were bold these days, driven by hunger, and had been known to rip a cardboard box to pieces or tear strips off a book's leather binding. There were too few cats to keep down their numbers and too many homes that could ill afford traps. On bare feet Caterina edged to the top of the stairs.

It came again, paper rubbing against paper. Then she heard a faint metallic chink as she descended in the darkness, mouth bone dry. She knew each stair, where one was bowed in the middle and would utter a soft groan when stepped on, so her foot stepped to the side to avoid it, and on tiptoe she missed out the next one that possessed a high squeak. The knife in her hand led the way to the bottom where she paused.

She blinked, her eyes fighting the darkness, and as she turned her head towards the kitchen, she saw the living room door ajar. *Saw* it. In the darkness she should see nothing, yet she could see the edge of the door, a black line against a blurred grey background. She knew what it meant. There was a dim light inside the living room.

She could turn. Walk away. Creep back up the stairs as silently as the mice, gather Luca and Nonno together and barricade themselves in the topmost bedroom. Wait till daybreak, when the intruder would have departed, if they were lucky. If not, and he came prowling upstairs, they would be ready for him, the long carving knife directed at his throat. Caterina cursed the fact that the Bodeo pistol was still in Leonora's bedroom on Capri.

She could turn. Could walk away from this. Instead she moved forward and placed a hand on the living room door.

The living room was not large and Caterina saw the figure immediately. It was hunched over her father's desk in the deep shadow of the far corner, its back towards the door, so confident of being undisturbed in the blatant act of thievery. By the dull glow of a torch Caterina could see a scene of destruction, papers thrown in confusion, drawers upended, pens scattered. Luca's collection of shells hurled to the floor. The sight sent a wave of anger through Caterina and she stepped into the room.

'Who are you?' she hissed.

The scream was high-pitched. Stifled almost before it was uttered. The figure straightened and spun round, the torch beam leaping around the room and clambering up to the ceiling before finding Caterina's face. For an instant it blinded her, but instinct took over and she flicked on the electric light switch by the door, flooding the room with light. Grimly she stared at the figure that was clutching a wad of banknotes. She lowered the knife.

'What the hell are you doing, Mamma?'

Her mother stood motionless, her face taut. Caterina could see her trying to work out which way to jump – to opt for bravado, brazen her way out of this, or to beg for forgiveness with tears. Caterina wanted to hate her, wanted to shout at her and point to the mess she had made of their father's belongings. She wanted to say what her grandfather had said: *Get out of my house.*

But she couldn't. The words were not inside her. The figure in black was her *mother* and she was here in this house after eleven empty years. Her blonde hair was pulled back from her face and tied with a black bootlace the way she used to wear it when chopping garlic to make her favourite *polpette di pollo.* In her mind, Caterina was back in the kitchen as a child, smelling the rich *sugo al pomodoro*, dipping a finger in it and receiving a quick rebuke from the wooden spoon.

She shook her head, dislodging the image. She put down the knife, walked over and inspected the disarray more closely. Unexpectedly the anger suddenly drained from her, slithering through her cold fingers, and she tried to grasp it back but it was too late. It was gone.

She asked once more, 'What are you doing, Mamma?' Her eyes settled on the money in her mother's hand.

'I'm not stealing, Caterina. I have a right to this. God knows, I earned it. For twelve years I was here in this back-end of nowhere.'

The insult stung.

But where had the money come from? Her eyes fell on a shallow drawer made from rosewood, lying on top of the mess of opened letters and papers on the desk. Caterina frowned. She had never seen it before. Then she noticed a thin gap under the shelf where pens and ink sat and realisation dawned. It was a secret drawer. One her mother knew about.

Caterina stretched out her hand, palm up.

'Give it to me, Mamma. It belonged to Papà, not to you.'

A thin bead of sweat clung to Lucia Lombardi's temple and she brushed it away impatiently with the back of her wrist.

'Come, my Caterina, let us not argue. After all these years, let's be friends. I have missed you.' She smiled invitingly. 'We can share it.'

But Caterina's eyes had returned to the secret drawer and she could see that one item still lay inside it. A key. A big iron key, the kind that would open a church or a wine cellar or a basement where fine artwork was concealed. She snatched it from the drawer.

'No, Caterina. That key is mine. Mine alone. Give it to me.' Lucia's eyes blazed for one second with a flash of rage, but as fast as it came, it vanished. An icy blue stare took its place. 'Let me have the key.'

'Mamma, I am not an imbecile.'

She started to walk away but her mother pulled her back.

'I am ordering you to give me that key immediately. I am your mother. Here, you can take the money, all of it. You can buy Nonno and Luca some decent food that will . . .'

'No, Mamma.'

The slap rocked her on her heels. Her mother's hand slammed into her cheek and pain flared up the left side of her face, slicing into her ear, but that pain was nothing compared to the one inside her chest where she felt something break.

Instantly her mother's arms were around her, holding her close, stroking the back of her neck. 'I'm sorry, Caterina, so sorry. Forgive me. I didn't mean it. I would never hurt you, my darling.'

Caterina felt her mother's tears wet on her cheek, but firmly she extricated herself from the embrace.

'Let's sit down,' she said, 'and talk about the key.'

'This wine tastes like piss.'

They were sitting at the kitchen table, facing each other. Caterina wanted the solid table between them, no more embraces. No more slaps. She wanted to look at her mother's face to see when she was lying. At first Caterina asked questions. What made you go? What made you come back? But once her mother had downed a glass of the sour red wine and started talking, the words kept coming of their own accord. She told Caterina that she had loved Roberto Cavaleri because he had all the energy and humour that Antonio Lombardi lacked. He knew how to have fun, she said. All Caterina's father knew was wood. She did not seem to notice Caterina flinch at that.

'But he was like your Papà in some ways, always full of ideas and ideals, the foolish donkey.' Yet it was said with an affectionate shake of her head. 'Roberto was forever fighting alongside the partisans, harassing the Germans, sabotaging their convoys and stealing their trucks of weapons. He had such courage.'

She knocked back another glass of the wine and pulled a face that didn't quite disguise her anguish. He was caught, and shot by a German firing squad. After that salutary lesson in warfare tactics, as she called it, she shifted allegiance to the winning side and became the mistress of a German general who was stationed in Rome.

'Klaus was kind, Caterina. Kind and generous. Those two

qualities go a long way in covering up a lack of love. We had good times, Klaus and I. Germans know how to party.'

She rolled her blue eyes dramatically and laughed, but it was thin, that laugh, so thin it slid under Caterina's defences.

'How was I to know,' her mother declared, 'that the big beefy Yanks and the stuffed-shirt British would go and march all over Italy with their Sherman tanks?' She shrugged one shoulder, expressing her opinion on that subject with eloquence. 'My Klaus was shot. The Allies put a violent end to our parties.' She lit a cigarette and watched the skein of smoke drift between them, a bitterness tugging at one corner of her mouth. Caterina listened in silence.

'I was tarred and feathered, Caterina. Can you believe that? Tarred and feathered by the ungrateful citizens of Rome for being a collaborator. That's what they called me, a collaborator. Even though a fair few of them had invited me earlier to sing at their parties.' She smiled now, a precarious smile that would fool no one. 'You should have seen me, Caterina. I looked outrageous in my stinking tar and feathers, like a lost soul from hell.' Another laugh, and the sound of it brought the last of Caterina's defences crashing down.

You *were* a lost soul, Mamma. Lost in your own betrayals. But she said nothing. How could she? If she started to tell her mother what was in her head, she would never stop.

'Where did the money and the key come from, Mamma? What was Papà doing with them?'

Caterina could guess. It wasn't hard.

The lire banknotes, tied in a bundle with a strand of green

375

wool, sat on the table between them, but the key lay clutched in Caterina's hand.

'The money is your Papà's savings. Escape money for all of us. That's what he intended it for if things went wrong.'

'What things?'

'Oh, you know, under Mussolini you never knew when you might be dragged out of bed in the middle of the night by his Blackshirts.'

Caterina stared. 'You admit Papà was doing something illegal even back then?'

Her mother didn't meet her gaze. 'No, no, of course not.' She flicked a hand vaguely through the air. 'You didn't need a reason to be hauled into the street and beaten with their bloody truncheons. They did it just for fun.'

The lie sat there on the table between them along with the banknotes. Neither of them touched it. Instead Caterina rose to her feet and dangled the iron key from her fingers. Instantly her mother's eyes grew suspicious, though a smile curved her full lips.

'Cara mia,' she murmured in a low voice, 'let me have the key.' She pushed the pile of lire nearer her daughter. 'Take it all. Your brother and grandfather would want you to. Think of them. Don't be selfish, Caterina. The key is meaningless to you.'

Caterina was thinking. Briskly she headed for the door. 'Come, Mamma. Time for us to take a walk.'

'What? Are you mad? It's the middle of the night. It's pitch black out there.'

Caterina held the door open. 'All the more reason to go now.'

*

At the top of the cliff in Piazza Vittoria, Caterina stood leaning out over the balustrade that divided the piazza from the sheer drop. The moon shed its light like lace over the black waves and a night wind tucked itself in the folds of her work-dress, but her gaze remained fixed on the pale oval that was her mother's tense face.

'Now, Mamma. What does this key open?'

Caterina made no fuss. Her voice was calm, but her fist was stretched out over the abyss that tumbled down to the sea, the iron key clearly visible in the moonlight. All she had to do was open her fingers. A quick release of her grip and the key would be gone forever.

'As you said, Mamma, it means nothing to me.'

'Don't.' Lucia Lombardi's voice was panicky. 'Don't, Caterina. You don't know what you are doing.'

But Caterina knew exactly what she was doing.

'Tell me what it opens.'

'Give it to me and then I will tell you.' Her mother held out her hand, soft and white in the darkness, and took two steps closer. The night had merged with her black dress, so that her face and arms seemed disembodied as they edged nearer her daughter. 'I promise I will tell you.'

A sceptical laugh escaped from Caterina. 'Better still, Mamma, show me.'

Limestone is made up of skeletons, millions of them. Fragments of long-dead marine organisms. The thought that Sorrento was built on skeletons rose in Caterina's mind when she was standing in front of a massive overhang of limestone rock. The beam of her torch cut a hole in the surrounding darkness and transformed the grey sedimentary surface to a dirty yellow, but she had a sense of something slipping, something that would slide out of her grasp if she so much as took her eyes off it for a second.

Beneath the overhang stood a heavy oak door.

'You see,' her mother said behind her with a note of triumph. 'I told you it was there.'

Long tendrils of ivy snaked from the knife in Caterina's hand and she could smell the pile of torn vegetation that lay on the ground. Excitement hammered at her. She tried not to expect too much, but failed. She didn't speak, just drew the iron key from her pocket.

Her mother had led her to a spot on the back edge of town where the houses squeezed up against a shoulder of limestone as it rose to form the mountains that threaded their way down the spine of the peninsula. The overhang protruded, causing the small road to dogleg around it, but underneath there must have at one time been a large gap, an inland cave of sorts, but the mouth of the gap had been boarded up long ago and a dense layer of ivy had grown over the timbers, making them virtually invisible.

'In there,' her mother had whispered. She was tense and nervy. They had walked in silence and Caterina could feel her mother's anger bubbling between them. Caterina had hacked at the ivy, tearing her hands as she ripped it off the wood and her mother had stood there and watched without lifting a finger. The door looked in surprisingly good condition and gave Caterina hope because it meant someone had kept it in good repair until not many years ago. Presumably her father.

She inserted the key and heard the lock turn. That was when her mother elbowed past her and pushed the door open. Her mother screamed and the high-pitched sound was sucked into the limestone walls, a thousand million dead creatures feasting on it.

'What is it, Mamma? Are you hurt?' Caterina touched her mother's arm.

'Look! Look!'

She snatched the torch from Caterina's hand and its yellow glare swept over the stone floor and up the walls.

The cavern was empty.

You have a week. One week. To find the table.

Drago Vincelli's words in the confessional box seemed to echo in the emptiness of the cavern and drip down the limestone walls, mocking Caterina. All the hope that had sparked into life the moment she snatched the key from the secret drawer had been extinguished.

She turned to her mother. Lucia Lombardi was standing in the centre of the cavern, rigid and silent.

'I am finished,' her mother whispered. 'I will starve. The contents of this place were what I . . .' Her words ceased.

Caterina stood close, so she would see the lie if it came. 'They were what you came for, weren't they? The reason you returned to Sorrento. Not for Luca. Not for me. You came for the valuable artefacts Papà had stored here.'

Her mother could have said no. She could have lied. Just a little lie. It would have hurt no one. But she didn't. Instead she let out a murmur of misery and gave the smallest of nods. But Caterina could not bear to see her so stricken. Gently she wrapped her arms around her slender frame and held her tight.

Caterina took her mother home with her.

The impact of the night breeze seemed to bring Lucia back to life and she walked with her arm tucked through her daughter's, clinging to her, their flesh touching, their voices muted. As they walked along the empty pavements Lucia admitted that the hiding place under the rocky outcrop had been a secret known only to Caterina's father and herself.

Without warning, Caterina experienced a flash of jealousy. It flickered behind her eyes, back and forth, startling her. Why had Papà never shared the secret with *her*? Did he not trust her? He had often rested his warm hand on her cheek and said with pride that he could always trust his Caterina with any job he gave her. Not only to do the job, but to do it well. Yet now she learned he had kept so many secrets from her, and that knowledge created a cold place inside her. He had laughed that he could trust her with his life, but he had not done so.

Her mother turned her head to look at her as they walked through the dark streets.

'Don't, Caterina, don't be hurt. Your Papà loved you.' She made a soft throaty sound. 'God knows, that man loved you far more than he ever loved me.'

'That's not true.'

'Of course it is, *cara mia*. The only reason he kept the store of antiques a secret from you was because he wanted to protect you. He always knew it was a dangerous business to be caught up in. And your precious father couldn't bear you to think ill of him. You were the centre of his world.'

'No, Mamma, you are wrong. You never saw how Papà was when you weren't here, when you disappeared for days or weeks at a time. He was torn to pieces. And when you ran off with Roberto Cavaleri, he was destroyed. You ripped the heart out of him.'

'Don't hate me, Caterina,' her mother whispered softly. 'I tried to make him happy.'

The lie was swallowed by the darkness. They walked the rest of the way in silence.

Caterina sat her mother on the sofa and put a glass of wine in her hand. The night was hot and humid but her mother was cold, so Caterina wrapped a blanket around her shoulders, tucking it under her chin and spreading it over her knees. Touching her. Patting her. It was as though Caterina's hands were trying to make up for all the years of drought, and no amount of reprimand from Caterina could stop them.

Caterina made herself take the seat opposite her mother, rather than sit beside her on the sofa. She didn't trust herself. Or her hands. So she sat up straight, not leaning forward, her fingers curled firmly around the wooden arms of her chair. Her mother began to talk. About her life in Rome with the German general, her lavish apartment, the clubs she sang in, the applause she received, the parties she attended, a dance with Crown Prince Umberto and her fingers dressed in diamonds. Her hand kissed by Adolf Hitler himself.

'And afterwards?' Caterina asked.

Thrown out on the street, stripped of all jewels, rebuffed by those who had been her friends but who now claimed no kinship with Nazi whores. It was the women who had corralled her in a backstreet, tarred and feathered her, spat on her, tore her clothes, stole even her wedding ring. The tar burned her skin and the humiliation burned her mind.

'Got a cigarette?' Lucia Lombardi asked.

Caterina fetched the remains of Harry Fielding's pack and lit one for each of them. Her mother drew on it as though it were her last breath.

'Don't look so sad, Caterina. Come and sit here.' She patted the worn green velvet.

Caterina sat on the sofa. A gap of eleven years stretched between them.

'You mustn't be angry with your father.'

'He was a thief.'

Lucia Lombardi sighed with exasperation. 'Don't be tiresome, Caterina.'

'Tell me how much you know about Drago Vincelli.'

Her mother's face went blank. 'Stay away from that man, I'm warning you. Your father had dealings with him but had the sense never to turn his back on the bastard.' Her ringless hand crept up to her mouth and stayed there.

'Mamma, he is threatening me and our family if I don't find

a certain table that Papà is supposed to have made just before he died.'

'No,' Lucia whispered behind her fingers. 'No. No. No.' She pulled the blanket tighter around herself.

'You knew him?'

'Yes, I knew that lying, murdering, thieving devil.'

'Where did he live?'

'Nowhere. Everywhere. Always moving around. Cunning as a snake.'

Caterina reached out and removed her mother's hand from her mouth, so that she could see her full face. 'Help me, Mamma. Think back eleven years. What was his weakness?'

'What?'

'What makes Drago Vincelli vulnerable? What does he care about? Everyone cares about someone or something. Is he married?'

'Yes.' Lucia waved a hand dismissively. 'His wife lived somewhere in Sicily with a clutch of Vincelli whelps. He didn't care for their whining.'

'Think, Mamma. What else?'

Lucia closed her eyes, sinking into the past, her head tilted back. Caterina allowed herself to lean a fraction forward in order to study the fine profile more closely. A high forehead crossed by a small crease of concentration, a nose that was no longer quite straight as if it might have been broken at some time. Caterina wondered how. Cheekbones that made other faces look shapeless, and full sensual lips. It was a beautiful face, but a selfish face. Even she could see that. But it didn't stop her wanting to touch those thick dark lashes that belied the blonde tint of her hair or to kiss the pale powdered cheek.

Abruptly Lucia jerked upright, blue eyes bright and sharp.

'His car,' her mother announced.

Caterina felt a thrust of excitement. 'What car?'

'Back then he owned a 1926 Rolls-Royce Phantom.'

'He might have sold it by now.'

'No. You don't know him. It was the love of his life. He treated that flashy car of his far better than he treated the women in his life.'

Lucia stubbed out her cigarette harshly and something about the movement made Caterina wonder whether her mother had been one of those women. The idea tasted bitter in her mouth.

'Where did he keep it, do you know?' she asked.

'No, I don't. But stay away from it anyway. It's too dangerous.'

'I'd take that risk.'

Her mother's gaze lingered on her speculatively for a long moment. 'Yes,' Lucia said, 'I rather think that you would.' She released a loud burst of laughter.

An angry rap sounded on the ceiling above them.

'Nonno's cane,' Caterina murmured.

'Time is up, I'd better leave.'

'No. Stay.'

Lucia Lombardi was curled up asleep under the blanket on the sofa. Her gleaming blonde hair hung loose and tousled, her face slack, the hardness having spilled out of the muscles of her cheeks and her jaw, leaving them soft and malleable.

Caterina knelt on the floor beside her mother and listened to her breathing.

She was more beautiful in sleep than awake. Caterina bent down and smelled her skin. There was the scent of jasmine on it and something else, something that carried her right back to when her mother used to come home from Naples. Restless as a cat. Flicking her hair off her neck. And with each flick the scent of cigars and hair-oil teased at Caterina's nostrils. Her father wouldn't look at her.

That's what she smelled of now. Cigars and hair-oil.

'Luca, come here.'

Her brother hung back in the doorway. He looked a mess. The dawn was only just creeping in with the first fingers of morning light and Luca had tumbled straight out of bed in order to hitch a ride on one of the fishing boats in the marina. He was doing what he'd promised, trying to help Caterina by earning money. He wore ragged shorts. Nothing else. No shoes. No smiles.

He stared at his mother with suspicious eyes, the way he would look at a scorpion in one of his comics.

'Say hello to your Mamma,' Caterina urged.

'Hello, my darling boy,' Lucia said with a smile that could melt lead.

She held out one hand, but he gave it a look that kept her at bay. Caterina could feel the turmoil within him.

'Luca, Mamma has come to see us.'

'So, Luca, how tall you are for eleven. You'll soon be taller than your sister. Come and give your Mamma a kiss.'

Kate Furnivall

He didn't move. 'You left Papà,' he stated boldly. 'You made Caterina do all the work when you should have been here.'

Caterina went to his side and rested a hand on the back of his neck to ease him forward. 'Luca,' she murmured, 'you have been looking forward to seeing Mamma again one day. Well, today is that day.' She lowered her voice. 'Be kind, Luca.'

'Why?' His glistening black eyes looked up at his sister. 'She is nothing to me. You are the only mamma and sister I want.' He wrapped an arm around her waist.

'Oh, Luca.' Caterina held him close. 'Mamma is helping me. Helping *us*. Come into the room.'

Caterina knew how much he ached for his mother's arms but he remained where he was.

'Holy mother of God,' Lucia burst out, 'you look exactly like your father when he was in one of his wretched moods.'

'Moods?' Caterina echoed. 'Papà didn't have moods.'

'Don't be foolish, girl. He was a man. Of course he had moods whenever he didn't get his own way.'

Caterina walked to the front door. She unlocked it and held it open, Luca at her side.

'Goodbye, Mamma. Thank you for calling on us,' she said.

Without a word or a look, her mother marched out of the house. Caterina shut the door.

CHAPTER TWENTY-NINE

Army boots were out in force on the streets of Sorrento when Caterina emerged from her house. A wave of soldiers had transformed the town from its usual mellow ambers and washed-out pinks into a sea of harsh utilitarian khaki. It felt solid and oppressive. Uniforms marched in pairs down the pretty narrow streets and stationed themselves on corners with rifles slung on their shoulders. These were soldiers with an alert and wary look, men who were expecting trouble.

Caterina felt an uneasy stirring. What had happened?

The pavements hummed with anxious voices and military trucks patrolled the roads. There was a sense of being caged. Caterina walked quickly through the morning's dusty shadows, cut down an alleyway where the smell of fresh bread set her stomach growling and arrived at her workshop.

It was the work of a moment to drag out the low handcart that she sometimes used for moving deliveries of timber. It was small but ran smoothly on miniature wheels and had a metal bar by which to haul it. She relocked the workshop and with the cart rattling along behind her over the basalt slabs, she headed across to the northern edge of Sorrento. She hurried past the deeply wooded narrow ravine that looked as if it had been sliced out of the limestone heart of the town with a sharp knife, a ravine she couldn't bear to look at. And then took the road back up to the cavern under the overhang of rock.

Daylight breathes life into places. When Caterina threw back the door of the cavern, sunlight immediately darted inside ahead of her. It gilded one dark wall and stretched out on the floor like a well-fed cat. She worked fast, eager to be out of there because she didn't want to remember the lies her father had told her, while all the time he'd been gloating over the hidden hoard he'd stored here.

'It was all that ghastly ornate antique furniture I hate,' her mother had announced. 'The kind that once belonged to a fat old cardinal wearing a red biretta or in one of those magnificent palazzos that smell of dirty money and even dirtier power.' That's how she'd described it. 'No taste, if you ask me, just greed.'

Her father had impeccable taste. But it seemed he also had greed.

Right at the back against the wall lay a tangled heap that the torchlight had skimmed over last night, just a mess of discarded and broken scraps from tables and cupboards. A snapped chair leg. A mahogany drawer. An odd finial. Wafer-thin ribbons of cracked veneer and a sliver of mother-of-pearl jumbled up with a short section of white holly on which there were dark stains. She threw them all into the small cart, so that it was piled high, and covered them loosely with a length of sacking she had brought with her. She slammed the oak door behind her with relief and hurried back into town, hauling the cart at her heels.

The street market at the end of Corso Italia was crowded, the cramped space between stalls buzzing with noise. Shoppers hung around in tight huddles, whispers and rumours were spreading like wildfire.

What had happened to bring the army out to Sorrento in force?

Caterina scanned the faces, nodding to those she knew, but all the time she was searching for one person as she squeezed past colourful boxes of sweet peppers, watermelons and blood-red tomatoes. Everywhere there were bright splashes of colour. Netting sacks of beans and papery onions spilled into the aisles catching her cart, and huge vibrant lemons scented the air. Local growers had turned out to feed those who were lucky enough to have a handful of lire in their pocket.

'Caterina!'

A hand touched her shoulder. It was her friend, Albertina Donati, whose brother, Paolo, was in the same class as Luca at school. She was wearing her waitress uniform.

'Have you heard?' Albertina asked, clearly upset.

'Heard what?'

'The terrible news.'

'What happened? Why are the soldiers here?'

Albertina shook her head in mute dismay. 'It's the Rocco brothers. They've been murdered.'

Caterina froze. The Rocco brothers? They had been card-playing friends of her father. Both were in the blacksmith business and lived together near the spot where her father's workshop used to be. She tried to grasp the fact of their death but her thoughts were scattering, fragmenting and coming together again in ways that chilled her blood.

Murdered.

Dear God, not more death.

Without warning, an image of the Rocco brothers shuffling along and carrying a rolled carpet over their shoulders rose from the depths of her mind. For a moment she struggled to place it, but then it came to her. It was the day she had taken Jake to Papà's workshop, that first day when all this started. She could picture them ambling down the street, their hard-drinking faces warm with smiles of greeting for her.

She forced her attention back on Albertina. 'What happened?'

'They're saying their throats were cut in their own back yard.'

A low groan escaped Caterina. Her mind was suddenly swamped by the image of a figure sprawled in the hot sun on a pile of Naples rubble, his throat cut into a scarlet smile. She swore under her breath, ferocious and profane.

Albertina was saying something more, but Caterina cut in. 'But why the army? Surely it is a police matter.'

Albertina's head didn't stop shaking. 'Two soldiers,' she wailed. 'Two American soldiers have been killed.'

Caterina gripped her shoulder, shook it hard. 'What, Albertina? Tell me.'

'The two soldiers were up in the area of Via Caldoni asking questions. Later a man was out walking his dog. He found them.' Tears spilled down Albertina's cheeks. 'Their throats were ...'

Caterina heard no more. She was running.

Via Caldoni was closed. A police car sat at each end of the street and a burly uniformed policeman barred her way, arms outstretched sideways to prevent her dodging round him.

'Go back, signorina.'

'I need to speak with ...'

'Go back, signorina.' His tone was becoming less polite. 'We are busy here.'

'I know. Please, just tell me the names of the American soldiers who were ...'

This time he put a hand on her shoulder and moved forward, solid as a truck, so she was forced to retreat. 'Go back, signorina. Do as I say, please.'

Caterina looked past him, up the street to the ragged mound of rubble where she had once worked on the scannella alongside her father. There were soldiers striding up and down the forbidden stretch of the street, talking in low voices. American voices. For a moment everything seemed to fade from sight except the khaki uniforms, the grim faces under the military caps.

'Jake,' she whispered.

'Go back!' the policeman ordered.

She registered that a crowd of onlookers had come to stare.

Women in black with cobwebbed cheeks hunched over their rosary beads, and men removed their caps as a mark of respect. The narrow street of workaday houses felt shabby and claustrophobic as Caterina turned her head to study the nearest soldier. He was seated in the front of a jeep, writing notes on a pad, three stripes were visible on his arm.

'Sergeant!' Caterina shouted in English.

The jeep was more than fifteen metres away. He didn't look up.

'Sergeant!' she yelled again. 'Come here.'

Others in the crowd swivelled to look at her. The policeman scowled.

'Stop that noise.'

She ignored him. 'Sergeant! You in the jeep.'

The soldier raised his head. A fine-boned face, more like a scholar than a soldier, his eyes scoured the crowd for the owner of the voice. She called again, and this time his attention fixed on her. He jumped from the jeep and came over at a half-run, picking up on her urgency. He swept the Italian policeman aside.

'What can I do for you, ma'am?' He spoke English.

'I look for American soldier.'

'Well,' he gave her a teasing smile, 'there are a lot of us to choose from.'

'No. I need names of soldiers who died. Here.' She pointed up the street.

'I'm sorry, ma'am.' The humour had drained from his face. 'I can't give out that information.'

'Please.'

'Tell me who it is that you are searching for and maybe I can help you.'

She opened her mouth to answer. To say his name. As if saying his name aloud would keep him alive, but before the words passed her lips, a voice behind her said, 'Hello, Caterina.'

She turned.

'Jake.'

He was standing there, tall and uniformed, his throat uncut. His face was solemn, his eyes dark and deeply angry. Her instinct told her to leave him alone, to move away and let him get on with his grim job without interruption. Now was not the time. She knew that. The air around them hummed with heat and horror, and five seconds slid by in silence, but she couldn't walk away any more than she could stop the beat of her heart.

In front of everybody she stepped forward and pressed her body against his chest, breathed in the scent of the skin of his neck, while her hands gripped his shoulders hard so that she could feel the living muscle and bone beneath his khaki jacket. She felt, more than heard, his intake of breath.

'I thought you were dead,' she said.

Caterina stood in the marketplace once more and thought about the look on Jake's face when he detached himself from her grasp and said quietly, 'I will come and see you at your workshop later, Caterina.' It was the look of a stranger.

She retrieved her cart from Albertina, and continued to

search for one particular black-clad figure but it was nowhere in sight. She waited, exchanging comments with the man who ran a stall selling inky aubergines, so silky it was hard not to stroke them. Thirty minutes she waited before she spotted a tall elderly woman swathed from head to toe in deepest black enter the market, her bearing erect. The lines on her stern face seemed to have grown deeper since Caterina last saw her and to Caterina they looked like lines of agony.

With her cart in tow, she approached, before the woman had a chance to start bargaining for the fruit and vegetables. She would be a hard bargainer. Caterina could see that. There was a quality of stone about her, stiff and unyielding. Caterina moved out in front of her, blocking her path.

'*Buongiorno*, Signora Cavaleri. No, please don't back away, I have something to say to you.'

'Nothing that a Lombardi has to say is of the slightest interest to me.' The woman started to turn, face averted.

'My mother has come back to Sorrento.'

An infinitesimal jolt passed through the woman's body as though something had snapped inside, something vital.

'I thought you would want to know,' Caterina added softly. 'Before you see her in the street or in a shop.'

'Go away.'

Caterina had no wish to hurt this old woman. She had been hurt and humiliated enough when her eldest son abandoned his family for Caterina's mother, and further disgraced by the suicide of her deserted daughter-in-law.

'I am trying to help,' Caterina said.

'I want no help from you.'

'Your son Roberto and my father were working together, weren't they? Secretly. Illegally.'

She kept her voice pitched beneath the noise of the sellers and the shoppers, who were bickering over the price of a box of tomatoes or a scoop of beans. A man pushed past with a chicken dangling from his fist by its yellow feet, its wings flapping in vain.

'Do not speak ill of the dead, girl.'

'It's true though, isn't it?'

Augusta Cavaleri did not confirm it. Or deny it. Her mouth sat closed in a hard line, yet her silence confirmed in Caterina's mind that her guess was correct and Roberto Cavaleri had been up to his neck in the criminal activity.

'And your other son, Stefano? Is he involved in it now?'

Augusta Cavaleri's stare was unforgiving. 'Go away,' she hissed again.

'I think we should talk,' Caterina responded. But she did exactly as the woman requested and walked away from the market to its edge, where a lime tree spread its branches like a dusty old umbrella. She stood alone in its shade and waited.

She watched the tussle unfold within the austere woman, saw her take two steps away, then turn back and stare first at the small cart and then at Caterina herself. The heat didn't seem to touch her. Her skin looked cold and joyless. She walked over to join Caterina, her long black skirt scarcely rippling as she moved.

'What is it you want, Caterina Lombardi?'

So Caterina asked her questions.

'Do you know of a place where your son, Roberto, used to store repaired antiques?'

'No.'

'Have you heard of a jewelled table my father made?'

'No.'

'Do the names Caesar Club, Aldo or Count di Marco mean anything to you?'

'No.'

Augusta Cavaleri refused to look at her interrogator. She gazed up at a riot of cherry-red geraniums in a window across the street.

'You've heard that the Rocco brothers were killed early this morning?' Caterina asked.

'Yes.' Augusta Cavaleri shook her head in its jet-black scarf. 'It is the work of the devil.'

'I believe it is the work of Drago Vincelli.'

It took a long moment for the woman to react. 'Do you?' She looked at Caterina properly for the first time. 'Do you also remember the day your grandfather was found?'

'Of course.'

How could Caterina ever forget? In the narrow ravine with its steep sides. Nonno lying there in pieces. She had been ten. Her blue dress was torn and shredded as she thrashed through the undergrowth, shouts echoing up the steep rise of rock like the voices of ghosts. The blood on his white hair. On his face. She had squatted beside him until the stretcher came, squeezing his fingers tight to hold on to his life.

'Yes, I remember.'

'Do you remember what your grandfather said caused him to fall?'

'Yes. He said he was out walking, saw a partridge with a broken wing and chased it. But he lost his footing and crashed down to the bottom.'

'And you believed it?'

A pain in Caterina's ribcage cut through to the bone. 'Yes.'

'Do you want to know the truth?' The words were relentless.

'Yes.'

Both were oblivious to the voices at the market stalls and the rustle of leaves above their heads. Somewhere someone was frying onions with garlic and it spiked the air.

'The truth. Tell me the truth, signora.'

'It was the work of that devil of yours,' Augusta Cavaleri stated, 'Drago Vincelli. Some say it was because he and your father had fallen out over work they were doing together. But I heard that it was because of your mother.'

'My mother?'

The woman's scar puckered across her forehead. 'Yes. Everyone knew she'd been seen having a good time with Vincelli in Naples for some time. But when he wanted your mother to leave your father and come to him, she refused.' Her voice was bitter. 'She had her eye on better. When she refused him, he and that henchman of his hurled your grandfather down into the gorge to show Lucia Lombardi and everyone else what happened to anyone who was stupid enough to thwart his desires.'

There was a whirring inside Caterina's head. She put out a hand. Felt the old woman grasp it.

'That same day,' Augusta Cavaleri continued implacably, 'your mother persuaded my son Roberto to run away with her and I never saw him again.' She spoke fast. Suddenly in a hurry. 'And now she's back.'

Her gaze drifted down to the covered cart at Caterina's feet.

'Tell Lucia Lombardi to stay away from Sorrento.' She exhaled so hard that the air whistled from her lungs. 'Tell that whore from me, she is not welcome here.'

Caterina had laid a trail. Straight to herself. She sat on the scannella in her workshop, cutting out the delicate shape of an eagle's wing tips from a rich walnut veneer, and she knew they would come.

The cart had been a lure. A tease. To draw them into the open and make them show their faces. She was sick of eyes hiding in the shadows. Whoever was watching her would be curious to know what it was she had transported from one end of Sorrento to another. Her foot pedalled in a comfortable rhythm, working the hair-fine steel blade that sliced through the veneer as she guided it around each miniature feather. The familiarity was comforting, her skill innate. Her fingers demanded no attention, but performed their task effortlessly.

All her thoughts centred on the door to her workshop and the metal bar she had fixed across it. Another iron pole leaned against the wall beside it. She may not have Nonno's gun, but she was ready. She understood now. She had compassion for the reason her grandfather wanted to sleep with a pistol tight under his pillow and a knife rammed down the side of his chair. She understood why his stick was so eager to lash out. To hurt.

'*Get out of my house and never come back.*'

Oh Nonno.

It is not her we have to punish. It is him.

They came. One by one.

The first was Carlo, Augusta Cavaleri's grandson. He banged at the door, called her name cheerily and looked askance at the iron pole but passed no comment. He breezed through the workshop, full of charm and stories to tell, like a beam of sunlight sliding unexpectedly into her day. He kissed her cheek, admired her work on the eagle design, stuck two of its wooden feathers above his lip as a moustache to make her laugh. But there was no laughter in her. Not today.

She asked him outright if he knew anything more about the murder of the Rocco brothers and the soldiers, but he shook his head in exaggerated sorrow, his long curls dancing around his handsome face. Caterina reminded herself that it was *his* father who had run off with her mother, and whereas for years when they were young their shared bewilderment and pain had bound them together, now it seemed to divide them.

'How is shoemaking going in Naples?' she enquired. The rhythmic hum of the treadle under her foot was the background music to her words, operating the tiny saw with a reciprocating motion. 'Do you use machines or is it all done by hand?'

His eyes shone as he described the process, but she was aware of the way he paid more attention to what was stacked in the corners of the room than to her. He prowled as he talked, prodding at things, fiddling with drawers, stubbing his foot against cardboard boxes.

'Carlo,' she interrupted, 'how do you know the Bartolis? Why did they employ you?'

'When my father lived here in Sorrento he used to be friendly with Signor Bartoli.'

'Did they belong to a club together?'

He jabbed an idle finger into a drawer and nodded.

'Was it called the Caesar Club?'

'I think maybe it was.' He gave her a smile, making light of it, giving it no importance.

'Do you know what the Caesar Club is about?'

'No idea. A place for members to go drinking together?'

'Carlo, did your grandmother send you over here?'

He laughed at that. 'Of course not. I came to say hello and to see how you are.' He lied beautifully. 'I heard about the Naples bomb.'

'Tell your grandmother that if she wants to know the contents of my cart, she'll have to come and ask me herself.'

She smiled at him and he had the grace to blush.

The second knock on the door was soft. More of a scratch, fingernails on wood. No voice to announce their owner. Caterina jumped off the seat of the scannella and stood just inside the door, listening. There was no sound, no shuffling of feet with impatience.

'Who is it?' she asked.

'It's me. Leonora.'

Caterina had not expected that name. She threw open the door and scooped the girl inside, slamming the door behind her.

'Leonora, how did you find me here?'

'I asked around.'

That was all she needed, a count's granddaughter chasing through the town, asking after her. The girl was wearing a white cheesecloth shirt and loose silky trousers, the white dog at her side, its muzzle held high as it drew in the strange mix of smells of wood and oil. An odd colourless couple that did not quite seem to belong anywhere.

Leonora immediately wound her arms around Caterina's neck and squeezed her tight. 'I thought you were hurt. That night in Naples. I was frantic when I couldn't find you. I came back to look for you.'

The girl kissed Caterina's hair and didn't let her go.

'It's all right, Leonora, I'm not hurt.' Gently she unwound her friend's arms. 'But what happened to you? Why did you run away? Before the bomb went off.'

'I was worried about Bianchezza.' Her hand slid along the snowy fur. 'I felt something was wrong and I had to get home to Capri. Forgive me for deserting you. I am not ...' she shrugged her slight shoulders, 'reliable.'

Caterina wanted to believe her. That it was nothing, just a sudden whim to flee home, back to Capri and to her dog. But she wasn't sure she did believe her. The girl was jumpy and excited.

'What is it, Leonora? What's going on?'

'I brought you this.'

She slid a strap off her shoulder and threw down Caterina's canvas bag on her worktable. It was the bag she had left in Leonora's bedroom when they changed into the elegant evening gowns for the nightclub.

'I thought you'd want it,' Leonora added, her dark bob swinging forward with excitement. 'You might need it tonight,' she whispered.

Caterina did not hesitate. She snatched up the bag. They both knew what lay inside it.

The third knock on the door was brisk and to the point.

But this time Caterina's heart did not leap to her throat and her hands lay calm in her lap, because this time they were wrapped around the Bodeo. Her finger carefully released the safety-catch, that was all. She and Leonora were sitting on two hard chairs, positioned to face the door, the metal bar securely in place while Caterina narrowed her eyes and considered the plan that Leonora had laid out with such eagerness.

'Let us go to the caves,' her friend had proposed. 'Tonight.'

She said it the way others would say *Let us go the bar tonight*, and Caterina loved her for that courage. Apparently men had been coming to the caves on Capri for the past two nights and Leonora described it in detail. The moonlight catching the prow of their boat and turning the spume to silver filigree over the waves. The rocks grating on the hull. The rumble of the engine. Crates coming and going, carried by figures in black with torches and voices puncturing the pitch-dark night at the foot of the cliff.

Leonora had lain flat on the damp grass of a ledge halfway down the rock face, Bianchezza beside her. Caterina could see it as she described it, could smell the animal's breath, could hear the crunch of men's boots on the stones below and feel the weight of the black sky pressing down on her back.

'Come with me tonight,' Leonora urged. 'Bring a sail boat. Pick me up from the quay on Capri when all is quiet and I will guide us around the island past the Faraglioni rocks to the cave. We will be as silent as night herons. They won't even know we are there and we can find out if they . . .'

'No.'

'Caterina!'

'I need to find the jewelled table my father made, not go chasing through the night after stolen antiques. It's the only way I can get to Drago Vincelli.'

The dog whined. That was when the knock came, brisk and to the point.

'A message?'

'Yes, I've come with a message for you from Jake.'

Just the sight of Harry Fielding on her doorstep lowered the tension in the workshop, and Caterina slipped the gun back in its bag before he caught sight of it.

'What message?'

'He will be delayed. He won't be able to come over till later. He has more questions he needs to ask you about your father's workshop, but I'm afraid that with two of our men down it means we are all flat out and he can't get away yet.'

'I'm sorry, Harry.'

There were no other words. She could see the shock etched on his face at the death of his comrades, but it wasn't something he was ready to talk about.

'I must go,' Leonora announced abruptly. 'Can you give me a lift down to the ferry at the marina?'

Harry looked surprised at the request but was as courteous as ever. 'Of course. I'd be happy to.'

As he turned to the door, noting the iron pole with a nod of approval, Caterina put out her hand and murmured, 'Take good care of yourself, Captain Harry Fielding. Someone is carrying a sharp knife around out there.'

He took her hand. 'Keep a tight hold on that pole, Caterina. Let no one in until we have ascertained who the murderer is.'

'For God's sake,' Leonora muttered as she walked out of the workshop, 'she can look after herself. And so can I. We're not the ones careless enough to get our throats slit last night.' She ignored the stony expression that descended on Harry's face. 'Tonight, Caterina,' she said over her shoulder. 'Ten o'clock.'

Caterina shut the door on them. Slid the metal bar back in place across it.

She was alone.

CHAPTER THIRTY

For a long time Caterina waited for another knock on the workshop door but none came. She lit a cigarette and walked over to the wall where the photographs of her father hung. One was of him laughing straight at the lens, taken years ago when he was a strong and vital man clearly in love with the person behind the camera. The second photograph was years later, with him in the centre, flanked by Caterina and Nonno on each side. She was no more than seven or eight, her bony arm and hip moulded to the robust shape of her father. Caterina yearned to slide her hand inside the picture and hold on to that moment when happiness still seemed as normal as breathing. She brushed the tip of her finger across her grandfather's eyes, still bright and black.

'Nonno,' she whispered, 'dearest Nonno, you should have told me.'

Tears pricked her eyes and she looked across at the third picture. It was of Papà at work on the scannella, cutting out a section of veneer, and as she stared at it she saw that behind him stood a blurred figure she had not noticed before. She bent down and inspected it more closely, her nose almost touching the glass.

For a moment she failed to recognise it but then it came to her. It was a young girl called Rosamunda who used to turn up at times to sweep out the workshop for a few lire, a grey, unobtrusive child who merged with the background. Caterina had forgotten about the girl because she usually came when Caterina was at the uniform factory.

She stared hard, trying to conjure up an image of Rosamunda. Maybe the girl might remember something. She was trying to recall where the girl lived when there was a thud and a crash against the door outside. Caterina leapt across the room to the gun and spun back to confront the door that was quivering on its hinges. But the metal bar held.

'Now,' she said softly. 'Now you are here.'

This was why she had laid the trail of the cart to *this* place. Here. Her workshop. It was the place that defined her, that spoke of who she was and who her father and her grandfather had been. This was where she was strongest. This is where she could confront him.

Another kick clattered against the wood, splintering one panel.

'Wait!' she commanded.

She removed the metal bar, turned the key and stood back. When the door crashed open, the business end of her grandfather's gun was pointing directly at the intruder's chest and her hands were rock steady.

It was Aldo. He seemed to fill the small workshop, sucking up all the available space for himself. His massive shoulders appeared to stretch from wall to wall, as he kicked the door shut and faced Caterina with no shred of fear on his broad features. The gun might as well have been a fly.

'I've been expecting you,' Caterina said.

She had known he would come, the trail she'd laid was too tempting. But she had to show him now that he was wrong not to fear her. With no hesitation she pulled the trigger.

Sound exploded around her. The Bodeo recoiled in her hand, knocking her off balance. She steadied herself and heard the bullet slam into the timber of the door behind the big man. The noise in the confined space set her ears ringing and there was a taste in her mouth that she didn't recognise. Hot and metallic. As if she could taste the gun.

'You bitch! *Stronza!*'

His eyes were black with fury, his teeth bared at her, but he didn't move. Not a muscle. That was good. He had learned to fear her.

She kept the gun aimed at the centre of his chest. 'I don't know where you come from or how you watch me, but I drew you here because I want some information from you.'

He chuckled, a nasty sound that rumbled deep in his barrel of a chest. 'I don't give out information.'

'This time you do. If you want to continue breathing through your mouth instead of through a hole in your chest, you murdering bastard.'

He blinked, heavy hooded eyelids. Surprised.

The words came easily to her. All she had to do was picture this man hurling her grandfather down into the gorge, his skull cracking on the rocks, his sight draining away to leave only darkness behind. That's all it took. This brute was lucky she didn't pull the trigger again. Finish it. Right now. She could feel the heat of anger, like molten lead in her stomach.

She fought it down and quietened her breathing. 'Tell me where he is.'

'Who?'

'You know who.'

The thick ridge of muscle across his forehead contracted. 'Signor Vincelli, you mean?'

'Where is he?'

His dark gaze drifted from her face to her finger on the trigger and back again. He didn't hurry, but took his time, his eyes slow and speculative. She had thought of him as all muscle and brawn but now she wasn't so sure. His voice when it came was deep and resonant. It vibrated the wood-scented air.

'I don't know where he is. Signor Vincelli moves around,' he said at last. 'It is safer that way.'

'So how do you communicate?' She jabbed the gun at the air between them.

'Sometimes by telephone. More often we use gutter-dogs as runners.'

'Gutter-dogs?'

'*Scugnizzi.*'

The street kids. Of course. But she didn't believe he didn't know where Drago Vincelli had his hide-outs or how would

408

the kids know where to run to? No, he still thought she was stupid enough to fall for his lies. She dipped the angle of the gun till it pointed at his kneecap.

'Have you ever tried running with one knee, Aldo?'

He moved, no more than a slight shift of his weight as though preparing to attack. He was wearing a black lightweight suit and for the first time Caterina wondered whether he had a gun under there. The thought jolted her into action and she moved half a step forward.

'Take your jacket off.'

He took it off. His gun was in a neat shoulder holster that crisscrossed his white shirt. There were sweat stains on the shirt.

He hesitated.

The Bodeo was aimed at his groin. 'Unbuckle the holster.'

He did as she ordered and lowered it to the floor.

'Kick it over.'

He kicked it towards her. She felt better.

'Now we can talk,' she said.

The talk was brief. She accused him of killing the Rocco brothers and the two American soldiers, but he denied it. He would, of course he would. She had no proof. She could get nothing more out of him about Drago Vincelli's whereabouts but gave him a message to take to his master.

'The jewelled table does not exist,' she informed him. 'It was never made. Tell him that from me.'

The big man's swarthy face grew wary, not quite certain of himself for the first time. 'So what was in the cart this morning?'

'Old pieces of wood. Nothing of value.'

'Show me the cart.'

It was under her worktable, draped in a tarpaulin. She removed the covering. The cart was empty. He stared at it, then back at her with a twisted smile that made his black moustache squirm. 'If there is no table,' he said in a voice so quiet it became a threat, 'Signor Vincelli will want the jewels.' He held out his hand, a huge muscular platter, as if he expected her to hand them over there and then.

'I don't know where they are.'

'Then find them.'

Suddenly he was moving. Not towards her, but towards the far wall where there was a row of storage cupboards. He was fast, despite his bulk. Within seconds their doors were flung open and he was sweeping all the contents on to the floor in a jumble of brushes and sandpaper, files, a torch and jars of varnish. She watched, stunned. He could not seriously believe the jewels were lying around at the back of a pile of pots of fish-glue. This was just for show.

It was when he opened the cupboard where her finished music boxes were stored, awaiting sale at the next market, that she shouted, 'No!' He grinned at her and at the muzzle of her gun, and proceeded to throw them on the floor with indifference, turning his back on her and pounding the wooden boxes with his heavy boot. He ground their fine inlay under his heel.

'Stop now,' she ordered. 'You vicious bastard.'

Could she shoot him? Like this? In the back? He knew her

limitations and she hated him for it. She saw her finger shaking on the trigger, desperate to pull it.

'You want to die?' she demanded. 'Because I can oblige.'

He turned and saw something in her face that stopped the carnage underfoot.

'Do you know what I hate?' he sneered. 'I hate small spaces like this one.' His glance flicked around the workshop that was too small for his bulk. 'I hate tunnels and I hate mouthy women. *Puttana*.' He flashed his chunky gold ring through the air in a mimed version of a slap.

She was almost distracted.

Almost.

But fear does strange things to you. It alters your senses. You see the small things. The hardening of the lips, the flare of a nostril, the expanding black pupils. The sudden small intake of breath and the tightening of the skin at the eyes. It all came together in Aldo at that moment, all registered in her senses. So she was ready for the attack when it came.

He charged. She fired the gun.

But when a bull elephant stampedes towards you, you are not human if you are not afraid. Her heart reared up into her throat and her hand jerked. The shot went wide. In the fraction of a second before he reached her, she saw the bullet rip the edge of the collar off his shirt and skin a strip of flesh from the side of his neck. A fine spray of blood arced like a crimson rainbow through the air. A finger's width to the left and he would be dead, but it didn't even slow his charge.

He lunged at the gun and the impact almost broke her arm.

His massive fist slammed her hand, still clutching the Bodeo, down on to the worktable. A scream ripped out of her and she heard a bellow of rage that she thought came from him but it came from her. He was silent. The gun fell from her numb fingers on to the table and he reached for it.

Time ceased. Each heartbeat slowed. Her other hand dived into her pocket, pulled out the scorper hidden there with its long thin blade, and plunged it with all her strength into the back of his hand. Through muscle. Through tendons. Through flesh. Pinning it to the worktable.

A roar broke from him and she jumped back out of reach, the Bodeo safe in her hand once more. He yanked the scorper free, dark blood spilling from the wound, and as soon as the tool was in his good hand, he hunched his huge shoulders and lowered his head, on the verge of coming at her. She could see it in every nerve of his body but they both knew she would not miss her aim a second time. Not this close.

'Get out,' she hissed at him. 'Get out and don't ever dare come near me again. Tell that boss of yours that if he ever threatens me or my family again, I will put a bullet in his brain.'

Aldo said nothing but he was breathing hard. He pushed his bleeding hand into his pocket, tossed the scorper to the floor and lumbered over to the door. He threw it open so violently it slammed against the wall behind. He looked back at her, eyes narrow slits of hatred.

'You should have killed me when you had the chance, you stupid bitch.' His heavy lips spread in a warning snarl. 'Don't ever leave a job half done.'

Next time.

She would have to finish the job.

The stench of blood still hung in Jake's nostrils when he walked away from the Rocco brothers' backyard and it took five minutes on Sorrento's narrow stretch of beach to drag clean air into his lungs.

Corporal Hardwick.

Sergeant Whitely.

Two names he would never forget. Two letters he must now write to their mothers. The wretched war was over and those same mothers would be celebrating their sons' safe survival. How do you tell a mother that her son's throat has been slit by the people he came to help?

Where are the words for that?

He walked fast, back up the steep road, the heat clinging to his shirt. When he arrived at Caterina's workshop, thankful for the shade, he found Caterina scrubbing her worktable. She opened the door to him with a wet brush in one hand, dripping on to the floor, and he noticed that the soapsuds on it foamed pink.

'I'm sorry I was delayed.'

But she had turned from him, back into the room, her face shut down and unresponsive. Inside the workshop he could now see that behind her on the floor lay a pile of smashed fragments of wood. He stepped closer. It was her music boxes. Or what remained of them. They were crushed, hinges snapped. Her painstakingly exquisite inlay work was destroyed, scattered in twisted scraps on the stone floor.

'Caterina, you had a visitor?'

Immediately she abandoned the brush and came over to him, wiping her hands on the folds of her navy skirt. She wrapped her arms around him without a word and he knew she'd seen things in him that no one was meant to see. She held him close, one hand gently stroking the purple bruise on his neck, soft sounds rising from her, her lips brushing his cheek.

'I'm sorry,' she murmured, 'sorry about earlier. I didn't mean to make things awkward for you in front of the soldiers.'

She tipped her head back, looking up at him with her intense blue eyes and he knew that all his defences were useless against this young Italian who was never fooled by his police officer face. She lifted her hand to run a finger over his cheek, across the dark scabs on his forehead, down his nose, touching his lips. Finding life in each part of him.

'I thought you were dead,' she whispered. 'I thought you were dead.'

Her voice reached right through him to the hidden corner that lay in the dense shadow of guilt. She had known it was there. He didn't know how, but she did.

He kissed her pale forehead and felt her skin hot.

'What happened here?' he asked.

Her answer was silence. A silence in which he could feel the beat of her heart against his chest and her breath coming slow and steady on to his cheek.

'Tell me,' she said, 'who killed those men.'

Quiet words, yet they seemed loud in the room. So he told her about the soldiers. He let their names pass his lips. Sergeant

Tom Whitely. Corporal Jonathan Hardwick. He told her how he had woken up this morning feeling so damaged from his injuries that he'd made the decision not to go to Sorrento himself as it was only to run some routine questioning. That's all. Interviewing the neighbours around her father's bombed-out workshop again. Often a second round of questions produced different answers, forgotten memories rising to the surface, but instead of going himself, he sent Sergeant Whitely and Corporal Hardwick to do the task. They were young and eager. They wanted the job. If he'd gone himself, they would still be alive.

'But you'd be dead,' Caterina said quickly.

'I'd have been more careful.'

'You are in no state to be careful. You should be in hospital. Even Harry said so.'

She drew him over to the two wooden chairs, sat him down and fetched a glass of water for him. He needed something a hell of a lot stronger than water but he drank it down without complaint and kept the rest of his account brief while she sat on the other chair close beside him. 'The Rocco brothers were found in their backyard with their dog. All with their throats cut.'

'The dog as well?'

'Yes.'

'The soldiers?'

'Throats sliced from ear to ear. No one saw anything. It was done quietly. One person heard the dog howl.'

'Whoever did it must have been strong,' she pointed out, 'to overcome two well-trained men.'

He stared at a bullet slug embedded in the door and then at the carnage of broken music boxes. 'You have someone in mind?'

'Drago Vincelli's strong-arm sidekick, Aldo. That bastard was here in Sorrento today.'

The thought of such a creature even breathing the same air as Caterina ripped open something inside him.

'What happened?' he asked.

'I let him in.'

'Why the hell would you do that?'

'Don't, Jake,' she murmured, and took his hand between hers, stroking it firmly over and over until their skin seemed to melt together. 'I found out that they use the street urchins to carry messages and I found out that I cannot shoot straight.'

He laughed at that, an unexpected sound that surprised them both, but it loosened something that had been too tight, and he leaned forward and kissed her. Not just a brush of lips. Not this time. He kissed her full on the mouth, a hard hungry kiss that tore away whatever lay between them. She uttered a moan of pleasure and cupped her hand round the back of his neck, her fingernails digging into the short thick hairs of his Uncle Sam army haircut in a way that set his skin on fire.

He stroked her silky throat, her naked arms, the immaculate neat hollow of her collar bones, and he committed to memory the softness of her, her smell of coal tar soap and some kind of fragrant oil that she used in her work. They sank deep into him and he knew he could never remove them, nor would he ever want to. He would remember whole pieces of her.

She slid from her chair to his lap, her small frame lighter than he had imagined, no heavier than the thistledown at home that blew in the wind off Lake Michigan. Her fingers undid his tie and the buttons of his shirt, her breath coming fast from her full lips as she sank them on to his chest. It felt like being branded. Imprinting something of herself on to his skin. His hands caressed the soft curves and sharp angles of her slender body, taut and aching with need, and he knew that the only way he could make himself stop was by letting his mind step again into that rough yard of the Rocco brothers in Via Caldoni. Letting the stink of blood in the air crawl up into his nostrils once more.

He closed his eyes. 'No.'

The word fell like stone into the workroom. The air around them glistened with heat and he could feel a layer of sweat shimmer to the surface of her skin. Her body grew still.

'No,' he said again. Softly. 'This is not the time.'

Her eyes were huge pools of sapphire blue as they locked tight on his, her cheeks flushed, lips parted and moist. He wanted to seize her and roll laughing on to the floor with her in his arms, churning up the dust motes.

'Whose blood is that on the floor?' he asked instead.

'Aldo's.' She paused. Then a second time, 'Aldo's.'

There was a note of triumph in the second statement and Jake loved her for that. Fear must be hiding somewhere underneath, but he couldn't detect it. He waited for her to tell him what had happened, but she didn't, and he knew it was something he would have to come back to. She half-lowered her eyelids, the way a cat does in the sun, and rubbed her cheek against his.

'When today is over,' she murmured.

'When today is over,' he echoed and kissed her forehead, letting his lips linger there in a silent promise.

'Today,' she said quietly, 'Augusta Cavaleri told me that the accident in which my grandfather lost his sight was caused by Drago Vincelli. As revenge on my family because my mother refused him, despite encouraging him earlier. But then Mamma would, wouldn't she? It's what she does with men.' She let her gaze rest on his face for a second before turning it to the photographs on the wall, and he recalled the soft feel of her mother's arm tucked through his own. 'I think,' she continued after a long pause, 'that she was frightened for her own life. She fled, but of course took a man with her.'

'Roberto Cavaleri.'

She nodded. Then turned and kissed his lips.

'The Rocco brothers,' she said in a change of voice. 'They must have known something. Or at least, someone had reason to believe they might know something damaging.'

Jake curled an arm around her waist on his lap, keeping her there. 'I interviewed them myself a week ago. I liked their round jovial faces wearing matching wire-rimmed spectacles. Today the glass in the spectacles was crazed with blood. But back then they told me they'd seen or heard nothing, except the sudden explosion when the American bomb dropped.'

She grimaced. 'Of course they'd tell you that. You're an outsider. Not Italian.'

'Neither were Sergeant Whitely and Corporal Hardwick. They were just outsiders. Trying to help, goddammit.'

She jumped off his lap and swung to face him. 'Italy is grateful, Jake. Italy is grateful to you all for fighting our battles for us, for dying for us in Italian mud.' Her eyes were intense, but he could see her exhaustion in the way she held her head. As if it were too heavy. 'We will never forget what we owe you.'

He stood up. 'All you owe me,' he said lightly, 'is a kiss.'

Her lips were on his before the words were even out of his mouth and he felt the fire of her reach deep inside him. Abruptly she pulled back and let her gaze study his face, seeking something, though he didn't know what.

'Go now,' she said softly, 'go and do the work you have to do.'

'I will come to you later, I promise,' he murmured. 'Caterina, there are greedy and savage men out there, so I'm asking you to be more careful. Don't make me fear for your life. Don't ever put me through such agony again.' He pulled her back into his arms and pinned her there.

'Now I will walk you home,' he said.

'There is no need.'

'Yes, there is.'

He walked her home and waited in the street until he heard her shoot the bolt into place inside. Now she was safe.

CHAPTER THIRTY-ONE

Caterina knocked on the door. A crack ran down through one panel and its paint was peeling, exposing parched wood underneath. The street smelled unpleasant and the tenements leaned towards each other, seeking support. As she looked around her she spotted two filthy children, each wearing a British Army cap, crouching on the cobbles and playing races with frogs, indifferent to the stifling heat.

Caterina knocked again. This time she heard the sound of a child crying. The door opened and a young girl of about twelve stood there. She had straight dark hair and the face of a doll, wide-set green eyes and a cupid's bow mouth that was already curved in a sweet smile. Except a doll does not have an infant clamped on her hip or a toddler wailing as it clung to her fraying skirt. Her limbs were thin and spidery and her head turned with the alert movements of someone always on the lookout.

'Signorina Lombardi!'

'Hello, Rosamunda. You remember me.'

'Of course.' The girl beamed at her. 'Of course. You and your father were kind to me.'

'May I come in, please?' Caterina asked.

The girl jiggled the infant on her skinny hip and blushed. 'It's a mess.'

'Don't mind that,' Caterina said cheerfully and handed over a brown paper bag that contained bread, cheese, tomatoes and half a dozen peaches. Instantly the toddler at her side – hard to tell if it was a girl or a boy – stopped its wailing and attached a small paw to the corner of the bag.

'*Grazie*,' young Rosamunda sighed with a mix of relief and embarrassment. 'Come in.'

Caterina followed her into a one-room apartment at the back of the house. It was dingy, shabby and airless, but clean, with two single metal beds and a nest of threadbare blankets in one corner. A boy of about six years old was curled up on it. He looked sick.

'Rosamunda, where is your mother?'

'She died last year. Typhoid fever.'

'I'm sorry. Really sorry.'

The girl's father had been killed at the battle of Anzio and the mother had struggled to feed her nine children. Caterina remembered her. Sharp-faced, bone-thin and begging Papà to give her daughter paid work. At that time Caterina used to be incarcerated in the hateful factory all day making uniforms, so Papà had taken on the child to amble around the workshop occasionally with a broom or run a few errands for him. Just to help the family. Caterina hardly ever saw Rosamunda back then, and had certainly seen nothing of her for the last two years. She had forgotten her existence until today when she looked at the photograph.

She reached out, took the infant off Rosamunda's hip and its solemn eyes with long lashes regarded her with serious interest. She smiled at the emaciated child in her arms and received a contented gurgle in return.

'Rosamunda, how do you manage? Nine of you in this one room?'

'Yes,' she laughed. 'It's noisy at times. But we get by.'

'How?' Caterina asked.

'We sing. All nine of us. As a choir.' The young girl grinned. 'Your father always said I could sing, so I taught my brothers and sisters. We go round the bars, singing for the soldiers. They like to hear us and pay us good money for the songs. They always ask for *Torna a Surriento* – Come back to Sorrento.' She ruffled the toddler's soft hair. 'You know all the words, don't you, sweetheart? Thank God for the soldiers. We would be dead without them.'

Caterina broke off a snippet of bread and handed a piece to the two youngest ones. In an instant it had vanished.

'Rosamunda, did you ever see my father working on antique works of art, statues or icon or—?'

'Oh yes. Often.'

The air seemed to tighten in Caterina's lungs. She had not expected that answer. She had seen the triptych with her own eyes in Jake's basement and had recognised Papà's work, so she knew her father was corrupt, yes, she knew it, but still . . . There was a small stubborn part of her that refused to believe it. But to hear this girl say so easily, 'Oh yes. Often,' was too much. The girl could be mistaken. She was only a child. Surely she could be mistaken.

'So where did my father keep these items? They were never in the workshop when I came back after my factory shift.'

The girl took out a peach and all of the children's eyes gleamed in the gloomy room, as she raised a knife.

'Of course they were there.' Rosamunda smiled at the peach in anticipation. 'In the hidden room.'

Hidden room? Caterina wanted to snatch the fruit from her, to make her rethink the words she had just spoken.

'What room?'

The knife shaved off a juicy slice of flesh from the peach and the air was suddenly thick with the scent of it.

'The room behind the shelves.' She flicked a dark glance at Caterina and ran her tongue along a trail of juice on her thumb. 'Didn't you know? The whole set of shelves swung forward on a hinge. Behind was . . .' she took a tiny morsel and popped it in the parched mouth of her sick sibling on the blankets.

'Was what?'

'A small storeroom.'

Oh Papà. Another lie. More deceit. More corruption. Did I not know you? It was like a veil in front of her eyes and piece by piece she was tearing it down.

'How did you discover the storeroom was there?'

'I crept into the workshop one day, so silently Signor Lombardi didn't know I was there. I was always frightened of disturbing his work, so I tried to be quiet. I watched him open up the secret

423

room behind the shelves. It was there, signorina, honestly it was. I am not lying.'

The overcrowded room felt like a furnace.

'Did you ever see a table there?' Caterina asked. 'One covered in jewels?'

'Yes.'

'Are you sure?'

'Yes.'

'What was it like?'

'It was the most beautiful thing I have ever seen in my life. Beautiful enough to give to God.'

As Caterina turned into her own street, a figure was leaning against the wall of her house, ankles crossed, cigarette in hand, looking for all the world as if taking a snooze. The sight did not slow Caterina's pace. She speeded up, approaching fast but up on her toes, her feet silent on the basalt.

'I thought you'd gone,' she said.

Her mother rolled her head to face her daughter but otherwise did not shift her position. It was the stance of a prostitute, Caterina realised, and hated herself for the thought.

Lucia Lombardi gave her a slow smile. 'So did I. But I remembered something and came back.' She glanced towards the front door. 'He's out, your Nonno. Your brother too. No one home.'

'Nonno will be in a bar. Luca on the boats.'

Caterina noticed she said *'Your brother.'* Not *'My son.'*

'What is it you want, Mamma? The rest of the money?'

Her mother had taken half, left half on the table. That was something. Not much, but something. But it seemed now she was regretting it.

'No, Caterina, that's not why I'm here, damn you.'

'What then?'

'Because I have something to tell you.'

'It's too late, Mamma. Far too late. Don't tell me things I don't want to hear. About Papà. About Nonno. About that day you left. It's over, Mamma. Finished.'

Lucia Lombardi studied her in silence for a long moment. In no hurry. Eyes a hard granite blue. 'Not yet, Caterina.'

Words started to come out of Caterina that were not meant to come out. 'Sometimes,' she told her mother, 'I used to write about that day. The day you left. The cruel things you said to Papà. In the hope that by emptying them on to a page, they would go away. But they didn't. They stayed. Nailed inside my head.'

Her mother's stance stiffened. She pushed herself off the rough wall and let the cigarette drop to the ground.

'I came here now to help you, Caterina. To tell you one thing. I remembered where that bastard Drago Vincelli kept his Rolls-Royce Phantom when I knew him. I came back to give you this.' She handed over a slip of paper, holding it between the tips of her fingers, so that their hands would not touch. Without another word, she marched away, swinging her hips. Like a prostitute.

Caterina leaned against the warm stone of the wall for a second, sagging under the weight of what had just happened.

She unfurled the piece of paper. An address in Naples, *22 Via Adduci*. But could she trust it?

If it was genuine, it meant she had somewhere to start, a way to get to him. This was her one chance. To save herself and to save her family.

She must not let it slip.

In the deep shade of the narrow street a sandy-coloured dog slunk along against the wall, then lay down opposite her, panting hard. She found herself panting with it, until she realised that she was leaning against the exact same spot where her mother had leaned. She pushed herself away from it in case part of her mother crawled under her skin.

Piazza Garibaldi was heaving with heat and noise. Its incessant flow of traffic never ceased. Its people were all in a hurry. Caterina emerged from the grand arches of the station's colonnade and dodged across to the central island where a dozen lime trees offered shade. She drew breath there while she regarded the pedestrians with a quick assessment. She needed information about the whereabouts of Via Adduci.

In front of her rose the towering monument and statue of Giuseppe Garibaldi, the great founding father of the *Risorgimento*, the unification of the Italian states into the Kingdom of Italy in 1870. But even now the city of Naples was rebellious. It had its own rules, did things its own way. The Allied Army had invaded to save the country from Hitler's forces, but who would save Naples from itself when the soldiers were gone?

The prospect of Jake leaving these shores was unthinkable.

She pushed it away. Because if she didn't, she couldn't concentrate, and right now she needed her mind to be sharp. She didn't *want* to push it away. The feel of his fingers spanning her ribcage, the taut skin of his throat tasting like sunlight on her tongue, the horror of what he'd seen in the Roccos' backyard still engraved deep on his face. His eyes bloodshot, his shoulder flinching when her weight pressed on it. All these things she had to tuck inside her mind for later, but it was hard to stop herself imagining what would have happened if he hadn't said 'No'.

She headed for a newspaper kiosk, the vendor cheerful and flirtatious even when he found out that all she wanted was directions. She hopped on one of the trams rattling to a stop in the piazza and headed for Via Adduci.

It wasn't what she expected. Caterina thought it would be a row of lock-up garages at the back of a shabby apartment block on the edge of town, somewhere where strangers came and went all the time and no one took a blind bit of notice. That was the kind of man Drago Vincelli was, it seemed to her, one who blended with the crowd, not sticking his head up in case it got blown off. A man no one saw.

But she was wrong.

The garage at 22 Via Adduci was more of a barn, long and well-tended, coral-coloured tiles sunning themselves on the roof above walls of red brick. Smart and expensive looking. Like the street. There were tall wrought-iron gates to the property and a short driveway into a gravelled courtyard. The villa was centuries old and built of yellow tufo stone that gave it a somnolent air, in contrast to the garage that ran at right angles to it and which was clearly much newer.

Trees and flowering shrubs lined the walls, purple bougainvillea was sprawling over the gateposts. The place smelled of money and servants and Caterina knew she couldn't hang around here without being spotted and reported, so she quickly lifted the latch on the gate, slipped through and moved briskly across to the end wall of the garage. It lay in the shade of a stand of oleander trees and was not visible from the house.

No one challenged her. No one came running across the courtyard. She crept as silently as she could on the gravel around the corner to the back of the garage block where there were bushes and spiky fan-palms. She crouched down under the fronds and studied the brick wall in front of her.

How to get inside?

She sat on her heels on the black loamy soil, her blood thrumming in her ears as she inspected the single-storey building in front of her. The Rolls-Royce Phantom might not even be stored there any more. He might have moved it. Or sold it. Along the top of the building under the guttering ran a line of thin windows to allow access to daylight. There were four of them, each one about a metre wide but no more than half a metre high. One problem. They were three metres off the ground. Never had she regretted her lack of height more.

There must be a way. She eased herself out from under the palms, moved quietly to the far end and peered around the corner. A quick glimpse. There was a lean-to out in the open and it was stacked with large logs for winter fires. She gave it three seconds' thought, then made a dash to the woodstore. Ten seconds, that's all it took. She hurled herself back behind the wall, arms full of logs, her mouth so dry she couldn't swallow.

She stacked the logs under the first window and was about to climb them when she heard something, a rustle in the undergrowth, the swaying of a frond. She plunged her hand into her bag, fingers struggling for a grip, but a high-pitched wail came from a clump of leaves and a cat emerged, a creamy Siamese with a cross-eyed blue gaze.

She was pointing the gun at a *cat*. The absurdity hit her.

'Shoo!' she hissed and the creature vanished but she knew how close she'd come to shooting it.

She clambered up the logs and peered over the edge of the sill. In the gloomy interior she could see that a sleek black beast of a car stood inside the building, with a bonnet long enough to sleep on and huge chrome headlamps. Above them on its giant radiator like an exotic silver nymph sat the Spirit of Ecstasy Flying Lady mascot. It was the Rolls-Royce Phantom.

Caterina worked fast. She rapped the window with the butt of the Bodeo and the glass shattered. Behind it was a layer of metal mesh, but it also caved in after numerous blows from the gun. She plucked out the shards of glass, and ignoring any scrapes and scratches, she scrambled through the opening. With a grunt of relief she dropped down to the cement floor.

She was inside.

*

There was no sound in the garage except her own impatient breathing for hour after hour. She counted each minute that passed because they might be the last minutes she could ever count. Time slowed to a crawl. When the door of the garage finally swung open, brilliant afternoon sunlight stumbled into the dim interior, so that Caterina had to narrow her eyes to keep the gun trained on the figure silhouetted against the light.

Only one figure? She had expected two.

It was male, she could see that much, slim and definitely not weighed down by Aldo's bulk. This man carried himself with a swagger that gave her hope. Drago Vincelli was the one she wanted. Anyone else would get in her way and she didn't wish that on them.

'What the fuck are you doing in my car?'

Bull's eye. She recognised that voice full of malice. Drago Vincelli himself.

'I've been waiting for you,' she said and her voice sounded calm.

She had been seated in the open-topped Rolls-Royce behind the giant black and chrome steering wheel with its centrally mounted gear shift for two hours. The big cream-faced clock on the walnut dial fascia told her that. In her head she had played out every possible scenario and none of them ended well. But at least they all ended with Luca and Nonno still alive and out of danger, and if she was lucky, who knows, she might be still standing too.

During those two hours she'd thought about hell and she'd thought about Nonno's milky eyes. And she'd thought about the man in whose shiny black car she was sitting. Its seats were a rich dark red and it was like sitting in a pool of blood.

'Get out of my car, you fucking bitch! Right now.'

He was carrying nothing in his hands. No gun. No knife. No weapon of any sort. He wore just a white shirt and dark trousers, a heavy-link gold chain at his neck to match the gold tooth that even now he liked to flash. No shoulder holster with a neat little pistol. That frightened her. Drago Vincelli unarmed was even more dangerous than Drago Vincelli armed. It meant he knew something she didn't.

She slipped out of the car, keeping her eyes fixed on him, the gun lined up with the button at the centre of his white shirt. He didn't move a muscle. Beside her stood another car. It was a distinctive french-blue, almost the colour of her mother's eyes, clearly a Bugatti, judging by its trademark horseshoe grille. It looked expensive, one of those luxury cars that men like to pamper more than their wives. Its sweeping bulbous front wings begged for a loving touch and a dorsal seam ran down its spine all the way to its fast-back tail.

For no more than a split second she swung the Bodeo away from Drago Vincelli and pulled the trigger. The explosion in the confined space was deafening as the bullet smashed through the bonnet of the Bugatti and screamed as it ploughed into the engine.

Drago Vincelli roared with rage.

She fired again. Into the glossy black coffin-bonnet of the Rolls-Royce Phantom. This time Drago Vincelli greeted the act of vandalism with dead silence. She was reminded of how he had manipulated the stark silences in the confessional box to unnerve her.

'The next bullet is for you,' she announced.

He didn't blink. He didn't beg. He didn't do a thing except curve one corner of his mouth into something she might have thought was a smile, if she didn't know better.

'You fight better than I anticipated,' he said.

It sounded amiable. Respectful even. But she knew it was neither.

'You fight better than some men,' he grinned, as though trying to distract her with his gold incisor. 'I've seen Aldo's hand.'

'He deserved it.'

She could pull the trigger now. Right now. End it all.

Take a man's life.

She told herself this was no man, this was a devil who had no claim on life. Not after all he'd done. She need show no mercy. But her finger froze on the trigger.

Drago Vincelli saw it.

'I knew you would be trouble,' he said. 'Just like your father was.'

Outside in the road the sound of a car's engine approached and Caterina felt a stab of dread, but the car drove past.

'You are only alive, Caterina Lombardi, because I want your father's table with its jewels and I am certain you are the one to find it.'

'When you are dead, Drago Vincelli, the table can rot in hell along with you, for all I care.'

She tightened her grip, the metal warm on her palm. She took a breath and slowly released it. Now.

'No.' The word leapt from Vincelli's mouth. 'If you wish your brother to live, take your finger off that trigger.'

His black eyes didn't flicker, and she could see a dark thrill in them. Fear clawed at Caterina's heart, raw and red-blooded because she knew this was why he'd come alone and unarmed. Unafraid. He had Luca.

'Where is my brother?'

'Somewhere safe.'

'You're lying.'

He wasn't lying. They both knew it.

'You are not a person who does what you are told, Signorina Lombardi. I saw that. There is steel in you. I decided to take no chances, so this morning I persuaded your brother to step aboard a boat bound for Naples.'

Persuaded.

No, no. She knew what Vincelli's *persuasion* involved and horror hit her. She prepared to pull the trigger but she caught the flash of his grin.

'If you shoot me,' he said flatly, 'you will never see your brother again. He will not die pleasantly, I warn you. Find that table for me and all will be well.'

'Where is he? Where is Luca?'

He chuckled, a thick slimy sound. 'He's with Aldo.'

The market in Via Verrazzano was crowded and crushed as shoppers fought to find the cheapest bargains. Caterina elbowed her way through the stalls, blind to all but the ones selling clothes. Some were on hangers, fur coats and beaded dresses, but no one wanted those. Food was what the hands grasped for. Bread. Flour. Potatoes. The stubby end of a salami.

Caterina's hand was clamped on her bag, aware that thieves stalked the shoppers. They pushed shoulder to shoulder, fingers trailing into pockets. She slapped away a hand that thought her attention was on a pair of sandals. It thought wrong. She moved fast, eyes darting from stall to stall until she spied what she was after. It was a bundle of work shirts thrown in a heap on an army blanket spread out on the cobbled ground. She crouched and dug out a shabby one, grey and threadbare. A patch of a different fabric had been sewn over a hole in the front of it, as if its previous owner had been shot.

She snatched it up. 'How much?'

The woman selling the clothes was squatting on a three-legged stool, past sixty judging by the lines of effort on her face, but with a tiny baby asleep and swaddled on her lap. She looked at Caterina quizzically.

'Are you all right?' she asked. The babe on her lap cheeped in its sleep like a bird. 'You don't look so good.' Her smile was laced with real warmth. 'Sit down a minute. Your skin is as grey as the shirt.'

'You are kind,' Caterina replied. 'But I am in a hurry. How much?'

'Take it. It is worthless. It is yours for nothing.'

In the midst of the vociferous noise of voices haggling over prices, the amorous cooing of pigeons on the rooftops, the shout of a barber offering his services in the street, and her own cry of despair echoing inside her head. In the midst of it all, when life seemed as black as it could get, she was being offered this brief moment of kindness. It gave her hope.

Caterina ran all the way across the vast Piazza Nazionale and down Via Casanova. When she reached the jeweller's shop, she pushed open the door and entered its gleaming interior. She was carrying a loaf of bread, still warm against her chest, and thrust it as an offering to Signora Bartoli who was polishing the glass of the cabinets as feverishly as if trying to polish the marks off her own soul.

'Caterina,' she declared with surprise. 'What are you doing here, my child?'

Caterina allowed herself to be swept into an embrace, folded into the warmth of the plentiful bosom, patted and fussed over. When she finally came up for air, she stepped backwards out of the jeweller's wife's circle of affection; she knew she was going to have to hurt this woman.

'Signora Bartoli,' she said, aware of the risk she was taking. 'I need your help.'

The scissors sliced off the trouser-leg just below the knee.

'It will look absurd,' Signora Bartoli declared. She huffed a grunt of displeasure. 'You should not be doing this.'

Caterina shook her head. She continued to attack the bundle of old clothes that she had brought with her and which now lay spread on the bed in the apartment above the shop. She hacked off the lower third of the second leg to match the first, followed by the cuffs of the shirt. They had been too long. Her fingers pinched out the cut threads, so that the ends of the garments were frayed and wouldn't look recently worked on. The trousers were dark and shapeless, and she had threaded a length of Signora Bartoli's string through the loops at the waist to act as a belt. Without it they would fall down on her. Five minutes later she stood in front of the dressing table and wasn't sure if it was her or her brother she was looking at.

The stranger in the mirror was a boy. Short and slight with cropped hair slicked straight back off his face with a handful of oil. It emphasised the cheekbones like blades and the harsh purple smudges under the eyes. The shirt and trousers looked ridiculously big, like on a child who had sneaked into his father's work-clothes. He shuffled his feet uneasily in boy's scuffed sandals with thick soles that were good for running. She had chosen them with care.

It was the eyes that worried her. They were like Vanni's. A man's eyes in a boy's head. She turned away so that she wouldn't have to look at them and pulled on a peaked cap that hid half her face when she ducked her head.

'This is all wrong,' Signora Bartoli moaned, but at her side her daughter, Delfina, grinned.

'I'll come with you if you like,' she offered.

'No.'

Signora Bartoli smacked Delfina affectionately on her cheek. 'You stay out of this, *mia bella*.'

Her daughter started to rub smears of black grease and cinders into Caterina's *scugnizzi* clothing and over the skin of her arms and legs, rubbing it deep under her toenails, enjoying the task.

Signora Bartoli stood with arms folded protectively over her bosom, eyeing the way Caterina's small breasts had been strapped flat under the loose shirt.

'You remind me of the boys in the air-raids,' she muttered, 'nervous as hell. During the war they used to come scampering down the stairs into the underground tunnels that were designated as shelters when I was a warden down there and had to keep the little wretches under control.' She sighed, remembering. 'Some of the children were scared witless, poor kids.'

Caterina could imagine this kind and generous woman giving comfort to the terrified lonely children when the skies spat down death on them. She angled her cap, put a narrow-eyed sneer on her face and swaggered across the room towards the door with a careless flick of her hand to clear her path.

Delfina laughed.

Signora Bartoli put a hand over her mouth, eyes full of things unsaid.

'I'm taking my bag. But . . .' Caterina hesitated, '. . . I'll leave my gun here, if I may.'

It was hard to abandon the Bodeo but any *scugnizzo* worth his salt would have it off her in seconds.

'Take them bread, *cara mia*,' Signora Bartoli said. 'It will help.'

'Help what?'

'Help you to come back.'

CHAPTER THIRTY-TWO

Living on the streets. Not *walking* on the streets. *Living* on the streets, Caterina saw things differently. Naples and Neapolitans become not a city with people, but a landscape of opportunities, a place where sharp eyes could mean the difference between living and dying.

Sharp eyes notice the niche that will keep you dry in the rain. The corner out of the wind. The bombed house with the basement where you can squeeze in at night. Sharp eyes spot the hand that carries something too loosely, or foolishly puts it down for half a second.

And then it becomes yours.

The *something* can be anything, it doesn't matter what because everything is of value. To be eaten. Bartered. Sold. Half an apple, a heel of stale bread. A spanner. A bucket of newborn chicks. A jacket on the back of a chair. A purse in a pocket. Best of all, a wallet from a fat man smoking a fat cigar, because it means the wallet will be fat too.

All these *somethings* crossed Caterina's path that first day on the streets. She saw them disappear into small hands and heard the running of feet. She forced herself to take it slowly, to be patient, but it was hard when every second she was imagining Luca in Aldo's clutches. And Aldo had a score to settle. She tried to tear those images from her mind, as she scoured the streets and the bombsites, head down, cap low over her face.

No sign of Vanni.

She loitered on the edge of other gangs of *scugnizzi*, her manner sullen and uncertain, the way she had seen so many of the homeless boys behave. She handed out chunks of bread from her bag in exchange for answers but the answers were always the same. Yes, we know Vanni and his wolves. No, we haven't seen him today. No, we don't know where he hangs out. Clearly, there were rules. There was a brotherhood on the streets. Of a sort. When they heard Vanni's name their faces tightened.

But not one of them doubted she was a street urchin. In her dirt and skinniness. She withstood their scalpel-sharp scrutiny each time, hardening her mouth, hunching her thin shoulders, lowering her voice. Each time they were more interested in her bag than in her, but they saw something in her face, something feral, something defiant that made them accept her as one of their own. And that scared her.

She hitched herself to a group of four at first. She found them roasting the carcass of a seagull over an open fire on a deserted bombsite off Via Amerigo Vespucci down by the harbour, where British and American troopships were already loading up military equipment to ship home. She crouched down in

439

the heat and the dust and handed out cigarettes. It was only then that she ventured to ask for the hundredth time that day, 'You know Vanni?'

The same answer. Yes, we know Vanni. No, we have no idea where he is.

In her head she could hear the clock ticking, the minutes running out on Luca's life. She tossed the whole pack of cigarettes at the feet of the youths sitting around the fire in the dirt.

'I'm asking again,' she said, more insistent this time.

Their eyes flicked to her face and down to the white packet with its red bull's eye. They were clearly family. All had the same narrow pointed face and heavy nose. The oldest, who wore the dried-out pelt of a black cat around his neck, gave the others a glare, to silence them, but the youngest, skinnier and slighter than the rest, spoke out.

'Vanni hangs out up at the Galleria Umberto on Corso Umberto. That's his pitch.'

'Pia, shut your mouth.' The oldest one's hand swung out and clipped an ear, but the cigarette packet was already pocketed.

Pia? Caterina stared. The youngest was a girl?

Caterina tore off another chunk of bread and gave it to the girl.

'Thank you. *Grazie*,' Caterina said.

She set off at a run.

Vanni was there. Outside the Galleria Umberto Primo. Caterina spotted his rangy restless figure at once. She leaned against a palm tree and dragged in a lungful of fumes, as traffic streamed down the wide boulevard of Corso Umberto, one of the main commercial arteries of the city, its tall elegant buildings pock-marked by bomb damage.

He seemed to be alone.

The Galleria Umberto had become the heart of Naples. Everybody came there since the liberation. All sorts, those with money and those without. Indolent women in black lace stockings and businessmen looking to fix a deal, all averting their gaze from the squalid beggars outside. It was an arcade in one of the finest buildings in Naples, but down at heel and seedy these days.

Caterina didn't move. Not till Vanni did. He ducked his head, reducing himself to little more than an oversized shirt, and shuffled through the towering archway of the entrance. Caterina gave him ten seconds, then scurried after him in what she hoped was a *scugnizzi* scuttle.

There used to be a magnificent glass domed roof over the building, but the Allied bombing had put an end to that. Yet Caterina could not help but be impressed by the nineteenth-century grandeur of its vast columns and its archangels, but it was fighting a losing battle against the shops specialising in stolen goods, in restaurants that served black market food, and in bars that were the dimly lit haunts of mobsters and whores and thieves. It was a cross between a cathedral and a brothel. Caterina regarded it warily with interest.

A sudden slap on the back of her head made her spin round.

'What the fuck you doing here? Get off my patch.'

It was Vanni. How had he got behind her? She had followed him in.

He was jumpy, hands twitching. The crowd had swallowed him, but he must have circled back without her realising and now stood between her and the entrance, pale-eyed and aggressive.

'I didn't know,' she muttered. Eyes on her feet. Head hanging.

Don't let him see you as a threat.

'Fuck off then,' he snarled. He didn't recognise her – not in her dirt and her rags. It was the elegant white evening gown he'd seen before, not *her*.

He punched her, a fist hard in the stomach. Never before had she been hit. Before she could stop it her hand had lashed out and smacked him across the mouth.

Right then, before he could knock her to the ground, there was a roar from behind him and a shout.

'That's him.'

A muscular arm wound around Vanni's neck, who kicked and screamed but was pinned in a vice.

'Where's my wallet, you stinking piece of sewer-shit?'

It was a workman in navy dungarees, face puce with anger. Caterina saw the outcome at once. Vanni would be carted off to the police station, thrown in a cell overnight to teach him better manners and Luca would die. Calmly Caterina took a pair of heavy metal shears that lay on a nearby stall and slammed them into the side of the workman's head. He dropped like a stone.

Before he'd hit the ground, Vanni and Caterina were running.

*

He didn't thank her. That wasn't his way. Instead he asked her name.

'It's Bruno,' she muttered.

And he let her stay. That was enough. As Bruno, she trailed along behind Vanni and his wolves all day, and with her cap pulled well forward, she ran the streets of Naples. She stuck to his heels and kept her mouth shut. She refused to steal money from people's pockets but she snatched an apple from a stall and a pair of sunglasses a soldier was foolish enough to put on the bonnet of his army jeep. In Naples anything that was not bolted down vanished.

Dusk crept up on her before she was ready. It slid through the back alleys and the last rays of the sun gilded the tip of the triangular pinnacle of the Gothic cathedral, so that it looked like a giant arrowhead plunged into the heart of the city.

Vanni changed when darkness came. He moved like a cat through the velvet blackness, all skin and bone but silent and sure, as he herded his pack of wolves tighter to keep them safe. With the stolen money he bought salami and bread, even a beer and he shared them equally between his pack, including Caterina and little Tino. She was concerned about the smallest boy. Tino had coughed all day, relentlessly until he was grey and exhausted, but he grinned at her as he sank his young teeth into the greasy sausage.

She had an odd feeling that he recognised her, but she said nothing. And neither did he.

CHAPTER THIRTY-THREE

The carved door closed. The key turned. The meeting began. The chairman was in an ill-temper but allowed no sign of it to show, except that the silences were longer, his sentences shorter. But none of the men around the table was aware of it. Except the one in the uniform. That one had quick eyes.

For half an hour he let them sharpen their claws on each other. Vent their bile. Settle their scores. He permitted them one cognac, no more. Enough to fan the flames but not enough to burn the house down.

'Mr Chairman, I say we close it down.'

All eyes turned on the speaker. A lawyer, a cautious man, a man who runs when a rabbit chases him. The chairman stared at him in silence, obliging him to lay his pale white neck plainly on the block for all to see.

'The danger is too great now,' the lawyer expanded. 'Too many people are asking too many questions and sniffing around in the right places.' He fretted at his gold cuff links.

'That girl. Antonio Lombardi's brat. She is stirring things up.'

Brat?

Caterina Lombardi was worse than a brat. Infinitely worse. Each time he turned round, she was there, a fucking stiletto in his side. One to be plucked out and destroyed.

She had damaged his Phantom and wrecked his Bugatti. The cause of his ill-humour, the reason for the acid burning his gut. It was not something the chairman liked the taste of.

The lawyer repeated, 'I say we close it down.'

'Shut down our network?' It was the banker, his voice high. 'Don't be a fool. We need to do more, not less. I say we expand.'

'Of course you say that. You are a banker. There can never be enough money in the world for you.'

'No, we have to tread more carefully.'

'I agree.'

'Don't be such an oaf. Now is the time to gather as many artworks as we can get our hands on. The troops are leaving. They don't care.'

'It's dangerous.'

'That American major.'

'He's digging too close.'

They all piled in. Voicing fear, exposing greed. But it was the wood-craftsman from Sorrento – the thin one who barely shaved and always drank his cognac in the first thirty seconds – who put words to the thoughts in the chairman's head.

'Get rid of the brat.'

Silence.

The chairman smiled. He passed the bottle of cognac down the table. He hadn't thought the Cavaleri craftsman had the guts. He didn't usually take after his mother.

The owner of an export company, a man with ships, leapt to his feet. 'I will be no part of such a thing. I agree that we should close the operation down. The war is over. We have done all we can. Time to stop.' He pointed a finger at the man in uniform. 'Go home, soldier.'

The shipping man pushed back his chair and strode to the door. He tried the handle but the door didn't open. He turned and held out his hand imperiously.

'The key, please, Mr Chairman.'

'You know the rules,' the chairman said mildly.

He let the man stand there, empty handed.

In the ante-room on the other side of the door, the drinkers of the Caesar Club could be heard carousing, unaware of the decisions of the eleven men in the banqueting chamber.

'The rules state,' he continued, 'that no one can leave or enter until the meeting is ended.'

'To hell with the rules. Open this door.'

The chairman was patient. Slowly he opened the buff file in front of him. Slowly he extracted a photograph of the exporter lounging on the deck of a ship and wearing no clothes. Surrounded by six exquisite naked boys.

'Sit down.' Sharp. Cold. Full of acid. 'I have a picture for your wife.'

CHAPTER THIRTY-FOUR

'What is it you want?' Vanni's voice came at Caterina out of the darkness.

She sat up, making her bed-nest rustle. A bundle of copies of *Il Mattino* acted as her mattress, betraying every twitch or shift of a limb. Vanni had led them into a tenement courtyard and slithered through a broken air-vent into a basement that stank of urine and rat excrement, where they laid claim to a pile of old newspapers kept there for sleeping nests, but Caterina could not sleep. Not while she thought of Luca with Aldo.

Tino was coughing, so she crawled over to his bed-nest, lifted his ragged shirt and rubbed his skinny little chest to help bring up the phlegm, the same as she used to do for Luca. When Tino finally fell into a fitful sleep, she felt her way back to her own newspaper nest, collapsed on to it, aching as she let her eyes sink shut.

'What the fuck is it you want, Bruno?'

Her eyes shot open. She rolled her head to face in the

direction of Vanni, though she could see nothing. It felt safer. Facing him.

'I am looking for someone, Vanni.'

'Who?'

'A man called Aldo. He's huge. An ox with a big moustache. Likes hurting people. You know of him?'

In the silence she could hear him thinking.

'You seen him around, Vanni?'

'You ask too many questions, kid.'

Earlier Vanni had got into a fight, some clash over boundaries. He and the leader of another group of street urchins had flown at each other like wolves, teeth and claws slashing. That's what she was aware of now, that ruthlessness of his, if she stepped out of line and threatened his pack.

'What happened to your parents?' she murmured.

'None of your fucking business,' he snapped.

'What about Tino's?'

'Dead. All our parents. All in the same street. Fucking British bombers came at night. Except for Meo's pa. He was shot down.' She saw the flare of a match as he lit himself a cigarette. 'It's kill or be killed. The bombs taught me that. Life is a shithole and you got to stay on top. You got to learn that, kid.'

'You watch out for your wolves.'

'Sure I do. They're . . .' He drew hard on his cigarette.

Family. That's what he was going to say. These orphans had become his replacement family and she knew he would spill blood for them.

'Vanni, I got family.'

No comment. The tip of the cigarette dodged like a firefly.

'A brother,' she added. 'Luca. Did you have a brother, Vanni?'

Still no comment.

'I need to find Aldo. Real bad. He's got something of mine.'

'What's that?'

'My Luca.'

Smoke curled around her nostrils, so he must be looking at her.

'Where is Aldo?' She could hear the urgency in her voice. 'Please, Vanni.'

There was a rustle of newspaper as he shifted position, turning his back on her.

'Like I said, kid, you ask too many questions.'

From nowhere the sluggish clouds came, bringing a dismal morning drizzle that constantly threatened worse. It swept through the harbour, blurring the hard edges of the cranes and trucks, turning the sea into a sheet of lead that nudged the grey troopships moored offshore. More military units were leaving.

Caterina pushed Tino's tattered cap firmly down on his head. His skin was burning up. He should be out of the rain, but he wouldn't let Vanni leave him behind. They had come to the docks to see if they could pick up anything the army wouldn't miss and while the rest of the pack sheltered in the ruined hallway of a roofless block of apartments, Vanni loped back and forth out in the rain.

To Caterina he did look like a wolf. That same ferocity, that same fixed focus. His long jaw thrust forward, and always the tireless stride.

Did he trust her? Did he trust Bruno?

She yanked her cap lower over her eyes and stepped out into the downpour, shoulders hunched, her shirt already soaked to her skin. Now was the time to find out.

Luca. Hold on, Luca. I'm coming. And if Aldo has laid a finger on you, my brother, I will put a skewer right through his heart.

She fell into step beside Vanni, though he didn't bother to acknowledge her. She could sense a tension in him, a restlessness as he paced, hands cupped around his eyes to help him peer through the rain, and she wondered what was going on in that head of his.

'What you need,' she announced at his elbow as he scanned the curve of the sea-road up past the grim medieval fortress of Castell Nuovo, 'is a pair of binoculars.' She gave a rough smile. 'You could spy on . . .'

Vanni jerked to a halt, seized her shirt front and yanked her to him. Not roughly but firmly.

'You got binoculars?' he demanded.

'No.'

'You know where to get them?'

'Yes.'

He shook her, rattling her teeth. 'You tricking me?'

'No.'

'Where?'

She placed both hands flat on his chest and pushed hard,

breaking his grip, and danced out of reach before he could lash out at her.

'I'll get them,' she said. 'And bring them here. Maybe two pairs of binoculars.'

He sneered at her through the rain, rivulets running off his chin. 'No, Bruno, you little shit. We're coming with you.'

Jake was seated at his desk, surrounded by papers, a cup of army coffee at his elbow and grit between his teeth. The grit came from his ride up to Sorrento. This morning he'd roared through the rain on the Harley, taking bends at breakneck speed, but still Caterina wasn't home. No sign of her. And now it had got one hell of a lot worse because there was no sign of her brother either. With a curse he flung the report of his latest interview across the desk, lit a cigarette and filled his lungs with smoke.

Where are you, Caterina?

Goddammit, why hadn't she stayed put in her workshop yesterday like he'd told her? They both knew this business with Aldo wasn't over. Jake and his team had spent yesterday interviewing half of Sorrento's inhabitants about the murders and Commissari Belzano had proved to be anything but helpful. To hell with the local police. In a case like this that involved both the army and the *polizia*, the Allied Military pulled rank every time. Everyone knew the police were corrupt. It was a fact of life in Italy. They were paid a pittance and were struggling to survive, just like everyone else round here.

But when Jake had finally reached Caterina's workshop it was late afternoon and it was locked. At her house her grandfather was a bundle of nerves, pacing the floor, cracking his stick down on the tiles as if it were somebody's head.

She had left a note. *Gone to Naples. Back soon. Don't worry.*

But she wasn't back. And now there was no Luca either. It was that note that convinced Jake that Caterina and Luca were not together. The note was obviously intended for her brother to read, not for her blind grandfather.

Don't worry.

Of course I worry, Caterina. I worry like crazy.

'Find her,' her grandfather had pleaded. 'Find my grandchildren, I beg you, Major Parr.'

This was not a man who found it easy to beg.

Rapidly and methodically Jake had interviewed the neighbours, even dragging them out of bed in their nightclothes. One piece of information emerged that he hadn't expected: Caterina and Lucia Lombardi had been seen deep in conversation yesterday outside her house. Jake allowed himself a sliver of hope. If Caterina was with her mother, they could be together in a bar somewhere and Lucia Lombardi was a woman who knew how to look after herself.

He had raced back to Naples and set about tracking down Lucia. It didn't take him long. He started by questioning Maria, the prostitute who hung out at Leo's Bar, the one who had recognised Caterina as Lucia Lombardi's daughter the first day he met her. It seemed Maria hadn't seen Lucia, but she gave him names of others who might have. So Jake had the prostitutes marched into his office, brothel by brothel. Blonde, brunette, flame-haired, sweet or sharp, yawning or sullen, it made no difference to him. He questioned them all. He had learned long ago that streetwalkers know the secrets of a city.

And all the time he'd handed out cigarettes as if smoking had just been invented, until a raven-haired fifty-year-old in a scarlet skirt had said, '*Si*, Major Parr. I know this Lucia Lombardi.'

He pushed a pack of two hundred Lucky Strikes across his desk and she wrote down an address.

Simple as that.

'Jake, you got a minute?'

Jake finished checking his .45 and slid it into its holster. 'Can it wait, Harry?' He picked up his officer cap and tucked it under his arm. 'I can't hang about.'

'No, Jake. It can't wait.'

Jake heard the note of urgency. 'Okay, get in here, but be quick.'

Harry entered the office and shut the door behind him.

'What is it, Harry?'

Harry stood to attention. Something he never did when they were alone.

'Spit it out, Harry.'

Harry drew in a deep breath. 'The painting of Mary Magdalene by Bronzino, the one that you retrieved from the brick factory. It is missing.'

'What?'

'It is not in the basement storeroom. Not any more. It has gone.'

'What the hell do you mean? Gone? How can it have gone? I put it there myself.'

'Someone has removed it.'

'Not possible. No one has access to those basement keys except you, me and Colonel Quincy.'

Their eyes fixed on each other, and Jake started to shake his head. Slowly at first, but then faster.

'No,' he said softly, 'not Quincy.' He began to prowl the room. 'No. Colonel Quincy has worked as tirelessly as we have to preserve this collection for Italy. Not Quincy.' The possibility stunned him. 'I informed him on the evening of the nightclub bomb that I had deposited the painting.'

He halted mid-stride.

'Colonel Quincy insisted I stay in hospital the next day.' He stared bleakly at his comrade.

Harry nodded. 'He ordered me to take the unit up to Sant'Agata to do a sweep of the place because of so-called *information* of a cache up there. Which I will remind you, Jake, we did not find.'

'We have no proof of criminal intent,' Jake pointed out. 'He may have removed it in order to . . .'

A knock sounded on the door and it opened.

'Not now, sergeant.'

'I have a message for you, sir.' The young uniformed soldier looked uneasy.

'Who is it from?' Jake asked.

'It's from one of the dirty kids that roam the gutters of the streets. He's out the front. I booted him away but he was insistent.'

'Deal with it, sergeant.' He turned away.

'But sir . . .'

'What is it?'

'He said it was important and that you'd want to speak to him.'

Jake was suddenly alert. 'What is the message?'

'He says he has information. About someone called Caterina Lombardi.'

The rain was lashing down, blurring the world outside, as Jake scanned the street outside the palazzo for the boy. A passing yellow bus sent a wave of water up over the pavement and a movement off to his left caught his eye. A skinny youth in rags was shaking his bare legs like a dog to rid them of the soaking, but his shirt and cap were already drenched. How long had he been waiting there?

'Boy!' Jake shouted. 'Get over here.'

Instantly the boy came scurrying over, head down against the downpour, dirt snaking down his limbs in dark runnels. Jake was sheltering under the portico that adorned the palazzo's façade and indicated for the *scugnizzo* to join him.

'Well? What is it you know about Caterina Lombardi?'

He put out a hand to grasp the boy because he knew how these street kids could vanish in the blink of an eye, but at that moment the boy raised his head and looked directly at Jake. Huge blue eyes stared up at him.

'Caterina?' he gasped. 'What . . . ?'

'Frown,' she hissed at him. 'Frown and smack me. We are being watched.'

It was hard to frown when he wanted to grin with relief and hug her soaked body to him, but he forced his face into stern lines and cuffed her lightly across one shoulder.

'Come inside,' he said quickly.

'No, I can't.'

'What the hell is going on?' He inspected the street, squinting through the rain. This time he saw them. In the doorway of a draper's shop, two lean figures, boys who would be men.

'Who are they?' He spoke in quiet tones, as if the watchers might somehow hear through the rain.

'Jake.'

One word. Desperation within it.

'Tell me what has happened?'

She stepped back from him. To stop them reaching out to each other.

'Aldo has my brother. Drago Vincelli arranged it.'

'Oh God, no.'

'It's true.'

He seized her thin wrist. She tried to pull away but he refused to let go. 'Where is he keeping him?' he demanded.

'I don't know yet. But the *scugnizzi* have some information and I am buying it.' She hung her head as though being bullied by him.

'Buying it with what?'

She flicked a glance up at him with the faintest of smiles. 'Two pairs of American Army binoculars. Cigarettes and aspirin.'

He didn't even blink. 'Wait here.'

Reluctantly he released her wrist and hurried inside, crossing the huge marble hall at a run. It had happened so fast. She had materialised on his doorstep looking like something dragged up from the bottom of the harbour, yet he wasn't able to give her the shelter he craved to give. Her skin was ashen, her lips blue and bruised-looking, yet her eyes still burned with that intensity that meant he could never look away.

He burst into his office, ransacked desk and cupboards, and emerged two minutes later with a pair of Bausch & Lomb binoculars in their leather case, a pack of aspirin and his last two hundred Lucky Strikes carton.

As the price of a boy's life, it didn't seem much.

'Harry.'

Jake barged into the English captain's office without knocking. 'I need your binoculars.'

'What for?'

'Quickly, Harry.'

Harry was on the telephone. He clamped his hand over the mouthpiece and mouthed, 'Colonel Quincy,' raising one eyebrow. 'Excuse me for one moment, sir,' he said smoothly into the telephone and pointed at a filing cupboard. 'Bottom drawer.'

Jake snatched from it a case of Kershaw binoculars, British Army issue, and headed for the door. With a sinking heart he heard Harry saying to their senior officer, 'Did you by any chance remove the painting to have it cleaned, sir?'

*

'Thank you.'

Jake handed over what she'd requested, plus his army rain-coat. He knew it would be far too big for her but he couldn't bear to watch her drown.

'Come straight back here,' he said. He hadn't meant it to sound like an order, but that's how it came out. 'When you know where Luca is being held, I'll find him for you. Promise me you won't do anything foolish on your own.'

She didn't promise. But she wrapped herself in his raincoat, pulling it up over her head, burrowing inside it so that only her dirty lonely face showed.

'Thank you, Jake.' She gave him a soft self-conscious smile that ripped his heart open. 'You've saved my life. Because otherwise I would have had to batter the information out of Vanni and I don't think his wolves would have liked that.'

'What do they call you, those wolves?'

'Bruno.'

'Well, Bruno, I intend to wait right here on this spot until you get back. Make it fast.' He risked a smile. 'I'll need my coat.'

She lingered another minute, reluctant to leave him, it seemed.

'I tell them you give me these things,' she whispered, 'because I found you down the side of the National Museum in Piazza Museo kissing your colonel's wife.'

It took an effort not to laugh. 'Come back to me, Caterina. In one piece.' He glanced in the direction of the huddle of youths in the shop doorway. 'Let me take them the binoculars; I could bring them in for questioning.'

'They'd be gone before you'd got within five metres of them.'

'Try me,' he said.

She shook her head heavily. 'I daren't. They are my only link with Luca. Give me a slap and then I'll go.'

Her reluctance to leave frightened him. As though she did not expect to return.

'I'd rather give you a kiss,' he said.

That made her smile. But then she was gone.

Jake stood there an hour and then another hour. The downpour stopped and the pavements started to steam.

Cigarette after cigarette hit the black basalt slabs under his feet. A mountain of paperwork sat on his desk demanding attention but he concentrated only on the mouth of the alley-way where she had disappeared. He stood there and willed her to come back to him and did deals with San Gennaro, the patron saint of Naples, if he would send her hurtling back around that corner.

He thought about her young brother, Luca. Terrified and alone, only eleven years old. Tied up. A prisoner of a man who took pleasure in inflicting pain, but if the boy possessed even half his sister's guts, he'd hold on. He'd know she would come.

When eventually she rematerialised it was without the rain-coat. She came from a different direction, tearing towards him at a run in her too-big shirt and cap, and if he hadn't had sharp eyes he'd have taken her for just another of the street youths fleeing from the *polizia* or from a rival gang.

'Jake,' she gasped. She was breathing hard and had a bruise ripe as a plum on the corner of her jaw. 'Quickly. Via Baldone.'

He nodded. He was ready, the unit on standby. This Via Baldone, this street that held her brother captive, it would not know where to hide when the might of the US Army hit it.

He made her stay. This was army work and she could be no part of it.

She argued. Of course she did.

But it wasn't negotiable. If he was taking a unit in there under the guise of searching for stolen artefacts, she was cut out. She had no place here.

She had traded the binoculars for a street name where Aldo could be found. But no number. It would take time and patience. He made her understand this.

Her hands gripped his shirt front, her face anguished, and he thought she was going to rend it into sackcloth. But she didn't. She stood close to him, her hair oiled back from her forehead, pain etched into its fine bones, and she locked her eyes on his.

'Find him, Jake. Find him alive.'

'If he's there, Caterina, I promise I will bring him to you.'

He made her stay. Safe behind the barriers.

Jake surveyed the dilapidated slum houses in front of him and recognised that this was not a safe place to draw breath. This was deep in Camorra territory, run by the mafia clans and by mafia rules. It dealt in extortion, protection, narcotics and prostitution, and not even the police risked confrontation here.

If you handed over money each week and did what you were told, you lived. If you caused trouble, you died. No exceptions. If Aldo was here, it had to be because Drago Vincelli had struck a deal.

But this was the US Army. It didn't do deals. It imposed its own rules. With a sense of pride Jake watched the platoon of beefy young GIs obey orders smartly and leap from the two olive drab 2.5-ton GMC transport trucks that were positioned across each end of the road. There was the pounding of buckled boots and the rattle of M1 Garand rifles in the hands of men who knew only too well how to use them, as they spread out along the centre of the street.

It was narrow and dirty, green filth skimming the puddles of rain, and the terrace of four-storey houses looked drunk and crumbling. Shutters creaked on broken hinges and faces with hostile eyes stared out from behind upstairs windows. A ripple of panic shot through the street, tight with tension. Jake took control, ordering a detail into each house to evacuate all the residents into the street, while the soldiers set about searching each room.

'Sir.'

'What is the problem, lieutenant?'

The young officer in charge chewed on his blond moustache uneasily. 'Some of the doors are locked, sir.'

'Open them.'

'Yessir.'

'Open all of them.'

'Yessir.'

There was the sound of splintering wood. All around the street echoed cries and shouts and Italian matrons screaming at their military overlords in words that few of the soldiers could translate but all understood. A loose-limbed GI hurried away from one front door with a cheek scarlet with the imprint of a slap on it. The Italian women voiced their objection loudly at being ousted from their homes; the Italian men were quieter, their deeper voices rumbled in huddles in the road, resentful at having their houses searched.

'So, Major, what in the name of Gesù Cristo are you looking for?'

The question came from a muscular man in a stained vest, with rapidly receding black hair and dark angry eyes.

Jake regarded him with mistrust. 'Your name?'

'Enzio Azzarà.'

'Well, Signor Azzarà, we are seeking a big bull of a man called Aldo.' His eyes scanned the string of residents who were being herded into the street, but no one there fitted the description. Ragged children were watching the soldiers with wide excited eyes. 'You know him, this Aldo? He may have a boy with him. Seen him around?'

'No.'

It came too quickly. Other discontented eyes in the street watched as men stood in silence, arms folded across their chests. Jake felt the hairs on the back of his neck rise.

'We also have word that there are stolen historic goods cached here,' he informed them. 'I intend to search every . . .'

'Major, every stinking house in Naples has stolen goods

hidden away. You know that and I know that. Are you going to arrest everyone in the city?' An unpleasant grin split the man's face and he tapped the side of his head. '*Che palle!*'

'Out of my way, signor.'

Jake strode over to the first house in the terraced row. Inside, the stink of bad drains hit him in the face and the smell of stale body odour was overpowering. Pallets and mattresses lay strewn on the floor of each room, crowded together. How people survived life in a hellhole like this in the heat of a Naples summer with only occasional supplies of water was beyond Jake. He inspected each tenement room with a burly Texan sergeant and a young lance corporal behind him, men he knew he could trust, rifles at the ready.

'Luca!'

He shouted out the name, listened to the empty silence and shouted again.

'Luca!'

He tried to picture the young boy. Tied to a chair and gagged or shut in a wardrobe, blindfolded and bloodied, each image getting worse inside his head. He'd seen kidnappings in Milwaukee and they always ended badly. That was something he didn't explain to Caterina.

They searched under beds. Found unspeakable things. Opened cupboards. Raked through filth, room after room. And they did it all over again in the next house. House after house. It was like striding back in time, tumbling back into a world before anyone had thought of such things as bathrooms and running water or electricity. It was no wonder these people stole. Took anything they could lay their hungry hands on. Prime Minister Bonomi and his government were going to need one hell of a sledgehammer to crack open this hard nut of poverty.

But of Aldo there was no sign. Was Caterina's *scugnizzo* a lying little skunk? Or had the big man got wind of the army sweep? The same way they had at Saint'Agata in the mountains. Jake cursed his luck. But he refused to abandon hope and personally conducted each house to house search with brisk efficiency, while Harry Fielding interrogated the uncooperative residents who were huddled in the centre of the blocked road.

'Major Parr, there you are.'

Jake's heart sank. He spun round to find Colonel Quincy at his shoulder, his ginger hair glistening with sweat below his cap. Christ, that was all he needed. Since when did the colonel come sticking his nose in operations? He stuck to his desk and his catalogues. What on earth had prompted him to turn up in this godforsaken backstreet from hell?

Jake saluted.

'Found anything?' Quincy demanded peremptorily.

'Not yet, sir.'

'You'd better not get this wrong, Parr,' Quincy warned. 'I stuck my neck out to get you the company unit you requested today for this search. I need results. Make certain you find some artefacts of whatever kind. That's what we're here for, isn't it? Don't you go making me look a fool, Major.'

'No, sir.'

In the prickly silence that fell, they both heard a cry from a child and for a moment Jake thought it might be Luca. Let it be Luca. Please let it be Luca and put an end to this charade of hunting for artworks here before Colonel Quincy realised what was going on. But no. It was another black-haired child of six or seven, frightened and fretful.

'Very well, Major. Carry on.'

Behind Quincy, Jake caught sight of Harry Fielding listening to the colonel's every word, a thoughtful frown on his face.

'Silence!'

Stillness spread through the room. No one breathed.

Jake could hear something, though it was faint and difficult to grasp. Too small to be called a sound. But it was there. The slightest of vibrations, but the harder he listened, the more elusive it became.

He was in a stark bedroom tucked high up under the roof eaves of a house at the far end of the street, and the heat trapped in the small space was unbearable. Sweat clung to his shirt. The sergeant and lance corporal working this house with him paused, to listen and wipe sweat from their eyes, but the only noise was the tramp of boots outside in the narrow street. Harry was down there, staring up at the window.

A thin stained mattress lay on the bare floor, a rough-hewn crucifix nailed to the wall and threadbare blankets were thrown in a heap in one corner. That was it. Except for a saucer piled high with cigarette butts. Worse, the window was broken, the glass smashed outwards. Jake quickly stuck his head through the empty frame and swore fiercely when he saw that a rope dangled down from an iron bracket outside, an escape route set up in case anyone came calling. So they had been expecting callers and someone had tipped them off. It sickened Jake. Was Quincy another one corrupted by Italy's treasures? The rope plunged down all four storeys to a tiny backyard below and Jake imagined the big man Aldo struggling down it at speed, sweat making his palms slippery, his wounded hand throbbing. Cursing Caterina under his breath.

So close. So close Jake could smell his oily sweat.

Had he taken the boy? Strapped on his broad back? Or thrown him out of the window. Or, God forbid, was Luca already dead and buried? He thrust away that thought.

He had promised to bring the boy to Caterina.

In silence he moved along the walls of the room, tapping, listening, and then he stared hard at the floorboards. He crouched, head cocked. Again there was the sound that wasn't a sound. He snatched his army clasp knife from his pocket, flicked out the blade and thrust the point into the edge of one of the floorboards. It didn't shift, but he tried another and another. The sergeant did the same, breathing hard.

'Christ Almighty!' exclaimed the sergeant. 'Don't let it be that. Not a child. No one would do such a thing to a poor child.'

'Luca!' Jake called out. He held his breath, listening hard.

That faint sound. It came again. Behind him.

He swivelled round and tried the board under the window. Let him be wrong, let it be a mouse. It lifted. He yanked it up and his heart jammed because inside the narrow gap between the joists lay what looked like a dead body. A mummified dead body. Bound in bandages from head to foot with only a tiny slit open across the eyes and across the nostrils.

'Luca!'

The eyes moved, glistening wetly. Jake's heart bounded back into action as he reached in and, with the sergeant taking the swaddled feet, they raised the child's body from its dark tomb. It smelled of urine and fear.

'Fucking hell and damnation!' the sergeant swore, a man with children of his own. A shudder ran through Jake as they carefully laid their light burden down on the floor.

'It's all right, Luca,' Jake said firmly, 'you're safe now. I'll have you out of this in no time.' The blade of his knife sliced through the cobwebbed bandages and he tore frantically with his hands at the frayed ends till the boy was free of them. 'You are Luca Lombardi, aren't you?'

The boy tried to nod and his young mouth convulsed in a spasm. Tears glittered in his eyes. His whole body started to tremble, his limbs jumping violently and Jake swept him into his arms, crushing him to his chest to press some of his own strength into the boy's fragile limbs. The worst thing was that Luca was silent. No words. His lips white and clenched tight, his teeth grinding. That was the sound, the faint noise that Jake had heard earlier and it raked at his heart.

What kind of person could torture a child like this? He kissed the boy's wet cheek.

'Come on, Luca, I'll take you to your sister. You'll be all right. No need to fear any more.'

Kate Furnivall

He lifted the boy in his arms as gently as he would a baby and carried him out of the room where he had been entombed. Outside, the air in the squalid street seemed fresh and clean by comparison, and Jake headed rapidly towards the army barricade, beyond which he knew Caterina would be waiting. He heard her voice cry out, saw her dodge under the truck.

'Major Parr, where the hell do you think you're going?' Colonel Quincy stepped into his path. 'Put down that filthy urchin and get on with finding the hidden artefacts. That's why we're here, let me remind . . .'

Jake swept past him and kept on walking, walking away from that room, the weight of the child's head tight against his chest.

CHAPTER THIRTY-FIVE

'Caterina.'

'What is it, my sweet?'

'I thought I was dead. I thought I had gone to hell.'

The darkness enveloped her brother's small bed, pressing closer, as she listened to the whispered words. She had lit a candle.

'The only hell, Luca, is in that man's evil head. You are here in Sorrento, safe and well.' She ran a hand along his arm, chafing its bare skin so that he would know he was alive. 'With me and Nonno.'

Silence. But she knew there was more to come. He had to let it out.

'He swore. A lot. He cursed you. He wanted to slit my throat. He described it to me in detail. All the blood.'

She didn't breathe.

'But his boss had ordered him to keep me alive until . . .' The words died.

She waited.

'Until you had done what they wanted,' he whispered.

'I'm sorry, Luca. Unbearably sorry.' She kissed his cheek. It was ice cold.

'He said he would crucify my hand.'

The weight of guilt descended on her chest.

'He said our mother is a whore. He said Papà died because he deserved to. He said the rats would eat my eyes under the floorboards. He said you are a whore-bitch who fucks with all the soldiers.'

He said.

He said.

He would die for what he'd said.

'He said he would hide me down in the black tunnels next time he goes down there; he would leave me tied up in the dark along with all the rest of the things down there, and I would die a slow and agonising death.'

Caterina drew her brother closer, fiercely pressing his face against hers to protect him from the thoughts rampaging inside his head.

'Listen to me, Luca. None of it is true. You know it isn't. He was trying to poison your mind. I will make him regret it, I promise. You're safe now.'

He tucked his head under her chin in the way he used to when just a kid. She stroked his hair, soft and reassuring, her breath easy and rhythmic. Only her heart betrayed her. Kicking against her ribs, hammering to get out.

Caterina could not drag her gaze from Jake's hands. They were square with thick pads of muscle and blunt nails, and right now the fingers of one hand were curled around one of Luca's ragged shoes.

Jake was seated in her grandfather's armchair opposite her, the lamps throwing his shadow in different directions, and he was talking earnestly about Colonel Quincy, the officer she had met at the nightclub. But his voice faded in and out of her ears. Instead her mind was filled with concern for her brother while she watched Jake's hand flex and unflex around the shoe, as though it were too precious to let go.

'I'm worried about him,' Jake said.

'About Luca?'

'No. I'm talking about Colonel Quincy.'

'Of course.'

They had talked about Luca and about Aldo till their tongues were sour from the subject.

It was late now. Her brother and her grandfather were in bed. The doctor had given something to help Luca sleep and outside, the night was hot and sultry with rumbles of thunder, but no rain. The hospital had been thorough with Luca and pronounced him fit to go home, just a few bruises and scrapes, but he had barely said a word, just sufficient to reveal he had been inside the cramped grave under the floorboards for almost twenty-four hours. A policeman had sat taking notes. Caterina had held Luca's hand the way Jake was now holding his shoe, and had felt his tremors shoot through her own body. She saw the mark, the small cross cut with the tip of a blade on the back of his hand, a pointer to the spot where to stab the knife later to match his own wound, before he bandaged Luca up like an Egyptian mummy, a filthy rag jammed in his mouth.

What kind of man did that to a child? Rage burned inside her.

'This Quincy of yours, is he clever?' she asked.

'Yes, very. He carries an encyclopaedia of art in his head.'

'So what is the problem with him?'

Jake paused and gave her a slow smile. 'I have just told you.' He moved from his chair and was suddenly on his knees in front of her. He touched the bruise on her jaw, his fingertips gentle. 'You have other worries on your mind. Forget Quincy.'

'No, Jake. Tell me again.'

So he told her again. It seemed a painting had gone missing from the basement storeroom, and on the last few missions houses or villages that they searched turned out to be dead ends, the stolen artefacts all vanished. As if they'd been forewarned. Just like Aldo had been.

'You think Quincy is working with the criminals? Maybe with the Caesar Club?'

'It's possible.'

He placed her brother's shoe on her lap, and she saw acute sadness in his eyes.

'You know, Caterina, Italy dazzles me with its beauty,' he said softly. 'Even after all the bombing, Naples is bewitching. We Americans have most of the riches of the world, but very little of its soul. It is all here in Italy, so other countries come to steal it.'

Caterina reached forward and let her hands touch him, which is what they'd been craving to do all evening. They caressed his face, her thumbs chasing the lines of tension from his high forehead, her fingers tracing the ridge of hard muscle to his jaw where late-night stubble pricked at her fingertips and made her want to rub her cheek along it like a cat.

'It's interesting,' she murmured, 'that Quincy left the nightclub just before the bomb exploded. As though he knew it was coming.' She kissed his cheek and breathed against his skin. 'As though he were in league with Drago Vincelli.'

She heard his tight intake of breath and felt him recoil inside, though his face remained warm against her lips.

'He is a British Army Officer, Caterina.'

As if that were enough.

'Is the army above corruption?'

His eyes focused on hers. 'There are so many temptations here.'

It was his look, rather than his words, that seemed to melt the barrier of ice that had formed around her heart the moment she'd seen her brother lying limp in his arms, his cheeks drained of colour. She clenched her fists on Jake's army shirt and pulled him close.

'Do you think of me?' she whispered. 'When you're busy waving your gun in somebody's face or ordering your men to seize a hoard of treasures from a cellar. Do you think of me, Jake, when you least expect it?'

'No.'

Her heart dropped.

'I think of you, Caterina, every waking moment. You are always there like sunlight in my mind. So no, I don't think of you when I least expect it. Because I always expect it.' He unlocked her fingers. 'No matter what, I cannot stop it.'

He kissed her hard and hungrily on the mouth, and despite all the pain and terror of the day, desire raced through her with a force that dragged a howl from her, stifled only by his lips. Nothing had prepared her for this, this seething, raging heat in her blood or this desire to devour him alive.

She slid off her chair, forcing him to fall backwards on to the cool tiles, just as the chime of the church clock nearby insinuated itself into the room as it struck midnight. She sat herself astride him on the floor, her thighs gripping his hips, and his eyes narrowed into dark slits of hunger.

'Jake, do you think your Colonel Quincy has taken secret possession of my father's jewelled table too?'

'What?'

But he saw her smile and realised she was teasing him. She bent down and kissed his throat, pressed her tongue on to its rapid pulse. Because right now there was no table to find. No dragon to kill. Time had stopped. It discontinued as abruptly as if cut by a knife and she floated free in his arms.

'Caterina.' His breath touched her skin. 'Caterina, promise me something.'

'Anything.' Her lips felt so heavy they could scarcely form the word.

'Promise me you will not put yourself in deliberate danger again.' His hand gripped her thigh and squeezed hard. 'The

way you did with the *scugnizzi*. With Aldo in your workshop.
With Drago Vincelli in the church. Promise me, never again.'

Her thigh hurt. The heat of it shot straight to her groin and
she moaned softly.

'You can't wrap me in cotton wool, Jake.'

'Promise me. Stay at home and lock yourself in with your
brother and grandfather until I can—'

She didn't promise. Instead she tore the buttons from his shirt
and kissed the gun-shot scar that lay beneath it. Her tongue
swept over the hard muscles of his broad chest and the taste of
him was seared on to her tongue. A taste of salt. Of strength.
And of something stubborn that made her whole body hungry
for him. She revelled in the long lean limbs of this man who
had so inexplicably become a part of the fabric of who she was
and she uttered a deep moan of pleasure as he slid her dress from
her shoulders and put his lips to her naked breast.

She felt a lurch of something deep within her. Something so
profound that it had no name. She knew she wanted this man
as fiercely as she wanted to go on living, needed him like she
needed to breathe.

The house was cooler now. The timbers creaked and clicked as
it flexed its beams, but it was hard for Caterina not to imagine
stealthy footsteps on the floorboards. Time and again her head
jerked round, chasing shadows. She reminded herself that Jake
was downstairs, a long-limbed guard-dog who would prowl
till dawn.

She was in Luca's bedroom and it smelled different. Even

though Luca had scrubbed his skin till it was raw, the stench of the foul floorboards under which he had been imprisoned seemed to cling to him as though it had seeped into his flesh. Into his fresh young mind.

In the darkness she caught the sound of her own breathing, a harsh enraged sound, and she forced it into a quieter rhythm. She didn't want to bring Luca her anger. Just her love. Her anger she would save for where it belonged, for the person who did this atrocity to her brother. She lay down on the bed beside him, curled her body in a tight ball around him and held him close, and as she kissed his hair, she felt the slight shift of his weight towards her, taking refuge.

Enough.

She wanted to scream the word. Enough. No more. She wanted to tear Aldo's eyes out and shred Drago Vincelli's heart into the gutter.

Today.

It must end.

Caterina felt Jake's lips brush hers, full and warm. He was leaving. They were standing beside the front door and dawn was only minutes away. Her arms encircled his waist, hands locked together, unable to let go.

'Don't open the door to anyone,' he instructed, his mouth still against hers. Eyes unwavering on hers.

'Don't go out.'

'Don't let Luca or Nonno go out.'

'Lock the door and stay here till I get back.'

Each instruction punctuated by a kiss.

Don't leave. The words were there on Caterina's tongue and she had to bite down hard to prevent them tumbling out. *Don't leave. Don't leave me to do the things I will do today. Save me from myself.*

'I'll be back as soon as I can,' he promised. 'As soon as I have news.'

She smiled. She nodded. She kissed him. She let him go. Wrenching her heart from her chest. Outside, the street lay in a muted pre-dawn greyness that swallowed Jake until all that remained of him for her to hold on to was the sound of his boots on the black slabs.

The wind whipped the sea into choppy wavelets that made the ferry crossing rough. The sea was laced with white caps that the early morning sun painted gold and scattered with streaks of crimson. Caterina turned away. It looked too much like blood.

The old ferryboat, smelling strongly of diesel fumes, was almost empty at this hour and the beauty of the emerald island of Capri rising out of the sea mist in the distance should have given her a moment of peace, but it didn't. It made her impatient. The clock was ticking fast. A pair of seagulls swung low over the boat and she envied them their wings.

Bait.

That's what she was setting herself up as. Not fish-bait for seagulls, but tunnel-bait for those who wanted her dead. She had not breathed a word to Jake about Luca mentioning Aldo's threat to hide him in the black tunnels 'along with all the rest of the things down there'. If she did, the army would pour down there in a wave of khaki and Drago Vincelli and Aldo would vanish like the mist, only to reappear one day with a knife at Luca's throat.

She had thought it through. She must be the bait.

'Leave,' Jake had said to her last night when she lay naked on the rug beside him. 'You must leave Sorrento. You and your brother and grandfather. I will help you to set up a new life somewhere else where . . .'

She had kissed the words from his lips. 'No, Jake. You don't understand. They would come after me. They would hound me down till they found me and then they would kill us all. That's what Italians do when it is a matter of honour. I cannot leave.'

She had rested her head on the jagged scar on his chest, a hairless silver platter that was a perfect fit for her cheek. She could hear the beat of his heart.

'No, Caterina.' His hand buried itself in her hair and she could sense the desperation in his words. 'I have some money saved. I could take you away to . . .'

'Jake, I don't want your money.' She stretched out on top of him, inhaling his breath deep into her lungs. 'I want you.'

'She's eating breakfast on the terrace.'

'I apologise for calling on you so early, Signorina di Marco, but it's urgent. May I speak with her, please?'

Caterina adopted a polite smile. She was wearing a dark green skirt and an olive short-sleeved blouse that she hoped had a military feel. She wanted people to do as she asked, no questions asked, like they did for the military, because today was not a day she had time to waste.

Octavia di Marco seemed to sense it. She was dressed as usual in a tapered black trouser suit, her sleek hair swept up, and after a moment's consideration led the way through the maze of white corridors, past the sunken pool and out on to the elegant terrace where Leonora was sipping a long glass of something that looked green and unappetising. Caterina was pleased to see the dog, and for once the dog seemed pleased to see her because it bounded forward with a wag of its plumed tail.

'Caterina!'

Leonora jumped to her feet, came over and hugged her visitor.

'I missed you last night,' Leonora said, lowering her voice so that only Caterina would catch her words. 'You didn't come to inspect the caves with me.'

'I couldn't, Leonora. Something urgent arose that took me to Naples.'

The young girl pulled a face, but she didn't take offence and slid her slender arm through Caterina's to lead her to the spot where she had been sitting.

'Signorina Lombardi. Here again. It seems you cannot keep away.'

It was Count di Marco who spoke. He was again reclining on his chaise longue, draped in white robes under the shade of the canopy. Its creamy fringe was ruffled by the wind off the sea, as the sky and the sea emerged reluctantly from the mist.

'So,' the Count exclaimed. 'What news of my table?'

From nowhere Octavia di Marco appeared at Caterina's elbow with a caffè espresso and laid it on the table in front of Caterina. It was the old chess table that her father had made before she was born, but it occurred to her that this terrace was one huge chessboard, with the Count as the white king and Octavia as the black queen. But the games were not with ivory and ebony pieces; they were with people.

'*Grazie.*' She nodded at the Count. 'You are right. I came back to Capri for a reason today.'

'What reason?'

'To tell you that I have found someone who has seen the jewelled table.'

All three di Marco faces stared at her, mouths open, perfect white teeth on show.

'Who?' The Count's frown deepened. 'Who is this person?'

'A girl who caught sight of it in my father's workshop shortly before he died. She claims it was the most beautiful thing she has ever seen. I thought you would like to know that it *was* completed, according to her. It did exist, not just on paper.'

'Did?' the Count demanded. 'Or does?'

'I don't know for certain but I believe it does still exist. Someone has hidden it.'

'Or sold it.' It was Octavia who spoke, remote in her own patch of shade under her brother's canopy. She waved a dismissive hand. 'It is probably out of the country by now in the back of some American's truck. Blood spilled over it.'

'Aunt Octavia! Don't be so morbid.'

'I'm not morbid, Leonora. I am realistic.'

'But it's mine by rights,' Leonora exclaimed.

'Indeed it is not yours, Leonora,' her grandfather pronounced. 'They are *my* jewels. Understand, young lady. Your marriage did not take place.'

'So what makes you think it was removed and secreted away?' Octavia asked in her cool voice. She didn't sit. Didn't look hot. Her black suit had no creases.

'Because,' Caterina responded, 'the Rocco brothers in Sorrento were murdered, as well as the two American Intelligence soldiers who had questioned them.'

'What has that to do with my table?' the Count demanded.

'The Rocco brothers' house was near my father's workshop.'

Leonora's eyes were appalled. 'You think they saw something? Somebody? Taking the table?'

'Yes, I do.'

The Count edged forward. 'Where,' he asked, 'is it now?'

'I don't know.'

'But you have a suspicion?'

She made him wait. Sipped her coffee. Did not wipe the sweat on her palms on to her skirt.

'Do you know anything about the tunnels under Naples, Count?'

A stillness descended on the terrace.

'Do you believe,' Octavia said in a sceptical tone, 'that the table is down there?'

Caterina said nothing. The Count was scrutinising her face, and then dabbed his forehead with a small white hand-towel at his side. 'Tell me more.'

Caterina put down her cup, slipped her bag on her shoulder and rose to her feet. She crossed the expanse of white marble between them and picked up the towel he had discarded. For a moment he was too surprised to object and by then it was inside her bag.

'I will tell you more, Count, when I have more to tell. I should know by the end of today. Good morning to you.'

She strode out of the shade into the dazzle of the sunlight and stopped in front of Leonora and her dog. She held out her hand.

'Come with me, Leonora, you and Bianchezza. Please, I need your help.'

CHAPTER THIRTY-SIX

'Take the gun, Leonora,' Caterina urged.

The girl reached for it eagerly, eyes alight. It was a Mauser HSc, a German pistol that was far smaller than Caterina's cumbersome old Bodeo, but much easier to fire. It was the one Caterina had taken from Aldo in her workshop. Leonora's hand wrapped around the well-designed wooden grip as though made for it and her fingers brushed along its richly-blued blunt muzzle.

'You know what you have to do?' Caterina asked.

'Yes. Sit here and shoot anyone who comes through that front door uninvited.'

Caterina kissed her cheek. 'You are a life-saver. Literally.'

A moan of protest came from a corner of the room where Luca was sharpening a long carving knife on a whetstone.

'I can defend us, Caterina,' he said. 'Especially if you let me have the gun.' He wielded the knife like a sword, slicing the blade through the air. 'I want to come with you to defend you. I don't want you to go alone.'

'I know, Luca. But I couldn't bear you to have blood on your hands too.' She walked over and ruffled his short hair, touched his young cheek. His skin was so taut she thought it might split.

'Let me come with you, Caterina, I can help you,' he insisted. 'I don't want you in danger. Let me meet him again face to face, but this time with a knife in my hand.'

'No, you are too young. It is dangerous.'

'Please, Caterina,' he whispered.

'No. You must stay here, my love, and help Leonora guard Nonno. Keep him safe for me.' She kissed his brow. 'And keep Leonora safe too, Luca. I'm relying on you.'

His voice sank lower. 'Don't die, Caterina.' His eyes clung to her face with a desperation that turned her heart over. 'Ask Major Parr to help.'

'I can't, Luca. At the first sound of army boots, everyone would flee. But don't worry, I'll be well guarded.'

She meant the gun but they both looked at the dog. It opened its mouth, showed off its white fangs and whined, eager to start. Leonora knelt down beside it and kissed the animal's muzzle, her arms wrapped tight around its muscular neck. Its pink tongue licked her bare shoulder and without a word she returned to her feet.

'You remember the command?' she asked Caterina.

'Yes. *Seek*. I won't forget.'

'Go then.'

Caterina made a rapid check on the contents of her shoulder bag and then looked around the room. Imprinting it on her mind. Nonno's chair. Luca's fishing rod lolling against the wall. Papà's pipe on the mantelpiece. Each one branded for one last time on her eye. On her mind. Just in case. Nonno had shut himself away upstairs, alone with his anger, so she didn't go to say goodbye to him, but she hugged the others. The weight of the Bodeo in her bag steadied her smile. Aldo's Mauser lay in Leonora's hand and Caterina did not doubt that her friend would use it if she had to.

Caterina picked up her cardigan, despite the heat of the day, and walked into the hallway.

'Caterina.'

It was Nonno calling her name. He was standing at the top of the stairs, with his white hair, white shirt and white eyes the only points of light in the gloom of the stairwell. His hand brandished his ebony cane in the face of invisible foes.

'I forbid you to go, Caterina.' He smacked his cane against the banister rail. 'I order you to remain here. In time Drago Vincelli will forget.'

'Nonno, no Italian ever forgets. I cannot stop now.'

She walked to the front door, and as it shut behind her she heard her grandfather shout, 'Caterina.'

Yesterday's rain had settled the dust. The road up to the Cavaleris' place on the far edge of town was steep, but up here the air was luminous and bees hummed in bright splashes of wild flowers. To Caterina's left loomed the blunt shoulder of the Monte Faito mountain with its emerald coat of beech and chestnut trees, and above it the sky stretched in a hard blue band. It felt like a day designed for peace. Not a day for death.

Bianchezza was padding silently at her side as Caterina entered the courtyard, but the dog flattened its ears, hackles raised, and thrust its white head forward when a barrage of barking erupted within the house.

'Get that creature out of here.'

Augusta Cavaleri had dragged open the front door.

'Good morning, Signora Cavaleri.'

'Get yourself and that animal off my property at once.'

'I need to speak to you about your son, Stefano. May I please come in?'

'No.'

The woman tried to slam the door in Caterina's face but she pushed her foot forward over the threshold, jamming it open.

'It's important, Signora Cavaleri. You wouldn't want me to go to the police instead, would you? Let me in.'

The woman hesitated. Just enough. Caterina took a resolute step into the house.

'Is Stefano here?'

'No.'

'I can speak to you instead.'

Another hesitation.

'Leave the animal outside,' Augusta Cavaleri ordered and backed down the hallway, her step heavy and reluctant.

Caterina crouched in front of the German Shepherd and stroked its creamy white head. 'Stay here, Bianchezza. I'll be back soon. Stay.'

The dog's pale blue eyes fixed on Caterina's.

'Stay,' she repeated and walked inside the house.

The living room was cool, shady, and smelled of dog, though the animals themselves were shut away in the kitchen, still voicing hostility to the intruder in their yard. Caterina recalled a time when she would run through this house as freely as her own, when it would be full of the scent of lilac and the sound of the accordion played by Carlo's father. Now the house had a neglected, unloved air to it and dirty clothes lay littered on a chair. Caterina stood facing the half-hooded eyes of the woman in the black mourning.

'Say it fast and get out,' Augusta Cavaleri snapped.

'My brother was kidnapped.'

'Am I supposed to care what happens to the Lombardi family?'

'He was taken,' Caterina continued, 'by a man called Aldo. The police say his surname is Facchini. He works for Drago Vincelli.'

Blank eyes stared back at her. 'What has this to do with my son, Stefano.'

'I saw Drago Vincelli's black Rolls-Royce at your garage last week. I believe your son could be working for Vincelli and could be involved in the kidnapping.'

'Do you have proof?'

'Not yet.'

'Then get out of my house.' Augusta Cavaleri walked stiffly over to the door of the living room and flung it open. 'Get out and don't ever come back. You don't know what you're doing, any more than your whore of a mother did.'

Caterina's cheeks flushed, despite her determination to brush aside the woman's insults, and unwillingly she saw herself as Augusta Cavaleri saw her. Fragile and foolish. Overreaching herself. She uttered a small suppressed moan, and blinked hard, as though her eyes had lost focus.

'What's the matter with you?' Augusta Cavaleri demanded.

'Nothing.' Caterina started to head for the door but her feet shuffled and came to a stop. 'I'm not feeling well,' she murmured under her breath. 'Could I have a glass of water before I leave, please?'

The woman strode from the room, her long black skirt rustling with impatience over the tiles. The second she had gone, Caterina darted over to the pile of crumpled clothes and extracted from it a man's vest that was stained with wood-varnish, which she thrust into her shoulder-bag. By the time the footsteps returned, she was seated on a chair, her head in her hands.

'Here.'

Caterina accepted the glass of water and drank it down. It had the cool tang of well-water.

'*Grazie.*'

'Now go. Your family has taken one son from me, Caterina Lombardi. Leave my others alone.'

'Do you or your sons know anything about the tunnels under Naples? I need to go there and—'

A hand like an eagle's talon gripped Caterina's shoulder and yanked her to her feet.

'Go!' the woman hissed. 'Or I will set the dogs on you.'

Without a word Caterina walked out, her bag firmly under her arm. It was a relief to get away from that house where the air itself tasted of poison. A relief to inhale the clean sea-breeze, to take Bianchezza's leash and to set off at a run downhill to the railway station.

The bait was set.

The Circumvesuviana train rattled Caterina's bones all the way to Naples. The dog hated it, but it laid its head on her lap and suffered in silence. Caterina could not shake Augusta Cavaleri's harsh words from her mind.

'You don't know what you're doing, any more than your whore of a mother did.'

She laid her hand on the dog's strong skull, trying to absorb a portion of the animal's instinct for survival.

'You're wrong,' she muttered under her breath as she watched olive groves shudder past the window and a farmer prowling with a shotgun to keep hungry scavengers off his land. 'You're wrong, Signora Cavaleri.'

She thought out each step that lay ahead of her.

'I know exactly what I am doing.'

A bell above the door tinkled when Caterina entered the jeweller's shop this time, making her jump. She was too tense. The dog padded in at her side, its claws clicking on the wooden flooring. The place looked the same as before, a thin smattering of jewellery in glass cases, shoes ranged on display shelves as though inhabited by phantom limbs, and the rich smell of leather hanging in the shop. The dog lifted its muzzle to scent the air, its black nose inhaling the musky scent of dead skins.

'*Bella* Caterina! You have returned to us.'

'This is my new friend, Bianchezza.'

Caterina allowed herself to be enveloped in the warmth and abundance of flesh that was Signor Bartoli, and she allowed herself to imagine what it would be like to have this generous woman as her mother. Behind the counter, Delfina grinned at her. Not a trace of jealousy. Her strong features were relaxed in the knowledge that there were more than enough of her mother's embraces to go round.

Caterina kissed Signora Bartoli on both cheeks, smelling the sweetness of peaches on her breath, and smiled through lips that felt stiff and unwieldy.

'I need to speak to you, Signora,' she said.

'About what?'

Caterina had transferred her gaze to the door to the back workroom. It was closed. 'Is Carlo Cavaleri here?'

'No, not today. My son is working there on his own.'

But Caterina walked over to the door, opened it and checked. Edmondo Bartoli glanced up from the pair of boots he was shaping at the table, surprised.

'Excuse me,' she said and closed the door.

Signora Bartoli had shifted to stand in the middle of her shop, hands on hips, scrutinising Caterina.

'Don't you trust me, Caterina?'

'Of course I do. That's why I'm here.'

The woman was still in mourning dress, but she had brightened the black garb with a long string of glossy jet beads. She twirled the end of them in a defiant gesture and turned her head to her daughter. 'Vermouth,' she commanded. 'Delfina, bring us vermouth. I can feel in my bones that we are going to need it.'

The sticky brown alcohol tasted sweet as it hit Caterina's stomach, burning away the tension.

'Signora Bartoli, tell me about the network of tunnels under Naples.'

Signora Bartoli's glass froze halfway to her lips, and the dark liquid swirled up the side and over the rim, spilling on to her fingers. They were seated in a small living room that was strikingly feminine, decorated with rich lace and dusky pink velvet, walls adorned with gilt mirrors and tortoiseshell-framed photographs. Elegant porcelain shepherdesses lined the mantelpiece and a songbird perched in resolute silence in a cage.

Signora Bartoli regarded Caterina quizzically. 'What's your interest in the tunnels, my girl? They are not pleasant, you know. Dark and forbidding, with a whispering voice of their own that can disturb those who aren't accustomed to it.'

Her drink resumed its path to her lips.

'You mentioned before,' Caterina said, 'that you were a warden down there during the war.'

'That's true. Sections of the tunnels were used as bomb-shelters during the bombardments by the American and British aeroplanes. Those were hard times in Naples.' She crossed herself devoutly. 'Many were killed. But thirty metres underground they were safe. Before the war my father was one of the maintenance men who were subterranean caretakers down there, so I knew the tunnels well. I used to play in them as a child.' She chuckled, one of her ready smiles finding its way on to her face at the memory. Caterina considered how much to reveal, how much to hold back.

'Signora, I have learned that it is possible that precious artefacts stolen from churches and palazzos are being secreted down there.'

The jeweller's widow burst out laughing. 'Don't be absurd, little one.'

'It is true.'

The laughter stopped. 'Are you sure?'

'Drago Vincelli's man, Aldo Facchioni, told someone that there were things kept down there.' She took a decent mouthful of vermouth. Her blood was singing in her ears. 'Help me, please. Tell me about the tunnels.'

Signora Bartoli emptied her glass. 'Do you need that dog with you? I could shut it in the yard.'

'Where I go, the dog goes.'

'When you are serious, you are so like your father.'

The words seemed to spiral inside Caterina's head and she wanted to catch hold of them, to feel their softness. Instead she focused on the tunnels.

'Tell me,' she said again.

'They are killers.'

'Vincelli and Aldo?'

'No. The tunnels. Sections of roof cave in. Walls collapse. Water floods when you least expect it. Don't go there, I'm warning you.'

'I have to. It's possible that my father's jewelled table might be hidden in one of the tunnels.'

Signora Bartoli sighed, long and hard, poured another slug of vermouth into each glass and downed her own at once. 'The first thing you have to realise is that there is not just one tunnel system under the city of Naples. There are three.' She ticked them off on her fingers. 'First there are the Catacombs of San Gennaro. These are under the Basilica of Madre del Buon Consiglio in the northern part of the city, inside the slope leading up to Capo-dimonte. I don't like them.' She shuddered. 'It is an underground burial site going back to the fifth century BC. Yes, it has beautiful frescoes and mosaics lining the walls, but honestly, Caterina, it is a gruesome reminder that that's how we will all end up. Nothing but dust and bones.' She rubbed a knuckle in one eye. 'Even my poor Orlando.'

Caterina gave her a minute of respectful silence, then pressed her further. 'So you think there would be no artefacts down there?'

'Not unless you count ghoulish rows of skulls and thigh bones. More than three thousand of the revolting things.' She crossed herself again.

'So what about the other tunnels?'

'There's the Bourbon tunnel.'

'Where is that?'

'It's an escape passage. It runs for more than five hundred

metres from the Royal Palace. It was constructed by King Ferdinand II in 1853 to create a fast route from the palace to the military barracks in Via della Pace. That's in the Chi-aia seafront district.' She chuckled to herself. 'He was no fool, that one. He wasn't going to hang around to be murdered in his bed by peasants with pickaxes. Anyway, sections of it were used as bomb shelters during the war and there's still a lot of rubbish chucked down there. The soldiers searched it, you know.'

'The Allied troops have searched it?'

'Oh, yes. They were hunting for the German soldiers who were supposed to be lurking down in the tunnels by day and committing sabotage by night. But also for booby-trap bombs and for any hidden treasures.'

'What?'

Caterina was stunned. Jake had not told her that. The tunnels had already been searched. It made sense, of course it did, but disappointment wrapped itself around her mind.

Jake. Why didn't you tell me?

She rose from her chair, no longer able to sit still, and paced around the dainty room, watched by the dog and Signora Bartoli. The soldiers didn't find anything of value down there in the tunnels. That had to be the answer. That was why he didn't tell her. She had not asked Jake where he'd found the triptych, the altarpiece her father had repaired.

Why hadn't she asked?

At the time she had been too shocked. Too angry. Unable to talk to him. But now she was . . . She sought after a word, but none came. Except *different*. She was different. It didn't sound much. But *different* was a big word. Did Jake see it too, that she had changed? Of course he did. Jake had eyes that stripped you right down to the underside of your skin.

She turned back to Signora Bartoli. 'Did your husband know my grandfather, as well as my father?'

'Yes, he did.'

'Before he became a jeweller, did he make shoes? Like your son does now?'

'No.' But she nodded her head. 'But his father did. His father was a cobbler.'

'My grandfather possesses many pairs of shoes in the bottom of his wardrobe, most of them unworn. So I assume they came from your husband's father. They must have been good friends.'

Signora Bartoli glanced at the vermouth bottle at her elbow but didn't touch it. 'Yes, little one, they were. I am sorry about Giuseppe Lombardi's eyes.'

She switched the subject back to the tunnels with a speed that Caterina didn't miss.

'The third tunnel system,' Signora Bartoli held up three fingers, 'is the massive network of aqueduct tunnels that were used to distribute water throughout Naples in wells and cisterns. These date back thousands of years to Ancient Greek and Roman times.' She paused and beamed her approval. 'You should see the brickwork they did back then. It is wonderful, as intricate as Venetian lace. But now many of the tunnels have collapsed or are blocked with rubbish thrown down there. It saddens me. And most of the entrances to the wells or access stairs are locked.'

'Is that where you played as a child?'

'Yes. I used to love to scare myself and my friends getting lost in the bowels of the earth.'

A boisterous laugh broke from Signora Bartoli but was abruptly choked off. 'No,' she said in a sudden whisper. 'Don't, Caterina. Don't even think of it.'

'I will go down there, Signora. With you or without you.'

For two full minutes the silence in the room seemed to solidify between them, disturbed only by the tick of a porcelain mantle-clock and the soft breath of the dog. Signora Bartoli then rose from her chair and bustled over to a delicate inlaid cabinet. She opened a drawer and removed something from it that she held aloft like a trophy. Her face was solemn, her eyes direct as she focused not on Caterina, but on the object in her hand.

'If you are not afraid of the tunnels, I still have a key.'

CHAPTER THIRTY-SEVEN

Jake entered the narrow street where Caterina lived and immediately he sensed that something wasn't right. A small pulse was thumping at his temple. The war had honed his alertness to danger during the street by street fighting, and he had developed a sixth sense that told him when he was in a sniper's sights. It had saved his hide more than once.

Yet he could spot no danger here, nothing out of place. The street lay in shade, a lazy and harmless scene. Two kids were dangling string for a kitten on a windowsill and a young man wearing an Italian army cap was sitting in a doorway, one leg missing below the knee. He was setting out tarot cards on a board and further down the street a woman hummed as she watered her geraniums. Nothing to fear.

So what was it?

Caterina. He moved rapidly to the door of her house and rapped on the door using the brass knocker.

No answer.

Images of Aldo Facchioni crushing Caterina's fine-boned skull between his massive paws leapt into his head, but he banished them fast. There was no sign of forced entry, no reason to believe she was in trouble. Except for that pulse at his temple that wouldn't stop.

He knocked again. Harder. Louder. Longer. He gave it no more than thirty seconds and then he called her name.

'Caterina!'

He had told her not to leave the house, instructed her to lock the door till he got back, to stay with her brother and grandfather. She had nodded. Nodded and smiled and kissed him. Not once had the words '*I promise*' passed her lips, but at the time he had been bewitched by her kisses and the scent of her skin and had not forced the promise from her.

Fool. Dumb fool.

'Caterina!'

The Italian soldier with his tarot cards was staring and Jake called out, 'Have you seen . . .?'

A voice came through the door, faint and female. It wasn't Aldo. Thank God it wasn't Aldo.

'Caterina?'

It came again, firmer this time. 'Go away.'

It wasn't Caterina.

His mind churned through the options. A neighbour? A friend? Her mother? No, that wasn't her mother's confident tone.

'I've come to see Caterina.'

'Go away.'

'Who am I speaking to?'

'Go away.'

'I am Major Jake Parr, a friend of Caterina's.'

Silence.

He put his mouth close to the door. 'Is she here?' he asked, curbing his impatience. 'If you tell her I called, she will want to . . .'

'Jake?'

A different voice. Immediately he recognised it as her brother's.

'Luca, yes, it's Jake here. Open the door will you?'

'No. Don't you dare.' The female voice once more, sharp and determined.

'Luca,' Jake called. 'This is important. Listen to me. I can't help your sister if I don't know where . . .'

A bolt slid across on the inside of the door, followed by the rattle of a lock, and the door swung open. In the hallway stood her brother, his dark eyes bright, his young face chalk–white and shaky.

'She's gone,' Luca said. 'You have to find her.'

Jake stepped inside the house.

The gun was six inches from his face and pointed straight at him. It was a Mauser HSc, a highly efficient 7.65 pistol made in Germany. One twitch of her finger and he could say goodbye to his brains.

Jake stood still, not even a blink, and waited for her to calm down. He wanted to tell her to take deep breaths instead of

499

standing there, rigid and unbreathing. He had recognised the young woman instantly as the friend with Caterina at the nightclub, rigged out in white again, a white wrap-around dress this time that emphasised her tiny waist. But right now he wasn't looking at her waist. Her pupils were huge, her arm stretched out stiff in front of her holding the gun. He could see she wanted to pull the trigger.

'I am a friend of Caterina's,' he told her in the kind of tone he'd use to a nervous horse that was threatening to kick him. 'Ask Luca.'

'It's true, Leonora. Major Parr is her friend,' Luca said.

Jake could have shot out a fist and slammed the gun from her hand before she had time to lick her dry lips, but he didn't. He needed her. He needed her cooperation. A broken wrist would not win him her trust so he stood there and stared down the black mouth of the Mauser, aware that Leonora's eyes were hating him.

'Put down the gun, Leonora,' he said quietly.

'She told me not to let anyone in.'

'I am a friend of Caterina's,' he repeated. 'She wouldn't want you to shoot me.' He risked a smile. Of sorts.

Slowly, reluctantly, she lowered the pistol but she maintained a firm hold on it. Jake didn't waste any time. 'Where is she?'

Luca came to his help. 'Caterina has gone to . . .'

'No, Luca,' the di Marco girl interrupted. 'Say nothing.' She waved the gun dangerously once again in Jake's direction. 'We don't know who to trust.'

Jake rested an arm around the boy's shoulders. 'You must tell me where she has gone, Luca.' He ducked down so that his eyes were level with the boy's and he could see the struggle in them to be a man. 'I can't help keep her safe if you don't tell me.'

Luca opened his mouth. The words that Jake needed were on the tip of his young tongue when Leonora reached out her free hand, seized the boy's wrist and yanked him away from Jake. Without tearing the kid down the middle, Jake had no choice but to let him go.

'We promised,' Leonora retorted, her face defiant. 'Remember, Luca?'

'What good is a promise,' Jake asked, his voice rising with impatience, 'if she is out there on her own in danger?'

'She's not on her own.'

'What?'

'She has Bianchezza with her.'

'Who the hell is Bianchezza?'

'My dog.'

'Christ! A dog? Are you crazy? She will need far more than a dog if she ends up in Aldo's clutches.'

Luca's face remained ashen, eyes sunk in deep shadows. 'We have to tell him, Leonora. We have to. She might be . . .'

A cane slammed against the door, making them whirl round, and Caterina's grandfather towered in the doorway. Jake breathed in air as if it wasn't going to be around much longer.

'Major Parr,' roared Giuseppe Lombardi, his white hair wild as though his hands had been tearing at it. 'What the hell are you doing here, you witless American? You should be in Naples.'

*

Naples seemed bigger. Busier, more crowded. Noisier and dirtier than before. As Caterina and Bianchezza hurried through the streets alongside Signora Bartoli, she saw the city through the eyes of a stranger. Because she knew she might never see it again, and without meaning to, her footsteps slowed.

'What's the matter?' Signora Bartoli asked.

'Nothing.' Caterina touched the solid weight of her bag as a reminder. 'Nothing at all.'

The entrance was not where Caterina expected. Not in the ancient historic heart of the city where the maze of alleyways tumbled on top of each other. She had heard of an entrance to the subterranean tunnels located in Piazza San Gaetano beside the towering church of San Paolo Maggiore with its ornate Corinthian columns, but her companion by-passed that route and headed north instead. Some of the entrances were the mouths of wells, Signora Bartoli informed her, deep shafts with metal ladders descending for thirty or forty metres, but the military had sealed most of them to prevent access. Too much rubbish was being dumped down there, too many 'accidents' occurring deep in the darkness.

Caterina imagined what it was like down in the aqueduct tunnels. Signora Bartoli said much of the system was bone dry, black and cold with the breath of the Ancients seeping into your lungs. It was a fitting place to die. Except she had no intention of dying.

They were in a street of ramshackle houses when Signora Bartoli halted. Caterina could see no obvious entrance to a tunnel, just a row of rundown houses that opened straight onto the pavement and a man shaving on a stool in the shade.

'Do the military troops know all the entrances?' she asked.

Signora Bartoli regarded Caterina with a patient smile that dented her round cheeks. 'Of course not. The military are simple-minded.'

She led Caterina down a narrow passageway, no more than a metre or so wide between two houses, the ground stony and full of litter, the smell vile. But at the end it opened on to a small rectangle of scrubland where wild flowers had taken hold and a coop of chickens clucked and fluttered as the dog approached. Off to the right stood an old stone hut with ivy sprawling across its roof and half a rusted bedstead leaning against the door. It looked like a disused outside privy.

Signora Bartoli walked up to it, kicked the bedstead into the weeds and held up the key, as a light wind stirred up the dust around them. Her gaze focused on Caterina, a concerned expression on her face.

'Time cannot touch the dead, Caterina. There is no need to prove your father to be a decent and honest man. He is beyond that now. You can still turn back.'

Caterina took the key from her and unlocked the door to the hut.

Darkness does strange things to you. Of course it robs you of the ability to see. But it gives eyes to your other senses. Darkness trebles the ability to hear.

After they plunged down more than a hundred rough-hewn

stone steps from a hole in the floor of the hut, they stood motionless thirty metres underground.

Listening.

The silence was total. Black as a tomb. Only the soft panting of Bianchezza disturbed the stale air. The dog had not liked the steps but seemed unconcerned by this underground world. Leonora had assured Caterina that it was used to exploring the caves on Capri and would enjoy the hunt. They had brought torches, but the flimsy beams of light scarcely dented this solid wall of darkness.

'All right?' Signora Bartoli called from out in front.

'Yes. Let's go.'

'Be careful.'

'I will.'

'Not just where you put your feet. These tunnels can unsettle your mind. I've seen it happen. Be careful of that.'

Caterina nodded, unseen. Her nerves were screwed tight, but her mind was settled and she intended to keep it that way. She slipped her cardigan over her shoulders against the cold, and they set off in single file.

They started slowly, chipping away at the darkness, allowing Caterina to grow accustomed to the ways of the labyrinth of tunnels. Signora Bartoli spoke of them as though they were alive, twisting and turning with a will of their own, some friendly, some malign, all exuding the same cold sour breath. At times the passages were so narrow they had to squeeze through them sideways, or so low they were almost on their knees, descending into the bowels of the yellow tufo rock upon which Naples was built.

It was hard not to feel trapped.

It was even harder not to feel that Drago Vincelli was three steps behind them. Caterina held firmly to Bianchezza's leash, her ears alert for the faintest growl of warning, while Signora Bartoli murmured contentedly about the legends and myths, the stories that were passed among Neapolitans about the miles of passages and vast chambers that crisscrossed each other under the city.

Caterina's mind fixed on what might be out there beyond the beam of the torch. She urged her guide to silence, but Signora Bartoli shrugged and said no one knew about this section of tunnel because it had been sealed off for years. Dimly Caterina heard mention of the Ancient Greeks being the first to hollow out the volcanic stone in the fourth century AD to build Neapolis, their New City.

A noise? Did she hear a noise?

She halted. 'Listen.'

They listened, even Bianchezza, but there was no noise.

'You're jumpy.'

'Maybe,' Caterina allowed.

She turned a tight bend where the ground rose unexpectedly and the ceiling swooped down, skimming her head. She wondered how in God's name anyone in their right mind would want to play down here. Signora Bartoli continued to pick her way steadily along the tunnel, still talking, but only snatches drifted to Caterina out of the darkness. About the Ancient Romans taking over the Greek quarries and creating this vast underground aqueduct system, building cisterns to deliver water to the city.

Abruptly the words ceased.

Caterina switched off her torch and Signora Bartoli did the same. Darkness came down on them as solid as a truck, but Caterina breathed calmly and reached out to the dog.

'This is where our branch merges with the main tunnel.' The words were whispered into her ear. 'So this is where you start.'

Caterina reached into her bag and, working by feel alone, drew out the leather gun-holster that Aldo had worn under his jacket and abandoned on her workshop floor. She crouched down beside the German Shepherd and scratched under its ear. Signora Bartoli was right. It was time to start.

'Now, Bianchezza. Now it's your turn to find the bastard who almost killed your mistress.'

She switched on her torch once more but this time it was swathed in a scarf, so that only a dull glow trickled through the fabric. She showed the dog the holster which it sniffed at with interest.

'Caterina.'

She looked up at the woman who had chosen to help her and whose face in the shadows had taken on the contours of a death mask.

'Caterina, are you sure? We can go back.'

'No, I have no choice. But you can go back. This is my one chance. If I don't go on, they will come for me with their knives and their guns and their desire to hurt. If not for me, it will be for Luca. Or for Nonno. Nothing will stop them, Signora Bartoli.'

'Nothing except you.'

'Stay here,' Caterina said, 'I will come back to you.'

She wrapped the holster straps around the creamy white muzzle that looked grey in the shadows and she held it there for a long moment while the dog inhaled its scent, then she pushed it back into her bag and stroked the dog's head.

'Seek, Bianchezza,' she ordered in the tone that Leonora had taught her. 'Seek.'

CHAPTER THIRTY-EIGHT

Jake kicked the Harley Davidson on to its stand outside Intelligence Headquarters. He was in a hurry and signalled to the GI on guard to watch that no one stripped it of its tyres or its seat. The city felt scorched. After the cool cliff-top breezes in Sorrento, Naples was a cauldron of heat that sucked all moisture from his veins. He could smell a fire somewhere close and white smoke drifted like a veil above the domed roof of the Teatro di San Carlo near the Piazza del Plebiscito. It had already burned down once during the bombing. There were always fires in Naples. As if it burned in hell.

He took the steps at a run and welcomed the cool interior of the marble hall, but he had no time to waste.

'Captain Fielding?' he asked the sergeant on duty. 'Where is he?'

'In Interrogation Room 3, sir.'

'Who is he questioning, sergeant?'

'A Signora Lombardi, sir.'

That took Jake by surprise. He strode quickly down the corridor and entered a room on the right. He found Harry sitting on the front edge of a metal table and lighting a cigarette for Lucia Lombardi who was seated in a chair, her slim legs elegantly crossed. As the door opened, she turned her head away from the lighter's flame and raised a speculative eyebrow at Jake.

'Good morning to you, Major. You look in one hell of a rush today.' She tipped one corner of her mouth into a half smile. 'Have you come to rescue me?'

He shook his head sharply. 'If you'll excuse me, signora, I need to talk to Captain Fielding.' His tone was brusque. 'At once.'

She rose, smoothed her black dress down over her hips and sauntered across the room towards him. Her blonde hair was loose, swaying around her shoulders as she moved.

'Are you trying to get rid of me, Major?'

'Yes, ma'am.' He did not have time for finesse.

But she remained stubbornly poised only inches away from him, the unlit cigarette still between her lips. 'Got a light, soldier?'

He took out his black Zippo and obliged without a word, then pointedly held the door open for her. She rolled a smile in Harry Fielding's direction, blew a perfect smoke-ring and watched it expand as it drifted up towards the cherubs on the ceiling.

'Seen my daughter recently?' she asked with studied casualness.

'Signora Lombardi, I suggest you go see your son.'

'Luca?'

'He had a run-in with Aldo Facchioni. He is at home again, but could probably do with his mother's attention right now.'

She drew hard on her cigarette. If he'd blinked, he'd have missed it, that moment when her face changed. As though the tendons that held it in place had snapped and it started to collapse in on itself. But the moment was gone almost before it began, and the blurred edges became bright and hard again. She walked quickly through the doorway and without turning her head said, 'If you see my daughter, tell her I'll be in Sorrento.'

He shut the door.

'Harry, what the hell was Lucia Lombardi doing here?'

Harry Fielding was gathering together his papers, putting the top on his fountain pen, but there was something not quite as neat as usual about him. Jake sought to pinpoint it. Hair carefully combed, regulation British army uniform smart and shiny as a new dime. But there was an uneasiness in his manner, an awkwardness, though he met Jake's gaze readily enough.

'Why did you pull her in for questioning, Harry?'

'After that terrible business with young Luca, I've been digging around and discovered that Lucia Lombardi used to be a friend of Drago Vincelli before she shot off to Rome eleven years ago. So I brought her in to question her. To see if she could throw any light on where Aldo Facchioni or Drago Vincelli might be found.'

'Any success?'

'Not really. Though she did say that Aldo used to hang

around Sorrento a lot in those days.' He paused and frowned at Jake. 'What is it?' What's the matter?'

'It's Caterina. She has gone to the underground tunnels, God only knows where.' He made his voice flat. No hint of rage. No whisper of despair. No indication that his breath had stalled in his lungs or that he had turned into a person willing to slice Drago Vincelli's heart out, one piece at a time, if he laid a finger on Caterina Lombardi. None of that was allowed into his voice, and yet Harry stared at him as if he had two heads.

'Jake, Colonel Quincy wants to see you in his office.'

'To hell with Quincy. I need you to . . .'

'Jake, he says you are stealing artefacts from the basement.'

'What? Is he out of his mind?'

But a chill gripped his gut. Quincy must be looking for a scapegoat to cover his own thefts. He saw the concern in Harry's blue eyes and realised it explained the earlier awkwardness.

'I know it's not true,' Harry stated loyally and held out his hand. Jake shook it firmly.

'Forget Quincy, Harry. We'll deal with him later. I need you with me, my friend.' Jake was already moving to the door. 'And bring a flashlight.'

CHAPTER THIRTY-NINE

Caterina stumbled over something underfoot, something soft. It jolted her and her heart jumped. She expected to strike against hard edges, against the stones and boulders as she clambered over rockfalls in the tunnels, but not something soft. Unless it was a rat. She flicked the veiled beam of her torch to her feet, turning the pitch black to charcoal grey, but it wasn't a rat.

It was a shoe. A child's shoe. She picked it up and examined it. Almost colourless in the gloom, but just a glimpse of pale blue when she peered closely, soft baby leather with a buckle. For a reason she didn't understand, it made her want to cry, but she discarded it quickly and walked on through the wall of darkness. She was moving forward faster than was safe, towed along by Bianchezza who was still fixated on the scent from the gun-holster, as though it burned inside its black nostrils.

The only smell that came to Caterina was the acid scent of fear. Was it her own? From her skin? Or did it seep out from the rock itself, absorbed over the years from all those who had ventured down into these black holes? She couldn't tell. Signora Bartoli had explained how Mussolini and his Fascist government in 1941 had cleaned up some of the tunnels and the vast underground caverns to make them habitable for Neapolitans sheltering from the bombs, even installing toilets and electricity in one section. But not here. Here the primal smell of fear was strong.

She passed through a massive cathedral-like chamber so high her torchlight did not reach its cavernous ceiling, where the soft yellow rock towered over her, and she wriggled through holes amid mounds of boulders, holes that were surely too small for Aldo to squeeze through. The blackness enveloped her the deeper she went and she saw it no longer as something to fear. No longer an enemy, but something to embrace. It was keeping her safe. The darkness was not the threat; the men inside it were the danger. When she couldn't see her hand in front of her face, she didn't panic, but welcomed it. It was protecting her.

Caterina heard a voice.

It sent dread sliding inside her.

There was the sound of running footsteps echoing through the dead spaces. From which direction? Impossible to tell.

The dog uttered a low-pitched growl and she gripped its muzzle to silence it. 'Quiet!' she whispered and the sound ceased in its throat but she could feel its shoulder quivering. The tunnel grew narrow here, too small to crouch behind an outcrop of rock.

The footsteps grew louder. Heavy boots.

She hurried. Her mouth dry. Keeping her footfalls soft and her eyes sharp to seek out stones lying in her path. She drew out the Bodeo from her shoulder bag, eased back its hammer with her thumb and flicked off the switch on the torch.

Darkness descended.

'You okay, Harry?'

Jake spoke in a low murmur. Sound carried strangely in the stone passages. At times it barely made it a metre from his mouth, limping across the heavy stale air, the words vanishing inside the rock walls. At others it seemed to drift and echo, swirling in confusing spirals that did not want to stop. Ever since they had entered the tunnels, leaving a back-up team of six armed soldiers outside the gated entrance, Harry had been ill at ease. Not obvious because he hid it well, but Jake knew his friend.

'I'm okay,' Harry nodded in the white beam of Jake's flashlight. 'Not keen on tight spaces, that's all. Forget it. Let's concentrate on finding her.'

Caterina had to be here. But where? Where to start?

Jake wanted to bellow her name at every turn, to roar a warning to let her know he was coming. To tell her: *Wait*.

But fear rose in his chest, fear for her. Fear he was too late. Too slow. Too lost in this serpentine labyrinth. He was angry that she chose to do this without him. He and Harry had entered the tunnel system at Piazza San Gaetano and one of the maintenance men had guided them down the rough stairs cut from the rock, forty metres down into the belly of the earth. They had shed the maintenance guy and covered a lot of ground, the two of them, hardly speaking, each one tense behind the glare of his torch as they hurried to check every passageway and chamber.

Only once did Harry ask, 'Do you really think Vincelli and Aldo are down here waiting for her?'

'She thinks so. So I have to think so too.'

The bearded official at the Gaetano entrance swore she had not come past him, but admitted that there were other entrances, not all of which had been securely sealed. There were forgotten wells she could have climbed down or ancient access points that only the locals knew about. Jake had to assume she was down here.

A sudden image flashed into his mind of Caterina taking one look at the menacing darkness and retreating back up into the light, but the image was gone as quickly as it came. Caterina would not retreat. Not when she knew the lives of her brother and grandfather depended on finding Vincelli and Aldo Facchioni.

There was one of her.

Two of them.

Professional killers.

And what did she have? What was she carrying into battle? A thirty-year-old gun and a dog.

He ducked under a steep overhang of rock and heard Harry's head collide with it behind him, followed by a grunt and a low curse that rumbled into the silence.

'This is too slow, Harry,' Jake whispered. 'We have to separate. It will double our search area.'

'Agreed.'

At the next fork in the tunnel, Jake's flashlight took the left hand black hole; Harry took the one on the right.

'If you find her,' Jake urged, 'fire your gun.'

Jake doubled his speed. He took risks.

The passageways darted off in different directions, a baffling maze that crept under the villas far above, where every courtyard had once possessed a well to the aqueduct below. In places his torch beam caught the metal of rungs set into narrow yellowish shafts that rose to the surface, but which had been built over long since, as the city expanded.

His boots made little sound. He'd had the sense to tie rags around them to muffle their tread. Time and again he halted, stopped breathing and listened intently. But all he heard was the ancient silence. It rolled over him and the thoughts of Caterina inside his head. Twice he almost knocked himself out on jutting projections and then without warning he ended up flat on his back when a sudden slope of scree beneath his feet skidded from under him.

The torch went out.

His ribs throbbed from their crack on the ground and granules of tufo gravel had embedded in his cheek. But as he lay there, winded, and silently cursing himself, he saw a line of light in the pitch darkness, a line no thicker than a hair and so dim that had his torch been on, he would never have seen it. It was a slit at ground level, at the base of the wall. The shifting of the scree must have uncovered it.

Jake rolled onto his side. He pressed his face silently to the line of light but he could see nothing through it. It was like trying to look through a thread of yellow cotton. He didn't breathe, didn't blink.

Then it came. A sound so faint it was scarcely a sound, but it had the cadence of voices, the rise and fall of two people speaking. Somewhere beneath him.

CHAPTER FORTY

Jake.

How do you do it?

Every day. How do you face your fear? Knowing a bullet could rip out your throat any moment and your blood arc in a scarlet torrent to drench the ground at your feet.

Tell me.

Every soldier in combat goes through this. Every soldier puts on his socks, combs his hair, picks up his rifle and instead of fleeing into the hills to hide, he stands and fights. Italy was forced into this war by Mussolini, Britain by Hitler, America by Hirohito of Japan.

None of you had a choice.

How do you live with death at your side?

The voice vanished and the footsteps faded. Caterina stood with her back flat against a rock wall in total blackness, breathing quietly, imposing a steady rhythm. Eyes wide and blind.

One hand rested on the dog's head for reassurance, whether for herself or for Bianchezza, she didn't care to ask. Only when some time had passed – she had no idea how short or how long – did she move.

She once more lifted Aldo's gun holster from her bag and placed it against the dog's nose, not because she doubted the animal's hunting skill, but because she wanted to start again and do it better this time. Without the fear.

The torch went back on, still wrapped up to keep its light muted, she shortened the leash in her hand and whispered, 'Seek.' Without hesitation Bianchezza resumed her task, her creamy tail high and happy. Caterina had expected the dog to work with nose close to the ground, but no, the long white muzzle was raised, nostrils twitching, as though Aldo had left a strong-smelling miasma in his wake.

They progressed faster, their pace smoother now. She was getting better at navigating around the obstacles and didn't have to keep reminding herself to breathe. There were fewer bumps and scrapes, until they came to a divide in the tunnel with a choice of two entrances. One was low and narrow, part of it blocked by rubble, the other wider and more inviting. With Aldo's size in mind and remembering that he'd told her in her workshop that he loathed small spaces, she automatically opted for the wider entrance but Bianchezza had other ideas. The dog drew her unerringly to the smaller one. The low passageway veered abruptly to her right, almost turning back on itself, and the dog was straining at the leash now, but suddenly the sub-terranean world changed.

In front of her there was a flight of steps descending into an abyss of darkness below and Caterina caught hold of the dog's collar to prevent it racing down. She listened hard but could hear nothing but Bianchezza's soft whine of eagerness and her own chaotic heartbeat. The dog was her canary in a coal mine. If Bianchezza felt it was safe to go on, so did she. She ruffled the thick fur. Overtaken by a rush of gratitude, she knelt and kissed the silky head, rewarded by a soft whine of pleasure.

'Come on, *bella*,' she whispered. '*Grazie*.'

Cautiously she began the descent, keeping the dog behind her, the gun out in front. The torch and the leash had to share the same hand, so the murky beam was erratic on the steps, walls looming up on both sides. She felt calmer here, despite a sharp and sudden drop in temperature as they plunged down, and she instantly knew why. It was the smell that rose to meet her, an odour she knew as well as she knew the one in her own workshop. The scent was unmistakable. It was the sweet aroma of wood.

The beat of her heart grew violent and intense because this was what she had come for. *This* is where they would be.

Caterina wanted her father. Now, here in this cavern, where the darkness was solid and unbreakable because even in the almost impenetrable gloom under her torch, the beauty within the chamber shone out and Caterina wanted her father here beside her. It would have made his heart sing.

The collection of antique furniture and priceless orna- ments lay shrouded in dustsheets and mystery. She spotted an exquisite dolphin foot that was part of a baroque secretaire, and she could not stop herself throwing back the sheet, so that she could shine her torch over the hoard of treasures. She had tantalising glimpses of ancient walnut and willow furniture piled on top of each other, rich with inlays of gold and ivory, decorated with carved mermaids, lions, eagles and smiling cherubim. There was a Venetian overmantle mirror with parcel-gilt frame and eighteenth-century mercury glass. But no jewelled table.

She found a table from Ancient Rome made of citrus wood with a swan's head rising from acanthus foliage. A medieval *condottiere* sword with an exotic blue mahoe wooden hilt and a rusty iron blade was propped against a graceful caryatid figure sculpted in marble. Off to one side stood a marriage *cassone* chest crafted for a noblewoman with the finest seventeenth-century ebony and satinwood veneers. All the sumptuous work of Italy's greatest master-craftsmen. Here it was, spread out before her like a feast.

All stolen. All pillaged. All disembowelled from Italy's heritage. And there, staring her in the face, was her father's work. She knew it instantly. In the side panel of a superb *cadenza* cabinet, a repair to an inlaid biblical scene, and it made Caterina ache with need to see her father's head bent over his work once more. Yet at the same time a sense of betrayal and disillusionment threatened to overwhelm her.

She needed to know if Stefano Cavaleri and the Count were involved, so she removed from her canvas bag the small towel she had taken from the Capri villa. She whispered to Bianchezza and held it in front of the dog's nose. Obviously the scent was familiar, but when told to *Seek*, Bianchezza walked among the antiques with no sense of direction. No connection. But when Caterina quickly did the same with Stefano Cavaleri's vest, the dog went immediately to a sumptuous silvered fauteuil. So Stefano had been here or at least handled the stolen chair.

She was in no doubt that some of these valuable works of art came from that lock-up hiding place to which her mother had hurried with greed dripping from her lips, the one they'd found empty. Vincelli had already got his hands on them. He and her Papà had been up to their necks in crime together and yet Caterina had trusted him and believed in him.

Bianchezza uttered a deep-throated growl.

Caterina had prepared herself for this moment. Talked herself through each tiny fragment of it. She was ready with the gun in her hand, no shakes, no regrets, no terror at the prospect of taking a man's life.

The hammer was cocked, safety off. Ready to fire.

The walls of the chamber were lined with planks of pine-wood and a section of it suddenly swung forward to reveal the gaping maw of another wide tunnel. Secrets within secrets. Now she understood better how they transported the furniture here.

'Signorina Lombardi.'

Shoot now.

Don't speak to him.

Just shoot.

It was Drago Vincelli, wearing a suit and white shirt covered in cave dust. He advanced into the shadowy light of her torch and Caterina could see the outline of a gun in his hand. It was pointing straight at her.

'Signor Vincelli. You came, I see.'

Pull the trigger. Pull it now.

'You knew I would come.' Vincelli gave a sour grimace. 'Once I heard you were going around announcing you were heading for the tunnels under Naples, I knew you had a death wish, you stupid bitch. I gave you a chance and you wasted it. So my friend and I are here to finish the job, because it's clear that you do not know where the jewelled table is hidden. Isn't that so, Aldo?'

The big man stood in his own circle of amber light behind his boss, holding an oil lamp in his bandaged hand, and an embroidered antique footstool with feet in the shape of ball and claw in the other.

Now, Caterina told herself, *now. While Aldo is unarmed.*

Her finger tightened on the trigger. A hair's breadth. But it froze.

The cavern was chill and she could hear death breathing in the dark corners.

His death?

Or hers?

'I know who has my father's jewelled table,' she stated.

'Lies! You know nothing.' Vincelli was angry. Not listening. She suddenly realised how much he wanted to pull that trigger to rid himself of her. 'Caterina Lombardi, you should never have put your fucking nose down here.'

He took two steps closer to her, his decision clearly signed and sealed in the narrowing of his dark eyes, and Caterina could almost see each tendon contracting in his fingers. Her heartbeat shut down.

'You do not have the nerve to shoot me,' he taunted her with a flash of gold tooth.

Caterina pulled the trigger of the Bodeo.

The white shirt erupted in a splash of crimson and Drago Vincelli dropped to his knees.

The noise of the gunshot ripped the air apart in the confined space. Caterina's ears throbbed and the dog threw itself under a beautiful gesso table.

There was blood. On the floor, on the dustsheet, spattered on Caterina's face. A bright vital red, as vivid as poppy petals. Drago Vincelli was somehow staying upright on his knees – Caterina had no idea how – swaying forward and back like a child's toy. His gun was discarded and both his hands clawed at his chest, his fingers drenched in scarlet, but he didn't fall.

His eyes grew dull and there was blood on his teeth, but he fixed his gaze on Caterina and mumbled words at her that she didn't hear because she was busy re-cocking the hammer and directing her gun at Aldo, who didn't move a muscle.

'No military bomb. Not ... from the planes.'

She caught Vincelli's whisper. 'What do you mean?'

'No military bomb,' he repeated slowly, 'on the ... workshop.' A crooked smile twisted his face. 'Police bribed. To lie.'

Bile rose into Caterina's throat. 'No,' she whispered. The Bodeo was shaking.

'Yes. To kill your father.'

'Who?' she demanded. 'Who planted the bomb in my father's workshop? You?'

He shook his head and an odd sound escaped that was meant to be a laugh. Each breath was loud and liquid.

'Why?' Caterina stepped closer. 'Why would anyone want to kill my father?'

But Drago Vincelli's eyes started to roll in his head. He was falling.

'See you in hell.' He spat out the words and a stream of blood came with them.

Still clutching his chest, he keeled over on to his side on the ground. His breathing stopped. His eyes glazed, but remained wide open, startled, as though he could not believe he had died.

It was Sal Sardo all over again. Without the sunlight and the crows.

Aldo crossed himself.

'Stay where you are,' she ordered.

He placed the lamp on a chinoiserie bookcase and lowered the footstool in his arms to the floor, but he had the sense to move no closer.

'Stay where you are,' she said again.

Nothing was functioning right. Her thoughts were backing into each other. Her pulse stopped and started, jumped and raced, forgetting how to work, and wherever she looked, she saw everything through a veil of blood. Even Aldo. The massive muscles of his shoulders were tense, the scab on his neck was black, his eyes kept flicking wildly between her and Vincelli, the ring on his finger glinting as he rubbed at the bandage on his hand, and she knew he wanted his hands around her throat.

'The first death-shot is the hardest, they say,' she warned. 'The second comes easier.'

He said nothing. He glared at her.

'You will be handed over to the police,' she informed him, 'and tried for kidnapping. Or,' she said softly, 'we can finish it here.'

Suddenly he was grinning, a sick greedy twist of his mouth and it scared her, just as something hard jammed against the back of her head, forcing it forward. 'Put the gun down, Caterina, or I will have to blow your brains out.'

It was Harry Fielding.

'Harry?'

Caterina placed her gun on the ground and tried to turn but the muzzle of his gun pressed harder, holding her there. He kicked the Bodeo away.

'What are you doing, Harry?' she asked, baffled.

'Ah, poor Caterina, you are too clever for your own good. I told you again and again to stay away from Drago Vincelli, but you wouldn't listen. Now look where it's got you.'

His voice was tight, but still the old Harry. He sounded almost compassionate, but she knew better now and swore at herself for being taken in by his English charm.

'You are working with them, aren't you?' she accused. 'Stealing Italy's treasures. Why Harry? We trusted you.'

'Why do you think, sweet girl? Because I need the money, of course.' He was standing far enough behind her to avoid any kicks. 'I told you,' he elaborated, 'that my Pa lost all our wealth in the 1929 Wall Street crash and shot himself, the cowardly bastard. What was my mother supposed to live on?'

'The same as the rest of us,' Caterina said quietly.

Harry paid no heed. Aldo edged over to the tunnel through which he'd entered, but he moved with a wariness that showed he was not certain of what Harry intended to do. Maybe they didn't get on. The thought gave Caterina hope.

'It's been absolutely vile watching my beloved Ma scrimp and save, the banks seizing our home, Bradeway Hall, and selling off her precious horses.' He jabbed at her skull. 'She lives in rented accommodation, you know, like a bloody fishwife.'

'So you decided to steal.'

'Just an artefact here, a painting there, nothing much.' She heard his voice soften. 'Enough to make Ma happy again.'

'Don't do this, Harry. You're better than the Vincellis of this world.'

He laughed, a soft affectionate sound. 'I really liked you, Caterina, if only you'd listened to me and steered clear. But now,' she felt him shrug, 'I'm going to have to kill you and that's a shame.'

A shame?

She tried to step away, telling herself he would not pull the trigger, not on a woman, but she knew he would. If he had to, he would. He was a soldier.

'Stand still' he said. Polite but firm.

'Does Jake know?'

'Good Lord, no. Jake is as straight as a die. But he started getting suspicious that someone was leaking information about where we would be raiding next, so I had to cast doubt on Colonel Quincy, though in reality Quincy is totally innocent.' He paused, uneasy. 'I then had to make Quincy suspicious of Jake to cover paintings and other things that were missing from our stores of artefacts. Damn bad, I admit.'

'Damn bad,' she echoed.

'You've really messed things up now, killing Drago Vincelli like that. Who is going to run the Caesar Club now?'

Vincelli's body lay half in shadow, already departed from this world. The stink of blood was strong.

'Listen, Harry, it's not too late to . . .'

The gun jabbed harder into the back of her head.

'Sorry, Caterina. Really sorry.'

Face to face with death, Caterina felt it strip her of everything except who she was. She slowed the wild panic of her heart, and held on only to what mattered to her. Her love for her family. For Luca. For Nonno. And yes, even for her dissolute mother. But it was the depth of her love for Jake Parr that took her by surprise. It was a fierce consuming thing that burned through her veins and devoured the best of her. It made her stronger in ways she did not know she could be strong and she knew she could not bear to let it go.

With a rapid step to one side, she jerked her head around to face Harry.

'At least look me in the eyes when you kill me, Captain Fielding.'

His handsome face looked sad. But nothing more.

'Goodbye, Caterina.' The black eye of the gun stared straight at her forehead. 'I'll miss you.'

The explosion of the gunshot crashed against the rock walls, but Caterina felt no pain, no splitting of bones and brain. Instead of crumpling to the ground, she watched in confusion as Harry Fielding twitched, as though a wasp had stung his neck, then folded his limbs neatly to lie flat on the stone floor. Blood, as black as ink in this unlit patch, spilled in a torrent from a raw hole in his throat.

Jake saw his friend fall. Instantly he was overwhelmed with grief. He had fired the bullet himself from his Colt .45, but he stared at his own hand in horror, appalled by its betrayal, sickened by what it had done.

But Caterina was still alive. Still breathing, still standing, and the relief of it outweighed his grief. He darted forward to Harry's side and saw Caterina scoop up her old revolver from the floor and point it squarely at Aldo.

'Don't move,' she warned.

Jake threw down his torch and tore off his jacket. He knelt beside his comrade and used the jacket to press down hard on the wound. If he could stem the flow of blood, there was a chance, but it kept coming and coming.

'Harry,' he said urgently, 'stay with me, my friend. Hold onto me.' He wrapped one of Harry's hands around his arm and saw the faintest flicker of his pale eyelids. His slack mouth opened but no sound emerged.

'Jake! Watch out!'

It was Caterina's voice. He wrenched his attention away from Harry and saw Aldo charging down on him, a knife in his hand, coming for his undefended back.

In that instant, Caterina stepped towards Aldo and pulled the trigger of her gun, but Jake heard the heart-stopping click of a gun jamming. The old Bodeo had failed. He snatched at his own gun which lay discarded on the ground beside him, but his hands were slippery with blood and he fumbled it.

When the massive shadow was about to crash down on him with the knife, he saw something leap through the air. A flash of white. A dog sank its fangs into the arm with the knife. Aldo roared and smashed the animal against the rock wall where it slithered to the floor, motionless.

Though it had gained Jake precious seconds in which to seize his gun, he knew it was too late. But out of nowhere the long thin blade of a sword arced up from the ground and bit deep into Aldo's armpit. He heard Aldo's scream, a sound that scraped the surface off the rock.

Jake leapt to his feet, but Aldo was already vanishing through the rear entrance to the cavern. He put out a hand to Caterina who was standing with a bloodied sword still in her grip.

'Give me your gun, Jake. I'll go after him . . .'

For half a second he pulled her close to him, touched his cheek to hers. 'No. Stay here,' he said. 'Try to slow the bleeding on Harry. Quickly now, while I . . .'

For the first time in the dim light he saw the body of Vincelli and his words dried.

What kind of hellhole was he leaving her in?

Without another word, he seized his torch and took off after Aldo.

CHAPTER FORTY-ONE

Caterina crooned to Harry. He was dead. He would not hear her song of sorrow, but she stroked his fair hair off his face in the subterranean gloom and quietly sang a psalm for him to ease his path from life. She crouched beside his body, head bowed, and held his chill hand tight between hers as if her warmth could delay his journey.

How long she crouched there, she didn't know. The psalm had ceased. Her fear for Jake prowled through the darkness around her and she did not count the number of times she ceased breathing to listen for his footstep.

He should be back by now. Had he found Aldo?

Was he safe?

Should she abandon her vigil and race through the tunnel?

She closed her eyes to shut out death and darkness, and summoned up instead an image of Jake alive and laughing, his skin naked and gleaming gold in the lamplight. As it had in her house last night when she had lain on top of him, skin on skin, life on life. Her American soldier, whom she would not allow death to lay a finger on, was now in danger of . . .

A murmur came out of the gloom. The unmistakable rustle of long skirts made her eyes fly open and she saw three women dressed in black, two tall and one short. Her mind must be playing tricks. The figures loomed over her like three witches and she was ready to strike out in panic, but a hand gently touched her head.

'Caterina, *bella*, hush that sound.'

It was Signora Bartoli, the jeweller's wife. Caterina was keening over Harry and hadn't even heard the mournful sound drifting out of her mouth. She jumped to her feet and by the light of the three extra torches that had entered the cavern, she recognised the stern faces of Augusta Cavaleri and Octavia di Marco. She stared at them open-mouthed, baffled by their presence.

'You didn't think I would leave you all alone, did you, Caterina?' Signora Bartoli spoke kindly.

'What are you all doing here?'

'We are here,' Octavia di Marco said with an urgency that Caterina had never heard from her before, 'because we three are friends, bound together by our oath to help liberate Italy.'

Nothing made any sense.

'Caterina,' Signora Bartoli explained, 'before you left my house with the key to these tunnels, I telephoned Augusta and Octavia. I knew they needed to be here.'

With a sudden intake of breath, Augusta Cavaleri broke the circle as she caught sight of the dead body of Drago Vincelli.

She strode over and stood beside it, gazing down without a word, just her robes rustling as she fingered the rosary beads that hung from her neck.

'Signora Bartoli,' Caterina demanded, 'what is going on?'

'It is time you knew the truth. You have come so close, far closer than we ever expected.'

Truth? Caterina's mouth went dry at the thought. Truth had a cold finely honed edge that could cut you in pieces.

'Yes, I want the truth,' she said.

It was Octavia di Marco who started to speak, calm and unhurried, her eyes fixed on Caterina's. Only the soft click of the rosary beads intruded into the cavern's silence. She talked of the agonies that Italy had suffered for more than twenty years under the Fascist dictatorship of Benito Mussolini. The killings. The beatings. The fear. And the destruction of the country's spirit till it was face down in the dirt.

But throughout the country brave men and women had fought back – the partisans. These rebels had sabotaged the regime in every corner with bombs, assassinations and secret spies. Many gave their lives, were caught and executed. And when the Germans came, the partisans fought again just as fiercely to rid Italy of the Nazi jackboot.

'In Naples,' she continued, 'there was a group of these men who met in secret under the guise of the Caesar Club, a drinking fraternity. Your father was one of them.'

'And my Orlando was another,' pointed out the jeweller's wife, 'as well as Augusta's son, Roberto, before he ran off to Rome with your mother.'

Augusta Cavaleri's voice cut in sharply. 'This man fought courageously at their side.' She pointed down at Drago Vincelli's bloodied body. 'He was an explosives expert, destroyed railtracks and bridges. But he grew greedy when one day he derailed a freight train and found it was transporting treasures stolen from Naples museum. That was the end of his loyalty to Italy.' She spat on the man at her feet and it slithered down his cheek.

Caterina could sense the hatred in the air as she turned back to Octavia di Marco. 'My father was a master craftsman. He knew nothing about bombs.'

'Yes, they were all getting older, so they switched to raising money to finance the guns and missions of the younger partisans.'

Realisation hit Caterina and a mix of anger and relief swept through her. 'By repairing stolen works of art and selling them to wealthy buyers all over the world. Using Italy's own wealth to build a new stronger Italy.'

'Exactly. But Drago got too greedy. He always wanted more and more for himself. And as chairman of the Caesar Club he persuaded other members to do the same, selling the artefacts to line their own pockets instead of to finance the resurgence of Italy.' Octavia stared at the inert body of Vincelli. 'He always feared you, Caterina.'

'Me?'

'He was afraid you knew too much because you worked so closely with your father. He was frightened you would betray the club.'

Papà, you should have told me. Warned me. So I would have been ready.

Vincelli's dying words came back to her. *No military bombs . . . not from the planes.*

'He claimed that the bomb that killed my father was planted by someone. The police were bribed to lie that it fell from a plane.' Caterina felt, rather than heard, the air escape from the women's lungs. 'Who?' she asked, her voice louder. 'Who did it? Tell me.'

There was silence. For a full minute no one spoke.

'I did it.'

Three small words of confession.

From beside the body, Augusta Cavaleri looked steadily into Caterina's face and said again, 'I did it.'

But this time there was fury in every syllable.

'If your father had kept his wife happy in bed, she would not have needed to steal my son. The day I heard of my Roberto's death in Rome, I knew his soul would demand vengeance. I begged a bomb from Drago and set it off in your father's workshop when he was busy in the back room.' She struck her fist against her own breast with sudden passion. 'I am Italian. We believe in revenge. An eye for an eye, a life for a life. It is the Italian way.'

'I believe in family,' Caterina declared fiercely. 'I have protected mine.'

Signora Bartoli nodded. 'You protected them well.'

Caterina advanced on the tall figure of Augusta Cavaleri. 'And the Rocco brothers too? Did they see you enter my father's workshop the day of the bomb?'

The scar on the proud woman's face gleamed silver like the mark of Cain. 'If your soldier friends had stayed out of it, and not come asking questions in the street, it would not have been necessary.'

No remorse. No shame. No guilt at taking a knife to the throats of four men who would let her come close because she was a woman. They trusted her. All Caterina could see was Augusta Cavaleri's pride that she had defended her family's honour.

'Who bribed the police?' Caterina asked.

'It doesn't matter. Not now,' Octavia di Marco murmured.

'It matters to me. Was it the Count?'

Octavia laughed scornfully. 'No. Count di Marco cares for nothing but his own ivory palace.'

'It was Drago,' Augusta Cavaleri replied. 'Drago bribed Commissari Balzano to report that it was a bomb dropped from an Allied aeroplane.'

'Why would Drago Vincelli do that?'

'Dear Mother of God, will you never understand, Caterina Lombardi? Drago Vincelli was my sister's son. My nephew. Even though he turned bad and stole Italy's treasures for his own selfish greed. Still, he was family.'

It was half an hour before Jake emerged from the maze of black tunnels back into the cavern with its treasures. His shirt was stiff with blood, but it was Harry's blood.

He could not bear the touch of it on his skin. He knew that the memory of that split second in his life when he was forced to pull the trigger and kill his friend would never leave him. It would stalk his nights, dragging its claws through his dreams. Caterina had been blocking his shot, her back to him, standing unknowingly between him and Harry. He'd had no choice, no time. It had to be a head shot or the neck. He chose the neck in the hope the wound would not prove fatal, but he knew the moment he saw the damage that it was a vain hope.

When he reached the cavern it was a blur of people in uniform. Someone must have alerted the authorities because they were here in force, police and army, dark suits and white medical coats, with voices raised and language barriers that made the confined space feel as if it would burst. But Jake's eyes saw only Caterina.

She stood tight against a wall, refusing with a shake of the head to leave each time she was ordered to do so. She looked small and resolute, her face drained of colour, her hands twisting together and covered in dried blood, but when her eyes found his, they came back from the dead.

She stood quietly while he cut a path through the crowd to her, and he wanted to take her into his arms. Instead he placed his hands on her shoulders and looked carefully into her face.

'I didn't find Aldo,' he said quietly. 'I'm sorry. He escaped. Even though he was wounded, I lost him. He turned a corner and vanished among the tunnels. I'm sorry.'

'He must know these secret passageways very well and have escape routes already laid out in his mind.'

'Were you frightened I was lying dead too?'

'You were a long time,' she said simply.

'You must trust me.'

'I do.'

She wrapped a fist into his bloody shirt front and held on to it. He kissed her forehead and they stood like that together, his lips on her skin, their hearts beating in rhythm.

'Outside, please, sir,' said a British corporal in an officious tone.

Caterina took Jake's hand and led him away from the darkness.

CHAPTER FORTY-TWO

The glass was cool in Caterina's hand, the prosecco dry and delicious. Her grandfather's hand caressed her cheek, reluctant to leave it, and his lips found her forehead and lingered there.

'You are your father's daughter,' he declared with pride. 'You possess his heart and his courage. He fought for Italy like a lion and now you, my Caterina, fight for the Lombardi family.'

'And you say that Signora Bartoli, Augusta Cavaleri and Octavia di Marco fought too? Alongside Papà?'

'Ah yes. You should have seen those three women in their youth. They were warriors.' Her grandfather laughed and Caterina realised it was a sound she had not heard since her father died. 'They handled a rifle as well as any man. Italy needs women like them. It is tragic that Augusta Cavaleri lost her reason after her son was shot and cared for nothing but vengeance.'

He was prowling up and down the room, swinging his long limbs, unable to keep them still, suddenly a man ten years younger. The smell of burning filled the room as Luca fed Harry Fielding's map to the flames in the firebasket.

'Nonno, why didn't you tell me the truth long ago?'

'Oh, Caterina, because I was frightened Drago Vincelli would come to kill you or your brother if you angered him, and I knew I would be unable to defend you. But now,' the smile would not stay off his face, resurfacing each time he tried to banish it, 'now you have done what I would have done years ago if I'd had my eyes. Put a bullet in Drago Vincelli's heart.'

Put a bullet in Drago Vincelli's heart.

The words lay heavy on her own heart. She would carry them with her for the rest of her life, just as she knew Jake would carry the guilt of killing his friend. But now she knew she *had* a life, and so did Luca. Her brother turned and grinned at her.

'Don't look sad, Caterina,' he said, 'I heard that a new troop-ship from Cairo docked in Naples today on its way home to England. Lots more customers for our music boxes.'

She heard the word – *our. Our* music boxes. And she smiled because she knew she would need a bigger workshop.

Nonno swung out his arm and pointed directly at where he knew his own carved chair to be.

'And you,' he said as he strode over to it, 'Major Parr, you have the respect of Giuseppe Lombardi.'

In the chair Jake was taken by surprise at the sudden approach and Caterina laughed when her grandfather swooped down on him, took his face between his two strong hands and kissed him soundly on each cheek.

'To you, Major Parr,' her grandfather announced solemnly,

'I give my thanks and my heart for saving my Caterina's life. You will always be welcome in this house.'

'Thank you, Signor Lombardi.' Jake smiled as he looked straight across at Caterina and said, 'I hope I will be.'

She didn't smile. Or laugh. Or make it easy. She nodded. And that was it. Caterina's promise to him.

Nothing had changed.

The mountain-top terrace of the di Marco villa on Capri still dazzled with its whiteness. Even Octavia di Marco in her black mannish suit hovered with a tray of freshly squeezed lemonade, silent and watchful as though the underground cavern had never existed.

'I'm so sorry,' Caterina said sincerely. 'I feel responsible. Is Bianchezza any better?'

Leonora was sitting cross-legged on the marble flooring beside Caterina's table on the terrace, her dark hair cropped much shorter as if in penance. Bianchezza's head lay across her lap and the girl's hand gently soothed the dog's painful ribs.

'She is getting better by the hour,' Leonora assured Caterina. 'The vet has given her an injection.'

'So, Signorina Lombardi,' the Count interrupted, 'are you here to visit the sick animal or are you here with news for me about my jewelled table?' He was again swaddled in his pristine white toga under his canopy.

'I am here to thank Leonora.' Caterina slid to the floor beside the dog and ran her fingers affectionately around its ear. 'Bianchezza was wonderful,' she said to her friend, 'and so were you.'

Leonora's pale cheek flushed at the compliment and she raised her glass in a toast. 'To us,' she grinned.

Caterina turned to take her own glass from the chess table and as she did so, from this low angle she caught sight of the underside of her father's table and her hand froze in mid-air. The maple veneer underneath was wrong. All wrong. The patterns and whorls on its surface did not flow into each other or mirror each other, as they would if veneer had been correctly applied. She opened her mouth to voice her astonishment to the Count, but stopped.

Her father would never do such shoddy work. It would break his heart. Unless he had a good reason. If he wished to indicate to collectors – or even to Caterina herself – that this exquisite chess table was not right. Telling them to look closer.

His voice speaking from the grave.

Without a word Caterina reached into her canvas bag and pulled out the sharp-bladed scorper she kept there now in case a wounded Aldo ever blundered on to her path. The Count cried out at the sight of the tool in her hand, but she sliced the tip of it through the veneer on the underside.

'No,' the Count shouted in horror and struggled to his feet.

Strip by strip Caterina peeled back the veneer and suddenly the table top was no longer secure. It was Octavia who lunged at her, but too late. Before she reached her, it was done and Caterina lifted off the table top.

She heard the gasps and was dimly conscious of voices raised, but all her senses were absorbed by the glorious work of art revealed beneath it. It was the jewelled table. Light and beauty leapt from it with a radiance that made her heart slow.

She heard again her father's voice in her ears. *'Be patient, my Caterina. Listen to the wood.'*

The scene depicted on the table was the one that had been described to her. The sapphire blue sea lapping around the isle of Capri with the Count's villa perched on the cliff. It was breathtaking. The inlay work was magical, a master craftsman at the height of his powers, using the finest jewels and exquisite woods to create a work of art that would rival the masterpieces of the ancient world.

Caterina laid a hand on its glowing surface, and only then did she become aware of the conversation around her on the terrace. The three members of the di Marco family were each claiming ownership.

'How in God's name did it get here?' the Count demanded.

Octavia was kneeling beside the table, her hand, like Caterina's, unable to resist touching the beauty of it. 'I brought it here,' she said, 'when you were sick in bed with pleurisy two years ago.'

She spoke to Caterina. 'Your father had hidden it in the lock-up storeroom, the secret one cut into the hills of Sorrento, but we feared your mother had a key, so we moved everything after your father's death. But before then I persuaded him to let me keep the table for Italy, instead of giving it to Leonora or to the Count. So he designed a cover for it using our chess table. It was brilliantly conceived and we were grateful to him.'

'We?' the Count queried. 'Who are *we*?'

'Augusta Cavaleri, Maria Bartoli and myself. Though I have no money of my own, I have always supported the partisan resistance.' She regarded the Count with distaste. 'Even though you chose to take no part in it all. No part in anything,' she added with a hint of bitterness. 'I'd even have taken part in the four-day rebellion battle against the Germans in Naples in 1943, if I'd been a few years younger.' Her face, usually so impassive, was alight with passion for her cause. 'All I could do was help supply money for weapons and radios. But we did it. We drove the Germans out of Naples and liberated our city.'

The Count shook his head in sharp sorrow. 'More than five hundred were killed in those four days of revolt. And you wonder why I will have nothing to do with the world any more.' A breeze ruffled his robes and he retreated to his chaise longue once more, deep in the shade.

'You have to choose life,' Octavia said urgently. 'Or what is the point of our being here?'

Leonora regarded her aunt with wide shocked eyes. 'So why did you keep this table, instead of giving it to the partisans?'

A trace of Octavia's old disdain returned to her expression. 'Because the partisan movement is run by men. And all they want to do is spend it on weapons and bombs. Augusta, Maria and I were preparing for peace. We kept this table to finance the election campaign for the partisan party next year.' She ran her long-fingered hand lovingly over the emeralds and sapphires that scintillated even in the shade. 'This table will buy Italy's future under Palmiro Togliatti.'

'Take it,' her brother growled. 'Take the table and be damned. Togliatti is a communist and will bring Italy to its knees before a year is out.'

Caterina let her fingers caress the table one last time and then she rose to her feet to leave.

Papà.
A good and decent man.

On the front steps of the villa Caterina turned to say goodbye to Octavia. Leonora had remained on the terrace to nurse Bianchezza, but Octavia grasped Caterina's arm before she could descend the steps. There had grown up between them an unexpected respect.

'What is it?' Caterina asked.

'It's Aldo Facchioni.'

Even now his screech of pain when the sword bit into his flesh would not stop hammering at Caterina's mind.

'Where is he?' she asked.

'He is with the Cavaleris. They are hiding him in the shed behind their garage.'

'Ring the police. Quickly. They can ...'

'No, Caterina.' Her grip tightened. 'Don't. He is dying.'

'Dying?'

Relief and horror both raced through Caterina together. 'Tell them to take him to hospital,' she urged.

'He wants to die with his family.'

'The Cavaleris?'

Octavia nodded.

Always there were webs within webs. Paralysing those caught in them.

'Let him die in peace, Caterina.'

Caterina drew her arm away. 'It's over now.'

*

'So it's over, Caterina.'

'Yes.'

'He's really dead,'

'Yes. Drago Vincelli is dead. No need to be afraid any more.'

Her mother gave a low whistle through her teeth, the kind of harsh sound a barrow-boy would make. 'I didn't think you had it in you.'

'You don't know me, Mamma.'

They were at the railway station, standing in a waiting room painted an ugly brown. Lucia Lombardi inhaled on her cigarette and regarded her daughter through the drifting veil of smoke. She was wearing what looked like a new eau-de-nil jacket and matching shoes and a ridiculous feathery hat. Caterina wondered who had paid for it all.

'You're right, sweetheart. I don't know you.' She gave an appreciative pout of her lips. 'Under all the unsightly hair and hideous clothes, you are more like me than I thought.'

A train growled to a halt at the platform outside the waiting room and grey steam belched from its heaving engine up into the sky, briefly blocking out the sun. Her mother picked up the same brown leather suitcase that had stood by the door eleven years ago, but this time without the scarlet umbrella. Caterina's stomach lurched.

Don't go.

Her father's words.

Stay. Please stay.

'Where will you live in Rome?'

'Oh here and there.' Lucia Lombardi gave a loose flick of her hand. 'I know some places.' She patted her handbag. 'Now that I have a little cash to keep me going.' Caterina had given her the other half of Papà's secret stash. It wasn't much, but it would keep her for a while until it ran out. What then?

'Will you sing in Rome?'

'Of course. They love me in the clubs.'

That's not what she said before, but truth was a movable feast where her mother was concerned. She stubbed out her cigarette and walked out on to the platform.

'Mamma, come and visit us. For Luca's sake.'

Her mother turned her blue eyes intently on her daughter, as though she too had heard the same echo that Caterina heard from long years ago. Her carefully painted mouth gave an odd little smile.

'Can't you bring yourself to ask for your own sake?' she said and Caterina was back on the stairs of her childhood watching the triangle of light.

She stepped close to her mother and put her arms around her, inhaling her musky perfume. She kissed her cheek and had to make herself pull away.

'Well,' her mother looked pleased, 'what was that for?'

'To thank you for coming back to give me the address of where the Rolls-Royce Phantom was kept. It helped me.'

The carriage doors were open. People were climbing the steps.

Don't go.

'Have a good journey.'

Lucia Lombardi was eyeing a good-looking man heading for the nearest carriage. 'I intend to.'

She was just about to step aboard when Caterina said firmly, 'Mamma.'

'What is it?'

'If you don't come to visit Luca in Sorrento, Luca and I will come to Rome and find you.'

'Of course I'll come, sweetheart.' But her attention was already on the good-looking man entering her carriage. She smiled at him and he carried her case on board, talking to her, so she forgot to wave.

As the door was closing, Caterina called out, 'Come, Mamma, for my sake,' and saw her mother stare at her from behind glass.

The train belched out a bellyful of smoke and the massive wheels started to move, smuts of ash billowing in the air. Caterina hurried alongside the train, moving faster as it picked up speed, then a window lowered and her mother's face was there with its feathery hat and beguiling smile.

'I'll send a postcard,' Lucia Lombardi called out. 'With my address. I promise.'

The engine pulled away and Caterina stood on the platform, waving a handkerchief back and forth, faster and faster, until the train was no more than a dot on the horizon. She lowered her hand and walked out of the station, conscious of a lightness in her chest that had not been there before.

It was time to open the workshop.

CHAPTER FORTY-THREE

A week later, the Bay of Naples shimmered out towards Torre Annunziata and Salerno, with the islands of Capri and Ischia drifting in and out of the distant blue haze. Caterina and Jake stood side by side. They were looking out to sea, drawing in deep breaths of the clean sparkling air, to rid their lungs of the corruption and canker that had crawled inside them when they were deep in the subterranean world concealed beneath the city.

The ancient fortress of Castel dell'Ovo reared up on their right and Castel Nuovo on their left, battle-worn monuments to Naples' violent past. And Caterina knew that the violence still smouldered here among the ruins and the alleyways, like a fire that could never be stamped out. Yet it was a city they both loved and that fact gave Caterina hope when she turned to Jake in his army uniform and asked, 'Will you stay?'

His hand brushed along her forearm, his thumb easing its way down the jagged scar of the dog bite. 'I have to be here to give evidence at Augusta Cavaleri's trial, just as you will have to. And at our own hearings too, though they have accepted that our actions were in self-defence. So yes, my Caterina, I will stay.'

That wasn't what she meant.

'And you?' he asked. 'Will you stay? Or will you pack up your wood and your dreams and travel to Rome and Paris with your beautiful furniture designs?' He smiled, and there was laughter in his voice as he added, 'Or to London? Even New York?' But the laughter was warm. The laughter told her he believed in her.

'I'll stay,' she said simply. 'If you're here.'

She studied his strong hands and watched the way he had of tightening the muscle above one eyebrow when deep in thought, as he was now, and without warning she felt something leap into life inside her. This was the moment to tell him what was in her head.

'Jake,' she said. The words were rising fast to her tongue but she kept them in check, aware that though Italian blood coursed through his veins, he had been born and bred an American. She chose her next words with care. 'Jake, Naples needs policemen. Good, trustworthy policemen to help bring honesty and decency into the running of this city after all the Allied troops leave. You speak excellent Italian. With your experience as a police officer in Milwaukee, you would qualify easily.'

His gaze locked on hers, eyes bright. 'Me?' he queried. 'In that fancy Italian *polizia* uniform?'

He raised one eyebrow, teasing her, and she burst into

laughter, fighting back the desire to wrap her arms around his waist and hold him here in Italy. In the harbour, troopships were being loaded for the journey home. Cranes swung jeeps up into the air like clumsy metal birds and men in uniform yelled instructions, eager to be on their way back to their loved ones.

Jake wrapped an arm around her shoulder and held her tight against him, and she felt the connection at some deep level. His dark eyes still gazed out to sea and she wondered what he was seeing there.

'Think about it, Jake,' she murmured.

'I love you, Caterina,' he said. 'And I love Italy. Far too much ever to leave either of you.' He turned and looked at her, eyes full of things she couldn't know but things that she would discover in time. So much was still unsaid, and she felt no need to say it. Not now. For now she stood beside Jake and accepted the simple pleasure of breathing the same good clean air he was breathing.

She loved him. That was enough. The future for Italy was a slippery road that shimmered as brightly as the Bay of Naples itself, and yes, it would be rough and chaotic and even danger-ous at times. After all, this was Italy. But Caterina intended to take her music boxes and her designs in a strong sack on her shoulder and walk along that road.

Acknowledgements

People say that writing is a solitary occupation but they're wrong. I am surrounded by a whole team of wonderful supporters who keep me getting out of bed each morning with a pen in my hand and I owe them all a great debt.

I want to thank my wonderful new publisher, Jo Dickinson, and all the fantastic team at Simon & Schuster. Your belief in me and this book got me over the yawning chasm at dark moments and safely into the sunny uplands of a final draft.

Huge thanks also to my brilliant incomparable agent, Teresa Chris, who is both inspiring and inspired.

I am also grateful to Marian Churchward for her winning ways with a keyboard and her constant good cheer, even at absurd hours in the morning.

Thanks also to Brixham Writers and David Gilman for keeping me afloat with life-rafts of wise advice, tea and biscuits.

And as always, my warmest thanks to Norman for understanding the weird life of a writer and offering love, chocolate and darn good ideas for filling in plot holes.

My thanks to you all.